VIRAL

a novel by J. T. Cooper

Viral

ISBN 978-0-692-11107-9 PRINT

May 2018

Published and Distributed by
IngramSpark

http://www.ingramspark.com/

1. FICTION / General / . 2. / Suspense. 3. / Pandemic.

For my dear friend and gracious mentor,
Gwyn Hyman Rubio

VIRAL

He'd expected them to order him into a lorry filled with explosives and send him off to crush a crowd of pedestrians or a building full of bodies. It would've been easier. Impact, explosion, Paradise. Instead, they'd punctured his skin with a syringe full of death and driven him to the Barcelona Airport.

The plane was far above the Atlantic now. The light hurt his eyes. Although they'd said he wouldn't have symptoms for another day or two, he knew his fever was soaring. His throat felt as though he'd swallowed a sword, and when he coughed, the sword cut his lungs.

He shouldn't complain. He'd pledged his life. How they chose to use it was their affair. He wondered if his cousin, seated several rows back on the aisle, felt sick yet. They were not to communicate nor acknowledge each other in any way, but he couldn't help but wonder about him. His cousin owned a sweets shop in Liverpool and had two children. His sacrifice was greater.

Ill as he was, he must obey orders. The young man seated next to him had a new iPhone on his tray table. The sick man turned away to lick his finger and then touched the instrument. "Nice," he murmured. The young man nodded.

Now he must go to the bathroom. Crawling over the passengers in his row, he exhaled on them, put his fingers to his mouth again, and touched seats and armrests as he staggered down the aisle. His cousin was asking a flight attendant for something. His hand touched her arm.

Once in the bathroom, the sick man sneezed into his hands, smeared the slime over his palms, and touched the faucets, the toilet paper, the flushing button. He coughed, making the sword twist in his chest, and tasted blood. He must not cover his mouth when he coughed. He must not wash his hands.

He could hardly pronounce the city where he was going: Cincinnati. A town in the midwest of the U.S., they'd said. And from there he was to go to Las Vegas, the most degenerate and evil of all American cities. His was important work, they'd said. His martyrdom would be exalted above all others. After a life spent among the filthy British, he would finally have his chance to punish the West.

He exited the bathroom, breathing on the old lady waiting outside. His cousin, his brother in this pilgrimage, was shaking hands with the man across the aisle. Other brothers on other planes were doing the same thing, although he'd not been told how many nor where they were going. It was a grand scheme, they'd told him, years in the planning and ultimately more devastating than the attack of 2001. He was honored to be part of it.

He climbed over the young man with the iPhone, touching his hand as he went, and collapsed into his seat. He coughed again and a flight attendant with long, dark hair offered him water. He made sure to press her fingers when she gave it to him. When they landed in Cincinnati, he was to hurry through Customs, easy enough since he and his cousin had checked no baggage. Once in Las Vegas he could get a hotel, but, no matter how sick he felt, he must go to restaurants, walk in crowds, touch everything. He wasn't sure if he'd have strength enough to do it. Maybe the tuberculosis he'd suffered as a child had weakened him. His cousin certainly didn't seem as ill.

Curling up against the window, he pulled his jacket over his ears and shivered. His heart was beating very fast. They'd said he'd live for five or six days, long enough to infect hundreds of people. He wasn't sure he'd last another five hours.

Chapter One

Luke didn't mind working Sundays. The airport had a different feel on weekends, like a mall full of hellos and good-byes where people hugged and gave each other flowers or balloons. He strolled through the main concourse. Drifting out from the food court, the scents of pizza, french fries, and cinnamon rolls mixed together to make him hungry, but there were still two hours until his four o'clock lunch break. Or dinner break. When he worked the noon to eight shift, he could never make up his mind what to call it.

Weekdays at the airport were all business. Suits and smart phones. Laptops and nerves. He wondered sometimes if pulling those rolling cases elongated peoples' arms. Maggie often joked that his loaded gun belt shortened him at least an inch, that he grew when he took it off. This always amused Luke since he reckoned that most of his fellow law enforcement types thought their guns made them as tall as Clint Eastwood.

He nodded at the cute girl in the sunglass kiosk. Some of the guys had asked her out, which was fine for them, he supposed. His rutting season had ended more than seven years ago when he'd married Maggie, and he hadn't been one bit sorry about it. He passed the bookstore, the pricey shops, and then the closest gates. This was his beat, today anyway, and it was easy enough work, especially on a Sunday. *Project an image of quiet confidence*, the training manual read. His dad hadn't ever worked in law enforcement, but he'd given him similar advice when Luke had trouble with some boys from middle school. "Stand tall, look 'em in the eye, and don't back down for nothing," Dad had said. "But put a little bit of a grin on your face. They'll wonder what you're up to."

For the most part, Luke had followed the advice, although he'd never thought there was anything wrong with people thinking an airport policeman was approachable, even if it did mean they were forever asking him where the nearest bathroom was. All in a day's work, he thought, as he noticed an unsupervised stroller. The baby inside was plugged up with a pacifier and had one bare foot. Luke frowned and was halfway to perturbed when the mother dashed up, looking apologetic and holding a tiny shoe. "She kicks them off all the time," the woman explained. He didn't bother to tell her that she should've pushed the stroller while she was retrieving the shoe.

He kept walking, watching, policing. Every day when he came home, Maggie asked how his day had been. Most times he said it'd been fine: dull and uneventful. He hoped they'd stay that way, but just as he was turning to go back the way he'd come, his radio squawked. Luke had hardly acknowledged the call before the dispatcher barked that Sergeant Davies was to report to Customs and help secure the area.

"What the hell," Luke murmured and set off for the stairway. He knew better than to run, but he strode on out. Something was cooking.

The fire doors were closed, which made sense, but he nearly knocked over two TSA employees leaning against them when he entered the area. They were young and had big eyes. "What's going on?" Luke asked.

They shook their heads. "Don't know," said one. "But we're locked down."

Luke marched through throngs of passengers, frozen where the process had halted, some with their belongings already in bins. But they were going nowhere; the TSA employees had left their lines and were manning exits. A few people clogged the declaration area although there was no Customs employee at the counter. He glanced to his left at a door that led to the elevator, but it was guarded by two Agriculture people.

No panic yet, he determined, although the passengers looked anxious, and several were jabbering on cell phones. Luke searched his memory. This was Flight 29, coming in from Barcelona, as he recalled. And since this was Cincinnati, right smack dab in the Midwest, he'd bet nearly every passenger here had a connecting flight to somewhere else. The natives would be getting restless soon.

He made his way back to passport control. Quite a few people crowded together there, although, unless it was a seriously underbooked flight, several had already cleared all the hoops before the lockdown. From this location he could see several entryways and doors, every one of them more than adequately manned. He was wondering why they needed him when a Customs officer motioned to Luke. "Can you take this area? I need to find out what we do next."

Luke nodded. "What's going on?"

She shrugged. "They called EMTs to the plane, and next thing we heard was to stop processing passengers and seal the area."

She sped off toward an office in the middle of the huge hall, and Luke planted his feet. It didn't look like anybody was going to start a stampede, but you never knew. The doorway behind him was the one passengers had come through from the plane. Unlikely they'd think of charging this direction.

The Customs Hall was gloomy. Its blue walls and carpet weren't exactly cheery, and the fluorescent lights in the cavernous room made him feel like his eyes were dilated. Some design person had probably argued that sleepy colors would keep everybody calm as they waded through the labyrinth of paperwork, and maybe the designer was right. The passengers were being good sheep, staying back and waiting to be called by Customs officers who weren't there. A sign said that they were to stand behind a yellow line until summoned forward, but there was no yellow line. The previous carpet had one, but the new rug, ugly as the swirly-patterned ones in most hotels, had no line at all. Luke couldn't help but smile at the passengers who kept looking down as if it would materialize.

It helped to be tall. At 6'2" Luke could see over most heads. There was plenty of supervision, probably a dozen or so Customs and Agriculture officers spread along the walls, and that didn't count the TSA people up front or the airline representatives who were taking most of the passengers' heat. Nor did it count the terrified girl caged in the cubicle for currency exchange. And there were probably more uniforms congregating in that office out in the middle. It had blind windows, so he couldn't see what was going on, but just then two officers came out, both talking on cell phones and walking in opposite directions. A uniformed female hollered out the door at them. "It's not just here," she said, her voice too shrill for business as usual. "Atlanta, Dallas, L.A., New York, and Chicago are all in it too. Two on each flight."

The officers stopped dead and walked back to her. Hushing up for about five seconds, the passengers who could hear her stared at the woman, and then a low rumbling came from the crowd in front of Luke. Stupid, he thought. All they needed was for people to panic. It reminded him of the wedding that'd turned nasty back when he was on patrol in Afghanistan. Some hyped-up buck had fired a rifle into the sky, and within two minutes there'd been a barrage of random shooting and a gigantic mess to clean up. No matter how much they tried to act civilized, people were nothing but walking match heads.

Wearing an airport volunteer's vest, a graceful older woman came up to Luke. He'd seen her wandering among the clumps of passengers but only when she came closer did he recognize her and realize why she'd be helpful. Nearly six feet tall with white hair swooped up into a twist behind her head, she'd been a language professor at Northern Kentucky University when he'd gone there. She'd taught him, or tried to, French 102, and he'd thought her ancient fifteen years ago. "We should let them sit," she said, gesturing at the passengers and then squinting at him. "I remember you. Always wore a cap and had the most appalling accent."

She must be eighty now, but her blue eyes were still sharp. He grinned. "Luke Davies, Professor Mayfield. Spoke French like a hillbilly, didn't I?"

As he recalled, she was German, a GI bride, and spoke French and English along with her native tongue. He guessed she came in handy around a bunch of international passengers, although a flight from Barcelona might tax even her impressive skills. Of course, Paris and Munich should be landing any minute. Luke looked at his watch. Actually, they should've landed already.

"Not many chairs," he observed. The chain of command was fuzzy, and the ones who should've been in charge were sequestered in that office. Luke moved toward the passengers and chose an elderly couple. "Would you like to sit?" he asked, pointing at the chairs against the wall. "I don't think anything's going to happen real soon."

Just his luck, the couple looked confused by his English, but Professor Mayfield glided up beside him and tried it in French and then, it seemed to him, perfect Spanish. He counted maybe twenty-five people clumped together in his area, and within two minutes, nearly all of them were sitting on the half-dozen chairs or the floor, leaning against their carry-ons. He could feel them relax, more from Professor Mayfield's presence than from sitting, although nearly all of them asked him for information he didn't have, and one man was getting fairly ticked off about missing his connecting flight to Minneapolis.

Down the way he could see Professor Mayfield working her magic on the passengers around the carousels. He wished she'd come back. One woman was giving an airline employee hell in rapid Spanish, and he heard a young man, maybe college-aged, insisting that the Customs people were terrorists. Luke didn't blame him. At least six cities with two people each? It sounded like terrorism even if the guy was pointing his finger at the wrong people.

Another passenger had figured out a different way to pass the time and was sneaking sips from a bottle of something in his duty-free bag. Luke didn't blame him either. "I have to get to Kansas City," one woman complained, her voice on the edge of hysteria. "My flight left thirty minutes ago," declared a trim businesswoman who was hugging her cell to her chest. Nearly all of them were working their phones.

Luke felt superfluous. If this was a terroristic situation, it would affect the entire airport and he could be of more use elsewhere. He got on his radio. "Davies," he said. "What's the story?"

The dispatcher spit out what she knew. "Dead man on 29. The EMTs think it was some kind of infection. The entire airport's locked down."

A chill hit the back of his neck. "Then you need me somewhere else. This area's secure."

She sounded harried. "Negative, Davies. Stay where you are."

The chill went on down his spine. "As near as I can tell, I'm the only airport policeman down here."

"Affirmative. The Lieutenant was just about to send more but got the word about the full lockdown."

"Lucky me, huh?"

Her voice softened. "Oh yeah. Lucky."

Then he saw a couple of Customs people emerging from the office. One waited while the other went toward Security. Infection. Maybe some kind of biological terrorism. That meant that every one of these passengers had been exposed, and, by being down here among them, he'd be at risk too. The one Customs officer returned with two bins. He shoved a full one into the office and handed an empty one to the other officer who motioned to Professor Mayfield to join him. Snaking their way around the passengers spread out on the ugly carpet, these two started collecting cell phones. People were protesting, but with Good Cop Mayfield and Bad Cop Customs, they were complying. Knowing he had only a couple of minutes, Luke reached for his phone. Adrenaline pumped into his bloodstream. Maggie said it was like an IV drug, and Maggie ought to know.

He pressed a button. Let her answer quick. Let her remember.

❖

Maggie Davies was pulling up impatiens. There hadn't been a frost yet, but the plants had gone leggy, the stems pulpy and yellow, and she thought they looked untidy. Jacob was playing in the yard with Amber from next door, both of them kicking through the bright, fallen leaves and hollering cheerfully. Any minute now they'd be asking again about going to the pumpkin patch. She'd promised that she'd take them but wanted to time it so she could hit McDonald's afterwards for their supper. Sometimes she gave herself a break from cooking when Luke worked the evening shift, and Jacob loved McDonald's.

Maggie glanced at her watch. Three-thirty. They'd leave in another half-hour. With any luck, Jacob and Amber would be pacified enough by pumpkins and Happy Meals that she could stop at the grocery. She had to work tomorrow and hated prolonging Jacob's stay at daycare by shopping late. Her phone, sitting on the back step, dinged, and she dusted dirt off her hands. Luke, the screen said. This was early. He usually called on his dinner break.

He spoke right over her hello. "Howdy there, Sugar Dumplin'."

Her breath caught at the peculiar greeting. His voice was odd, strained and oozing with a country accent stronger than when she'd met him. Luke complained that living near Cincinnati had leached the honest twang out of his voice, but now it was back, more than ever. And she knew why.

He didn't wait for her to reply, but she remembered what his next words would be. "Gonna be late, so don't wait supper." He paused. "And hurry ever' chance you get." He clicked off before she could say anything, even if she'd known what to reply.

It was a code. Back when they'd first married, back when he'd still been in the National Guard, he'd told her that, if he could, he'd warn her if something big was happening. She'd laughed, accusing him of being one of those paranoid survivalists who built bomb shelters and stockpiled dehydrated food, but he'd asked, "Wouldn't those people in the Towers have welcomed a little advance notice?" And he'd outlined the plan she should follow if he ever called and started the conversation with "Howdy there, Sugar Dumplin'."

As fast as you can, he'd said, get in the car and drive down home to my parents' house. It's so far back in a holler that nothing can touch it, and my mother always has enough food put up to last out a nuclear attack. Maggie's hands were shaking. Nuclear attack. What was happening? She glanced at Jacob. He was safe and she could watch him through the kitchen window. Going inside, she turned on the television, clicking between network stations and CNN. Nothing but the usual stuff for a Sunday in October: politics and football. No startling alerts crawled across the bottom of the screen. She was tempted to ignore Luke's call but could almost hear his slow, ironic drawl: "Well, if I didn't get in before the news people, it wouldn't be much of a heads-up, would it?"

Her mind juddered around like Jacob's radio-controlled car. Should she call people? Luke had said she shouldn't. "Let them wait on the big guys to handle the situation," he'd advised. "You'd just be causing panic." Her sister was at the Bengals game with her husband Andy, and by this time of day, Maggie's mother had probably drunk herself halfway to a stupor. No point. Besides, what if Luke was overreacting? She took a deep breath. Think, she told herself. Organize.

She called Amber's mother and apologized, saying she couldn't take the kids to the pumpkin patch because there'd been an emergency with Luke's parents. It wasn't quite a lie. Calling Jacob in the house, she countered his disappointment with news that they were going to see Granny and Pop and got him started packing toys in his book bag. She flung clothes into suitcases, remembering that the weather forecast had called for cooler temperatures later in the week. Luke teased her about her obsession with the Weather Channel, but she liked to be prepared. She packed sweaters and light jackets, warm pajamas and socks, and took the bags downstairs.

Jacob dragged his bag behind him into the kitchen. "Why are we going to Granny and Pop's?"

She was stuffing a tote bag with granola bars, fruit snacks, and juice boxes. "Because Daddy said we should."

He accepted this. Because Daddy or Mommy said so. She'd used that inconclusive reply on him dozens of times, and he rarely questioned it. But here she was, a grown woman, doing nearly the same thing.

"Is Daddy coming too?"

"No. Go potty," she ordered.

Maggie ran back to the bath off her bedroom, and, with a couple of swipes, emptied the medicine cabinet into the tote with the food. Medical care was spotty enough down in the country. If there were some kind of disaster it might be non-existent. This made her think about her job. She couldn't possibly get to work tomorrow if she drove to Henley County this afternoon, but she didn't know what she'd tell Dr. Harris if she called in now. "Oh, by the way, my husband says there's a national disaster coming, so all the pregnant ladies will have to do without my care tomorrow." They had four due this week, and she'd worry about them. But she was a mother too. From the bedside table she threw in her contraceptives. It looked like she still had a couple of weeks' worth. Plenty. Picking up her nursing bag, the one with her stethoscope, hemostat, pin light, and scissors, she carried it and the tote bag downstairs.

"I'm ready, Mommy." Jacob stood by the back door. He had her ability to seem perfectly still and calm, although, in Maggie's case, it was an act, useful with patients and intriguing to Luke. She hoped Jacob's serenity was genuine.

"Okay, sweetie. I need to get the bags in the car, and then we'll go. Why don't you pick out a few of your books to take? And maybe your crayons." If she followed Luke's instructions, she had one more thing to do.

Years ago, when he'd outlined the emergency plan, he'd said for her to take the gun, the one he'd bought for the house, stored high up in the coat closet away from Jacob's reach. "I keep it loaded," he'd said, "but take the box of ammo next to it. You know how to use it."

She supposed she did; Luke had taken her to the range twice, back before Jacob had come along, but she'd never gotten over the urge to blink when she squeezed the trigger and the whole idea of shooting appalled her. Unlike Luke who'd handled guns since he was no older than Jacob, she'd never touched anything more lethal than her toy laser pistol until she'd met Luke.

Maggie stretched to reach the Smith and Wesson 38, hidden behind Luke's collection of ball caps. She'd just as soon handle a snake. The gun and shells weighed down her purse, making her worry about the straps snapping, but she'd done what she'd been told. If it was all foolishness, that was Luke's fault.

Chapter Two

The Customs and Border Protection people let Luke help them herd the passengers onto the plane, the same one that had carried them across the Atlantic. After four hours of waiting in Customs, most of the passengers were too worn out to get cantankerous, but a half dozen or so had jerky movements and darting eyes that kept Luke alert. The Customs Supervisor had told Luke and the other officers that he'd talk to everyone once they were airborne. About time, Luke thought.

They'd filled the plane with passengers first, leaving Luke a window seat near the middle. He wondered if it was the same seat where the man had died. He'd heard a flight attendant say the man had huddled down, head pressed against the window and face covered by his jacket. It made Luke want to wash his hands. Hell, it made him want to shower continuously for a week. The plane was messy; none of Flight 29's trash had been removed. And it smelled bad, or maybe that was his imagination.

Despite his queasiness, he'd been the one to ask about food. His stomach had been growling for hours, and he had no idea how long it would take to reach their unknown destination. Besides, people could get mean when they were hungry. Someone had sent down a cart of soft drinks while they were still waiting in the Customs Hall, but they wouldn't get food until they were in flight, the supervisor said.

It looked like everyone was on board, from the EMTs to the terrified girl from currency exchange. Lots of ominous empty seats. The same pilots and flight attendants, looking anything but fresh and friendly, manned the plane. He wondered if they'd serve alcohol. The one guy who'd been sipping from his duty-free bag all afternoon had hardly been able to walk onto the plane. Four or five Customs officers prowled up and down the aisle, watching and waiting. Maybe they'd be the ones to offer blankets and check seatbelts.

The plane's engines roared to life, and at that moment Professor Mayfield slipped into the seat next to Luke. Despite her age, she looked more serene than anyone else on the plane. To make conversation as much as anything, he said, "Know where we're going?"

She surprised him. "Somewhere in Illinois."

"Really? How do you know that?"

She clasped her hands in her lap. An old-fashioned wedding ring rested below her knobby knuckle. Luke wondered if Mr. Professor

Mayfield was waiting at home or deceased. "I'm not official. I move around. I hear things."

"What else do you know, Professor Mayfield?"

She gazed out the window, beyond Luke, at the lights on the ramp. The sky was black behind the sodium glare. "We're a long way from the classroom, Luke. You may call me Ilse."

He bobbed his head as formally as she'd spoken.

"We're going to an unused military facility to be quarantined until they discover the cause of the man's death." She frowned. "They've sent his blood to Atlanta."

"The CDC," Luke said. Her eyes clouded for a second. "The Center for Disease Control."

She nodded. "They do not think this was the only plane carrying infected passengers."

"I heard that much," Luke said.

She closed her eyes, her lean face as composed as a corpse, which she, and everyone else might be soon. Luke rested his head against the seat, ignoring the possibility of the dead guy's germs. A crapshoot, his dad would call it. He could worry about how exhausted the pilot was or where they were going. He figured he could worry about how well the government was going to handle it all. Or, he could worry about getting sick. Usually he left worrying up to Maggie; she was good at it. He made an effort to picture Maggie and Jacob locked up secure in the cocoon of their car, speeding through the darkness to the mountains where he hoped they'd be safe.

❖

Nothing seemed unusual in River Hills, Kentucky as Maggie stopped at an ATM for cash and gassed up the car. Until she'd married Luke, she'd lived her entire life across the river on the west side of Cincinnati, an area known for bingo, tight families, chili parlors, and Pete Rose. Her family didn't go to Kentucky, even to shop or eat, and they'd never flown anywhere either. Some of them didn't even realize that the Cincinnati airport was actually in Kentucky. Where it belongs, joked Luke, who'd been as adamant about living in Kentucky as her family had always been about Ohio. You'd think the river was an armed border, she'd told him when he found their first apartment in Kentucky. Isn't it, he'd asked, his eyes dancing.

She wasn't happy about passing the ramp for South I75, but she followed Luke's instructions. Take the back roads, he'd said. The interstates might get clogged up. That was fine for Luke; he'd grown up driving on roads so narrow and winding that the back of the car nearly met the front. Maggie wasn't comfortable with it, and she missed the dependable availability of McDonald's and Speedway. But she obeyed because Luke had said so and because she guessed she liked having someone tell her what to do.

So far, Jacob was happy running his newest truck up and down his jeans. It wouldn't last. She turned on the radio, switching from station to station to hear what was going on, but she couldn't get any news at all. Sports and sports talk on AM and music and ads on FM. If Luke had jumped the gun on this one she was going to kill him.

He loved going down home, as he called it, and his parents, Roy and Oleatha, loved seeing him. They tolerated Maggie because she was Luke's wife and Jacob's mother, but she wasn't really family; she was a stranger, and even worse, she was city. It wasn't fair, but then she didn't suppose any kind of prejudice was. When they visited Henley County, Maggie tried to help out, to be cheerful and willing, but it didn't matter. She would never fit in.

She drove. The weather was beautiful, and no more cars populated the narrow road than there would've been on any pretty Sunday. Falmouth was quiet, and she was nearly to Lexington when both Jacob and the traffic started snarling up. "I'm hungry," he whined. "Are we going to stop for burgerfries?" It was one of the few baby expressions he'd kept, probably because he realized his parents thought it was cute.

"Not just yet," she said. "Here." She handed him a granola bar and a juice box.

"I want real food," he protested, his voice threatening to turn into a full-blown tantrum.

"Jacob." Luke would've had him quiet in a minute; he had that policeman's way about him, even with a child. But Maggie dreaded Jacob's infrequent outbursts, knowing they sometimes made her as blindly angry as the child. This was one of the reasons she'd held firm about not having more children even though Luke wanted them. Jacob settled down this time, though, and she heard him slurping his juice.

She wondered if Lexington's heavy traffic had anything to do with the disaster, whatever it was, but couldn't see any signs of it. Parking lots were full, and people looked relaxed as they stopped and started. Going by Luke's route, she had to drive straight through town with every shopping destination known to man as well as fast-food restaurants on every corner. She expected Jacob to start up any minute, but he'd opened a book and was turning pages while he chewed. She relaxed an inch; she wanted to get past the traffic before she stopped.

Glancing over at her phone, Maggie considered if it would do any good to call Luke. Probably not, but she did it anyway, getting only his voice mail. Her stomach knotted up with thinking about what might be happening. After seven years of marriage, she pretty much knew what he'd say about that: most things in life are small potatoes, Maggie, but you turn them into Idaho bakers. She smiled at the Toyota in front of her.

By the time they reached the other side of Lexington and crossed the Kentucky River, Jacob had fallen asleep. It was nearly dark, but she could see the steep palisades knifing into the river and make out flames of color from the trees that had turned. It was beautiful country, bold and flamboyant compared to Ohio's bland simplicity. Maybe it was the land itself that made Luke and his family so original and eccentric. Or stubborn and odd, she thought. She scrunched her neck, hearing pops and cracks. She'd stop in Salton, maybe another ten miles or so, and they'd eat at the little diner Luke liked. Maybe she'd hear something there.

❖

They'd barely reached altitude when the flight attendants handed out drinks and dry turkey sandwiches from a bin. No cart, no please, no thank you. They got to choose Coke or Diet Coke, both warm. Luke didn't care. He kept eying the front of the plane where he expected the Customs supervisor to start talking any minute.

For a few minutes, all Luke could hear were tops being popped and wrappers crumpled, but it didn't take long for the thrum of conversation to start up again. And it was getting louder toward the back, one or two voices especially. Ilse Mayfield looked at him, and he nodded. Somebody better say something soon. Finally the supervisor stood. He was a sturdy man, not fat but deep-chested, with a ring of graying hair around his bald head. On his dark blue uniform was the same insignia as an Army major. Come on, Major, Luke thought, give us the scoop. The man's lips were working like he was trying to dredge words up from his stomach.

"My name's Allen," he said. "Frank Allen, and I'm a Customs Supervisor for the port of Cincinnati. I'm going to tell you folks what we know, which isn't much."

He paused, not a good idea in Luke's mind, and there were some shouts from the back about letting them go home or making calls or getting off the plane. Allen talked over them. "A man died on Flight 29. The EMTs, who are here with us," he gestured to his left, "determined that he died of some sickness, probably an infection. Now, we don't know what kind of infection, and we won't know until they've done lab tests at the Center for Disease Control. But we're playing it safe. Based on where this man was coming from, his ticket, and the fact that he had a partner on the plane who didn't die and was able to exit the airport, we think it might be a planned attack. We also know there were similar passengers on at least five other flights, all of which landed considerably before Barcelona."

Murmuring jumped to a roar at this. Luke heard "anthrax" and "biological warfare." Someone was sobbing.

Allen waited and then started again, speaking no louder so the passengers had to quiet down to hear him. "We are, all of us, quarantined until we find out what we've been exposed to. The government is sending us to Ft. Rieselman in Illinois, where we will wait for news. The post was in the process of being closed down, but they're preparing it for us with food, comfortable quarters, and expert medical care. Once we get to Ft. Rieselman, you can have your belongings and phones back. The president's speaking to the nation here in a few minutes, but we have someone recording that so you can hear it after we land."

The man looked tired. Everybody on the plane looked tired. Allen rubbed the back of his neck with a fleshy hand and went on. "I'm just as upset about this as you folks are. Normally I'd be setting up camp for the evening in my recliner if I were home, and . . ."

Noise from the back of the plane escalated. A woman screamed, a child cried, and there was the sound of what might've been kicking. Ilse Mayfield gulped air like she was drowning, and Luke stretched to see the rear. The agitated young man Luke had noticed back in the Customs Hall stood in the aisle waving his hands and exhorting the passengers to listen to him. His voice was high, electric. "He's a damned terrorist. This is a fucking hijacking, and we're the hostages. We need to make them take us back to Cincinnati right now!" Then the man reeled down the narrow aisle, his feet smacking the floor. Over the headrest of his seat, Luke could see him: slim with wavy blond hair and a contorted face. His fists were clenched, but Luke couldn't see whether they held anything but air. "Are you going to let them get away with this?" the angry guy shouted, cheerleading the passengers as he passed them. "Let's roll!"

Luke's first thought was how inappropriate, how all but sacrilegious it was to reference the heroes of 9/11, who'd demonstrated their bravery when this guy was a toddler. Then Luke glimpsed something metal between the man's bunched fingers as he waved his hands up and down. So far none of the passengers had joined the guy, but it could happen. Trapped in the window seat, Luke sprang his seatbelt loose, stood hunched down under the overhead bin, and was ready to break Ilse Mayfield's toes if he had to. She'd scrunched until she looked like a praying mantis. The screaming man was nearly to Luke's row, and nobody'd done a thing. Allen was saying something like "See here," or "Settle down," and the uniforms ahead of Luke were unbuckling seatbelts and glancing first at Allen, then at the screamer. The man charged on, whipping his head from side to side, but the passengers were ignoring him or covering their faces. Just as Luke hitched his leg to clamber over Ilse, the Customs officer in the aisle seat behind them stood. He hesitated for one second to let the man get in front of him, then grabbed the guy's arm and swept his leg. The agitated passenger was down before he knew what'd hit him and was cuffed and back in his seat, blood streaming from his nose, in seconds. He'd been grasping car keys; they lay on the floor beside a spot of blood.

Luke sat and Ilse Mayfield slowly released her long legs. Frank Allen sent two of the younger, burlier Customs people back to the angry man's area, and two passengers, looking like they'd cry if somebody said "boo" to them, crept toward the front to take empty seats. Allen went on like nothing had happened. "I'm sure you are feeling unlucky as all get out, but the other folks who flew with the terrorists on either their transatlantic or connecting flights are scattered all over the country. We'll be able to help you the minute there's a symptom." Nobody reacted to this. He went on. "We're doing our best to take care of you folks. I understand how anxious and unhappy you must be, but we'll be a lot better off working together than against each other. Professor Mayfield?" He raised his bushy eyebrows.

"He'll want me to translate." She unbuckled her seatbelt.

And calm people down, Luke thought.

When the Customs officer who'd brought down the screamer returned to his seat, Luke caught his eye. "Nice work."

The man picked up the keys and shrugged. He was probably fifty judging by the wrinkles on his neck and the gray in his hair, and no more than five, nine or ten with a wiry build. It hadn't mattered. Luke had learned that in the National Guard. The skinny guys were often stronger than the beefy ones. Luke glanced at the man's name badge: Briley. He said, "The guy never even saw me."

Luke heard the hills in the man's voice and was tempted to ask where he was from, but Briley had already sat down. Luke figured there'd be plenty of time at Ft. Rieselman to strike up a conversation. If they weren't sick.

❖

Maggie's fingers itched to try the radio again or maybe the phone, but she resisted. Jacob was sleeping, and if she woke him, he'd start in again about stopping to eat. She should be hungry too, she supposed. Her stomach was growling, but it was also so tensed up that eating seemed absurd. There was no traffic now in either direction. The solitude was eerie, reminding her of spring break her senior year in college. She'd never had money to make hedonistic pilgrimages to the beaches like most of her friends. But that spring had been her last chance, so she'd saved her money and driven to Virginia, to William and Mary where a high school friend went to school. Maggie remembered the trip, the first long one she'd taken by herself. Most of it had been fine, but as she'd neared Williamsburg, she'd been on a lonely, two–laned road like this one, with no lights, cars, or signs of civilization. She remembered how tall pines had loomed over the narrow road. She'd barely been able to see the sky.

Shivering, Maggie looked ahead for the turn to Salton. The highway bypassed the tiny town, but it was hardly a half-mile to its center and the cozy little diner. She squinted at blue lights at the intersection, and as she neared it she saw that they were flares, set up in front of a police, or, in this area, probably a sheriff's car blocking the turn-off. She slowed and then stopped, rolling down her window. Two men stood by the cruiser, blue flames licking at the rifles they held.

This was a bad idea, Maggie thought. She remembered the .38 in her purse. She didn't have a permit; it was registered in Luke's name and paperwork had been the last thing on her mind when she'd left home. She didn't need some kind of legal hassle, or worse. Stopping woke Jacob who yawned, looked out at the uniformed man, and said, "Daddy?"

"No, not Daddy."

The man in uniform approached the passenger side window, so she lowered it. He kept his distance. "We've got the road into Salton blocked, ma'am," he said. "Where you heading?"

The other man was in civilian clothes, holding his rifle at the ready. He made her nervous. "We're going just beyond Catesboro." She hoped the sheriff wouldn't ask for identification. She wasn't sure she could get her wallet out of her purse without him spotting the gun.

The sheriff tilted his head and hunkered down in an attempt to see her, but he stayed better than four feet from the car. It looked like his mountie hat might fall off any minute. He seemed to have the same thought and raised his hand to the brim. "So why were you coming to Salton?"

"To eat," she replied, hoping her voice wasn't shaking as much as her hands. She gripped the steering wheel. "At the diner by the hardware store."

"I'm hungry, Mommy," Jacob complained from the backseat.

The man took his time, looking first at Jacob and then at her. He took off his hat and brushed his hand through hair as short as velcro. "Don't you know what's going on, ma'am?" The flares made him look cyanotic.

"No," she said, more loudly than she'd intended. "What *is* going on?"

"They closed up the Cincinnati Airport. Man died on a plane, and they think it might be plague or something like that. Radio said everybody on the plane was exposed, and a bunch of 'em got off and flew other places or went into the city. That's why we're not letting nobody into Salton. Trying to protect the town."

Dear God, Maggie thought. She could feel her heartbeat in her neck. The sheriff was staring at her, and Jacob was kicking at the seat, declaring he was *famished*. Where had he picked up that word?

"Ma'am?" The sheriff's eyes were all squinched up like he was afraid she was going to faint or something. She heard the sound of the car's motor coming and going. Maybe she was going to faint. She took a deep breath.

"Ma'am," he said again, "where are you all coming from?"

She exhaled. "From Northern Kentucky, River Hills. It's close to the airport." The man was staring at her, and she'd bet he was itching to move even farther away. The civilian guy cleared his throat and spat.

She went on. "My husband is an airport policeman."

Both men swore in hushed voices.

"He called and told us to get out of town."

The sheriff stood and turned to the other man. Maggie wasn't worried about the gun now; these two would probably think it was smart for her to have it. Besides, Luke always said there was a fraternity among law enforcement people, not that he'd ever take advantage of it. The two were conversing in low tones, and she couldn't have heard them anyway for Jacob's complaining. "Hush, baby," she said. "I can't do anything about this."

Something in her tone must've struck the child for he stopped whining. She glanced in the rear view mirror and saw that his dark eyes were wide. "We're all right," she said, reaching back to pat his leg.

But were they, the demons in her head asked. And was Luke? The man had said plague. Was that a generic term for illness or did he actually mean bubonic plague? She searched her mind to remember what she'd studied about it. The Middle Ages were long gone; bubonic plague wasn't much of a challenge for today's drugs and besides, there weren't usually fleas on airplanes. Of course, diseases could be created in labs. Whatever it was, Luke had been exposed. God.

The civilian walked back to a pickup parked behind the sheriff's cruiser, and opened the door. He was fiddling with something he put into a Wal-Mart bag and brought back to the sheriff who stooped again. "J. D.'s wife packed us some sandwiches. He's put a couple in this bag along with some pop. Maybe that'll hold you until you get to Catesboro."

"How kind," Maggie breathed.

"You got people there?"

She nodded but wasn't sure he could see her. "Yes," she said. "My husband's relatives." She should've said "kin," but he'd know what she meant.

The sheriff walked around to her side of the car and placed the bag on the pavement. "No offense, ma'am, but I don't want to get too close. If you'll just hold on a second."

She nodded again and waited until he'd gone back to stand by his cruiser. Then she retrieved the bag and called, "Thank you. Thank you both very much." The sheriff touched his hat, and she drove off.

The sandwiches were ham and cheese, Jacob's second-best favorite, and after peeling off an offensive leaf of lettuce, he forgot all about burgerfries. He liked the can of Coke even better. Maggie took one bite, but her stomach wanted nothing to do with food. The road seemed darker and more tortuous than ever, and they still had over an hour to get to her in-laws' house. She should call them; they had no idea they were getting company, but she didn't know what to say. Did they know anything about the situation? Some evenings they didn't bother to turn on their television. Lots of nights they were in bed by nine. She glanced at the clock. It felt like midnight but was only a little after seven.

Happy now, Jacob was going on about the sheriff, the twisty road, his soft drink bubbles, and Maggie made the right comments without thinking about them. Back when she was a girl, it seemed like she fought fear all the time, but when she'd married Luke, his big, confident presence had banished all those dreads and dangers. She didn't have him now. She'd have to dredge up her defenses again, and she could. After their father left them, she'd protected her ten-year-old sister from their mother's drunken rampages. She'd called the fire department when Mom's cigarette set the apartment on fire. She'd managed to go to college. Why, she'd even faced off an angry monkey. She almost smiled.

"Jacob? Did I ever tell you about the time I had a fight with a monkey?"

He giggled. "Was it Curious George?"

"No, I don't think so. He didn't wear a little red hat." She'd been working at the VA hospital, where she'd eventually met Luke right after his time in Afghanistan. "I was working nights at the hospital," she told Jacob. "And when I got off work, it was dark outside. Kinda spooky and lonesome."

"Like Halloween." Jacob slurped more Coke.

"Right. Well, one night I went to my car and sitting right on the hood was a monkey."

"Was he big?"

"He seemed pretty big to me, chattering and banging on the hood."

"Was he someone's pet?"

"No. The hospital was right next to the zoo. Remember when Daddy and I took you to the zoo last summer?"

"Uh huh. I liked the giraffes best."

"Well, I think this monkey had escaped from the zoo. And I think he was scared. He screeched at me and looked like he wanted to bite."

Maggie glanced back to see Jacob's open mouth. "What did you do?"

"I said, Mr. Monkey, you're sitting on the wrong car. Then I shook my finger at him and banged my purse against the hood. He stared at me as if to say, who do you think you are, and then he screeched and scampered off." She used a funny voice and got a hearty laugh from Jacob, who said maybe the monkey had learned a lesson and wouldn't run away any more.

As they drove deeper into the Kentucky mountains, she coaxed Jacob into singing all the baby songs they'd shared for years: "Itsy, Bitsy Spider," and "Little Bunny Foo Foo," and others she'd nearly forgotten. Her phone beeped with a text. Her sister. Maggie didn't want to text on this road, and she didn't want to talk about horrific things in front of Jacob. The road was deserted, and the only lights came from houses buried deep behind the trees in an occasional valley or up on a narrow ridge. Leaves blew onto the road and her windshield, making Jacob exclaim, "It's raining leaves, Mommy!"

The tiny town of Catesboro was just as silent as the hills. Leaves skittered across the empty main street. The Dairy Bar was dark and closed, and even the church parking lots, usually full on a Sunday evening, were empty. The news was out to everybody now.

She'd wondered if the sheriff of Henley County would try to block off Catesboro as they'd done in Salton, but she saw no sign of it. The effort would've been futile anyway. The county was honeycombed with little roads, usually with picturesque names of gaps and creeks or, sometimes, the people who lived on them. Luke knew all the roads, and most trips down here he would take her exploring them. Maybe he knew how long the hours at his parents' house were for her, or maybe he wanted to reclaim the territory that had once been his. She made a sharp right just after Catesboro and then, after five contorted miles, took a left onto a narrow track that Luke said had once been a logging trail. Trees canopied the road as she went down a hill and made one more turn. After thirty or forty yards, the road, not much more than a path, changed from pavement to gravel and twisted down a sharp hill. She slowed to nothing as the gravel shifted under her tires. An even narrower gravel track led off to the left, to Crazy Annie's house, Luke'd said, and then she saw the lights at Roy and Oleatha's, peeping through the trees. She'd made it. Maggie pulled her car up behind Roy's truck and turned off the engine. "We're here!" Jacob exclaimed, and Maggie straightened her shoulders.

Chapter Three

Luke woke with a start and reached over the side of the bunk for his M203 before he remembered where he was and why he was there. He reckoned it was the military setting that had taken his instincts back to Afghanistan where his rifle had been like a third arm. The tiny room was pitch dark. He could hear Bob Briley's breathing from the other bed. At least he was breathing.

It'd been past nine o'clock last night by the time they'd gathered everyone into the mess hall for food and information. They'd served themselves lukewarm spaghetti and meatballs from the chow line. He'd been thinking how much better he felt for eating when two men showed up in moon suits, and the meatballs turned to depth charges. One was from Washington, and he'd tried to put a good spin on everything despite the fact that he looked like a poster boy for HAZMAT. He'd told them to choose partners for their rooms. He'd kept saying that they'd be cared for, that the government was going to do everything they could to keep them comfortable and healthy.

Luke had heard nearly the same thing when they brought in a television and played the president's speech. Don't panic, the president urged, but then he'd gone on to say that all schools and non-essential businesses were to close. All air, rail, and public means of transportation were shut down. The stock market and banks were closed until further notice. The country was under lockdown, but they weren't to panic. Right.

Somebody'd asked if the other airports had passengers in isolation, and the Washington guy had ducked his head. No, he'd said. Only Cincinnati. Their Passenger of Death had been the only one to die early. But this was good, he'd insisted. "If it hadn't been for him, we'd still be in the dark." Which was supposed to make them feel special, Luke had thought. Bob Briley was sitting next to him mumbling cuss words. Out there, across the nation, people were breathing the same air as the terrorists, sharing droplets from their coughs and sneezes. And the germs were hopping from host to host, gleefully spreading disaster.

The other guy was a doctor, but he hadn't taken Spin 101 in med school. No, he said, we have no idea what the sickness is and won't for a while. Yes, they could all become infected. And yes, they could die. Millions could die. Across the table he'd seen Ilse Mayfield holding the currency exchange girl's hand. One of the flight attendants had covered her face. For some reason the scene made Luke think of church back home when the spirit seized the congregation and people were moaning and crying. Except this was the Apocalypse rather than Pentecost. "We're set up in the building with the big red cross. Let us know," the doctor had urged, "if you even have the slightest twinge of a headache or any other symptom."

Everybody'd been too tired and disheartened to say much after the doctor left. Until the Customs dudes handed back the phones. Not two minutes passed before people began roaring. No wireless. No internet. The guys in charge kept saying this would be remedied soon, but several people were shouting, hollering, cussing. But at least they could make calls. Better than nothing, although not for him. He'd turned his on, but it was out of bars. Unless he found a way to charge the thing, it was useless.

Luke got out of his bunk, his feet sliding against cold tile. He still felt dirty. Only the fact that others were waiting their turns had rousted him out of last night's shower. Outside the bathroom, someone had placed boxes of new undershirts and boxers, and these were what Luke was wearing. He couldn't abide the thought of putting his uniform back on and would've felt naked in it anyway: they'd taken away his and the other armed officers' weapons, cuffs, and sprays.

When Luke opened the door to the hallway, Briley groaned at the light. "Rise and shine, soldier. The Easter Bunny's been here," Luke said, tossing Bob one of the two plastic bags that hung on the doorknob. Inside were toiletries, toothbrushes, sweatpants, sweatshirts, more underwear, and socks. He reckoned they'd have to wear their own shoes.

"Good God," Briley moaned. "What time is it?"

Luke grinned at him. They'd decided to bunk together just after Bob had said he was from Tennessee, not 50 miles from where Luke had grown up. "It's nearly seven," he replied. "You're ornery as catshit, Briley."

Bob sat up. "But I'm still healthy. Wasn't sure we'd see morning."

While Briley showered, Luke glanced at his roommate's belongings on the chest of drawers. Comb, wallet, pen, badge, and a curious, little leather packet about big enough to hold more pens. He got caught in the act when Bob walked in, toweling his sparse hair.

"Snooping."

Bob grinned. "Know what those are?"

Luke opened the leather pouch. "Lock picks," he said.

"Yep. Used them to open unclaimed luggage." Briley pulled his sweatshirt over his head. "Handy for other stuff too," he said with a wink. "Ever fooled with them?"

Luke shook his head. "I've seen them before. Played with them a little bit. Tougher to do than you'd think."

"For certain." He pointed out two little wrenches. "You use these to hold things in place and the others to move tumblers." He slid his fingers over two of the skinny tools. "These are for padlocks; the others are for doors."

"Could be useful around here."

Briley nodded. "Never know."

The two of them made their way to the mess hall along with bunches of people who emerged from theirs and other barracks. It appeared that one of the buildings housed males and another females and couples.

"Looks like shirts versus sweats," Bob observed. The passengers and flight crew had retrieved their baggage after last night's meeting and were dressed in their own clothes. All the others were wearing gray sweats like Bob and Luke.

"Miss my gun," Luke complained.

"Thought you were in the military, boy."

Luke frowned.

"You know." Briley started reciting, pointing first at an imaginary firearm at his waist and then at his crotch. "Here's my weapon; here's my gun…"

Grinning, Luke joined in. "One's for shooting; one's for fun. Yeah, I remember. Okay, I wish we had our weapons."

"Me too. I ain't sure it's a good idea that none of us have them." Briley nodded toward a clump of people going into the mess hall. Their chatter was high-pitched, indignant. People didn't take kindly to confinement.

Briley turned serious. "One bag belonging to someone here had an orange tag on it."

"Packed weapon?"

Briley nodded. "But the tag was gone by the time they loaded the baggage back on the plane."

"I don't like that."

"Me either. I'm going to have a word with Allen."

Luke nodded. "Makes me even more uncomfortable not to have mine."

A woman wearing sweats stood outside the mess hall marking people off a list as they went inside. "Taking roll?" Briley asked.

"Yep." She made a mark for Bob but had to ask Luke his name.

"She's Agriculture," Bob explained. "How many of us are there?"

"Ninety-seven. Fifty-two passengers, six flight crew, two EMT's, one airport policeman." She nodded at Luke. "One volunteer, one bank employee, two airline representatives, and the rest TSA or Customs and Agriculture."

Luke and Bob were holding up the line but neither moved. "That means a bunch of people got through Customs," Bob said, his voice tight.

She looked down at her list. "Allen says over eighty. And one volunteer who just walked out onto the ramp and disappeared."

Luke let out a deep breath. "Over eighty. Out there spreading it to the world."

She nodded.

Bob whispered, "Anybody sick yet?"

She shook her head. "Get your nametags. We're supposed to be friendly."

They picked up the sticky-backed tags, scribbling their names on them, and went into the mess hall. Like the night before, food was set out on the cafeteria line, but, again, there were no people serving it. Luke put a couple of limp pancakes on his plate but all that was left of the bacon was grease pooled in the pan. "Reckon we're out of luck if they run out," Briley said.

"Then we better get up earlier tomorrow."

They chose seats near Ilse and the currency girl, whose nametag said she was Alicia and who'd shared a room with Professor Mayfield. The girl looked better this morning; although, without makeup and her carefully styled hair, she didn't seem much more than a child. "Have you ever been to Disney World?" she chirped. "They say the park is honeycombed with tunnels for the people working there. I almost wonder if there are tunnels here." She blinked several times. "We haven't seen the cooks or anybody."

Bob smiled at her. He probably had kids her age. "Services provided by the Easter Bunny and Mickey Mouse." He looked pleased when Alicia giggled.

Ilse stared at her coffee cup. "We have a schedule," she said, pushing a couple of papers toward Bob and Luke. "For meals and medical checks."

Luke glanced at it. People with last names between A and F were to go to the medical building at 10:00. That would include Bob and him.

"I think we could do more," Ilse announced. "We should organize into teams for serving meals. Some people took obscenely large portions this morning, leaving little for the latecomers." She sniffed.

"Come earlier," Luke said, stuffing pancake into his mouth. They were awful compared to Maggie's, but he ate them anyway.

"They don't unlock the door until seven."

Alicia giggled again. There were nerves in it. "That's so Mickey Mouse can escape before we see him."

Ilse went on. "We could institute some portion control and move the line more quickly."

You couldn't beat the Germans for organization, Luke thought as he wiped his mouth. "Sounds like a plan. No news on Wi-Fi?"

She shook her head. "I'll be talking to Mr. Allen about that and meals this morning."

"Yeah, we have something we want to discuss with him too," Bob said, slurping down the rest of his coffee. "Where is he?"

Ilse looked pale to Luke, but maybe he was seeing goblins under the bed. Maggie always said that the mind played a bigger part in illness than the body. He'd heard somebody complaining about achy legs in the cafeteria line.

"He's probably in the recreation room," Alicia offered. "There's a TV over there and a pool table." She shrugged. "Don't know what we're going to do all day."

"Hustle pool, I reckon," Bob said. "Might make me some money."

Luke grinned. "I need to find a charger that'll fit my phone. That'd be entertainment for me."

Alicia jumped up, all bright eyes and energy. "Maybe mine will work. Could I have your phone?"

"Sure." Luke smiled and handed it to her. She seemed to need smiles.

After she left, tottering on high-heeled sandals that looked absurd with her sweats, Ilse sighed. "Youth," she said. "She cried half the night, but this morning she's bright as a new penny."

"She's probably just glad to be healthy," Briley said.

"I suspect we're luckier than the people outside." Her eyes followed Alicia as she moved between the tables. "Shoes," she mumbled. "We also need shoes and feminine hygiene products and. . ."

"Shoes would be good," interrupted Luke. "But as to luck, I figure it'll be about the same here as out there. Some of us will catch it, some won't. We might get better care in here. Might not."

Bob frowned. "However it goes, I'd bet they're going to use us as lab rats to figure out what to do with the rest of the country. We're the only ones they can put under a microscope. That makes me a little anxious."

Luke felt his shoulders twitch. "Everybody here's as anxious as whores in church. And that makes *me* anxious. Let's go see Allen, okay?" He stood.

Most people had left the mess hall, but the blond guy, the one who'd made a scene on the plane, stood and moved to one clump of people near the door, most of them talking on their phones. No one seemed to be babysitting him. No one was paying any attention to him either.

"His name's Todd," Briley said. "According to his baggage tag, he was heading to Detroit."

"Could he be the one with the firearm?"

"No way of knowing. I heard that he was sitting next to the dead guy. That'd make anybody a little hinky, wouldn't it?"

"Yeah, but armed and hinky is not good." Alone, Todd walked over to the food line and got a cup of coffee. "Not too popular, is he?" Luke said.

Snorting, Briley said, "Not likely to be, is he? But I can't help but feel sorry for him."

❖

The red-eyed clock said it was five-ten. Maggie rolled away from Jacob's warm, damp body and stared into the darkness. She'd never been one to sleep late, and nerves made it worse. Besides, Roy had said last night that they'd need to set out by six-thirty. Getting up this early would give her a little time to herself.

She fumbled around in the dark to find her clothes, swiping on a little deodorant and grabbing her hairbrush. This was the strangest house. She had to go through the kitchen to get to the bathroom, so she started coffee on her way and then dressed, splashing water on her face and brushing her teeth. She hated the water down here, even if, as Roy always bragged, it was from the cleanest well in the county because it was filtered through sand. She didn't care if it'd come through a beach: it smelled like metal and minerals and she'd always brought bottled water for her and Jacob to drink when they visited. They'd have to risk it this trip.

Pouring herself a cup of coffee, she sneaked out the kitchen door and crept around the house to the front porch. Dark had a whole new meaning down here. It was dense, almost tangible. She stumbled on a step, slopping hot coffee on her hand and stifling a curse. The porch swing was damp with dew, and the air was thick, like it'd been bottled up in this hollow and steamed.

If Roy and Oleatha had been up she would've turned on the television to see if anything was new. Craving information, she also wished she could get a clear signal for the internet down here in the boonies. She doubted the CDC knew anything yet but wondered if anybody had sickened. They'd be able to tell a few things from symptoms. She wished she still had her nursing books, especially the one that had spent thousands of words on each communicable disease. But she'd always sold her books as soon as a class was over, desperate for the pittance they'd contribute to the next quarter's expenses.

Roy and Oleatha hadn't been surprised to see them last night. They'd been watching television and knew about the Cincinnati Airport. Roy'd said that Luke had been smart to send them down. Oleatha had given them the back bedroom like she always did. She'd been the one to answer the call from Luke. It made sense that he'd called their home phone, but Maggie had begrudged Luke's mother the two or three minutes he spoke to her before she gave the phone to Maggie. His phone had died five minutes later, before she could ask how long they said he'd be there and before she could say she loved him. He probably didn't know the answer to her question and knew how she felt, but it bothered her.

From the porch swing, she couldn't see the tops of the trees across the track. The Davies' house sat in a narrow ravine with hills rising both in front and behind it. That's what a holler is, Luke'd remarked the first time he'd brought her down here. She'd figured it out. "Oh, a *hollow*," she'd said.

He'd grinned. "Yep, a holler."

Compared to Cincinnati or River Hills, it was quiet as a cave, although as she peered into the dark, she heard soft, secret sounds. A light breeze swished the trees, and birds were tuning up. Luke thought it was peaceful, but the absence of people made her feel like nature was going to grab her up and smother her. Those soft sounds could be animals prowling through the woods and not escapees from the zoo either. Maggie smiled at how Jacob had laughed at her monkey story. Then she heard other noises, the sounds of people stirring in the house behind her, and before long Roy stepped out on the porch and lifted his coffee cup.

"Nice of you to start the coffee," he said. He went to the edge of the porch and craned his neck to see sky. The sun wouldn't touch the house until mid-morning.

Roy was a tall man, like his son, and he had a full head of wavy hair like him too, although Roy's was white and worn a little long, like a television evangelist. Oleatha's cooking had thickened his waist and time had creased his face, but he was an imposing man, even a handsome one for all his seventy years.

"You sure you can drive my pickup?"

She'd told him so last night, but he'd been a truck driver for who knows how many years, driving eighteen wheelers between Knoxville and Detroit most of the time. "I can drive it," she said. She'd managed with any number of strange and broken-down vehicles her mother had owned.

His shoulders shrugged inside his plaid shirt. The buttons were working a little harder than they should've. "I was supposed to have my cataract surgery the end of this week. Man from church was going to drive me down for it. But I reckon they won't be doing surgeries now."

"I doubt it."

He took a swig of coffee and squinted back at the road. "I hate not being able to drive, especially since Oleatha quit ten years ago. Said driving made her nervous. Folks from church have been taking us to the store for the last several months. We don't have as much laid in as usual."

Not a good thing, she thought. But she also felt bad that she and Luke hadn't known his vision had deteriorated. "You should've told us."

He shrugged again. "Wasn't nothing y'all could've done about it. You've got your work up in the city."

They would've found a way, Maggie thought, but Luke's parents would rather die than ask for help, unlike her mother who thought the world and all its social agencies had been established for her benefit.

Oleatha came to the door and whispered that she had breakfast ready, that they should let little Jacob sleep. Over fried eggs, sausage, and canned biscuits, Oleatha listed all the things they should buy. Last night Roy had said that food trucks probably wouldn't be able to deliver their goods, so he and Maggie should head out early and stock up before everything was gone.

"Luke says you always have enough canned and in the freezer to last for months," Maggie said, scribbling down item after item.

Oleatha shrugged. She was a serious little woman, big-chested and round like a pigeon. "I have some," she said. "But a body can't freeze eggs and milk. You can freeze bread, but it's not much count. Write down juice too. Jacob drinks juice like water."

She and Jacob were trouble for these old people, Maggie thought, but she didn't know what she could do about it.

"You done?" Roy looked at Oleatha.

"I reckon. Get that boy some candy, Roy," Oleatha said. "He'll be missing his daddy."

Roy's truck was a big red Chevy with a touchy clutch, but Maggie eased it up the gravel track and headed back the way she'd come the night before. Roy still seemed nervous about her driving, but she'd do fine unless she had to share the narrow road with another vehicle as big as Roy's. "What do you think this sickness is?" he asked.

"I don't know." She slowed to avoid a mongrel standing in the road. People down here just let their dogs roam. "If they're right and it's terrorism, they could've created most anything in a lab."

"But we're safe down here." He meant to declare it, but a question tinged his voice.

"For now." They passed a few houses with lights on, but there was nobody on the road, thank God. "All it takes is one infected person." This was true, but she wished she hadn't said it. She didn't want to scare him any more than he already was. "It depends on how the disease spreads."

"Like coughing and sneezing?"

She nodded, not sure he could see it. Dawn was breaking, but that wouldn't help his blurry eyes. "That's the most contagious way, but some infections are spread by body fluids, and they're easier to contain." She could get into viruses and bacteria too but didn't think he'd want to hear all that.

Roy turned his head. "I guess we're lucky to have us a nurse down here."

She tried to smile even though she knew there was little she could do to fight a deadly disease. If it comforted him, though, she was glad.

"Course I bet Luke wishes he had you to nurse him."

"I'm sure the quarantined people will get excellent care, and he may not get the disease. We just don't know."

"That's the hell of it, ain't it? We don't know a blessed thing."

It was just about daylight when they pulled into the Catesboro Wal-Mart and discovered that the whole county had been thinking the same thing. Cars crowded the lot and a huge throng gathered at the front doors. Roy squinted. "What's going on? It's past seven, ain't it? They open at seven."

"Twenty past," Maggie said. "But the store's dark." She wasn't sure how much he could see.

They had to park at the end of the lot and more vehicles were pouring in as Maggie and Roy hiked to the store. The crowd was rumbling and a couple of people were banging on the glass. Maggie figured the number of trucks and cars in the lot holding a rifle or shotgun was better than two to one.

As they made their way up to the doors, Roy spoke to several people. He was like Luke: big enough to clear a path for a woman who wasn't but five feet, four inches tall. "Howdy, Bill," Roy said. "What's going on?"

"Ain't nobody come to open up," replied an old man with pants hitched nearly to his armpits.

A hefty woman with a sleepy toddler on her hip complained, "This is a crime. People got to have food." Angry mumbling agreed with her.

A young man fiddled with the brim of his cap. "I reckon we could open the store ourselves. I got a tire iron in the truck."

Somebody laughed, but another man said he had something better than a tire iron. The murmuring grew to a rumble. Roy raised his head like a dog catching a scent. "I don't like the looks of this," he muttered. "Let's go, gal."

There was nothing wrong with Roy's pace. She had to sprint to keep up with him. "I know someplace else," he said when she started the engine. "I'll tell you where to turn."

She thought she'd ridden every secret, winding mile in the county, but Roy had her turning and twisting down paths she'd never seen. Daylight helped, but it was still a harrowing drive. Finally they stopped at the top of a rise in front of a concrete block building with a sign saying it was Hazel Varney's store. Roy grunted as he got out of the truck. "I figured the little stores had been hit hard and early. That's why I decided we'd go to Wal-Mart. But Hazel's so tucked away back here, not many would think of her."

"What's this place called?" Leaves untouched by tires carpeted the gravel around the store. Maybe three or four other buildings were visible from where she stood: a couple of frame houses, one with a trampoline in front, and a rusty trailer with a porch full of logs. The view from the store was open and breathtaking. Although Luke's county felt like a foreign country, Maggie had to admit it was beautiful.

"Pig's Eye. Roy had a sly grin on his face, reminding her of Luke when he was in a teasing mood. She smiled back. "I reckon it was Pisgah to start out with, but somewhere along the line it became Pig's Eye." He waited for her to process this. "You know where Pisgah was?"

She shook her head. This was a test and she was failing it.

"Moses stood on Mount Pisgah when he looked out over the Promised Land." Roy gestured at the post card view, but she doubted that he saw much of it. He turned toward the store. "We'll do as well here as we would've at Wal-Mart and without all the people shoving and shouting."

Maggie wasn't so sure, but she followed him into a store about the size of Kroger's produce section. It was dim and smelled of onions, cheap candy, and tobacco. The floor, made of wide wooden planks, was uneven and ancient. It reminded her of the general stores in cowboy movies.

"How do, Hazel?" Roy said to a skinny old lady standing behind a counter. "Reckon you're still healthy, ain't you?"

She nodded, her wrinkled hand pressed against her mouth. "You?"

"Hunky dory," he replied. "This is Luke's wife. She and the baby come down here to get away from it."

The woman frowned, and Maggie wondered if Hazel thought she was carrying the disease. She spoke in an accent so thick Maggie could hardly understand her. "Where's Luke?"

Roy dropped his head. "He was at the airport. They took him away with the people from that flight."

Hazel shook her head mournfully.

"You got any food left?"

"Ain't nobody been in yet this morning. S'pose they all went to the Wal-Mart."

Roy snorted. "They'll be here soon. We just come from Wal-Mart and they haven't opened up."

"Land!" the woman declared. "Well, get what you need, Roy, before they get here. The truck'll be here directly. It always comes on Mondays."

"I wouldn't count on it." Roy leaned over and hitched up two ten-pound bags of potatoes. "Don't think there'll be anything moving for days."

Hazel mumbled something, but Maggie was concentrating on Oleatha's list. She picked up ten pounds of sugar and five pounds of pinto beans. Jacob wouldn't touch those. Roy joined her as she was looking at the eggs. There were only six cartons. He and Maggie hesitated. "Take all you want," Hazel offered. "That truck will come."

Roy shook his head. Maggie knew how much he loved his morning eggs. He picked up two and walked over to Hazel. "Got to leave some for other folks," he muttered.

"They wouldn't do it for you," Hazel retorted, but Roy said no more.

"Milk won't keep," Maggie said as Roy came back to her side. Hazel had plenty, but there was no point in taking too much.

"No."

Maggie turned to one of the sagging shelves where, on the bottom, there were several cans of condensed milk. "It's no good for drinking or cereal, but you can cook with it."

Roy nodded. "Good idea." He grabbed several loaves of bread. "Guess we can freeze these."

"Yes, although as Oleatha said, it's not much good." Maggie hesitated. This was his store, his home; she wasn't sure how far she should go. "Or we could make bread. I know how."

Surprised, he looked down at her. "You do?" He rubbed his chin. "Don't think Oleatha's ever made anything but cornbread. Well, what do you need?" He put all but two of the loaves back on the shelf.

Maggie was thinking. Yeast, of course, and she could make a starter that would last for months. And tons of flour and more sugar. Who knew how long this would go on? She'd already picked up several jars of peanut butter. With that and bread and Oleatha's homemade blackberry jam, Jacob could eat indefinitely. She silently blessed her Grandma Hauser, her father's mother, who'd taught her how to make bread.

She and Roy had just finished loading up Hazel's counter when another truck pulled up out front. "Good timing," Roy whispered. "What kind of candy does that boy like?"

"Skittles." Maggie opened her purse to get her wallet.

Roy grabbed two bags of candy and gave her a hard look.

"I want to help," she said.

"I take care of my own." He started laying twenties onto Hazel's counter.

"Leave anything for the rest of us, Davies?" A man called as he came through the door.

"A sight more than you'd find at Wal-Mart."

Maggie couldn't get over how everybody seemed to know each other. And how suspicious some of them were. This man had truly meant his comment. His eyes darted over their purchases as well as the contents of the store. Maybe it was just fear.

"It's damned near a riot down in Catesboro," the man said. "Wal-Mart finally opened up and people were nigh on to killing each other to get at the food. There weren't no bread nor milk by the time I got in the store. You'd think it was Doomsday."

Roy took his change from Hazel and gathered up the groceries. "Maybe it is."

Chapter Four

"No need for it," Oleatha said after Maggie offered her help in the garden. Jacob pestered his grandfather until he took him fishing. The lunch dishes were done. Maggie had unpacked and tidied their room and knew better than to do anything more. Oleatha regarded mess and dirt as the Devil's own excrement and took offense if anyone implied she didn't keep a spotless house. By herself.

Maggie had calls she needed to make if she could get any kind of signal. Grabbing her phone, she went out the kitchen door and climbed the hill behind the house, passing the derelict outhouse that Roy wouldn't tear down and the remnants of a small barn nature had demolished for him. Right beside it was a shed, fairly new and painted white like the house. At the bald crest of the hill she could look down on the house: the garden with Oleatha's broad backside bumping along between the tomato plants, and Sloan's Creek, the lazy stream that gave the road and hollow their names. Somewhere along this creek, on down the road and toward the foot of the hollow, was where Roy and Jacob were fishing.

It was bright and warm up on the hill. Maggie exulted in the wide expanse of sky and the breeze on her face. Her excuse for coming up here was that her phone might get better reception, but, in truth, she felt like she'd escaped from a lidded kettle. First she called her sister Tina, who was home. Both she and her husband were teachers. Tina was sure the whole mess would be over in a week. She hadn't heard of anybody getting sick. They'd finally let everyone leave the airport. Tina thought Luke had overreacted by sending Maggie and Jacob to the hills. "Have you heard from him?" she asked.

"Just for a minute last night. He's at a military base in Illinois."

"I'm sure he'll be fine."

Maggie didn't reply. Finally Tina said, "I guess you want me to go check on Mom."

"Someone has to."

"You know how I hate to go over there."

"I don't exactly enjoy it."

"She's always drunk."

Maggie looked up at buzzards wheeling on the thermals. "You're not teaching; go early, around lunch. Sometimes she's not too far gone then."

Tina sighed. "Okay. Otherwise she'll be driving, and we don't need that again."

We, Maggie thought. She'd been the one to bail her mother out of jail last winter when she'd been caught driving drunk. Tina avoided it all. Maggie had always made sure Tina could avoid it all.

Tina asked, "Have you called Dad?"

He'd avoided it too, leaving them for another woman just when Mom was starting to get bad. He'd sent money and presents, along with divorce papers from Colorado, but she hadn't seen him but twice since he'd left, twenty years ago.

"No." Maggie couldn't keep her voice from turning hard. "You can handle that too, if you want." Tina had always made more of an attempt to contact their father. Maggie had washed her hands of him when, at fourteen, she'd realized that she was holding what was left of their family together.

Tina changed the subject. "Have you been watching the news?"

"No." Oleatha had forbidden it, saying that all the gloom and doom got on her nerves and wasn't good for Jacob. There was little of substance there anyway, just paid experts hypothesizing about terrorism, disease, and disaster. They didn't know anything. The internet, on the rare occasion she could access it, didn't either. "Do they know what it is yet?"

"No, but they found another one of the terrorists dead in Dallas. What kind of people would do this?"

"I don't know."

For all her bravado, Tina's voice rose higher and higher, and Maggie spent another five minutes calming her down before hanging up and calling Dr. Harris. There was no answer at the obstetrician's office, so Maggie called his home number. No answer there either. Maggie left a message.

Then, in a fit of guilt, Maggie called her mother, told her where she was, and advised her to stay home. Donna was lucid, not even slurring yet. Like Tina, Donna insisted that all this would all blow over in a day or two. She thought Maggie should come home. Her disability check was due. Would the banks be open? Maggie said no, but maybe she could get Tina to bring her some money. Donna said she'd try an ATM, which drove Maggie to near panic at the thought of her mother in a car.

❖

It'd warmed up enough during the day that Luke had changed into his tee shirt, but when he went walking after supper, the early dusk made him shiver. He strolled along the wide avenue between the buildings and watched the sun disappear below the flat horizon. It looked like a crayon drawing by a six-year-old. Sitting on a concrete wall by the mess hall was Bob Briley. He had a bottle of wine in one hand and a cigarette in the other. "Where the hell did you get wine?" Luke asked.

"You can get anything if you've got money," Bob replied. He offered the bottle to Luke who shook his head. "I bought this off a Spanish gentleman who wanted U.S. currency for cards. I've been making money all afternoon."

"Pool?"

Bob nodded. "I figured the only one around here who might beat me was another country boy, but you weren't anywhere in sight."

Luke sat down. "I'm lousy at pool."

"What did you do for entertainment when you were a rebellious young hill jack? Chase women?"

Luke grinned. "A little. And every now and then we hot-rodded down to the line and bought beer."

"Reckon you spent the rest of your time in church."

"More than I wanted." Luke reached for the wine. What did it matter? Maggie hated for him to drink, couldn't blame her with that mother of hers, but he liked a sip now and then. He didn't even wipe the lip of the bottle.

"So, you think Allen's going to do anything about our guns?"

When they'd finally seen Frank Allen in what he joked was his "office," a coat closet off the recreation room, he'd been concerned about the passenger with a weapon and agreed he'd feel better if his people had their firearms. Luke wasn't one of his, but he supposed Allen had adopted him. He'd said he'd talk to people but wasn't optimistic, and he wasn't going to mention the mysterious firearm. "This Homeland guy would probably do a mass interrogation and get people all wound up. Not good," he'd said.

"So, who's in charge? The medical staff are part CDC, part military. And Allen said the cooks are military too, but is Homeland running this?"

Briley shook his head. "Hell, I don't know. I've even been wondering if they've got guards around this place. Wouldn't surprise me."

Luke's head jerked up. "Do you reckon?"

Bob grinned.

"A little reconnaissance?"

"Why not? I'm up for anything." Bob took a final puff from his cigarette and shredded the butt with his heel. "I quit smoking ten years ago, but when one of the passengers offered to sell me a pack, I up and did it."

"Why start again?"

Bob shrugged, his movement hardly discernable in the dusk. "Figured as how we're all gonna die anyway."

Luke wasn't anywhere near that pessimistic yet. Nobody was sick. The doctors had taken ninety-eleven tubes of his blood, pronounced him fit and healthy, and said they were ready for anything. It might turn out okay.

Neither of them knew where the main gate was, but instinctively they turned away from the simmering sunset, away from the airfield, mess hall, and their bunkhouse, as Briley called it. Passing first the recreation hall and then the medical building, they met up with a breathless Alicia. "I've been looking for you everywhere," she declared to Luke. She put cold fingers on his hand. "I wanted to give you my charger."

"That's terrific," Luke said.

She wore jeans, tight ones, instead of her sweat pants, and Luke could smell perfume. "One of the flight attendants had an extra so you can just keep it," she said, pushing back a lock of blonde hair. "She's so sweet. She let me borrow a pair of her jeans." Alicia smiled up at Luke. "I couldn't stand those sweatpants. Made me feel like I was sick."

Ironic. "So where's the charger?"

"Oh." She took a step away from him and grinned over her shoulder. "I found out from Ilse what building and room you're in and took it there. I plugged in your phone."

This bothered Luke a little, but he smiled. "Thanks. Who's the flight attendant?"

"Cynthia. She's the one with the long dark hair."

"I'll make sure to thank Cynthia."

She giggled, waved, and tottered off in her high-heeled sandals.

"I think my sister's Barbie doll had shoes like that," Luke muttered.

Briley's eyes followed Alicia's tight little rear end which did look real good in her borrowed jeans. "You just got flirted with," he said, taking a drink. "I believe you could have some of that."

Luke's mind flew to a picture of Maggie's face, her blue-green eyes, her golden skin. "She's a child."

Briley's eyes were still following the girl. "Not that much of a child." He smirked. "Thought you used to chase women."

"Used to." He started walking. "And 'used to' died."

It was fully dark by the time they got to the gate, but lights flooded the entrance until it was bright as daylight. The gate was secured and reinforced with barriers on the other side. Half a dozen soldiers stood sentry by the barriers, and Luke saw two more in front of a truck parked nearby.

"Whoo-ee," Bob breathed. "Armed to the teeth. Army, right?"

Luke nodded.

The guards faced the road, not the camp, but neither Luke nor Bob went right up to the reinforced gate. Bob held his bottle behind his back. "You do a tour?"

Luke nodded. "Afghanistan." He'd all but lived in an MRAP like the one parked beyond the barricades.

The soldiers didn't act like they'd noticed them, but Luke was sure they had. He was reminded of his father's advice about snakes: they're probably more afraid of you than you are of them. "I was in the National Guard. For college. Henley County kids don't have trust funds." He shrugged. "Our unit got retrained as IED patrol boys."

"Hot?"

"Hot enough."

"You ever heard of this camp?"

"Nope. It's small; maybe they did some kind of specialized training."

Beyond the modified MRAP were several vehicles, including buses, probably belonging to the medical staff and the people who brought their underwear and socks. Or cooked their meals and emptied their double-bagged trash. "Guess that's where Mickey Mouse parks. But how does he get in? It doesn't look like they plan on opening this gate for anybody."

Bob rubbed at a drop of wine on his shirt. "Surely there's another gate."

"Where?"

"I don't know, but I'm not walking the perimeter of this place tonight."

"Seen enough?"

Bob nodded, but he had an odd look on his face. "Why the everloving hell do they need such big guns? Christ, I wonder if they're keeping others out or keeping us in."

"Both."

"Yeah, but it doesn't make sense. The germs are everywhere. I heard them talking on CNN about how twelve terrorists could've infected enough people on those planes to spread whatever sickness this is all over the country. You gotta figure that every plane had some people going into the cities where they landed but even more catching connecting flights. It's not like we're the only ones exposing people."

They turned back. It was early, but Luke wanted to call Maggie. Bob went toward the recreation building. A passenger stood outside. He nodded at Luke and Bob. "They just said the CDC's going to make an announcement at eight. We got time for another game, Briley."

"You all are just dying for me to take your money, ain't you?" Bob dumped his empty bottle in the trash. "Might as well. Can't dance." He looked back at Luke. "See you later."

When Luke reached his room, he saw that Alicia had even figured out which bunk was his. His phone was sitting on the floor next to his bed, plugged up to the charger. On his pillow was a note written in curlicued letters. "I'm in Building G, second door on the left if you need me." He shook his head. He might have to get Ilse to help him with this little problem.

Maggie answered after only one ring. "Are you all right?" she asked.

"Fine, honey. The docs checked me out today and said I was a healthy boy. Nobody's sick yet." He heard the screen door squeak and knew she'd gone out on his parents' porch to talk. "You all doing okay?"

"Yes. Another of the terrorists died."

"I know. Some of the people down here camp out in front of the TV. Others are using up their phone minutes. We hear all the news."

Her voice was tight. "The CDC has a news conference at eight."

"I know that too, Maggie. Don't worry."

"I can't help it."

"How's Jacob doing?"

"Better than I am. He's been fishing with your dad, and Oleatha's made him cookies even though she never quits complaining about how picky he is about vegetables."

Luke chuckled. "Sounds about right." With the charger giving him all the power he needed, he told her about what had gone on at the airport. Her voice faded occasionally, but that was okay. He described Briley and Ilse. They talked until the phone was warm against his ear. He imagined her on the porch with crickets chirping in the shrubs. He never wanted to hang up, but Maggie was the one who said they should.

"I want to hear what the CDC says and if there's anything new." Her voice was softer now. "Your mother doesn't let us keep the television on very much. Says all this worrisome news would be bad for Jacob."

"She's got a point. Does he understand what's going on?"

"No. I'm going to talk to him tomorrow. I wanted to hear what we're fighting first."

"Makes sense."

"I love you."

"I love you too, Sugar Dumpling. I'm glad you remembered the code."

❖

In the recreation room people were sitting on the floor and standing against the walls. Ready to translate, Ilse grouped the people who didn't speak English around her. Luke scanned the crowd for Todd and spotted him by himself near the pool table. Briley stood close by, a cue stick in his hand. Alicia sat on the floor next to Cynthia, the dark-haired flight attendant. Good. Allen and a couple of his Customs people leaned against the wall by the pop machine. It'd been empty since mid-morning. Another job for Mickey.

All their faces were tense with the same kind of expression Luke imagined cancer doctors saw when they called people in for results. He figured the whole country was watching. Even the Moon Suits, down in the medical building or wherever they hid out, were probably glued to their screens. The way he saw it was that you could handle anything, good or bad. It was the not knowing that made you crazy.

Chapter Five

Spanish Flu. The words formed in Maggie's brain before she was totally awake. Jacob still slept, although he wouldn't for long. She could see a sliver of light under the door and smell coffee brewing. Creeping to the window, she parted Oleatha's ruffled curtains and stared out toward the garden. There should've been daylight, dim, but daylight; however, dense fog choked off her vision. It lay like a plague, like the flu itself, over everything.

She wished she could remember more of what she'd read about the 1918 pandemic. Oleatha had let them leave the television on for a while after the CDC spokeswoman had announced that the dead terrorist had been infected with an influenza virus "very similar to the so-called Spanish Influenza." Maggie wondered how many people had understood what the woman had explained: that the virus's genome had adapted and was unlike anything they'd ever seen. It had mutated, Maggie thought, with a flare of dread leaping up from her stomach. Whether it had changed on its own or through genetic tinkering was anyone's guess, but the fact that the virus was both very old and very new didn't foster much optimism for natural immunity. The CDC woman had skirted that question.

Maggie glanced over at Jacob, his hair dark against the pillow. He needed a haircut. She supposed she could try to cut it, but she'd never done that before. From the other side of the door she could hear Roy and Oleatha murmuring. They'd been cheered by the news, and Maggie guessed that compared to what they'd feared, strange, horrific diseases like anthrax and ebola, any type of influenza sounded mild. "I had the Hong Kong Flu back in 1968," Roy'd said. "It was rough, but I survived."

Maggie had caught the flu two years ago and, although she'd spent a miserable three or four days fighting aches and fever and had coughed for two weeks, she'd survived too. "They didn't have antibiotics back in 1918, did they?" Oleatha'd asked. Maggie had said no. "We'll be all right," the woman had said. "God willing."

God willing indeed. For the first time in twenty years Maggie's fingers itched for the feel of rosary beads. Antibiotics fought only secondary, bacterial infections, she'd wanted to scream at Oleatha. This was pandemic flu, not the seasonal variety. And, although anti-viral drugs might ease the symptoms, producing vaccine took months. The CDC woman had admitted as much.

Maggie threw on jeans and a tee shirt. She'd need to do laundry soon. Did Luke have clean clothes? She shut her eyes. She missed him so much it hurt. He'd called again, just for a few minutes, after the news conference, and had sounded as optimistic as his parents. "It's just the flu, honey. Just a little bit of misery. And maybe I won't even catch it."

But the man on the plane had died, hadn't he? And the demons who'd sent him on his suicidal mission had probably wanted him to live a while longer so he could spread his foul germs to more people. She figured his quick death had taken them by surprise. And that wasn't encouraging either.

Maggie sat on the bed to put on her shoes. "Mommy?"

"Good morning, baby boy. Get your clothes on and we'll eat breakfast."

In the kitchen, Oleatha was plopping dollops of oatmeal into bowls. Over the last few days Maggie'd decided that her mother-in-law contradicted all the rumors about country women being fine cooks. Oleatha kept them fed, but she was perfectly capable of ruining good food. Roy grimaced when his wife set a bowl in front of him, but Maggie wasn't sure whether it was because the gray stuff looked unappetizing or that it wasn't fried eggs. She went to the other end of the long kitchen and got into the pie safe Oleatha used as a pantry. Jacob would eat oatmeal but not without incentives, and Jacob's picky eating invariably led to disparaging remarks from Oleatha about Maggie's parenting. She couldn't swallow those along with gooey oatmeal. She grabbed a box of raisins and poured brown sugar into a custard cup. "Here you go," she said, spooning a good bit of brown sugar into the child's oatmeal and then using raisins to make eyes, a nose, and a mouth on top of the cereal.

He grinned. "It looks like a jack-o-lantern, Mommy." He ate a bite, more raisin than oatmeal, but at least Oleatha couldn't start in on him.

"Pretty cute," Roy said and reached for the brown sugar himself.

Jacob fished around for more raisins. "When is trick or treat?" he asked.

Oleatha sprinkled raisins on her oatmeal too. "Today's Halloween," she said, stirring them in. "October the thirty-first."

Jacob turned a grief-stricken face to Maggie. She should've known this was coming. "But my costume," he mumbled. "And trick or treat and candy." His eyes overflowed and he set off into a full cry.

She hugged him. "I know, little guy, but it can't be helped."

"I want to go home," he wailed. "I want to trick or treat. I want to be a pirate."

There was nothing she could do. Roy rubbed his face and looked at Oleatha. She pressed her napkin to her mouth and waited until Jacob's sobs slowed a little. "We don't trick or treat down here," she said. "Leastwise, not here in the holler. Land, the houses are too far apart for that." She looked at Roy again, and he gave her a tiny nod. "But sometimes folks do have Halloween parties."

Jacob was too deep in his mourning to pay much attention.

"I was thinking we might have us a Halloween party right here," Oleatha said. "I reckon we could dress up. How does that sound?"

He looked up, his face wet and pitiful, and nodded, just a little. For once, Maggie could've hugged Oleatha.

"And maybe we could have us some refreshments. Not candy, but something special." Oleatha gave Roy a sharp nod. It was his turn.

"I reckon we could conjure up a pirate costume," Roy said. He curved his index finger and pawed at the air. "Were you going to be Captain Hook?"

Jacob shook his head but seemed fascinated. "A pirate with a hook?" The tears had stopped.

"Yep. We'll make you a hook," Roy declared. "You eat your breakfast and we'll see what we can find." He gestured at Oleatha and Maggie. "These two'll need to be working on the refreshments."

Maggie glanced over toward the back door where a rickety table covered with oilcloth held dozens of late tomatoes. She knew Oleatha had planned to can them today. Well, maybe they could do that too, if Oleatha'd let her help for a change.

She suggested this while she was washing the dishes, and Oleatha started like she'd been stuck with a pin. "Do you know how to can tomato juice?"

Maggie shook her head. "No, but I thought you could tell me what to do." It was one of Oleatha's chief talents.

The older woman hesitated before mumbling that she guessed she could. "I thought we'd make popcorn balls," she said, speaking up now. "And I've got some lemonade mix we could add a little food coloring to. Call it alligator juice or something." She grinned.

Maggie had seen Oleatha grin like that about twice in the seven years she'd been married to Luke, and both times it'd been about Jacob. "Sounds like fun," she said, smiling back.

There was no microwave, just like there was no dishwasher. Maggie vaguely remembered an old hot air popper her grandmother had used, but there was no sign of that either. While Maggie was washing the tomatoes, Oleatha disappeared and returned with an odd apparatus that looked like a metal basket with a long handle. "For popcorn," she said, wiping it with a rag. "Like we did it in the old days." She fetched a coffee can full of popcorn and put kernels in the basket. "Low fat too," she quipped.

Not only had Oleatha grinned, she'd actually made a joke. The world must be coming to an end. Oleatha turned on a burner and jiggled the metal basket over the heat. Before long the corn started its cheerful popping, filling the kitchen with delicious scent. As Oleatha had told her to do, Maggie cored the tomatoes and quartered them, putting them into a huge kettle Oleatha unearthed from what she called the Big Room.

"Did you always call that the Big Room?" Maggie asked. She was scrubbing out a huge aluminum dishpan.

"No. It was called the 'young'uns' room' when Roy was a boy." She shook the corn. "This house is Roy's homeplace. His parents moved out when we got married. Hasn't Luke told you none of this?"

Maggie shook her head.

"Well, he should've. Dry that dishpan real good now and do it quick." Oleatha held the full popcorn popper in front of her like a sword. "Back when we moved in, the kitchen was at the front, right off the porch."

Maggie set the pan on the table. "Where the front room is now?" She would've called it the living room, but she was trying, Lord, how she was trying.

"That's right." Oleatha dumped the popped corn into the dishpan and slid it into the oven. "Our room was to the left, just like it is now, and then there was the Big Room behind the kitchen. You've noticed how the fireplace goes through, how it opens in both those rooms?"

Maggie nodded.

"Well," Oleatha poured more corn into the popper, "that made it warm in the winter, so the Big Room was a bedroom for the children. Roy and his three brothers and sisters all slept in there when they were growing up." She started shaking the refilled popper over the burner again. "Roy and me didn't have babies right off." Her voice got low. "I'd about decided the Lord had made me barren, but then Curtis came along. Now, I wasn't no snob, but all of my kin had indoor plumbing, and I thought I should have it too. Besides, I had a dickens of a time trying to take care of a baby with no bathroom. And Roy gone most all the time."

Maggie was standing right next to her, stirring the seething tomatoes while Oleatha popped more corn. How had the woman managed? Luke had told her once that his father was usually gone for six to ten days at a time. Oleatha would've been stuck down in this hollow with no plumbing or neighbors or anything. "I can't imagine."

Oleatha gave a little snort. "Don't suppose you can. Anyway, I started plaguing Roy to run plumbing and get us a bathroom. He finally allowed he'd do that and add on at the same time, so I got this kitchen and bathroom and the bedroom you and Jacob are sleeping in. And I kept the Big Room."

Loud guffaws were coming from that odd room, where Jacob and his grandfather were rummaging through the chests and chifferobes crowding the walls. There was also a twin bed in there along with a big dining room table that Oleatha cleared off for holiday dinners. Just now it was piled up with half-finished afghans and stacks of catalogs.

After pouring the second batch of popcorn into the dishpan, Oleatha started more. "Curtis died when he was fourteen months old, and I reckoned it'd been foolish to enlarge the house. But then we had Marla. She stayed in the big room until Luke arrived." She smiled. "He was kindly a surprise."

Maggie lifted her eyebrows.

A whisper of a smile crossed Oleatha's face but faded fast. "Marla slept in the room where you and Jacob are staying until she run off with that foolish boy who thought he was going to make it big in Nashville. I planned to move Luke into her room and turn the Big Room into a dining room. Even bought the table and chairs. But Luke didn't want to leave it. He kept saying Marla'd be back." She shook herself along with the popcorn. "So we left it pretty much the way it was," she said. "I never did get around to changing it out."

Jacob burst into the room. "Pop says we need some anumimum, alumi-, some kind of foil, Granny. Can I have some popcorn?"

Maggie gave him the foil while Oleatha dumped a couple of handfuls of corn into a bowl for him. "That's all," she warned. "We're doing something special with this popcorn."

When Oleatha decided she had enough corn popped and she'd shown Maggie how to strain the tomatoes through a food mill, she started a pan of sugar, water, molasses, and butter. She stirred and then turned to look out the window. The fog was lifting, but the sky still seemed to be sitting on the house. "Anyway," Oleatha said, "that's the story of the Big Room and this house. You getting all the juice out?"

Together they worked on the tomato juice and then the popcorn balls, greasing their hands and making baseball-sized treats. Oleatha joked again, saying that she'd always heard that you were allowed to eat any of the popcorn that stuck to the backs of your hands. Jacob and Roy came through the kitchen a time or two, going from the cellar to the shed to the Big Room and back, and the phone rang several times. Maggie always jumped, wondering if it was Luke, but the calls were all for Oleatha, church people and others seeing how they were doing. Everybody felt isolated, she supposed.

Oleatha cut most of the callers short, saying she was up to her elbows in Halloween nonsense, but one time she stayed in the front room for a good fifteen minutes before returning with an odd look on her face. Maggie was washing out the dishpan. Twelve gigantic popcorn balls sat on waxed paper in the middle of the table.

"You want a cup of coffee?" Oleatha asked.

"Sure."

Oleatha poured it and sat with a long sigh. "That was Marla."

"Is she all right?"

Oleatha nodded and pushed her trifocals up her nose. "You remember her daughter Carrie?"

Maggie had seen Luke's sister Marla maybe four times, most recently at the seventieth birthday party they'd thrown for Roy back in the spring. Marla's daughter Carrie had been carrying around her baby girl. As far as Maggie knew, Carrie had no husband or even a live-in partner. Luke had said that in most every way Marla was raising her granddaughter. "Yes, she's a pretty girl."

Oleatha sniffed. "Pretty on the outside don't mean pretty in the soul. Carrie's wild as a hoot owl, even if she is my own grandchild. Of course she's young, not but nineteen, but still." They both sipped their coffee. It was left over from breakfast and thick as sludge. "Anyway," Oleatha continued, "Marla's not working, reckon everything's closed, so Carrie up and decided she could leave town and dump little Savannah on Marla. Not so much as a good-bye. Carrie just took off in the middle of the night."

"Does Marla know where she's gone?"

Oleatha waved her hand like she was shooing a fly. "Said she figured the girl went off with this man she's been seeing. They'd been talking about going to Florida."

"That's rough for Marla." Luke's sister hadn't had an easy life. She'd married a Henley County boy who'd dragged her to Nashville, and she'd had Carrie by him before he left her. Somehow she'd managed to get by, working nights as a waitress until finally becoming manager of a restaurant. Luke said that she should've come home after her husband left her, but she was too proud. It didn't seem like she'd passed that trait to Carrie.

"Marla says about half the filling stations in Nashville are out of gas. Guess the trucks aren't delivering anything. People are panicking." Oleatha fiddled with her cup. "This is worse than what they're letting on, isn't it?"

Just then she looked every one of her sixty-seven years, her shoulders slumped and hair frazzled by the morning's work. Her arms were freckled, red-head's skin, but Maggie'd never known Oleatha's hair to be anything but gray. She didn't know whether to tell Oleatha her fears or spout the same eternal optimism as the government. "I don't know. I'm not sure they know."

"I hate to think about Marla and that baby all alone in the city."

Maggie hesitated and wondered what Luke would say about what she was thinking. He'd probably remark that it was just about as wrong as it was right. "Why don't you tell Marla to bring Savannah up here?"

Oleatha stood. "I studied on it but decided not to. I think that might've been what Marla had in mind when she called. Reckon she was thinking you could take care of the baby if she got sick."

Maggie's throat tightened.

"But the way she was talking, they've been all over the city the last two days trying to get money and food. I'll not have them bringing sickness down here." She rubbed at her nose. "It don't matter for Roy and me; we're old, saved, and ready to meet the Lord. But I don't want anything happening to Jacob."

Maggie remembered the term, uttered with a defiant reverence when it came from Luke's mouth. "They're blood kin, Oleatha."

"So's Jacob."

Chapter Six

Luke woke up in a good mood for two reasons. First off, the disease was only flu, at least this was what he was telling himself, and, as they'd promised, the Easter Bunnies had left a brand-new pair of Nikes outside his door. He put on his new shoes. After breakfast duty, he was going to take a lengthy stroll around Ft. Rieselman. It wasn't like it made any difference, but he wanted to get the lay of the land.

After waking Bob, he went to the mess hall, arriving at the same time as the morning roll call person, this time one of the passengers, and another server, the EMT named Jack. He'd been popular with those who wanted to know all the gruesome details about the terrorist's death. Jack spoke but seemed quiet. Maybe he was tired of talking. They heard a key in the door and rushed it, hoping to see someone. It'd become a game. Briley swore he was going to stay up all night sometime just to see who came and went. Luke caught a glimpse of a soldier in camo's underneath surgical garb.

Luke served strange pre-formed patties of scrambled eggs and sausage links, while Jack manned the toaster and orange juice pitcher. Briley came through the line joking that there weren't any biscuits and gravy for hillbilly boys, but Ilse took her food without comment. Her nose seemed to be riding a little high. The family, the ones from Indianapolis who had a little girl younger than Jacob and a boy about eight, came through next accompanied by Drew, the other EMT. The eight-year-old had decided that Drew, who was tall, lanky, and black, must have connections to the NBA, and clung to him like a bur on a sock. "Hey Jackie," Drew said to the other EMT, "you're not looking too good this morning. You all right?"

Jack laid a piece of toast on Drew's plate. "Just tired, man. Maybe it's all catching up to me."

Drew lost his usual smile and scrutinized his buddy. "Five went down in the night," he murmured to Luke.

"Damn. How bad are they?"

Drew shrugged. "Once they go in that medical building, they might as well be in Los Angeles."

"Hey Drew," said the little boy "We gonna shoot some hoops after breakfast?"

Drew got his grin back. "Sure thing, but I'm gonna eat with my friend first. I'll catch you later." He leaned toward Luke. "I didn't even make the high school team, but you'll never convince little Zachary of that. White boys think we can all play ball."

"Would you move it along, people? Some of us are hungry here." The passenger behind Drew gave Luke an exasperated sigh.

"Sorry," Drew mumbled, turning away from the line.

"Here you go, sir." Luke placed one link and one egg patty on the angry man's plate. "What's your name? I don't see your tag."

"It's because I'm not wearing one. And I want two eggs and two links." The man was probably forty, medium height, a little chunky but not obese. His hair was thinning, making his face look rounder than it was. His dark eyes challenged Luke to defy him.

"I'm sorry, but we're not giving out extras until everyone is fed. There are still people in line. You can have another if there are any left."

"You won't let me have another stupid, little egg?" His voice rose.

Jack frowned. Across the room, Briley stood, sniffing out trouble like a hound.

"No, sir, I will not."

The man stormed off, kicking the nearest chair and sitting alone at a table. Across the room, Allen craned his neck to see what was wrong. It turned out that there were just enough eggs but only one sausage link for Luke and Jack, who waved it away, saying he wasn't hungry. The angry guy watched them take their plates and got up to look at the empty pans. Then he threw the egg spatula on the floor.

Luke sat by Briley who said, "That's a weird one."

"Yeah. Hey, anybody know who got sick in the night?"

Bob shook his head.

"More to the point," Ilse said in a brittle voice, "has anyone seen Alicia? She didn't come to bed last night." Her bright eyes raked Luke.

His hand froze over the toast he was buttering. "She didn't come through the line." Then he sputtered, "You think I . . ? No, Professor Mayfield. I didn't and I wouldn't."

She raised a haughty eyebrow at Briley.

"Luke was alone and sawing away when I came in," Bob said. "I can usually sleep through a root canal, but I believe I'd notice that kind of activity."

"She has a fondness for you, Luke," Ilse said with old-fashioned formality.

"Drew said five got sick in the night. Maybe she's one of them."

The mess hall was nearly empty. Luke wondered if the Mickeys would chase them out if they stayed too long. Despite his date with Zachary at the basketball court, Drew was still sitting with Jack who wasn't eating. He sipped some juice and then rubbed his hand over his face. Luke figured Jack had caught it. It had started with a vengeance, he thought.

And then Alicia ran through the door, her heels loud as jackhammers. She all but threw herself at Luke who stood with his hands out, afraid she'd fall. Burrowing into his chest, she started sobbing.

"Child, what is it?" Ilse asked. She grabbed some napkins from the table and handed them to Luke, who was patting the girl's back and feeling awkward.

"It's Cynthia," Alicia wailed.

"Sit down," he said. "Come on. I'll get you some coffee."

She shook her head, but Luke was able to maneuver her into a chair. Bob grabbed her hand. "Settle down, honey. Is Cynthia sick?"

Rivers of black mascara, probably borrowed from Cynthia, snaked down her face. She was crying too hard to talk. Luke stood behind her making "do something" faces at Ilse who finally went to the food line and poured a cup of juice. "Here," she said, putting Alicia's trembling fingers around the cup. "Drink."

She did, and the hiccoughing sobs subsided. They waited. Finally she took a deep shuddery breath. "She got sick. Last night. We were in her room giving each other manicures and talking." She held up her hands, the nails shiny and deep pink. This upset her all over again and she pressed a napkin to her eyes. "One minute she was fine, and then she said she was chilling and aching all over. I made her go. Walked over to the medical building with her, but they wouldn't let me in."

Luke broke in. "Who's her roommate? Why wasn't she there?"

Alicia crushed the sodden napkin in her fist. "Oh, another flight attendant. She's hooking up with the co-pilot. You know, that good-looking guy who's so full of himself. They spend most of their time in his room."

"Great," murmured Bob. "Romance in hell."

Ilse folded her hand around Alicia's fist. "We knew people would get sick. Several others have come down with it too."

Staring at Luke's unfinished breakfast, Alicia nodded. "I know. I watched them all come in. The lady who was worried about her children in Louisville, a TSA lady, the others. I sat on the steps and saw them come in."

"Did you sit there all night?" Luke softened his voice. Drew and Jack were looking at them.

She nodded.

Ilse still held Alicia's hand, bright fingertips glowing against the napkin. "The doctors know what they're fighting now," she said. "I'm sure Cynthia will get good care."

Alicia shook her head wildly, breaking away from Ilse's grasp and covering her face. "You don't understand. She's dead." Her voice rose to a keening wail. "I was sitting there and one of those people came out and asked if I was sick. I said no, I was waiting to hear about Cynthia and he told me. She died an hour ago." The sobs started up again.

Luke looked first at Ilse and then at Bob. Their eyes were as dead as Cynthia. Across the room Luke saw Drew reach under Jack's arm to help him up. Another one. Ilse had her hand on Alicia's shoulder and was coaxing her up. She was probably going to put the girl to bed. Luke stood. "Where you heading?" Bob asked.

"Walking."

"Want some company?"

"Not really. No offense."

Bob stuck his hands in his pockets. "None taken. I'll wander over to the rec hall and see what's happening in the rest of the world. Not that I really want to know." He frowned. "You know, you can't close Pandora's box. Eventually those fucking terrorists are going to catch this thing themselves."

"Unless they've already got a vaccine."

Briley rolled his eyes.

Once outside, Luke turned left, away from most of the camp. In light of Cynthia's death, his little quest to discover the secrets of Ft. Rieselman seemed trivial, but he didn't know what else to do. He'd love to call Maggie but didn't want to worry her with the news of a death. When they'd met he'd been astounded by her cool expertise. It'd been at the VA hospital in Cincinnati. He'd come home from Afghanistan with a nasty cut on his leg from falling from the MRAP steps and meeting up with an evil piece of scrap metal. He'd been due to go home the next day and didn't want anything to delay it, so he and his buddies had bandaged the wound as best they could. Then the injury had become infected with pretty pink streaks surrounding it. He'd known he had to get help and had figured free was good.

In the Cincinnati VA examining area, he'd noticed Maggie right away, not only because she was the prettiest woman he'd seen in five years but because she seemed to have a bubble of serenity around her. It'd fascinated him. He'd always admired confidence, but the whole time her gloved hands worked on his leg, he'd also wondered what might be hiding behind her calm, seawater eyes.

It'd all been an act. He'd soon discovered that underneath the façade, Maggie seethed with anger and insecurity and guilt, mostly because of her useless father and drunken mom. But by that time Luke had been lost, and it didn't matter. They'd surrendered to each other, faults and all, in more ways than one, he thought with a little smile. He remembered how her mother had gone on a bender four days before their wedding, and how Maggie had banged on the door of his apartment, kicking a chair and slamming her purse on the floor before she'd sat on his sofa. "She ruins everything," Maggie'd shouted. She hadn't cried, but she'd shut her eyes and turned very pale. "She's screwed up every important thing in my life, and now she's doing it again."

Luke had held her, asking what he could do. Maggie had opened her eyes. "If we have a prayer of her being at the wedding, she's got to go to detox right now. I know the routine. I've done it before." He'd seen every one of the disappointments in her eyes. "Please," she'd said. "Could you do it for me this time?" He'd told her he would; of course he would, and then she'd cried, saying she'd never had a hero before.

Damn, he missed her, but he was stuck in this stinking camp, feeling like a useless fool in the middle of a world-class disaster. Trudging on, he walked across tough grass to the fence that enclosed the camp. He'd parallel it for a while. Maybe it would keep his mind off Cynthia and Jack. And the strange guy who'd had the tantrum over breakfast.

The sky was dingy as dirty linens, and a breeze was kicking up over the prairie. It was ugly country: no trees or hills or anything of interest. He'd give anything to be down in Sloan's Holler with Maggie and Jacob where he could hear the creek and birds and feel the honest pull in his legs when he climbed a hill. The leaves would be putting on a show by now. Maggie hated it down there. She never said anything, but he could tell. And his kinfolk hadn't made it easy on her. She was city-bred, Catholic, and might as well have been from Mars as far as they were concerned. He wasn't sure his mother would ever cut Maggie a break, even if she had given her a grandbaby. Of course that was another bone of contention with his mother. She'd often said, in Maggie's hearing, that having an only child was unnatural.

The airstrip was on his left. It was deserted and bare, although there was a hangar big enough to accommodate a small plane. He wondered what they'd done with the plane they'd arrived on. He also wondered how their pilot had managed to set down the big transatlantic jet on such a small runway, but he hadn't been paying much attention Sunday night. Night before last. It seemed like they'd been here a week, but it wasn't even forty-eight hours. Already one was dead. He'd never heard of flu killing people that quickly. It was usually the very old and very young who died of influenza, Maggie'd said. And that was usually from pneumonia.

Following the fence, Luke came to a corner. More than likely the dull country outside the fencing belonged to the post too, but this marked the perimeter of their area. He almost turned back but chose to turn left instead, again following the fence. He was noticing that the dusty, clotted weeds had dirtied his new shoes when he heard a sound. Up ahead, Todd was shaking the fence. It looked like he'd found another gate, unmanned but locked up as tight as the front.

Luke stopped. Damn, he wished he had his gun or a radio or something. He was in the back of beyond with nobody within shouting distance except the crazy kid who'd gone bonkers on the plane. Luke didn't think Todd had seen him yet, so he slowed his gait, not wanting to startle him. Once again Todd rattled the gate, and then he looked up at the fence that rose several feet above his head. Christ, was the guy thinking of climbing it? Luke would have to stop him. He speeded up and called out, "Hey, Todd. How you doing?"

The young man looked around as calmly as if they'd happened into each other at the grocery. "You know my name," he said.

Luke pasted a grin on his face. "Yep. I'm Luke." Todd would know that Luke was a uniform; the sweats guaranteed that.

But Todd didn't move. He thrust his hands into the pockets of his jeans. "Guess everybody knows me." He sounded more forlorn than dangerous.

"Well, that's a fact." Luke tried to keep his pace slow and even. Todd looked like a kid who'd had his nose bloodied. When he'd been screaming down the aisle of the plane he hadn't seemed so harmless.

"I'm not trying to escape," Todd said.

Luke stopped just short of him. "That's good. You wouldn't have any place to go if you did."

"I was just looking to see if there was another gate to this place for deliveries and staff." He sounded like he'd been caught without a hall pass.

"Me too. Besides, it's exercise, and I just got me these new shoes."

Glancing down at Luke's dusty feet, Todd's face relaxed. "My mom always said I couldn't keep a pair of shoes looking new. You're just like me."

Luke chuckled, but he was waiting for Todd to say or do something. Finally the young man shrugged and turned away from the gate. "I don't think they use this one. The road up to it is overgrown with weeds. There must be another one somewhere."

They both walked over the bumpy ground, straight down the middle of the field toward the center of the post. "The currency exchange girl swears there are tunnels, just like Disney World," Luke said.

Todd's head jerked up, and then he saw Luke's expression. "Yeah, right," he replied, with a hint of a smile. "I still think it's all spooky."

Luke bobbed his head. "It is. But I don't think anybody's out to get us except the terrorists."

Todd shook his head and coughed. Luke had started noticing coughs.

"They're playing with us," Todd said. "You know those pills they gave us last night?"

"The anti-viral drugs?"

"Yeah, those. Did you notice how some of us got bottles with red stripes on top and some with blue?" He stopped, forcing Luke to listen to him.

"I never noticed."

"Well, look at them. Why are they different? Are some of the pills dummies? What do they call those?"

"Placebos." Luke frowned. "Surely they wouldn't do that."

Todd gave him a sideways look and started walking again. "Look, on the plane I was a jerk, an asshole. But having that guy die right next to me freaked me out. There was blood on his jacket. Lots of blood. I didn't know what was happening."

Luke had heard more than he'd wanted when people asked Jack and Drew about the dead man. He'd hemorrhaged; his lungs spewing blood, the EMTs had said, which sounded like a damned scary kind of flu. "I can understand that," Luke said. He'd relaxed his guard a little, but it tightened again as Todd became more agitated.

"But I'd still rather take my chances out there than at the mercy of those government guys. Too late now." He coughed again and wiped his mouth with the back of his hand. "Notice those pills, Luke. Really."

Luke stopped. "You getting sick?"

"Been feeling bad since I got up this morning, but I didn't want to let them have me."

"What other choice do you have?"

"That's just it, isn't it? We don't have any choices."

They kept walking, Todd moving more and more slowly as they went. He was breathing hard but kept muttering, "No blood yet. At least there's no blood."

Luke walked him all the way to the medical building. At the steps, Todd turned and tried to smile, his face gray now. "You know, just because you're paranoid doesn't mean they're not out to get you."

Even after Todd went through the door, Luke stood in front of the medical building, thinking how easy it would be to dismiss the guy's theory. It would be much simpler to go to the recreation room and join the others who sat around the television like they were hatching the shabby old sofa. He didn't blame them. Everybody wanted to know what was going on, he supposed. Not that there was a thing they could do about it. Instead, Luke walked back to his barracks and looked at his bottle of pills. Just like Todd had said, there was a line across the cap. His was drawn in red marker. Luke picked up Briley's bottle. His was blue.

❖

Jacob had nearly worn himself out with Halloween fun, and his grandparents looked absolutely shot. To give them a break, Maggie took him out on the porch and had him write numbers on a tablet. She worried about him missing school. Through the window she could hear Oleatha reading the Bible to Roy; she said he couldn't make out the words even in a large-print version. Maybe scripture comforted them. Maggie hoped so, but she'd never found much use for what she'd been taught in catechism class. Even as a child she hadn't been able to get past the commandment about honoring her mother and father and remembered how a nun had scolded her about showing proper reverence when she spoke of her parents. She'd wanted to screech, "What if they don't honor me?" But, of course she hadn't and felt bad for a week for even thinking it.

"Is that enough, Mommy?" He'd been laboring with his thick pencil for fifteen minutes.

"Sure. Your seven is backwards, but we'll fix it later. Want to go for a walk?"

He jumped up and pointed to the right. "We have to go that way. Pop says we should never go up around Crazy Annie's house."

"He's told me that too, but maybe we should just call it Annie's house. It's not nice to call people crazy."

Jacob kicked through the bright leaves. "I could show you where Pop and I fished yesterday."

"Sounds good."

Creepy kudzu curtains strangled the trees on her right. She had to crane her head far back to see the treetops supporting the rampant vines. She saw a large bird wheeling above the treetops. "Look, Jacob." She pointed up.

He shaded his eyes. "It's a hawk."

"How did you know that?"

"I saw it yesterday, and I told Pop what it looked like. He said it was a hawk."

Perhaps she shouldn't worry about him missing school. For nearly a mile, they strolled down the leaf-strewn track, the creek on their left winding and widening as they came to the foot of the hollow. As far as she knew, nobody lived down here. It felt lonesome and quiet. Jacob led her off the track, through weeds and Queen Anne's Lace to the creek bank. There the land opened up to a shallow valley full of ragweed, which Luke called goldenrod, and purple flowers he said were ironweed. Far across the creek Maggie could see pasture land. Jacob ran ahead and planted himself on a smooth rock by the side of the creek. "This is where we fished," he announced.

The water wasn't deep, but it would've covered Jacob's head. "You know not to come down here without Pop or Granny or me, don't you?"

He gave her an automatic nod. "We didn't catch anything, but Pop says we'll come back early some morning or in the evening. That's when the fishies are biting he says."

She sat beside him on the rock. The water was sluggish, but its movement slowed her breathing. She was a born river rat. She'd always loved looking at water, especially the wide, muddy Ohio. When she was little, her father used to take them to a restaurant that stretched right over the river, and she remembered seeing barges drifting by. Her dad had always bought her a kiddie cocktail, and, for a while, she'd had a drawer full of paper umbrellas.

Maggie could've sat by the creek for hours, but Jacob was jumpy. "When's the party?" he asked. "Should we go back to the house?"

"No. We have plenty of time. Look." She took off her nurse's watch, one with a second hand and clear numerals. "You know about big hands and little hands, don't you?"

He nodded.

She was in the middle of telling him that it was three-thirty when her phone rang. She saw that it was Luke. "Hello."

Seven years had taught her every nuance in his voice. He said cheerful words, but she knew better. "Are you all right?"

"I'm healthy." He paused. "Tell me where you are right now. Describe it to me."

She told him. "Jacob's here too. Do you want to talk to him?"

The boy grinned and put the phone to his ear. "Hi Daddy. We're having a Halloween party."

Maggie listened to Jacob tell his father about his costume and popcorn balls and that Pop was going to be a cowboy. "What?" Jacob said. "I don't know." He turned to her. "What are you going to be?"

"I'm not sure yet."

"She'd better hurry, hadn't she, Daddy? Granny says her costume's gonna make us laugh."

This could all be nearly normal if she forgot about the sickness and the quarantine and nearly everything else she knew. Luke was all right. If she could freeze time, this could be tolerable, even if they were separated. "Here," Jacob said, handing her the phone. "Daddy wants to talk to you."

He asked, "Have you seen the news this afternoon?" There it was, that taut wire in his voice.

"No. Oleatha won't even let me watch the Weather Channel, and my phone cuts out when I try to get online." She tried to joke. Luke ignored it.

"Thousands of cases. All over the country. They've caught four of the terrorists. And there've been horrific bombings. In the Middle East, Africa. Military's on alert everywhere. Ships have to remain at sea. Saber-rattling from China, North Korea. The President seems to be focusing on retribution rather than the flu."

"Dear God." She mustn't say too much. She mustn't upset Jacob. "And what about where you are?"

"There were seven sick this morning. Four more this afternoon."

"What about your professor friend and your roommate?"

"They're okay so far." She heard him swallow. "One girl's already dead, Maggie. Ten hours. She was dead ten hours after it hit her."

Maggie stood and turned away from Jacob. "What are they doing? Do they have doctors and equipment?" The pulse in her throat was jumping hard enough to shake her voice.

"There are plenty of doctors and nurses. Last night they started us all on anti-viral medicine. Said it might help prevent it or at least alleviate symptoms."

Jacob had climbed off the rock and walked farther down the creek where he was picking up pebbles and sticking them in his pocket. "Yes. Those can help."

"I guess they have good equipment. I don't know."

She'd never heard him like this. His job had always been to reassure her. "What about on the news? Any deaths reported there?"

"Bob says the government's trying to put out wildfires with a teacup. They're being cagey, not saying much. There've been riots all over the place. A bunch of National Guard units have been called up."

"I'm glad you're not in one anymore." She leaned over to pick up a yellow leaf. She noticed its veins, useless now for anything more than a pattern.

"I'd be glad to go if it meant getting out of this place."

"Is it so bad?"

"No. They try to give us what we need. There're two kids here, and at lunch someone had the bright idea that we should have a Halloween party for them and everybody else for that matter. Otherwise, there's nothing to do but shoot basketball or pool or sit around waiting to die."

This was completely out of character. "Luke Davies, you are not going to die," she declared and then looked around to see if Jacob had heard her. "Maybe that girl had some pre-existing condition or a weak heart or something. You don't know."

"You're right. I'm sorry. It's just pretty grim."

She softened. "I know, honey. But you're the tough guy, right? You're my hero."

He chuckled as she'd hoped he would. "I guess I need a Superman suit to wear to the party tonight, don't I?"

"Hmm. I'd like to see you in those tights."

This brought a full laugh. "Now that would be a picture. You really don't know what you're going to wear for Jacob's party?"

"No. I said something about being a witch, but your mother told me witches are satanic. I'll root around in Marla's stuff and come up with something. Do you realize that your mother hasn't thrown away anything you all wore as kids?"

"I doubt if she's thrown away anything in her life."

Jacob wandered back, his pockets lumpy with stones. "Do we need to go to the house now?" he asked.

"Soon," she said. "I guess I do need to go. You'll be all right, honey. I have to believe it."

"I do too, sweetheart. I love you."

"I love you too."

She and Jacob climbed back up the hill. Sunshine glistened off the leaves, and the air smelled of pine and spicy weeds. Earlier in the day Maggie had told Jacob that his father was taking care of sick people. He'd scrunched up his nose and asked if Daddy had become a nurse too.

She'd laughed. Now she wondered if she should've told him more. Even the bits and pieces he might glean from phone calls and television might worry him. Kids always knew more than adults realized. Her father had tiptoed around her mother's drinking for years, calling it "nerves" or "fatigue." Maggie'd figured out the truth when she was seven. "Daddy may be gone a long time," she said.

"I know," he said. "Pop said so."

"Did he say why?"

"Because Daddy's been where he might catch the sickness, but if we stay down here we won't get it."

"That's what we're hoping." She shortened her stride to match his.

"Will Daddy get sick?"

"We hope not."

Jacob seemed to consider this. He touched his pocket to make sure he still had his pebbles and then grabbed her hand. "Don't worry. Daddy's too strong to get sick."

"You're right." She squeezed his hand. "What are all those pebbles for?"

"Pop's going to make me a slingshot."

Great, Maggie thought. These people had an absolute fixation with weapons. Just then she heard an engine, a truck, she thought. Surely Roy wouldn't be trying to drive. Maybe someone had come by, but she'd thought everybody was too scared of the flu to visit. But when she and Jacob got far enough up the hill to see it, Roy's Chevy was where they'd parked it yesterday, and there was no sign of a vehicle.

Chapter Seven

In the mess hall, people were rooting through boxes of junky costume stuff. Some were talking about the ones who'd come down with the flu, but others were giddy about costumes and the beer Allen had promised for the party. Luke didn't care about a costume or beer but sorted through the stuff anyway. He saw fangs and a couple of witch's hats, googly glasses and boas. He picked up a tin badge and a cowboy hat that would've fitted Jacob better than him. He'd be a cowboy, he supposed, since there was no Superman suit.

Thinking of Maggie, he smiled to himself and sat for supper with Drew and a couple of passengers. Alicia was across the room with a swarthy man in a purple polo shirt. She seemed to be doing all the talking, but every now and then the man looked at her with an intensity Luke didn't like. Not that he was going to do anything about it. He didn't want to encourage her, even though it looked as though she had a new target. Drew was expressing his surprise at how someone had found party things so quickly. "My mother says most of the stores in Cincinnati are closed."

Luke swallowed a bite of meat loaf. "Other towns too."

"Who's getting this stuff for us?" the male passenger across from Luke asked. He was the guy who'd drunk up all his duty-free while they were in the Customs Hall. Luke recalled that his name was Pete. "Is it the military or the government or what? You got clothes and shoes and now costumes and beer. Can we ask for anything?" He grinned. "You know, dancing girls and Scotch?"

"Frank Allen passes along the requests to the government guy, the one who talked to us the first night. Who knows where it goes from there," Drew said. "I don't know about dancing girls, but that professor lady is always bending Allen's ear for something. She was asking him for warm jackets."

"It is getting chilly," the female passenger said. Her nametag said she was Jill. "But what I'd like most is a wireless signal. I'll never be able to pay the overages." Her IPhone was lying next to her tray. She probably slept with it.

"Business?" Drew asked.

She nodded. "I'm business development representative for medical facilities here and in Europe." Although she was a pretty woman, her mouth was set in an unattractively tight line, and she looked like she was wired as tight as a Jack Russell terrier.

Luke asked, "Does all that really matter now?"

A forkful of mashed potatoes was halfway to her mouth. "Well," she stammered. "I don't know."

"The professor asked Allen to get us a chaplain," said Drew.

Everybody got real busy chasing peas around their plates. They all knew about Cynthia, but no one mentioned her. Finally Luke asked, "Know anything about Jack?"

Drew shook his head. "That's what I'd like to ask for—news about the sick people or permission to visit them. It's not like they'd be spreading anything in there that we aren't trading around out here."

Pete pressed his napkin to his mouth. "I went over to the medical building this afternoon." Color came up in his cheeks. "My arms were aching and I was sure I was coming down with it. They checked me out, took my temperature, and said it was my imagination." He shrugged. "I felt like a fool, but they said several people had come in thinking they were catching it."

"A fool but a happy one," Drew said.

Pete nodded. "Anyway, I couldn't see any of the sick people. They took me from the front hall straight into an examining room, and that was it. I was hoping I could check on my roommate. He got sick earlier this afternoon."

Drew looked down at his half-eaten food. "I'm not sick, folks, but I don't feel much like eating."

"Me either," said Luke. "But I reckon we'll put on our costumes and make happy for those little kids tonight."

Jill's face relaxed. "Sure. We can do that."

❖

When Luke and Briley, both dressed as cowboys, walked over to the recreation hall, they met Frank Allen who was got up the same way.

"Hello Sheriff," Bob said.

Allen was smoking a cigar and showed no eagerness to go inside. "Good evening. You two my deputies?"

Luke grinned. "Sure, but even Barney Fife got a bullet."

Allen shook his head. "I haven't gotten anywhere with them about the guns, boys. They'll get me shoes or Halloween crap. They'll even get me beer—there's a keg inside—but they won't hear of giving our guns back."

"Probably no need," Luke said. "But we country boys get anxious knowing there's someone here who has one."

Blowing a cloud of pungent smoke into the air, Allen said, "I haven't told the Homeland guy about that yet. Counting on you two to smell it out."

Briley said, "Could even be one of the people who got sick today. Then it's not an issue."

"How do you contact Homeland? Do you have meetings with the Moon Suits or what?" asked Luke.

"I just talk to one: Fister out of D.C. He works on post, but he's never told me where. He doesn't want people bothering him." He rubbed at his face. Luke wouldn't have wanted his job. "So I call him. Not supposed to give out that number either."

"Well, they've been decent about getting what we need," Bob remarked.

"Yeah, anything we want as long as we stay put." Allen narrowed his eyes against his smoke. "I see no reason for them to hold us. They know what they're up against now."

Drew and a woman wearing a witch hat passed them and waved.

"I'm surprised people haven't tried to leave," Briley said.

"They have. A few have come to me and demanded transport. One of them made a huge scene and lost his shit over it. Kicked stuff. The same one who threw a fit this morning."

"Know his name?" Luke asked.

"Had to make him tell me. Joshua Monroe. You two might want to watch him."

"You think he's the one with the gun?" asked Briley.

"No, I think he's nuts." Allen stuck his hand in his pocket and squirmed a little. "You tell anybody I did this and you die, guys." He thrust a slip of paper at Luke. "This is Fister's number with a little code word we arranged to let him know it's me." He shrugged. "Silly shit, but he insisted. If I get sick, you're the boss, Davies. Since you have the code, he'll know I gave it to you."

Luke didn't take the paper. "Why me? There are others, Customs people." He gestured at Bob. "Briley for example."

"He'll help you."

"For sure." Bob was nodding.

"You're the only one of your type here," Allen said. "I think that's probably a good thing, and Ilse Mayfield thinks you're top notch. I've learned to pay attention to the professor."

Luke shook his head but put the paper in his pocket. "I hope I won't need it."

Allen gave him a crooked grin. "Me too. Go party, you two. Drink one for me."

There was a crowd around the keg. Drew bared his fangs at Luke and Jill patted his sheriff's badge. A dozen or so construction paper jack-o-lanterns were taped to the walls, and for once the television was turned off. Ilse Mayfield wore a shiny plastic tiara and nodded like a queen when Bob handed her a cup of beer. She sipped and made a face, muttering something in German. "Bad?" Luke asked.

"Dreadful," she replied.

The two little kids, the boy dressed as a pirate—Luke thought of Jacob—and the tiny girl as a princess, circulated around the room with bags in their hands. On the tables in the room, along with chips and crackers, were big bowls of candy the adults grabbed from and deposited in the kids' bags. Their parents seemed very grateful.

"Where's Alicia?" Luke asked Ilse.

She pointed. "Over there." Still wearing Cynthia's jeans along with several strands of Mardi Gras beads and a bright pink boa, Alicia leaned against the pop machine drinking a cup of beer and talking to the passenger she'd been with at supper. He was old enough to be her father but strikingly handsome. He'd changed to a dark shirt and tie and looked like he belonged in a gangster movie. Maybe it was supposed to be a costume, but Luke thought it looked a little too real.

"Is she all right?"

Ilse took another sip of beer and grimaced. "No."

Alicia was flirting up a storm, biting her cheap beads with even, little teeth and pawing the dark-haired man's sleeve with her bright pink nails. Cheerleader pretty as she was, Alicia was out of her league with this guy who was watching her with the same expression a fox gives a chick.

Pete, the passenger from dinner, came up and gestured toward the pool table. "Hey, Briley, you ready to take some more of my money?"

"Reckon so," Bob said. "Can't dance." He grinned at a couple of people moving to the music. Someone had scrounged up speakers, and heavy bass flooded the room.

Loud laughter came from the crowd around the keg who were pumping and pouring cup after cup. Luke let them stick one in his hand but after one sip had to agree with Ilse. Impervious to all the noise and frenetic gaiety, the Spanish couple and another pair were playing bridge at a card table over in the corner. Bob had said they were camped out there every time he came in the recreation hall. People were taking pictures of little Zachary and his sister Emma with their phones. "Just a nice little party," Luke observed.

Ilse surveyed the room. "For now."

Just then the co-pilot, who looked like a movie star without donning a costume, and his flight attendant friend came into the room. She drew every eye. Her outfit was little more than a bra made of some sparkly fabric and sheer harem pants pulled way below her jeweled navel. Gold bracelets snaked up her bare arms and pinched her flesh. Luke was reminded of the old *I Dream of Jeanie* show, but the television genie had looked as wholesome as oatmeal compared to this woman. Luke tried to remember if he'd seen the two of them at meals before. Maybe. But if what Alicia had said was true, they'd been having private fun and games.

"*Gott im Himmel*," Ilse murmured.

The harem girl or belly-dancer or whatever she was dressed up to be, slithered over to the keg and asked one of the guys for a beer. Honest to God, he dropped his cup. Far from disapproving of the attention his companion was getting, the co-pilot wore a benevolent smile. Across the room, Briley was grinning at Luke like a demon. Pete mouthed the words "dancing girls" and laughed. Luke knew she couldn't possibly have produced such an outfit from the box of Halloween crap in the mess hall. Did she carry belly-dancer wear in her flight bag?

Before long Zachary and Emma were scooted along to bed, which was good, because after a couple of quick beers, the belly-dancer started doing her thing, undulating to whatever music was playing and tossing her long, blonde hair until it whipped her face. Luke was speechless, as were most of the men in the room. The co-pilot leaned against the back wall and watched her, a sleepy smile on his face. Even the bridge players stopped and stared.

The girl danced in front of the couch, where track lights caught her glistening skin. She smiled, holding her arms out and then above her head until her breasts lifted and threatened to escape the skimpy bra. Luke had seen belly dancers when he'd been overseas. She was good. But she could've been lousy and the men in the room would still have been salivating. She was all skin and secrets under gauzy chiffon. He downed half his beer.

While Luke was watching, Allen came in and joined him. "Quite a show," he mumbled, shaking his head when someone offered him a beer.

"More like trouble," Luke replied. The atmosphere in the room was running as hot as tires at Talladega.

"No sign of Joshua Monroe," Allen said. "That's a good thing."

"Yeah. He'd probably be complaining about the size of the beer cups," remarked Luke.

When the music changed to a slower song, the girl extended her hand toward the smirking co-pilot. They danced in a more conventional way, his hand large and dark against her bare waist. Luke let out a big breath he hadn't realized he'd been holding. "Maybe it'll be okay," he said to Allen.

Alicia had persuaded her gangster to dance too. You couldn't have slid a dime between the two of them. Shaking her head, Ilse moved to Luke's side. "You can't protect her," Luke said.

"No, but that's what she's looking for."

The next song was a rowdy country one, and more people stood to dance, some of them by themselves. Even Luke felt an urge to click his heels against the floor, but evidently the harem girl didn't care for banjo-picking; she moved toward the keg with the co-pilot trailing behind her.

"You staying a while?" Allen asked Luke.

"I can."

"Keep an eye on things, will you? I'm whipped." Allen shook his head when he saw Luke's concerned look. "I'm fine. I just need about fifteen minutes to myself."

Luke nodded and threw away his cup.

It wasn't a half-hour later when the sparks caught. Some people had been drinking steadily for nearly two hours, and the dancing girl was still doing her thing, encouraging different guys to dance with her, if you wanted to call it that. She set them in front of her and gyrated while they stood there looking stupid, about bursting their pants to touch her but not daring it. One guy in particular, a TSA named Derek, had claimed several dances. Luke figured tempers were about to flare. For a while now, Alicia's gangster had been talking to the co-pilot who listened but never took his eyes off his girl. As best Luke could tell, the talk wasn't idle chitchat, and Alicia wasn't admitted to the conversation. Her face had drooped into a pout, and her arms were crossed over her beads.

He patrolled the room, and although she stood in one place, Ilse's eyes did the same. The co-pilot mystified Luke. Despite the gangster talking in his ear, he kept smiling at his woman like her antics were amusing the hell out of him. Luke wondered if he got off on watching her tease and titillate. The harem girl had beckoned to Alicia's gangster several times, but he'd ignored her. Finally, the co-pilot himself pointed at the dancer and seemed to be urging the older man to dance. He shrugged and gave the co-pilot the only smile Luke had seen on the man. Although Alicia grabbed his arm, he shook her off and did it with a little more strength than Luke would've liked. Unlike the others who'd made some weak attempts at dancing, the gangster stood in front of the dancer like he was challenging her, his legs wide, arms dangling at his side. She laughed and raised the tempo of her gyrations to a frenzy, the jewel in her navel winking as she moved. Unlike the others, the gangster wasn't shy about touching her. Languid as snakes, his hands caressed her waist as it undulated. She smiled and moved closer, inviting, suggesting. Most every eye in the place was watching them, but Luke kept his on Alicia who was fuming, and the co-pilot who was all but laughing.

Something real strange, almost creepy, was going on. Derek, who, after a couple of dances, must've decided the dancer was his, charged up from over by the keg and pushed the gangster. The couple ignored him at first, but then Derek grabbed the girl's arm. Her eyes glittered as bright as her jewelry. In one smooth motion, the gangster punched Derek in the chin, and the younger man went after him like a maniac. People gasped, someone screamed, and Luke flew toward them. The dancer stepped aside to watch, a greedy smile on her lips.

Luke tried to get between them, but Derek was punching in a white heat. His face set and inscrutable, the gangster was handling him, parrying the blows with a cold professionalism. Luke took a glancing hit on his arm and a pretty good one in the shoulder before Briley stuck his cue stick under Derek's chin and pulled him back. "You need to settle down now," he said, his Tennessee drawl thicker than usual.

Growling "Ease up," Luke pinned the gangster's arms behind his back. The man's shoulders immediately relaxed. He hadn't even broken a sweat. "The party's over in fifteen minutes," Luke said, loud enough for the whole room to hear and released the man.

Acting like she was all concerned, the dancer sashayed over to the gangster, joined by the co-pilot who looked as if he'd been watching an Easter egg hunt. She squeezed the co-pilot's arm and then ran her fingers over the gangster's face. Unruffled, the gangster turned to go, the other two following him. Too, too weird, Luke thought.

Briley still had hold of Derek who was struggling to get loose. "Hold on there, boy," Bob said. "She's already got two men; she don't need any more." The guy quit wiggling and hung his head. A bruise was blooming on his cheekbone. Noise picked up again and the bridge players started dealing a hand. Alicia hovered near the door and reached out to the gangster as he passed, but the man smacked her hand and muttered something over his shoulder that stopped her dead.

When Briley let go of Derek, the young man shuffled over to the keg where some of his buddies commiserated with him. Others left, some of them stuffing their pockets with Halloween candy, Bob went back to his game, and Luke lost sight of Alicia. He crossed over to Ilse to ask if she'd seen where the girl had gone. She shook her head. "Books say that debauchery flourished during the Black Plague," Ilse recited. "People were certain they were going to die, so morals and standards had no meaning for them. Maids wore their mistress's clothes. People fornicated on tavern tables and even monks and nuns performed depraved acts."

"You saying that's what we got going on here?" Luke asked. He was a little out of breath.

"I think we're seeing a bit of the same thing. Fear can remove inhibitions just as much as alcohol."

"Yeah, and you put the two of them together and it's a powder keg." Luke spoke to the bridge players. "You all come to a stopping point, okay? And then we're closing up." They nodded. The guys over by the keg were mopping up, and a few people were collecting trash.

"Can we watch television?" It was one of the passengers he and Bob had christened the "Broody Hens," the ones who left the TV only for meals.

"Sure. Somebody douse the music, okay?"

Luke stayed until the Broody Hens were the only ones left. Bob had walked Ilse back to her barracks but returned. "I'm all het up," he said. "Fighting always does that to me. I'll watch the tube for a while." He grinned. "Get the nightmares out of my system before I go to bed."

Luke nodded. He was ready to go. Outside it had dropped at least ten degrees and was spitting rain. Down at the medical building lights blazed. They probably would all night. He wondered if anybody else had sickened. Not everybody had come to the party. Some may have been lying in their bunks, shivering with fever and fear. He went into his room without turning on the light, pulling his phone from his pocket. He'd like to call Maggie, but it was too late. He was undoing his trousers when from behind thin arms reached around his waist and fingers snaked below his unhooked waistband. He remembered the long, pink nails. "Alicia."

She slid around in front of him and pulled his head down, kissing him before he could stop her. For about three seconds he allowed himself to feel warm breasts against his chest and a hot tongue in his mouth. For about three seconds he let the heat take him. Ashamed of it, he admitted he wasn't immune to what had been going on at the party. Then he said, "No." He pushed her away, gently he hoped. "No, Alicia. This isn't right." She was in her underwear, scanty stuff Maggie would've called useless. Her head hung down, curtained by her hair. "I know you're sad and scared. We all are. But this isn't the way to make it better."

Luke turned on the light. Her clothes were on Bob's bunk. "Get dressed. We can talk if you want. We could even go for a walk if you don't mind getting wet." He thought about her Barbie shoes out on the slippery pavement.

She still hadn't raised her head. He grabbed her shirt and started working it over her head like she was a child. All he needed was for Briley to come in about now. She let him get her arms into the sleeves, and then she raised her head. Her eyes were glassy. "Just for now," she said. "I won't bother you when we get out of here." She waited.

Shaking his head, Luke held out Cynthia's jeans. "I'll take care of you," he said. "You don't need to trade yourself for that."

She took the jeans and slipped into them and her ridiculous shoes.

He opened the door more widely, letting the hall light shine on the tawdry beads and boa on Bob's bed. "Want me to walk you to your building?"

She grabbed the gaudy stuff.

"We'll get through this." He knew it sounded feeble.

Heels clattering like a child in her mommy's shoes, she left without saying another word.

❖

"Someone either had access to preserved Spanish Influenza viruses or mutated an existing avian flu virus to make them similar," the newsperson said. "Or prepared a recombinant virus that is completely new." It sounded like a blurb for a TV thriller.

Maggie knelt by the television. Turning the volume way down, Maggie scanned the screen to get what she could before Oleatha caught her. She was finishing up her Halloween costume in the bathroom, and Roy and Jacob were doing the same in the kitchen.

"Where are preserved Spanish flu viruses kept?" the interviewer asked.

"I'm not at liberty to say."

Or you don't know, Maggie thought. She fiddled with the half-dozen or so strands of beads around her neck. Desperate to come up with a costume, she'd riffled through the drawers and closet in her room, finding, as she'd expected, many things Marla hadn't bothered to take when she left home. With the beads, a bold shawl, a peasant blouse from the eighties, and a scarf wound around her head, Maggie had become a passable gypsy.

She read the scroll across the bottom of the screen. They'd apprehended two more of the sick terrorists, leaving at least six of them either at large or dead, whereabouts unknown. Even the exact number of terrorists was unknown. The newsman asked if there were any things they'd learned about the virus. Somehow, the expert was able to keep emotion out of his expression. "Very contagious, as one would expect. This has influenza's usual respiratory symptoms. The especially dangerous cases involve pulmonary hemorrhaging. Those patients die quickly." Just a little bit of misery, Maggie thought.

Hospitals were reporting vast numbers of people crowding their facilities. The Red Cross was setting up mobile units in many cities. The U.S. Postal Service was discontinuing mail service until next Monday.

Maggie heard Oleatha coming out of the bathroom and clicked off the television. She'd learned more than she wanted to know. Jacob was giggling when he came into the front room. "Ahoy, maties!" he shouted, brandishing an aluminum foil hook. Roy had drawn a ferocious mustache on Jacob's upper lip and somehow managed to make him a black pirate's hat. Right behind Jacob, grinning for all he was worth, was Roy, done up like a cowboy. He had a tin foil badge and what Maggie figured was a real gun in a holster that looked like cardboard covered with electrical tape. He was carrying a guitar. She clapped her hands. "What great costumes!" she exclaimed. "The pirate and the singing cowboy."

Roy ducked his head. "Well, I figured since Roy Rogers and I share the same name. . ."

He quit talking when Oleatha came into the room. Even Jacob was speechless. Nobody would have recognized her. She'd attached red yarn to an old farmer's hat for hair, whitened her face, reddened her nose, enlarged her lips, and painted lines around her eyes. With what looked like baggy red and white polka-dotted pajamas and bright red ribbons tied through the eyes of a pair of Roy's huge shoes, she was the most bizarre clown Maggie had ever seen. Jacob couldn't quit laughing. And neither could Roy.

"Happy Halloween," Oleatha crowed in a funny, high-pitched voice. Jacob collapsed onto the floor, laughing too hard to stand up.

Roy finally recovered himself enough to sit and put the guitar in his lap. He started singing "Happy Trails to You," and Maggie remembered her father telling her how much he'd loved Roy and Dale and Trigger and Buttermilk when he'd been a boy. This Roy had a nice voice too, and his gnarled hands did fairly well with the guitar. Jacob was mesmerized. "Pop," he said when his grandfather finished, "can you teach me how to play that?"

"Well, your hands are still a little small, but we can try. Sure."

The villain of the seas was temporarily transfixed and reached over to touch a string. Roy said, "What else did I tell you to say, Pirate Boy?"

Jacob straightened and declared, "Yo, ho, ho, and a bottle of rum!"

Maggie laughed, but the clown made a disapproving noise. "Roy," she warned.

He winked at her.

Jacob finally noticed his mother. "What are you, Mommy?"

"I'm a gypsy, but my costume's pretty lame compared to the rest of you." Maggie picked up a shoebox she'd laid on the coffee table amid the crocheted doilies and china candy dishes. She'd covered the box with freezer paper, cut a hole, and stuck a light bulb into the top of it. "See my crystal ball? Would you like to have your fortune told?"

Jacob grinned.

"I see, young man, that you will be a famous astronaut." That was his current ambition, although it might change to Daniel Boone down here. "You will see the stars and travel to the moon," she said in a deep voice.

Nothing doing but she had to make up fortunes for Roy and Oleatha, so she predicted that Roy would meet a good-looking blonde woman named Dale, and Oleatha would do a lot of traveling with wild animals. They started in on the popcorn balls soon after that and drank tinted lemonade that turned their tongues green. Jacob was gnawing on his second popcorn ball while Roy strummed the guitar. "I didn't know you could play," Maggie said.

He was picking a soft little tune that Oleatha must've known. She was humming. "Oh, I don't play much anymore," he said. "I used to take it with me in the truck and play of an evening. Took the road out of my ears."

Luke would enjoy this so much, Maggie thought. He'd never believe how his mother had dressed up. All of a sudden Maggie rushed back to the bedroom for her phone. "I'm going to take pictures and send them to Luke," she said, making Oleatha stand on one side of Roy's recliner and Jacob on the other. "Smile."

They all thought that was a fine idea and insisted she send one of herself. Jacob clicked the picture, and Roy continued to play. He seemed to enjoy it, and any kind of a musician would've had a hard time resisting Jacob's whole-hearted admiration. At one point Roy went into a fast tune, a breakdown, he called it, and Oleatha suddenly stood, clicking her feet against the linoleum floor with those absurd shoes. With all the face paint, it was hard to read her expression, but her eyes were dancing as much as her feet. She reminded Maggie of the Irish dancers she'd once seen, and she wondered if the two types of dancing were related somewhere back in time. Breathless, Oleatha stopped after a minute or two, and Jacob and Maggie clapped for her. "Pretty good clogging for an old woman," Roy said. "Especially one who don't believe in dancing." His eyes were full of mischief.

Oleatha tossed her head, setting her yarn hair to waving. "I wasn't dancing," she said with a loud sniff. "The clown was."

It took nearly as long to get the costumes off as it had to put them on. "What did you use for his mustache?" Maggie asked as she scrubbed at a squirming Jacob.

"Burned a cork," Roy said.

"He may have this until he grows one of his own."

Once he was clean, Maggie sent Jacob to bed, and the old people followed right behind him. But Maggie went outside, craving fresh air. She looked straight up, into the cleft of sky she could see. It was cloudy, the sky pale with wind-blown clouds. Normally down here she could hear trains in the distance, tooting their baritone horns at a crossing not too far away, but she hadn't heard any since she'd come Sunday night. Crickets were chirping. Her heart was beating and the clouds were moving. But the world seemed very still. She touched her phone and wondered why Luke hadn't called to comment on the pictures.

Chapter Eight

It was afternoon before Maggie got around to starting her bread. The morning had flown with laundry and kindergarten lessons. Luke had called before breakfast, contrite about not phoning the night before and tickled about the pictures. He said he'd been a cowboy too, and asked to speak to his dad to tell him about it. Then Tina had called, complaining that their mother was all but comatose and not eating. She'd tried to get her into a rehab facility, but every one she'd called had been converted to caring for the ill. Maggie had sympathized but said there was nothing either she or Tina could do. "You can't worry about it, Sis. Don't feel guilty." She was telling herself as much as Tina.

"Have you talked to Dad?" Tina had asked.

"No."

After lunch Oleatha again marched off to her garden, declaring it would frost in the night. Maggie wondered if the Weather Channel was still on the air. It seemed like every station was devoted to the flu crisis, but Roy'd finally found one with old reruns that Oleatha deemed acceptable for Jacob. He and his grandfather were in the front room watching.

Maggie'd thought she wouldn't have to bake for another few days, but they'd gone through all the bread from Hazel's store. There was always toast at breakfast and sandwiches at lunch. And for dinner every night, unless she made cornbread, Oleatha invariably put a saucer stacked with slices on the table. "Light bread," she called it. Maggie dumped her dough onto the floured countertop. She'd been feeding her starter every day, but for as long as it held out, she was going to use regular yeast. She wasn't too sure about the starter.

Grandma Hauser had taught Maggie how to bake bread when she was no more than eight or nine years old. She remembered her grandmother's kitchen, crowded with eggs on the counter and sacks of flour and sugar waiting to go into canisters but never quite getting there. In Maggie's memory the room always smelled of cinnamon and nutmeg or onions and sage. Grandma Hauser had been a heavy, patient woman. Maggie had loved staying with her.

"Use the heel of your hand, child," she'd advised and Maggie did, kneading the dough and turning it.

In the summers she'd sometimes stayed as long as two weeks, sleeping in a tiny room upstairs on a bed covered with a peacock spread. A crucifix hung on the wall behind it. "The Blessed Virgin is watching over you," Grandma Hauser would say every night as she tucked her in.

Little Maggie had thought her grandmother was doing a pretty good job of that herself.

She smelled the yeast under her hands. "The dough is alive," Grandma Hauser had said. "It's your job to help it grow." Maggie turned the shapeless lump. Her grandmother had taught her how to make cinnamon rolls too and, later, cookies and pork roast and noodles. When they'd cooked, they'd listened to a radio tuned to an old-fashioned station with more talk than music and ads for baking powder and laundry detergent. After the cooking was done, Grandma Hauser sometimes set Maggie down in front of her sagging armchair and brushed her hair. As the brush pulled at Maggie's hair, making her boneless as a kitten, Grandma Hauser had hummed German songs she'd learned from her parents.

Maggie'd always hated going home to the arguments and slammed doors. There was a crucifix over her bed at home too, but she felt no protection from it. When she was thirteen, Grandma Hauser had died and there'd been no shelter from the battles at all. A year later her father was gone.

From the front room she heard Jacob laughing. She'd promised him, when he was no more than an hour from her belly, fresh and red and smelling of the womb he'd just left, that he'd have her protection. He'd never hide trembling under the covers while his parents destroyed each other. She'd make sure of it. Plopping the dough into a greased bowl, Maggie covered it with a towel and cleaned up her work. Oleatha had chosen to be agreeable about the bread-making, maybe even a little impressed by it, but Maggie knew that a dirty dish or skim of flour in Oleatha's kitchen would set her off.

The air outside was chilly enough for a jacket. Maggie grabbed her hooded sweatshirt and escaped to the front porch. Jacob was too enthralled by ancient *Leave It to Beaver* episodes to follow her. She took a deep breath of sharp air. Strands of eerie kudzu floated in the breeze, and golden leaves skittered down the road. Her mind was calm, more peaceful than it had been in days, but then baking always made her feel good.

She leaned against the porch rail, letting the wind blow her hair and listening to the gurgling creek across the road. Last night's rain had swollen it nearly to its banks. Then she heard another sound: a crowing rooster. Generally roosters meant hens, didn't they? And hens meant eggs. They were down to less than a dozen with Roy complaining on mornings when he didn't get them for breakfast. Maggie dashed back in the house, stuffing her wallet in her pocket and grabbing an enamel pan. She'd get Roy some eggs.

The crowing was coming from up the hill, so she climbed that way, thankful the rooster's rusty notes were frequent so she could follow them. When she came to the narrow path that led off to the right toward Crazy Annie's house, Maggie turned. Oleatha had whispered that there were men growing pot down there, but Maggie wasn't going to bother their crop.

The crowing sounded closer, but she couldn't tell exactly where it was coming from. The left side was sheer rock with bits of weed and lichen dotting its boulders. On the right, trees, some bare and some with gaudy leaves still clinging, shot up into the sky with scrubby bushes and honeysuckle swaying at their feet. Her foot slipped. The track was covered with leaves, slick and leathery from the rain. Then, along with the constant crowing, she heard another sound—somebody whistling. She remembered her father whistling when he washed his car or cleaned out the garage. He'd be listening to the Reds on a little radio and whistling.

Maggie walked around a shallow bend and saw a tiny, beaten-down house, Crazy Annie's she supposed, although she really should get out of the habit of calling it that. A bearded man in a ball cap and jeans was painting the weathered boards of the house. Sheets flapped on a makeshift clothesline that stretched from a porch post to a dogwood branch. He quit whistling and looked at her. "Hello." His voice was wary.

"Hi," she said, just as cautious. "I heard a chicken and thought somebody might have some eggs for sale."

"More specifically, you heard a rooster."

Well, of course she had. Picky, wasn't he? Maggie nodded.

The man was probably about her age, or Luke's, three years older. He wasn't as tall as Luke, but then not many men were. She didn't think he was the pot farmer.

Still leery, he said, "The people down the road have fighting cocks. Hens too, I reckon, but you don't want any eggs from them."

"Why not?"

He scrunched up his nose, making his mustache move. "They're no good for eating, dark and gamy like the meat."

"Oh." She didn't know what else to say. He was holding his paintbrush like he'd just as soon get back to work, so she turned.

He said, "I'm Travis Parker. Are you kin to the Davies?"

It was an easy enough guess. Other than the villainous pot-growers there wasn't another house for two miles up the hollow. She nodded. "I'm Maggie, Luke's wife."

A grin transformed his face. Bright blue eyes lit up in the shadow of his Pennzoil cap. "I'll be damned," he said. "I'd heard that old Luke married. Good for him."

She gave him a weak smile.

"Is he down at the house?"

"No. He was working at the airport in Cincinnati when they closed it. He's quarantined at an army camp in Illinois."

Travis set down his brush and came over to her. Closer up, she noticed broad shoulders under a flannel shirt and wide hands flecked with paint. "I'm mighty sorry to hear that. Is he sick?"

She shook her head.

"So you came here to hole up until the sickness passes?"

"Yes. With our son Jacob."

The grin came back. "Luke's got a kid?"

Maggie nodded. "He's five."

"I bet Oleatha and Roy think he set the moon in the sky. I'll be damned." Still smiling, he rubbed at his dark beard. Maggie figured his hair was dark too, but she couldn't see it for his hat. "This is my Granny's house," he said. "I used to come down here when I was a kid. Luke's younger than me, but we used to play and get into trouble all the time." He paused. "I reckon I'm hiding from the flu too, but mostly I'm waiting for my granny to die."

Maggie's head jerked up.

"Well, you can't tell me you haven't heard of Crazy Annie." Maggie could tell that he didn't like people calling her that. "She's my grandmother. Been in a mental institution for years, but she had a stroke last week. They sent her to the hospital, but there wasn't much they could do for her. Said her brain kept swelling." He looked down at his scuffed black boots. "My sister wanted them to put in a feeding tube and send her to a nursing home, and they were fixing to do that on Monday. I didn't think much of that idea to begin with, but when the flu hit I couldn't see keeping Mamaw alive just to have her get sick." He hitched his shoulders up like he was trying to ease a load. "So I drove up to Lexington, made them disconnect the tubes they had running into her, and brought her down here where she can die in peace."

It was like someone turned on a faucet. He'd been waiting to tell this.

"What did your sister say about that?"

He turned his eyes to the white strip he'd painted on the house. "She didn't like it, still doesn't, but she's speaking to me." The paint seemed to hold his interest. "Maybe I didn't do the right thing. Sometimes I think Mamaw might be hurting."

"Would you like me to look at her? I'm a nurse."

His eyes darted to her face. "Really? I'd be mighty grateful." They walked to the porch. "Watch your step," he said. Several of the floorboards were rotted through.

The house was warm, although it smelled like burned dust, the way houses do when the furnace comes on for the first time. Ahead of her, Maggie saw a closed door. To the left was a kitchen with a rickety table and no chairs; to the right a large living room was furnished with a twin bed pushed against the wall, an air mattress on the floor, and a worn, plaid recliner. There wasn't much light.

Maggie went to the bed and saw that he'd set two kitchen chairs against it to keep his grandmother from falling out. He'd wrapped an old blanket over these, probably so she wouldn't hit her arm against them. Maggie looked at her. If Crazy Annie had been a creature of terror at one time, she certainly wasn't now. The old woman lying under a crisp sheet and quilt was tiny, wizened with age, and probably weighed no more than ninety pounds. She wore a pink cotton gown that looked as new as her bed, and her sinewy arms lay on top of the quilt. One arm had a three-inch long gauze bandage, and there was a gash on her forehead. Maggie asked, "May I examine her?"

"Please," Travis said. He went over to the front windows and pulled up shades. There were no curtains.

The contusion on Annie's forehead was raw and seeping, well on its way to becoming infected. Maggie held the woman's bird-like wrist and took her pulse: slow but fairly steady. Wishing she had her stethoscope, Maggie leaned over and put her head against the sunken chest. The beat was faint. She noticed the bruise where an IV had been and red marks under Annie's nose. "They were using a nasal feeding tube?"

Travis nodded.

"Did she get these wounds when she had her stroke?"

"Yeah, she fell. Bumped her head and scraped up her arm. It was in the day room at the institution."

As gently as she could, Maggie peeled back the adhesive attaching the gauze. Annie's closed eyelids didn't flutter. Whoever had bandaged it, probably Travis, had done a neat job but could've used the kind of tape that didn't cling so harshly to skin. Annie's was as fragile as tissue. The scrape was deep and angry. "When did she have the stroke?"

"Last Wednesday."

Maggie patted the tape back in place and straightened. "I have some supplies at the house. I'd like to come back and dress her wounds." She ran her fingers over the woman's sparse white hair. "I know she's dying, but we might as well make her as comfortable as possible."

His hands were fisted at his side. He nodded.

"Are you giving her anything for pain?" Maggie looked past Travis to the kitchen table. On it she saw gauze, tape, and a bottle of alcohol. At the end of the bed was a box of adult diapers. She didn't see anything that resembled injection equipment.

"She can't swallow."

"No, I thought you might be giving her shots."

He shook his head.

"I have to get back; they don't know where I am and I have bread to bake." She smiled at him, wanting to give him comfort as much as his grandmother. "What if I come again after supper? I could bathe her, dress those scrapes, and examine her a little better."

He took a deep breath. "I'd like that." And then he exhaled. "Bring a flashlight. I'll be watching for you. There's some nasty characters around here."

"We eat early. I won't be late," she promised.

❖

Luke woke with a jerk. He'd been dreaming, one of *those* dreams, full of steamy sex and sweaty flesh. The woman was faceless, not Maggie, but not Alicia or, even worse, the belly-dancer. As he'd left the party last night, he'd heard another flight attendant call the sexy chick Amanda. He grabbed some clothes and his phone and went to the bathroom. It was early, too early, but he didn't think he could go back to sleep after the porn movie in his head. Opening the phone, he saw the pictures Maggie had sent: Jacob grinning and his parents looking goofy. Luke laughed. Then there was the photo of Maggie, all got up like a gypsy. Maggie. He called, even though it wasn't but seven-fifteen in Henley County. She answered on the first ring, although it took two more tries before he could hear her, and apologized for missing her call. She sounded good, so good he wanted to run all the way to Sloan's Holler.

After he talked to her, Luke took a shower, and, as he left the bathroom, he noticed a large box full of jackets at the end of the hall. The Easter Bunnies had been generous again. There were several coats in different colors and sizes, all bearing tags from Wal-Mart. Luke wondered who was paying for all this. Probably our tax dollars at work, he thought. He grabbed a navy blue extra- large for himself and a tan medium for Briley. He'd best wake his roommate; Bob had breakfast duty today.

Briley was sitting up, blinking at the light. "The Easter Bunnies brought us some jackets. Good thing; it's cold as a witch's tit outside." Luke tossed the jacket at Bob. "I figured a medium would be about right for an old banty rooster like you."

"Ha, ha, funny boy."

"There's also a sign on the bathroom door saying we're supposed to go to the mess hall at 2:00 to get flu shots." Luke ran a comb through his wet hair." How do you figure they have vaccine this soon?"

"They don't. I heard last night that they're going to use a different process to make vaccine, a quicker one using animal tissue rather than eggs. But it's still going to take months."

"So what's this stuff they're giving us? Something they just happened to have in the can?"

"Who knows? Experimentation again, I guess." Bob grabbed his things and headed to the bathroom, leaving Luke to think about their day, flu shots being the highlight of it. Maybe, though, he and Bob could work out a plan for finding the mysterious firearm.

Luke had just finished what passed for French toast and an odd little slice of ham when Briley sat down. "Man, they've got this down to exacts," he said. "Not a piece of anything left after I got my food." He eyed his plate. "Reckon they need to ration us this close?"

Ilse said, "They might. Food is going to become a problem, I suspect."

Before Luke could process her dire prediction, Jill and a Customs guy rushed up to the table and sat on either side of him. Jill had the clipboard. "Lots of people didn't show up this morning," she said.

"We need to get people to check on those who haven't shown up," Briley said. "I bet some of them are sleeping off last night's beer."

Luke tried to smile, but his mouth was having a hard time. "Where's Frank Allen?"

The man said, "I'm his roommate. I took him to the medical building at three o'clock this morning."

"Damn." Briley put down his fork.

"He was turning blue," the man said. "We had to get a gurney for him."

Luke pushed his plate. "Now what?" he asked himself as much as them.

Briley sighed. "You know what."

"He left a note saying you were in charge," said the man. Maybe this guy wanted it. If so, he could have it.

Luke looked at Ilse. Her steely gaze didn't leave his eyes. What was she trying to tell him? "Okay, Jill. Let me see the list."

He noticed that Alicia wasn't marked off and asked Ilse about her. "Still asleep, and healthy as far as I know," she said.

Luke made a mark and then took a deep breath. "Okay, let's get this going."

He looked around and saw Pete, Drew, and Derek, who looked sheepish when Luke caught his eye. He didn't see Amanda, the co-pilot, or the gangster. With a deep sigh, he stood and hollered, "Listen up, people." They immediately got quiet. "I don't know if you've heard, but Frank Allen got sick last night. I reckon the man must've already been delirious at the party because he said he wanted me to pick up where he left off if he got sick. For those who don't know, I'm Luke Davies from Northern Kentucky, and I'm an airport police officer."

There was some murmuring, and Luke waited for it. If anyone protested his elevation to big, giant boss, he'd hand it over in a minute. They didn't. "We've got a lot of people who didn't show up this morning. Now, I don't know if they've all got hangovers from that fine brew we sampled last night or they're just snoozing in, but we need to know if they're healthy. Drew? Would you find a couple more people, two females please, and go check on these folks? I hate to interrupt their beauty sleep, but we gotta look out for each other, right?"

Drew and the Customs guy nodded, and Jill said that she'd go. Luke waited until they left. "I've got to make contact with the Head Moonsuit," he said, and a few chuckles broke out, "and then I need to get my bearings. But I'll stop by 'the office' every now and then. You all did get jackets this morning, didn't you?"

They nodded.

"Well, I'll see you at lunch," he said, trying to smile like he loved what he was doing. "Don't forget to be here for your shots at two." Then he sat down.

"You'll do well," Ilse said.

"I understand it was your doing that I got this job."

Briley snickered.

Ilse dipped her head. She really could play the part of a duchess even without last night's tiara.

"We need a better system for checking on each other," said Luke.

She nodded.

"We need somewhere to go now that it's cold outside," added Briley.

"Make notes," she urged.

For the next half-hour, he jotted down ideas. Damn the Mickeys if they wanted to clean up the chow line. Everyone but Drew had come back to report. Jill said, "It's not good."

Luke took a deep breath.

"I haven't seen Drew, but the rest of us found out that five more went down during the night, and we found four more sick ones."

"Jesus Christ," whispered Briley.

"Why didn't their roommates check on them?" Ilse sounded perturbed.

Jill shrugged. "Guess they thought they were sleeping in or felt funny asking. Not everybody has buddied up." Her voice lowered. "One was all but unconscious."

"Who was that?" Luke asked.

"An airline representative. Her name is Cathy. Red-headed woman."

Ilse said, "I know her."

Frowning at her clipboard, Jill said, "This one's odd. Gene Costanza. His roommate said he never came to bed last night. He was the one who was fighting with Derek over the dancing girl."

"Amanda," Luke murmured.

Jill said, "Those two are missing too: the co-pilot and the dancing girl. Craig Salyers and Amanda Schultz. There's no sign of them."

"Did they get sick?"

"No way of knowing. I guess they could've walked over to the medical building sometime in the night. Costanza wasn't injured was he?"

"Not that I could see. The roommate doesn't know anything?"

"Nope. He said that the man's barely spoken to him the whole time we've been here. Just said he was from Las Vegas."

Bob raised his eyebrows. "Sounds more like fun and games than illness."

"I wonder if Alicia might know something," Ilse said. "She was talking to him last night."

Luke nodded. "I'll ask her."

Just then a grim-faced Drew walked in with the two children. Both had been crying. "Could somebody find these babies something to eat?" he asked.

Ilse stood and held out her hands. "I believe they have some bread left. Would you like toast and milk?" She stooped to hear them and Luke heard her say, "Juice? Certainly you may have juice."

"Both parents," Drew murmured when they were out of earshot. His voice was shaking. "The mother's sick, but the dad's dying. Cyanotic like Allen." He shook his head. "Dear merciful God."

Jill's hand shook when she made notes. "Did you find any more?"

"No. The others were just skipping breakfast. They can't do that to us, guys. I don't want to make breakfast mandatory, but it's scary as hell knocking on doors thinking dead people might be inside."

"That makes twenty-three sick and one dead," Jill said. "Out of ninety-seven." She sounded like a businesswoman but lowered her head and whispered, "Lord help us."

Luke couldn't sit still another minute. "If you all would see to those children for a little while," he said as he rose, "I'll come up with something more permanent in a little bit. I've got to call Fister and find out some things."

Drew nodded. The kids were walking back to the table with Ilse, all three faces solemn. "We'll need to get out of here soon for the Mickeys," he said. Everybody had picked up the expression. "I'll take them down to the recreation room."

"And I'm going to work on our other problem." Briley asked for Jill's list and left.

When Luke had walked a few yards beyond the mess hall, he pulled out the paper Allen had given him and dialed the number. A voice said, "Yes?"

"This is Luke Davies. Are you Fister?"

"What's the code?"

Luke read it. "Sanctuary." Of all the silly-assed notions.

"This is Fister. I heard that Frank Allen's sick."

"Unfortunately," Luke said. "We've got a few problems here."

"So do we." Fister paused. "What?"

"Now that it's cold, we need more space for people to congregate. The rec room's crowded, the mess hall's locked up a good portion of the day, and people don't tend to stay in the barracks." It was hard talking to a disembodied voice. Luke wondered if Fister wore his Hazmat suit all the time. "Seems to me there are plenty of unused buildings here."

"True."

The man didn't make it easy. Luke wondered if he'd been this difficult for Allen. "I was thinking someplace with fair-sized rooms, like classrooms."

"We can do that. It'll be another area for you to police, however. Like the barracks."

Police? Luke hadn't realized anybody had been doing that. "Do you mean watch over to see if people are sick?"

"Yes. And clean. We don't have personnel for that."

"Okay, but there's another problem. The buddy system isn't working very well. We've got people missing, and there's no way we can tell if they're in the medical building or out roaming around. Costanza, Salyers, and Schultz. Are they sick?"

"I can't say."

Or won't say? Luke was getting perturbed. "Look, fella, we're doing the best we can out here, but we can't keep tabs on everybody. We want to know who's in the medical building. And we'd like to know how they're doing, like an update posted somewhere. Maybe something as simple as the hospitals do: stable, critical." Luke took a breath. "Or deceased."

"The medical staff is overworked as it is."

"Give them a clerk. You've got plenty of soldiers guarding this place. Seems like one of them could type up a list once a day."

"I'll look into it. But you need to find those missing people."

Jesus, Luke thought, trying to keep his temper. "Okay. We also could use a preacher, priest, a rabbi or something. Even a counselor."

"I doubt that could be arranged."

"Well, try. We appreciate the food and jackets, but you know that line about living on bread alone."

There was silence. Luke tried again. "Mental health is important too. And there's still no Wi-Fi. We also want our weapons returned."

"Unnecessary. Find those people, Davies."

Chapter Nine

A cold wind whipped across the plains and fought to creep under Luke's jacket. He didn't care. He was still hot after talking to Fister. Besides, he was determined to find the three missing people so Fister would shut up about it. Up by the barracks he saw Alicia crouched on a step, wearing a blue jacket. The wind tossed her light hair. Did the wind ever stop blowing in Illinois?

"Just the person I need to see," Luke said, giving her a smile.

She scowled. "To scold me?"

"No, no." Luke sat down beside her. "I need your help."

Her face was stony as he informed her about Allen's illness but crumpled when he told her about the children's parents. "I was wondering if you could take a shift with the kids. Drew's got them now, and I'm sure somebody else will volunteer. Maybe you all could work it out; take mornings or evenings or something."

A little light came into her eyes. "Sure. Where are they?"

Luke told her. Then he said, "That man you were talking to last night, Gene Costanza, do you know where he is?"

Her face tightened again. "Why should I?"

"He and the couple are missing. I'm trying to find out if they're sick, but nobody saw them going to the medical building."

She shook her head. "All I know is that he said he was getting out of here. He didn't tell me how. I asked if I could go with him, and at first he said I could. Then he blew me off as he was leaving with Amanda." Her voice went funny. She'd had two men reject her last night.

"I don't see how he could've gone through a gate," Luke thought aloud. "And why did he get chummy with the co-pilot and flight attendant? It's odd."

Alicia shrugged. She was wearing sweats rather than Cynthia's jeans and had traded her Barbie shoes for Nikes. "He said he was going to Vegas; that's where he's from. I wanted him to take me back to Cincinnati, but he said it had to be Vegas. When he left last night he said he wouldn't take me at all." She made a face. "Cynthia couldn't stand Amanda. Said she was a bitch."

Even if the man had escaped the compound he'd have no transport unless he stole one of those vehicles at the front gate. And walking was out of the question. As he'd told Todd, Ft. Rieselman looked to be miles from any town except for the couple of strip centers to the north that had the usual pawn shops, bars, and used car lots that always sprang up around a military base. Rieselman had been empty for months. Luke doubted those businesses were still operating.

Alicia stood. "I'll go find Drew," she said. "Those poor little kids."

Luke nodded. "I know you'll take good care of them."

She gave him a stingy smile; he wasn't quite forgiven. "I'm glad to have something to do."

Her words started him thinking. Maybe that's what everybody needed: something to do. He could manage that. Walking on toward the airfield, Luke's mind spun with ideas. Fister called, telling him that Building A4 was being unlocked. They could turn on the heat themselves. Luke thanked him.

"The missing people are not in the medical facility," Fister reported.

"I've heard that Costanza was planning on escaping."

Fister didn't answer.

"Did the soldiers at the front gate notice anything last night?" Luke was tired of the man's reticence.

"Not that I've heard. An escape is disturbing."

Luke frowned at the phone. "Why? Everybody in the country has a good chance of being exposed even with us locked up." Luke wanted the mystery solved, but he didn't really care where those three had gone. It would make his life easier if they disappeared. It also made sense that Costanza was the passenger with the weapon.

"It's breaking the quarantine." Fister's voice was stern.

"Yeah well, all of this is a lot like closing the barn door after the cows escape, don't you think?"

"There are protocols."

"I understand. I operate under protocols all the time, but I fail to see the logic in what's going on here." Still walking, Luke was nearly to the airfield. Up ahead, a man was sitting on a bench.

There was another long pause. Finally Fister said, "I'm checking into generating a daily report on patients, but we do have four deaths now."

Luke closed his eyes. "Who?"

The bodiless voice listed Cynthia, whom they knew about, a passenger from the first bunch, and the kids' father. "And Frank Allen," he said.

"Jesus," Luke murmured. "Already?"

"The doctors tell me he was in respiratory distress when he arrived." Luke couldn't detect even the tiniest bit of emotion in Fister's flat baritone. "I have instructed the medical staff to post a list each morning."

"I appreciate that," Luke said.

Fister clicked off. The guy was a charm school dropout.

He recognized the man on the bench, a passenger from his clothes, but Luke couldn't recall speaking to him. He'd have to learn their names now and wondered how Ilse had done it with her students. Damn, he thought. Allen.

The man was reading. Probably in his forties, he had short brown hair and a ruddy complexion. It was hard to tell with him sitting, but Luke didn't figure the man to be very tall. "Hello," Luke said and introduced himself.

The man shook his hand, smiled, and said, "Jim French."

Luke suddenly remembered. "You're the pilot."

French nodded. He had an open, good-natured face and eyes so blue it was as if they'd taken on the color of the skies he flew. "And you're in charge now," he said.

"Yeah well, can't dance." That was Briley's line. Luke wondered why he'd picked it up. The man closed his book, and when Luke saw it was a Bible, he got an idea. "I haven't seen you around much," he said.

"I'm sort of a loner," French said as if he were apologizing. "Not much on socializing. Why? Do you need my help?"

"Well, since you asked, do you know the whereabouts of your co-pilot or Amanda Schultz or Gene Costanza? We can't find them."

Shaking his head, French said, "I don't know Gene Costanza."

"Passenger."

"No, I don't know where any of them are. Sick?"

Luke shook his head.

"Salyers is my co-pilot, but we don't have much in common except work. We roomed together at first, but I ended up moving elsewhere." French looked uncomfortable. Luke figured he probably knew who'd moved into his spot, and why. "He's a hard-working guy, started out as a mechanic to save up for flight school. Ambitious. But we don't think much alike." He rubbed a finger down the leather cover of his Bible.

Luke nodded and stared at the runway. "Bet it was a job putting that big plane down on this."

French smiled. "A little bumpy, wasn't it? And even harder for the pilot who took off from here."

"I hadn't thought of that." Luke frowned. "Do you suppose he had to fly in a biohazard suit?"

"Don't know. But I'd call it hazardous duty, wouldn't you?" He chuckled.

Luke joined him and then was silent. He was having a hard time starting what he wanted to say. "As you can imagine, people are getting awfully scared. I'm scared myself." He paused. This man had said right off the bat that he was a loner, but Luke needed him. "Folks don't have anything to take their minds off the sickness except television, and I'm thinking all the grim news does more harm than good."

The man nodded and Luke knew his instincts were right. "So, I thought I might organize a few activities. I'm going to ask the bridge players to give lessons, and maybe Ilse Mayfield could teach French or German. Or Spanish for that matter, she knows all of them."

French smiled. Everyone knew Ilse.

"I've pestered the head Moon Suit for a chaplain, but he's ignoring me. I think we need somebody to take care of us spiritually as much as physically. So I was wondering if you would head up a Bible study or a prayer group once a day." From the time he was twelve, Luke had resented every hour his mother had forced him to spend in church, but he knew this was important, at least for some people.

French flinched. "I'm no clergyman," he said, looking down. He shut his eyes for a second. "I guess I could do it. With some help. Is there someplace we could meet?"

Luke nodded. "They've just opened up another building for us."

"I don't know enough to teach the Bible, but I'd be happy to talk about scripture and lead some prayers. It would be a privilege."

"Fantastic. Did you say you needed some help? I can ask people."

A warm smile lit up French's remarkable eyes. "I do, but not from anyone here."

❖

By two o'clock when Luke joined everybody else in the mess hall for their flu shots, he felt as though he'd done a good day's work. Jill had volunteered to handle the record keeping, including duty rosters for serving meals and cleaning and roll taking at breakfast each day. She would also keep tabs on who had sickened, and, God forbid, died. Along with Alicia and Drew, Connie, a motherly British lady who'd been on her way to visit family in Michigan, offered to help with little Zachary and Emma, whom they all agreed should be kept in the dark about their father's death, at least for a while. The three adults worked out a schedule, and Connie even produced some toys and books she'd intended for her grandchildren.

Luke announced times and places for bridge lessons, Bible study, and conversational French and German. They planned to make one room a library consisting of all the passengers' books and magazines and a game room. The last had been a suggestion from Derek who said he'd ask people to pool their laptops, hand-helds, and cards. He'd found both chess and checkers sets buried in a recreation room closet. Luke told him to run with it.

The medical people had set up two tables and were urging people to roll up their sleeves and line up. Feeling like he was back in the National Guard, Luke stepped behind Jill. "Everything going okay?" he asked.

She nodded without looking at him. "If there's anybody left to keep track of," she said. "Two more have gotten sick since lunch."

"Who?"

"Female Customs person and a TSA."

Luke took a deep breath, but it didn't ease the tightness in his shoulders.

Jill frowned. "As I was walking over here I met that angry guy, Josh Monroe. He told me he absolutely refused to get a flu injection. Said it was probably poison."

Luke shrugged. "It's a free country. But he's tough to work with."

"That's an understatement."

The line moved slowly, but as Luke neared the tables, he noticed that the left line was getting injections from a blue box of serum and the right, his line, from a red one. They were making people get shots the same color as the line on their pills. "Wonder what the difference is?" he muttered.

"Who knows? It won't matter. There's no way they've had time enough to make an effective vaccine. They're probably testing something on us."

Jill wore tailored slacks and a suit jacket, probably packed for her European meetings, but her professional polish was fading. Her hair was caught up in a messy ponytail and her shoulders slumped against the jacket's crisp seams.

"Great." Luke shifted his weight to the other foot and thought about what Todd had said. All the satisfaction from his morning's work hissed out of him like air from a balloon. People were waiting quietly. Connie had the two kids just then, and they protested when the Moon

Suits separated them into the two lines, blue and red. All this reminded Luke of something other than lab rats, but he couldn't think what it was.

❖

Maggie waited until supper to tell Roy and Oleatha about Annie and Travis. And she waited a little longer to say she was going back up there to care for Annie. She didn't figure they'd like it. But at first all they could discuss was Travis and how he'd sprung his grandmother from the hospital. "Where there's life there's hope," Oleatha declared. "He should've left her alone and let the doctors treat her."

"She'd never recover from a stroke that severe," Maggie murmured, wondering why she was defending Travis. She'd been brought up to think passive euthanasia was as bad as abortion. It didn't matter; her in-laws were paying no attention to her.

"You call that life?" Roy asked, his voice a little too loud. "Laying in a nursing home with tubes sticking into her body?" He put down his fork.

Oleatha sniffed. "It's God's will who lives and dies, not people's."

Jacob was ignoring the discussion, digging into his chicken and dumplings like they were the best thing on earth. Maggie had never seen him eat anything like that. At home he would've called them "sloppy" or "slimy," but if Pop liked something, Jacob did too. Except for beans.

"A hundred years ago folks would've had to let her go. If she couldn't swallow, then she couldn't live." Roy popped another doughy chunk of dumpling in his mouth.

"But it's not a hundred years ago," Oleatha retorted. "God gave us brains and expects us to use them to make people better."

Roy stared at his wife, his gaze sharp despite the cataracts. "It would take Jesus Himself to say whether all this medical stuff is God's will. Maybe letting people go was the way God intended it, and using tubes and respirators isn't. Ever think about that?"

Oleatha obviously hadn't. She raised her chin.

"I want to get this straight," Roy declared. "You mean to tell me that you'd let me linger? If I had a stroke you'd let them poke tubes into me and let me live like a vegetable?" His voice rose with every word. "For God's sake, woman, don't you ever do that."

"So you'd want me to starve you to death?" Oleatha's eyes shot sparks.

"For dang sure." He reached for the bowl of green beans. "We come in hungry; we might as well go out hungry."

That, Maggie supposed, was his final word on the subject, and Oleatha seemed to realize it. "I haven't seen hide nor hair of Travis Parker in years," she said, buttering another slice of bread. Maggie had pulled it from the oven just before supper.

Roy was still riled up. "I never liked that boy."

"Oh, you did too, back when he was a young'un. You always said he was a spunky little cuss. It was when you found out he was Billy Jenkins' best friend that you decided not to like him."

It took Maggie a minute, but she finally remembered that Billy Jenkins was Marla's ex-husband, the boy she'd run off to Nashville with.

"Well, you have to admit the Parkers were always queer folk: poor old Annie, and then that son of hers, Travis's father, who locked her up and then went around the country playing like he was a Civil War soldier."

"I don't reckon there's any harm in dressing up and playing soldier."

Roy crinkled his nose. "A grown man?"

"Well, they're odd; you're right about that. Everybody hoes their corn a little different. You can't hold that against folk, and Annie had to go somewhere. She couldn't live alone once her mind was gone."

"I'm done, Granny. Can I have a cookie now?"

Oleatha smiled at Jacob's empty plate. "Sure, honey. Law, that child loves chicken and dumps."

Jacob giggled.

"Wipe your mouth," Maggie murmured. When he'd grabbed two cookies and left the room, she said, "I thought I'd bathe her. He's kept her clean, but I don't think it's right for a man to wash his grandmother if he doesn't have to."

Oleatha's cheeks colored. If she'd wanted to oppose Maggie's plan, this changed her mind. "Well, you'd best go before it's dark. Get the flashlight for coming home. I don't much like you being out after sunset."

"Me either," Roy muttered. "But I reckon Travis will walk you to the end of his lane anyway."

Maggie hadn't thought about it. "I'll help with the dishes first," she said.

Shaking her head, Oleatha pointed at the door. "Go on. I'll wrap up your bread directly when it's cool."

What sky Maggie could see had gone pink, but there was still some light. The breeze had calmed, but it had done its work; the path was damp but not as sodden as it had been that afternoon. She carried her nurse's bag along with Roy's flashlight and some folded towels.

Travis had obviously bought sheets and nightgowns for his grandmother, but she wasn't sure what other supplies he had. And Maggie had gathered a few first aid items she'd brought from home. Shifting the bag to her shoulder, she climbed. The hill stretched her muscles and shortened her breath. Moving around in this hollow was as good as joining a gym.

Luke had called not long after she'd put the bread in the oven. Full of news about his "promotion," as he called it, and all the many things he'd been planning and doing, he'd not said much about the Parkers. Unlike his parents, he'd called them eccentric rather than queer. Maggie grinned about how the meaning of that word had changed. But he'd said Travis was a bit of a hermit, a real mountain man, but a good guy. Luke had seemed glad that Maggie was helping him. And then her phone dropped the call.

At the turning, Maggie stopped and looked back. You'd never know a house sat on down the hollow. She wondered if it would be visible once all the leaves had fallen. Of course, from here she'd have never guessed Annie's house was around the bend. Maybe these people liked being hidden. After her parents divorced, she'd lived in a series of apartments, hearing arguments and music, closet doors and babies. She remembered how embarrassed she'd been when she realized what the rhythmic thumping against her bedroom wall meant. She understood the luxury of privacy.

She was nearly to the house when Travis met her. With his ball cap pulled low over his eyes and his abundant facial hair, he was nearly as concealed as the house. "Howdy," he said. "I'm surprised Roy didn't walk you up."

"I think he wanted to, but his cataracts are so far gone the bad guys would get us before he knew it."

"Wouldn't count on that."

"How's she doing?"

"About the same."

He'd finished painting the side of the house and brought the sheets in from the line. She wondered if he had a washing machine. He'd placed a floor lamp near Annie's bed to help Maggie see, she supposed, and laid out a stack of new washcloths, a bar of soap, and a towel on one of the chairs by the bed. Maggie held up her towels. "I didn't know," she murmured.

He shrugged. "You left your little pan down here this afternoon. I figured it could hold your wash water."

"Oh, I did forget that, didn't I?" She gave him a nervous laugh. Spreading one of her towels on the old recliner, she set out what she'd brought. A rifle leaned against one corner of the room, and in another, two shotguns rested against the paneled walls. Maybe the marijuana farmers were more dangerous than she realized.

He was running water in the kitchen sink. "Getting it warm for you," he explained. She filled the pan and set to work, washing the old lady in pieces and keeping the rest of her covered for modesty and warmth. She talked to her as she washed, feeling more comfortable conversing with the dying woman than her grandson.

"You reckon she can hear you?"

"I don't know," Maggie said, patting one withered arm dry. "But if she can, I want her to know who I am." Annie's nails were yellowed with age, but they weren't blue yet. Maggie washed carefully around the cuts and changed her wash water. Travis stood by the stove watching her. Then she moved to the lower half of the woman's body, cleaning emaciated legs and gnarled toes, changing her diaper and cleaning her private parts. "How old is she?"

"Eighty-seven."

He took a frozen pizza out of the refrigerator and slipped it in the oven. "I guess you've eaten."

"Yes."

"Probably better than cardboard pizza."

Maggie wrung out her rag. "Chicken and dumplings, but Oleatha's not really. . . ," she faltered. It was probably rude to criticize her mother-in-law's cooking, especially since she was an uninvited and, mostly, unwanted guest.

He grinned. "Much punkin in the kitchen?"

Grinning back at him, she said, "Well."

Turning serious, he asked, "Are you all okay for food? You were looking for eggs." His voice trailed away as hers had. He seemed embarrassed.

"We're fine. Oleatha has a freezer full of food. It's just that Roy complains about not having eggs every morning." Maggie finished up the washing. "Do you have a clean gown for her?"

He pulled one out of a basket on the kitchen floor. "Do you want clean sheets too?"

"Sure."

Although she'd eaten plenty, the pizza smelled good. She was already getting tired of plain, country food. Travis lifted his grandmother so Maggie could change the sheets and then Maggie doctored the woman's wounds, used her stethoscope to listen to her slow heartbeat, and brushed her hair. She'd stuck a bottle of lotion in her bag and rubbed the fragrant stuff on Annie's arms and hands. "There. She's clean and fresh."

Travis was cutting the pizza. "Sure you don't want some? I got plenty." He turned on a radio that sat on a shelf behind the stove and opened the refrigerator to get a Coke.

"Oh," Maggie said, transfixed by the familiar red cans. "I don't want pizza, but I would love a Coke."

This pleased him. He opened hers and brought the chairs from beside his grandmother's bed. "I figure if I'm in the house I'd notice her thrashing around, but when I'm outside or asleep, I feel better if there's something keeping her in bed."

Maggie sat. "We could tie her in, real loose."

He shook his head. "You didn't use the alcohol on her scrapes?" He pointed at the bottle on the table.

Maggie took a long drink. It was nectar. "Awfully harsh," she said when she'd swallowed. "I used an antibiotic cream. I'll leave it here."

The pizza was gooey, cheese dripping and stringing off the crust, and the smell of it made Maggie's stomach think she hadn't eaten in a week. He noticed. "I know you want some of this."

Grinning, she nodded, and he cut her a slice.

The radio was all talk but not really news; once again a panel was discussing whether the flu virus had been created in a lab or stolen from viral archives. The president had vowed to hunt down the terrorists to the very ends of the earth, the announcer said. Maggie didn't care. "It seems like all they can talk about is the terrorism part of it," she said. "Who's to blame and how to catch them. I want to know what's going on with the sickness."

"Don't you all watch TV?"

"Oleatha doesn't let us." She took a bite, burning the roof of her mouth but savoring the squirt of sauce against her tongue. "I turn it on every now and then when she's busy."

"I didn't bring a TV down here, but there's plenty on the radio." He got up again to bring each of them a paper towel. "They won't give numbers; reckon they think it'll panic folks, but they're figuring at least forty percent of the population will catch it. Hospitals are already overflowing. They're short on respirators."

She wiped her mouth. "Four have already died where Luke is." He looked up from his pizza. "They've given them flu shots, but they're probably useless," she said.

Travis frowned. "Yeah. Nothing they can do yet. The president closed schools and government offices for another week, and said non-essential businesses should voluntarily close for that long too. But this isn't going to be over in a week by a long shot." He drank. "Of course, I don't guess businesses have much to sell. There are still restrictions on transportation. No gas. No food." He put a bit of crust in his mouth. "I got plenty of pop and beer." He grinned and pointed to a case of each on the floor over by the closed door, which, she figured, might enclose a bathroom.

She tried to return his smile, but panic was coagulating in her stomach along with the pizza, and she laid down her slice. Most of the time she battened down her fears, diverting herself by thoughts of making bread or entertaining Jacob, although Roy was doing most of that. Only when she talked to Luke did she allow herself to think of the devastation the epidemic would cause. Without meaning to, Travis had set the terrors free. "I guess I should go," she said.

He stood and grabbed a flannel shirt off the counter.

"I have a flashlight," she said. "Finish your pizza."

He ignored her. Shrugging the flannel over his tee shirt, he moved the two chairs by his grandmother's bed, pausing to look down at her. Maggie wondered if he said good-bye every time he left the house.

"She could have another stroke," Maggie said. "Or her heart could fail; that could happen any time. But I think she'll live until morning."

With his back to her, she could barely see his nod, but his shoulders relaxed. He chose one of the shotguns from the corner and turned. "I'll walk you home."

She didn't protest again. It was fully dark outside, that ponderous, solid dark of the hollow. Her flashlight's beam was an insignificant flicker, not much more than the burning tip of his cigarette. "I'll come back tomorrow," she said. "In the morning."

"I'd appreciate that."

Although he'd conversed easily enough in his kitchen, on the path he was silent. She wanted to talk to him; more than that, she wanted him to talk to her, but he didn't speak until they stopped in front of the house. Light from the living room pooled onto the porch where Roy sat on the swing. "Safe and sound," Travis said.

"Thank you, boy." The old man's body hitched as he stood.

Maggie almost commented on Roy's term for a forty-year-old man or on the irony of Roy waiting up like she'd gone to prom, but swallowed her words at the sight of Travis's solemn expression. He touched his hat, the way she'd seen old men acknowledge an acquaintance or a favor. And then he turned to climb the hill.

❖

At Ft. Rieselman they'd also had pizza for supper along with salad that tasted grassy, like the kind that came out of a bag. Nobody had eaten much. A few people had come up to Luke where he sat with Ilse, Jill, Bob, and Drew. They'd wanted to know how their friends and partners were, but Luke had been unable to give them news. Since lunchtime, five more had sickened, including Pete and the two American bridge players. Even worse, people had been hearing from their families all afternoon, and nearly all the calls had reported new cases of the flu. "Do you need to call anyone?" he'd asked Ilse. He'd never seen her with a phone.

"I called earlier in the day," she'd said. "I've been using Alicia's phone."

"Is there a Mister Professor Mayfield?"

She'd smiled a little. "Not any more. But I do have a son in Chicago, and a daughter in Virginia. And three grandchildren. Everyone's well so far."

But Drew's sister was ill, as was his girlfriend. And Jill couldn't reach her mother. Both of them had picked at their suppers and left, Drew to spell Connie with the children and Jill to check for a list on the medical building for about the fifth time that day.

"Let's head to the bunkhouse," Briley said. "Something to show you."

The sun was sinking ahead of them. Walking into the red gold light, Luke saw Joshua Monroe speeding toward them. "Might be something left on the chow line, Josh," he said.

The man was sweaty and breathing hard. "Had to finish," he said, pulling out his phone and typing in something.

"Finish what?" asked Briley.

"Walking around the perimeter." He smiled. "That makes four today."

"Fitness plan?" Luke was glad to see him smiling.

But the smile faded to an intense look. "Of course not. When I complete sixty-four perimeters, they'll let us go."

Briley's head jerked up. Luke said, "Why sixty-four?"

With exaggerated patience, Josh said, "Because six and four are ten and ten times ten is a hundred, and then a thousand, and so forth. Simple."

Luke hesitated. Briley said, "I see."

The smile returned. "I know you guys are counting on me for this."

"Sure thing." Briley gave him a hearty nod.

"Absolutely. See you later." Luke watched him stride to the mess hall. "Uh, we got a problem here," he whispered to Briley.

"Crazy as a junebug, but not belligerant."

"This time."

Once they were in their room, Briley gave Luke a clipboard with the list of Rieselman people on it. He sat on Luke's bed and pointed. "I've been trying to keep this current with info from Jill." He pointed. "These are the passengers, the only ones who could have the tagged bag."

Lots of possibilities, thought Luke, as he looked down the list.

"Subtract out the kids and probably the women."

Luke said, "You can't count out women."

Briley shrugged. "Okay, but less likely. The ones I've starred are in the medical building."

"Yeah, but one of them could still have the gun."

"Hold up, hillbilly. Sure they could, but we could search their rooms and bags." Briley held up his lockpicks. "That would reduce the list. I say it's unlikely that Jill has it or the little British lady, if you don't mind me crossing off a few women. Wouldn't mind seeing what's left in Costanza's room anyway. What do you think?"

"It's invading privacy."

"You gonna get a warrant? It's better than telling this Fister guy and having interrogations and, you can bet, thorough and unpleasant searches."

"True." Luke thought a minute. "When?"

"Have to spread them out. Mealtimes are best. That's about the only time people are definitely not in their rooms." Briley stood. "I'd like to do a couple now, though. Costanza for sure."

"Okay. Which do you want me to do?"

Briley grinned. "Neither, Mayor. I'll do the dirty work, if you'll just hang around outside and delay folks from coming in the building. Give me, say, fifteen minutes."

Luke nodded and went outside to lean against the side of the barracks. He saw no one. The sky was violet now, and the breeze had picked up.

Chapter Ten

Oleatha hadn't needed the Weather Channel to get the forecast right. During the night, frost crept into the hollow. Maggie wondered how it had wormed its way in. "Won't show up until later," Oleatha said at breakfast. "But when the sun hits the plants, they'll be booglified."

"Booglified?" Maggie had never heard the term. Jacob giggled and kept saying the word.

Nodding like a wise woman, Oleatha said, "Booglified. Gone all limp and wilted."

It was oatmeal again that morning with reconstituted canned milk and toast from Maggie's bread. Nobody was going hungry, but fixing meals had become a challenge. Jacob spread a thick layer of jam on his toast. "Are we going fishing this morning, Pop?"

Although the kitchen was cozy, Roy shivered. "Not until it warms up a mite. We might go after dinner."

Jacob's eyes clouded with confusion. "Lunch," whispered Maggie. When she'd first married Luke, his names for mealtimes had bewildered her too.

"Reckon I'll do the wash this morning," Oleatha said, stacking dishes.

"I'll help." Maggie stood to take the butter and jam to the refrigerator.

"No need. Why don't you go up and check on Annie Parker?"

So, after stripping sheets and piling their dirty clothes by the washer in the cellar, Maggie put on her jacket and went outside. Frost filmed the grass and fallen leaves. It was a beautiful, clear morning. She inhaled the crisp air and told herself to ignore the fact that Oleatha seemed to prefer that Maggie help anybody else but her and how Jacob wanted Roy's company a whole lot more than hers these days.

She climbed the hill and strolled down the track, noticing more today. She supposed she'd seen Travis's blue truck, a big Dodge, but she hadn't really registered it. She also noted a small outbuilding so ramshackle she was surprised a squirrel hadn't knocked it down the hill. She shouted hello. Luke once told her that people tended to call out when they visited down here, mostly because they didn't want to be met with a shotgun, she supposed. And Travis certainly had an arsenal.

"You came back," he said as he opened the door. Today's hat was a blue one with UK Wildcats on it, and he wore a flannel shirt tucked into worn jeans.

His greeting annoyed her. "I said I would." She slipped out of her jacket and went straight to Annie. "How was her night?"

"All right." He turned to face the sink where he was washing out the sheets Maggie had changed the night before.

"I could wash those up at Oleatha's," she said.

"No thanks."

Somebody had gotten up on the wrong side of the air mattress, Maggie thought. She murmured to Annie, checking her pulse and listening to her heart. She couldn't see much change from the night before. Removing the dressings from Annie's wounds, Maggie went over to the sink to get wash water. Travis raised a soapy hand to push the faucet toward her. "Have I done something wrong?" she asked.

"No." He agitated the sheets with his hands, big hands, wider and sturdier than Luke's.

After rolling her eyes at his back, Maggie set to caring for Annie, washing her face and hands, changing her diaper, cleaning her, and then putting ointment and gauze on her wounds. There wasn't much more she could do, and she was thinking she'd leave when Annie's eyes shot open. They were the same bright blue as her grandson's. "Travis," Maggie murmured.

He hurried over, wiping wet hands on his jeans and leaning over the old woman. "Mamaw," he crooned. "It's Travis. Little Scooter. I'm taking care of you, Mamaw, me and this nice nurse." He waited. Then he repeated what he'd said. Annie blinked but didn't speak. "Can you hear me?" Travis grabbed her claw-like hands. "I love you, Mamaw."

Maggie stepped away to the window and looked out at the rocky cliff across the lane. Rank weeds tangled at the bottom of it. She wondered if the frost had killed them or if they were too tough for a single cold night. With all her heart she wished Annie would say something to Travis, but she didn't. Finally he stepped away from his grandmother. "Want some coffee?" he asked.

"If you have some made." Oleatha had been fretting about their coffee supply, although it looked to Maggie like there was plenty. Still, she'd been drinking tea the last couple of mornings. It was bad enough that Roy didn't have his morning eggs.

Travis handed her a thick mug and started to get the chairs. "I don't need to sit," she said.

Leaning against the counter, he sipped, looked at the beat-up linoleum at his feet, and mumbled, "Maybe I did the wrong thing. Maybe she'll wake up again. She might live after all."

"They said her brain was still swelling, didn't they?"

He nodded at the floor.

"She couldn't survive that. Really. Sometimes they just open their eyes. Sort of a reflex." She almost said that most of them died with their eyes open, but he looked so wounded she couldn't do it.

"You're sure?"

"Positive." The house was silent, no radio this morning. "I was wondering," she started. He raised his eyes. "I was wondering how in the world you got her out of the hospital." Maggie nodded at the shotguns in the corner. "At gunpoint?"

He smiled. "Would you be too cold outside? I don't smoke around her."

Maggie put on her jacket. Her parents had found comfort in their cigarettes. She'd never understood, but she wasn't going to deny it to Travis. Once outside, he lit up and adjusted his hat, like he was getting ready to tell a long story. "My sister called on Sunday morning to tell me they were planning on putting in a permanent feeding tube on Monday and then moving Mamaw to the nursing home. I begged her not to do it; I said what about hospice or something that could just ease her out, but she wouldn't listen."

"What about your parents? Your father's her son isn't he?"

He exhaled a plume of smoke. "Yeah, but years ago he made the big decision about putting her in the mental institution. He said that Glenda and I should decide." He shrugged. "Dad sort of buried Mamaw a long time ago."

Leaning against his truck, Travis went on. "I didn't like it, but Glenda was up in Lexington with her. I reckoned she should decide. Then Sunday night I heard about the sickness, and it didn't take a doctor to figure out it was gonna spread like wildfire. I made up my mind that Mamaw wasn't dying from some infection that would cause her more pain. And she was gonna die at home. She hasn't been home in nearly thirty years." He flicked his cigarette toward the road. "I packed up what I thought I'd need and went to Wal-Mart to get stuff." A smile flickered across his face. "I heard there was nearly a riot there Monday morning."

"There was," Maggie murmured.

"There wasn't anybody there Sunday evening. Strange, huh? Anyway, I drove down here and unloaded stuff and then took right off for Lexington. By the time I got there, it was three o'clock in the morning, and I figured it was a nice slow time for hospital security."

Maggie remembered those shifts. "You were right," she said.

"I didn't see a soul when I went up to the room. I pulled the IV out of her arm, but I was afraid to take the tube out of her nose." Setting his empty mug on the grass, he stuck his hands in his pockets. "So I found me a nurse, and I said I was going to take Mrs. Parker home. I was her grandson, and I had the right to do it. She could check her chart and see that I was listed on it as a contact. Of course she fussed. Said she was going to call the doctor and security. It was against the rules and that kind of bullshit." He grinned at Maggie. "I did have a shotgun in the truck, and I thought about bringing it in the hospital. I didn't though."

Maggie grinned back. She wondered what she would've done if she'd been the nurse.

"Finally I talked her into taking the tube out and giving me a box of those diaper things. I hadn't thought to buy them at Wal-Mart. And I carried Mamaw out to the truck and laid her down in the cab. I'd brought pillows and blankets." He tilted his head at Maggie, waiting for a reaction.

"You've got nerve, that's for sure. And Glenda isn't too upset about it?"

"Nah, I talked to her again last night, and after all this influenza news, she's come around to agreeing with me. She's glad you're helping."

Maggie ducked her head. She was doing little enough.

"So am I, even though it makes me feel beholden." He gazed at the sky.

Maggie knew the word, even if she'd never quite grasped its power. "Oh, you're doing me a favor," she said. "And Oleatha. We're better off staying out of each other's way."

He chuckled. "Fair enough. You want to go back in?"

As soon as they entered the house, Maggie could see that Annie had been moving. Her body was lying askew in the bed, and one arm was over her head. "Jesus," Travis muttered. "We're gonna have to tie her down, aren't we?"

Maggie nodded, trying to think how they'd do it. The woman's skin was as thin as paper.

"I got rope."

"No, way too hard on her." She considered what she might find up at Oleatha's that she'd be willing to part with. Everything Oleatha had ever touched was sacred. "We could cut a sheet into strips and tie those, but you just have the two sets, don't you?"

Frowning, he nodded. "Let's see what we can find." Opening the door to the room off the front hall, he flipped a switch that turned on a dim, bare bulb in the ceiling. It was, or had been, a bedroom. An old iron bed frame leaned against the wall. Next to it were a duffel bag and a pile of Travis's clothes along with boxes of motor oil, canned goods, and paint. It was a fairly large room, but a good bit of the space was taken up by a motorcycle, gleaming in the dull light. Travis went to a shallow closet and started pulling out clothes and boxes. "There used to be some dress goods in here," he said, pawing through a box. "Would that do?"

"Yes, if it isn't rotten with age."

"Here."

He held up a neatly folded square of yellow gingham, and Maggie fetched her scissors. Laying it on the kitchen table, she cut it into lengths. "Even these aren't long enough; we'll have to knot two together," she said, testing the fabric. It seemed sturdy enough.

Tying one length above Annie's waist and another at her thighs, they knotted it at the edge of the mattress. "We'll have to untie it every time we change or wash her," Maggie said. "But you won't have to worry about her falling out."

"That's no trouble."

She put her scissors back in her bag. "Is that your motorcycle?"

"Yep. My baby. I wasn't about to leave it outside the apartment in Catesboro."

"You live by yourself?" She was probably meddling, as Oleatha called it.

"All by my lonesome. I've been divorced nearly ten years now."

"I didn't mean to. . ."

"Oleatha would've mentioned it eventually. It's a sin." He grinned.

"Her daughter's divorced."

"Yeah, but Bill was the devil incarnate, so that's okay. You got to shun the devil."

Maggie chuckled. "It's about that logical, isn't it?"

He seemed pleased that he'd made her laugh. "And I was Bill's friend so that's another mark against me. I'm surprised she lets you come up here."

Lifting her head, Maggie said, "Well, she's not my boss, even if she thinks she is, but she seems pleased that I'm helping. Figure that out."

"Can't." He grinned again.

Picking up her jacket, Maggie said, "I'll come back this afternoon. Before dark this time. Do you have a phone? You could call me if you need me."

He turned skittish again. "You're mighty kind," he mumbled, head bowed over the Wal-Mart receipt he used to write down her number.

❖

Luke wasn't sure what had awakened him, but he knew it was still pitch dark. Moving the window shade, he held his watch up to the streetlight burning outside the barracks. A little after five. Then he heard something outside, a rattling, a shuffling. Stepping into his sweatpants and throwing on his jacket, he went into the hallway, light from the fluorescent tubes stabbing his eyes. Everything was quiet in the barracks. Ignoring his bare feet, he crept outside and caught a glimpse of soldiers moving down the street. They were in uniforms, not hazard gear, but wore gauze masks that glowed in the dark. Bypassing the barracks, the soldiers entered a building that Luke had tried the previous afternoon and found locked. He reckoned they were searching for the missing trio.

Suddenly there was a shout and another shout. Luke walked toward the soldiers and heard them command poor, old Josh Monroe to stand down, move, get to the barracks. Josh was screaming something about the soldiers wanting to shoot him for his perimeters, and Luke knew he had to intervene. Holding out his arms, he slowly walked to where Josh stood, his breaths and shouts coming in ragged bursts. "Hey, Josh. They're not going to shoot you," Luke said. "Settle down."

"Take him inside, sir," said one uniform.

Another, maybe their patrol leader, barked, "Get him out of here. We have orders."

Luke took a few cautious steps toward Josh. "Do we have a curfew?"

No response.

Josh was hysterical, crying that he had to walk. It was his job.

"Then Mr. Monroe has every bit as much right to be here as you do." Luke's bare feet were freezing. Two more baby steps and he was by Josh's side. "It's cold, fella. Why don't we go in for a while and let these guys finish up. Then you can come back out."

"They'll shoot me in the back. They will."

Luke put a tentative hand on Josh's shoulder, surprised that the man allowed it. "Tell you what, I'll walk right behind you, so if they shoot, they'll hit me. Sound like a plan? You're too important to lose."

Josh nodded, his eyes wide and scary. "You're counting on me, aren't you?" Josh asked. "And you're the boss. Big Luke, right?"

"That's right. Okay. I'm putting my hands on your shoulders and walking behind you. Head straight to the barracks. When we get inside, we'll both be safe." Josh's back was trembling, but as soon as he felt both Luke's hands, he started walking.

In the hallway, Luke lifted his hands, but Josh screeched, "No, no." So Luke put them back. "Which room is yours?"

"At the end." His voice shook.

"Who's your roommate?"

"Don't have one. Todd got sick." Josh turned his head toward Luke. "Brilliant guy. He knew we were prisoners. We had worked out an escape plan, but then he got sick. So I have to do it myself now."

What a pair, thought Luke. "I guess so."

They arrived at Josh's door. Luke turned the knob. Josh froze. "You can't come in. No one is allowed inside."

"Okay. You find me if you need me, you hear? I have a nametag on my door. You going to be okay?"

Josh slid inside without saying anything, and Luke took a shaky breath. He had to get this guy to the medical center, but not just now. He figured the soldiers were searching for the missing people, and he had to admit he was mystified too. Briley said he'd searched through Pete and Dan's belongings and found nothing, but Costanza's and the lovers' rooms were stripped bare.

Hoping not to wake Bob, Luke eased their door open, but the light was on. Briley sat on his bunk, wrapped up in his jacket. "You're up early," Luke said. "Too bad you missed the excitement." He sat, massaging his cold feet. "A patrol was out there looking for the missing three and happened upon Josh Monroe who totally freaked out. They weren't too friendly about it. I finally got him to his room."

Luke looked up. Briley's face was the color of cream and he coughed, a hideous spasm that seemed to come from his toes. "You're sick."

Bob was shivering despite the jacket. "I reckon so."

"Then let's get you over to the medical building. Where are your shoes?"

Briley didn't move. "Can I use your phone? Want to call my daughter."

Luke handed it to him. "I didn't know you had any family. I asked you Monday if you wanted to call anybody."

A faint smile lifted Bob's lips. "Two ex-wives and a daughter. Rarely see any of them, let alone call, but I still remember the second wife's telephone number. My girl lives with her. She's sixteen. Anyway, that's where I send money every month." He coughed again.

"I'll get you some water," Luke said.

There was a stack of those useless little mouthwash cups in the bathroom. He filled four of them and waited, wanting to give the man a little privacy. He'd miss Briley. When folks went into that medical building, they seemed to disappear. Luke carried the water back, setting it near Bob who was croaking into the phone, talking mostly about business and bank accounts. Luke wondered what he'd say to Maggie when he made the same call. It seemed inevitable.

"I love you, baby girl. Probably never seemed like it, but I do." He listened another few seconds and said, "All right. Bye now." He handed the phone back to Luke. "Okey dokey. Shoes."

He moved like everything hurt. It probably did. From under the mattress Briley pulled a wad of money, probably what he'd made from hustling pool. "Take this," he said. "It's of no earthly good to me."

Luke shook his head. "I'll keep it until you get out."

Briley's hand was shaking. "Take it. I won't be coming out."

Luke shook his head and stuffed the bills under his mattress. Bob stood, wobbling a little. "You gotta find that gun. It's going to be important down the line." He coughed so hard, he had to lean against Luke. "And do something with that poor, crazy guy. He's as contagious as the flu."

❖

Luke showered, dressed, and sat on his bunk, looking at the empty one across from him. They had made a good team. He glanced at the clipboard. Five people cleared. He'd try to continue the searches when he could, and he'd take Josh to the medical people after breakfast. Maybe the guy would be calmer then.

He put his jacket back on and walked down the hall. Every occupied room had a sticky nametag saying who was living there. It'd been Jill's idea, but he'd presented it. "I don't care who rooms with whom, or if you want a room to yourself," he'd told people at supper last night. "But I need you all to put a nametag on your doors and arrange with someone to check on each other every morning," he'd said.

Outside the air was still and frosty, and he saw no signs of the soldiers. Stars dotted the darkness, reminding Luke of the clear skies down in Henley County. A body couldn't even see stars around Cincinnati. He went straight to the medical building, hoping there'd be a list, but he saw no signs of one. Damn Fister, he thought. He'd sent soldiers out to search for the three missing people but couldn't be bothered to come up with a list. People were counting on getting some news.

He thought about going to the recreation room but didn't. Instead, he walked, remembering how he and Briley had been determined to find another gate. Josh probably knew, but it was difficult to get much sense out of him. No time like the present, Luke thought. He turned toward the front gate.

Despite the early hour, sentries were at their posts. Luke gave them a wide berth and kept walking, following the fence. It was dark, and he stumbled a few times, but it was no challenge for a country boy used to walking on wild terrain. Anyway, the sky was lightening, turning a pearly gray, and after he turned right he could make out a building that looked different from Ft. Rieselman's utilitarian architecture. As Luke neared it, lights came on in windows shielded by blinds. It was a house, one with a porch and a tree or two out front. He stopped and focused. Fairly large, frame, and painted a light color. In the one room without blinds he could make out opened drapes and a bookcase. He'd bet all of Briley's pool money this was where the CO had lived and was now Fister's headquarters. He grinned. Gotcha.

Staying close to the fence, Luke kept walking past the house, again turning right when the fence did. After a while, he heard the gusty sound of a big vehicle and loud talking. There wasn't a damned thing for him to hide behind if the dark wasn't cover enough. He stopped.

To his left, headlights bounced along what must be a bumpy road. He heard brakes whining and then the deep rasp of moving metal. Another gate, he guessed. As the headlights approached, Luke could see a couple of soldiers standing on the other side of the fence. The headlights stopped, illuminating the two as they opened the gate, and Luke could tell that the vehicle was a van, olive drab and smaller than a school bus. Three military people, all wearing what looked like surgical garb over their camos, got out and walked through the gate. He'd found the kitchen staff.

One of them must've seen him and said something because a guard shouted, "Stay away, sir! Stand back."

Luke wasn't moving, but again he held out his hands to show he was harmless. He'd probably have to quit breathing for them to think that. He waited. The cooks walked across the scrubby grass, heading for the mess hall, a fair-sized walk across a rough field, and the guards closed up the gate and jumped on the van. Evidently they didn't feel it was worth guarding all the time, but now that they'd been seen, Luke bet they'd start patrolling it. Revving its engine, the vehicle turned and headed away. Only then did Luke approach the gate, rattling it as Todd had done to the one at the back of the post. It was, of course, firmly locked.

Briley would be tickled to hear all this, Luke thought, as he used the same dusty path toward the mess hall as the Mickeys had done. He wished he could tell him. Sitting against the wall of the mess hall, he watched Jill take roll. "Well," she said, her tone the one she probably used when her company's profits were in the basement. "Where are the lists?"

Luke shrugged. "Not there. I'll call Fister"

"He promised." She was all but baring her teeth.

"I'll call," Luke repeated. "Can't do any more than that." He waited until several people had checked in and pointed to her clipboard. "Briley's sick." She winced. "So, Bob and one other person sick since supper last night. Maybe it's slowing down."

"Maybe."

Jill shook her head. It was a shame she couldn't ease up a little; she was really sort of pretty when she smiled. "Until we get a list of the dead."

❖

It was late afternoon when Maggie escaped up the hill to check on Annie. The honey-colored sunshine was nearly the same hue as the leaves. As she neared the house, she heard Travis whistling again, and it made her smile. He was painting, finishing up the front now. "Hello," she called.

"Hello yourself." He waved his paintbrush at her but kept working while she went in the house.

After listening to Annie's chest and heart and taking her pulse, Maggie changed and cleaned her and then took a clean washcloth and gently wiped the inside of her mouth. At first she had trouble opening the old lady's jaw, but once inside it was easy enough to clean around the toothless gums. "If you had teeth, Miss Annie, you'd be a handsome woman," Maggie murmured. "Look at those cheekbones." She stuck a gentle finger in the woman's cheek, pushing it out as teeth would've done. "I bet all the boys admired you back in the day."

Travis came in. "They did," he said. "Dad said she was a beauty."

"I don't doubt it. What color was her hair?"

"Coal black and curly. I've seen pictures of her and my grandfather. She was as tall as he was and slender with a big, old smile that lit up her eyes." He opened the refrigerator. "Beer?" he asked.

Maggie shook her head. "Oleatha'd have a conniption. Besides, I don't drink."

"No?" He chugged down about a third of the bottle. "Luke used to."

She finished her work, retied the restraints, and washed her hands. "Still does, every now and then. I drank a little in college. Not since."

He leaned against the counter next to her. She could smell paint on him and that scent of wind and outdoors that reminded her of little kids and dogs. Turning off the tap, she explained, "My mother's an alcoholic. I didn't want my child to live through what I did."

"Are you an alcoholic?" He asked it and then colored. They both seemed to get a little too nosy sometimes.

"No, I don't think so, but I didn't want to risk it."

"Coke then?" His eyes were dancing.

She smiled at him. "No, thanks. I have to hurry back for supper." But she lingered, looking over at Annie. "What happened to her? How did she end up institutionalized?"

"Oh, it's almost like one of those movies on the women's channels." Maggie tilted her head, encouraging him to go on. "She's from Kentucky, but not around here; she grew up in Evans County. When World War II started, she and her sister went to work at one of the plants up in Ohio. My dad's father grew up here. His mother was a Sloan, like the creek and the holler's named after, and he'd lived down here his whole life until he went in the service. He ended up in Ohio, near where Mamaw was working. Well, they met and married right away. For a while she lived close to where he was stationed, and then she got pregnant and he moved her down here. Back then his parents had a big house on down this track. It burned down in the fifties. His kin looked in on her from time to time. And he was able to get leave sometimes, but then he shipped out. Died in Italy before my father was born. So Annie lived alone down in this holler, grieving and taking care of her baby. My dad."

He upended his beer and finished it. "The Sloans and the Parkers looked after her, but it must have been lonesome. She had insurance money, and I think her folks sent her some too, but after a while she took in sewing and did other little things to get by." He looked over at his grandmother. "She still had a bunch of chickens and turkeys when I was a little kid. I'm surprised people would come all the way down here to bring their sewing and buy eggs, but they did. And she made quilts: beautiful quilts." He pointed at the one covering Annie. "She made sure my father got his schooling, sent him to Berea College, and did without, but from the time he started school, he said she was more and more odd. Alone too much is what I think. By the time I came along, I remember her being happy one minute and depressed the next. They took her to doctors, but nothing helped." He looked down. "They even gave her those shock treatments, made her real quiet, like a puppy someone's been whipping, but they didn't help either. Finally she got so bad my dad had to put her in an institution. She'd gotten to where she wouldn't eat or keep herself clean. It about broke his heart."

"Where's he now? Does he live around here?"

"No. After he retired, he and my mother moved to North Carolina."

Eyes shaded by his cap, Travis gazed out the window. "Before they put her in the institution, they used to send me down here to keep her company and help out. Some days she'd bake me cookies or play catch with me; she had a good arm." His mouth smiled, but his eyes were wistful. "I'd help her gather eggs and wash them, and of an evening she'd quilt and tell me about the old days back in Evans County." He shrugged like his shirt was too tight. "Other times she'd sit and cry, and I heated up soup for her and made her go to bed."

He shrugged again, shedding memories like a dog does water. "I suppose back in college you were testing yourself to see if you were an alcoholic. My whole life I've been checking to see if I'm crazy."

Maggie hardly knew how to reply. She smiled, flipping his confession into humor. "And are you?"

He grinned, his teeth very white against the black beard. "No crazier than the next son of a bitch, I reckon. You better skedaddle or Oleatha will have your hide."

Chapter Eleven

Friday started out foggy at Sloan's Creek, the hollow holding vapors like a lidded pot, but by mid-morning when Maggie had already gone to visit Annie and set bread to rising, the day turned fair. She sat up on the hill behind the house, fiddling with her phone and trying to decide whether to call Luke. Most times he called her since she was never sure if he was busy being the Mayor of Mickeyville. She smiled. He seemed determined to find humor in a horrible situation.

Most of Oleatha's garden as well as all her flowers had been booglified by the other night's frost, but the kudzu still hung in resilient curtains. She wondered how cold it would have to get to tame the vicious vine, even for a season. Fingers hovering over the buttons, she made up her mind and pressed the one for Luke. He answered on the third ring. "Hey, honey."

"Hey yourself. How are you?" The greeting wasn't trivial these days.

"Hale and hearty. How about you all?"

"We're good. Your dad and Jacob are fishing this morning, and your mother's doing her Friday cleaning. She won't let me help, but I've got bread started."

"Didn't you just make bread?"

She'd thought the same thing. "Yep, but we kind of go through it down here. You know how much pb and j Jacob eats."

He chuckled.

"So how is it?" She couldn't bring herself to ask how many were sick, how many had died.

"Only one got sick last night. But my buddy Bob Briley came down with it this morning. We were supposed to get a list of the sick, but we didn't."

"Oh, that's a shame about Bob. Hope he comes through it. Some people will, Luke. Really."

"Maybe."

She could feel his hurt. "Why wasn't there a list?" Diversion was good.

"I think this government guy's more interested in the three missing people than the ones who are here." He'd told her about them when he'd called the night before. "They had soldiers out looking for them this morning."

"Is it that important?"

"That's what I'm wondering, although I'd hate to think of them sick somewhere and needing help."

Good old Luke, she thought. He took care of people more than she did, and she was a nurse. "I don't think it's likely that all of them would get sick at the same minute."

"I guess not." His voice sounded marginally lighter. "Hey, I wanted to ask you something."

He described a man named Josh, whose erratic behavior had convinced him that mental illness was the cause. "I'm going to try to get him to the medical people. Aren't there meds that can help?"

"Sure. But a diagnosis is critical for choosing the right one." She had little experience with psychiatric care. "Are you sure he isn't on medication? Maybe not taking it? With all the stress. . ."

"Hmm. Hadn't thought of that. I'll check into it."

"I'm sure everyone there is nearly crazy with anxiety. What about your preacher pilot? Is he helping at all?"

"French? He's great. Nearly everybody's going to his prayer group, even a couple of Jewish people and Ilse, who I think is all but an atheist. We had to move more chairs into the room."

"Have you been going?"

"Both days." Neither of them said anything for a second or two. Then he asked, as he had the other day, "Where are you?"

"On the hill behind the house. It's sunny here, and I can hear some birds making a racket." She scanned the horizon to give him more. "Since the frost, your mother's put her garden to bed, but the kudzu's still thriving."

There was a weak chuckle. "Of course it is." He paused. "How's Annie?"

"About the same this morning. Travis is still painting the outside of the house. Do you suppose he's going to live there after she dies?"

"I don't know. Last I heard, he was working as a mechanic at a car dealership in Catesboro and living in town."

"Sometimes he's real friendly and sometimes he's not."

"I told you the Parkers are odd. I had Travis's dad in school. U.S.History my junior year. He always wore these funny little bow ties and threw chalk at us if we weren't paying attention."

"Did he ever throw it at you?"

He laughed. "Lots of times. It stung too. He made us draw maps and all but act out the battle at Gettysburg. Hell on the Civil War."

"Poor Luke."

He chuckled again. "So the boys are fishing this morning?"

"Yep. It's warmer today. Oh, Oleatha dug up some of your old readers, and Jacob and I have been working with them. Your son's reading now."

"Well, that's fine. That's real fine."

"Yeah, he told your mother that he wanted to be the one reading the Bible to Pop, and Oleatha got right on it."

A full laugh this time. They talked a while longer until Luke said he needed to check on Josh. "Call when you can," she said. "I've been going up to Annie's around ten and four most days, but otherwise I'm not busy."

"Stay healthy."

"You too. I love you."

As she walked up to Annie's that afternoon, she carried a foil-wrapped package of her bread for Travis. Oleatha hadn't blinked an eye when Maggie had suggested it, which surprised her. As the house came into view, she saw Travis sitting on the front porch smoking, waiting for her.

"Bread," she said, holding out the loaf.

"I thank you," he said, taking it, but he didn't smile. "She's worse."

As soon as Maggie went in the house she could see there'd been a change. Annie's color had faded to the shade of old piano keys, and her breathing was erratic. Cheyne-Stoke respiration, Maggie thought, whipping out her stethoscope. Annie's heart was weakening, and her pulse was thready. Maggie checked Annie's nails, and, as Maggie suspected, a bluish tinge tinted them. Travis came in and stood behind her. "Well?"

Folding up her stethoscope, Maggie nodded. "She's going, Travis. It may not be for several hours yet, maybe even another day, but soon."

He fiddled with the brim of his cap. Today's had "Ford" written in its distinctive script. He was still holding the bread. Maggie took it from him and set it on the counter. Opening the refrigerator, she handed him a Coke and got one for herself. "Let's go out on the porch." She knew he'd want to smoke, even if he'd just finished one.

Travis followed her and took the icy can without saying anything. Instead of sitting on the porch step, he went over and leaned against his truck. Maggie did the same. The metal was warm from the sun. "Have you made any plans for her?" she asked.

He raised a shoulder. "Yeah. And no. I don't want a funeral where people could gawk at Crazy Annie."

Maggie nodded but wasn't sure he noticed.

"And the radio's saying people shouldn't be gathering now anyway." He looked up, his eyes climbing to the top of the stony cliff across the road. Maggie bet he'd known for a while exactly what he wanted to do with his grandmother; he just didn't want to tell anyone. "I'd like to bury her right here," he said, turning to stare at Maggie as if he were daring her to object.

"There does have to be embalming and a death certificate. It's state law," Maggie murmured, hoping her tone was gentle.

"Who's gonna know? You, Roy, Oleatha? You gonna tell on me?"

"Of course not, but you'll want a casket, won't you? How are you going to get that without anybody figuring it out?"

An unpleasant grin crept from under his bushy beard. "I got ways."

She didn't want to know his ways. "Do you have a spot picked out?"

He pointed behind the house. "There's a nice little place up there, flat and dry, with a couple of redbuds beside it. I pulled some stones and dug the grave the first couple days I was here."

"Well, I guess you're going to do what you're going to do." She couldn't quite approve, but she couldn't see that it mattered either. Years ago people had buried their folks this way.

"I gotta be gone for a while this evening, though. I didn't get everything done ahead of time." His eyes met Maggie's and burned into them.

"You want me to stay with her?"

"I don't like to ask, especially after all you've done." Only then did he raise his soft drink to his mouth.

"Sure. When?"

"Could you come back up after you've had your supper? Just before dark? I'll walk you home when I get back."

❖

After breakfast, he'd opened Josh's door and found him sleeping. Probably exhausted after all his walking. He'd come back after lunch. Then he called Fister and gave him hell about the list. Luke was getting as nervous as Jill about what the body count might be. Trying to walk off his anxiety, he hiked toward the airfield and was relieved to see French there, sitting on the bench, writing in a notebook, and consulting his Bible. He was one person Luke wouldn't mind talking to. "Hey," he said, sitting next to him. "Prepping?"

"I am." French smiled. "I've taught Sunday School and listened to thousands of sermons, but I'm still a little nervous about this."

Luke waved a hand at him. "You're doing fine. People just need to talk."

"And pray."

"I imagine a lot of them were already doing that."

French put his pen down but didn't say anything. Across the way, Luke watched a cloud shred in the breeze. "I wonder if the soldiers will search again tonight for your co-pilot and the other two," Luke said. "I guess they figure it's safer at night. We're not out to breathe on them."

French rubbed at his nose before he replied. "I know where they are."

"Really?" Over the last two days Luke had imagined everything from a secret escape, to a tawdry *menage a trois*, to three people dead of the flu.

"Listen," French said, cocking his head toward the hangar.

Sure enough, once he put his mind to it, Luke could hear faint noises coming from the building. It sounded as though metal was being dropped on concrete. "Do you suppose they've been hiding in there the whole time?" Luke asked. "Why? There wouldn't be food or beds, would there?" With Amanda around, he figured there'd be a pressing need for beds, and the thought brought color up in his cheeks. Jim French was all but a preacher.

The sunlight caught an amused gleam in French's eyes. He knew what Luke was thinking. "They've probably managed," French said. "There's a plane in there. I peeked in a window the first day."

It all became clear to Luke. "And of course Salyers could fly it."

"It's a small Army plane, a C12. Beechcraft, probably used to ferry the VIPs around. I guess the military didn't get around to moving it before we came. Different from our big boys, but sure, Craig could fly it."

"And this Costanza, from everything I hear, has money. He's probably paying Salyers a ton."

"Good guess." French chuckled. "And maybe offering Amanda a job in Vegas at the same time."

Luke was appalled. It was a flagrant disobedience of rules; hell, it was theft. He reached for his phone, but French touched his arm. "Why? Besides, it's too late anyway." He pointed at the hangar. Someone was raising the door, and Amanda, dressed in tight black slacks and a sweater, was hopping into the cabin of the olive drab plane. Costanza, holding a briefcase, was behind her. He looked over at French and Luke and stared for a few seconds. They'd be noticed, Luke thought. All air traffic was at a standstill, and they'd be spotted. But it was a U.S. Army plane with an expert pilot. They had a chance. He waved and didn't do a damned thing.

Even though it was a small airplane, when Salyers fired up the engine, the noise thundered over the Illinois prairie. Surely even the guards at the front gate could hear it. "They'll make calls," French said, thinking along the same lines. "But there's no way they can get back here in time to stop them. And what would they do, shoot them? Someone may think it's worth sending out fighters to force them down, but I doubt it."

The plane crept out of the hangar and onto the runway, taxiing awkwardly along the bumpy concrete. Luke thought he saw Salyers wave from the cockpit. "It's wrong," he murmured.

"Is it?" French watched the plane. "It's not evil; no one's being hurt. The flu's out there as much as it is in here."

Luke watched the man's face rather than the plane. French's expression became thoughtful. "I suppose it's theft, although I doubt they'll keep the plane. I don't blame them. My little girls are sick. I'd like to be home myself."

"Then why didn't you do it?"

The plane was picking up speed, and as they watched, it took off into the sun. No alarms went off, no troops came storming onto the strip. French stood. "I don't know. Didn't really consider it." He looked at Luke. "Being law-abiding gets to be a habit, I suppose."

❖

"Did Roy and Oleatha say anything about you coming down here?" he asked. He wore a black leather jacket and a dark hat. His breaking and entering clothes, Maggie supposed.

She shed her jacket. "Nothing much. Oleatha said she was sorry to hear about Annie." This wasn't the whole truth. There'd been a discussion at the supper table. Roy had asked Oleatha why she was acting kindly toward Travis Parker when there was a time she'd just as soon smacked him as look at him.

"The Good Book says we should turn the other cheek," Oleatha had replied.

Roy'd said, "They's people who made you mad that you haven't spoken to in twenty years." His eyebrows had risen nearly to his hairline.

Sniffing and all but wiggling before she'd answered, Oleatha had murmured, "I keep thinking about Luke. About boys who don't have family to help them out." Maggie didn't want to tell this to Travis.

Rocking from heels to toes, Travis said, "I reckon you didn't tell them I was leaving you here."

"No, I didn't." Maggie figured he was going out to steal a casket for his grandmother, and she wasn't about to approve of it. Turning her back to him, she got very busy tending Annie whose breathing was even more erratic than it'd been that afternoon. Maggie could tell he was anxious to leave, but it was still light outside. Surely he needed darkness for his criminal activities. Annie's heartbeat was as irregular as her breathing, and her color had gone from pale yellow to gray. Hours, Maggie thought; she'd be dead in a matter of hours.

"I won't be gone too long," Travis said. "There's food and Cokes. Eat anything you want. I pushed the recliner over near her."

Maggie had seen it, along with the afghan lying across one arm.

"I figured you might want a cover if it gets chilly."

The room grew dimmer as he pulled down the window shades. "Do you know how to shoot a rifle or a shotgun?"

She turned at this. "No. Will I need to?"

He'd walked over to the corner where the rifle was and stopped, rubbing his hand across his hairy cheek. "I guess not. It's just if that crew down the road sees that my truck's gone, they might try to get in."

"Why?"

"They grow weed and they cock fight and they do most anything they can to raise money. Welfare don't go far when you're hooked on oxycontin, or more likely heroin now." He looked like he was about to change his mind about leaving. "Most people know I have a bike. They might steal it to sell."

"Go get your grandmother a casket. I'll be fine. I'll lock up tight."

"You sure?"

"Positive." Turning again to Annie, she added, "I'll take care of her."

Travis walked over to the bed and squeezed Annie's hand. "Do you think she'll last until I get back?"

He was close enough for Maggie to smell leather and tobacco and nerves. She softened her voice, but she wouldn't lie to him. "I don't know, but go on. Be safe."

Jerking his head once, he left, looking back to make sure she locked the door behind him. Maggie secured both locks and listened as he started up his truck. She wasn't afraid, and this surprised her. But she was restless. Although Travis had obviously intended for her to sit by Annie's bed, she didn't feel like sitting. Roaming into the kitchen, she opened the refrigerator. Besides the beer and Cokes, she found margarine, jelly, an opened can of pineapple, and a half-full jar of spaghetti sauce. In the freezer were more pizzas and several pre-packaged meals, fancied up now from what her mother used to call TV dinners. On top of the fridge was her bread, greatly reduced in size, a box of saltines, some peanut butter, and a box of Little Debbie cakes. She remembered when she'd had a Little Debbie in her lunchbox every day. That was back when Donna had still been capable of packing lunches. Maggie picked up the box. Nutty Bars. Those had been her favorites.

She turned on the radio. Hungry for news, she changed the station from country music to talk, but again she was disappointed. The reporter was talking about what the flu would do to the economy and then discussed how the rest of the world was preparing for its spread. She wasn't sure what she needed to hear, but this wasn't it. She caught sight of the Little Debbie box again and wanted a Nutty Bar more than anything. Despite feeling guilty for taking Travis's food as well as eating junk, she grabbed one from the box and peeled off the cellophane. Then she took a Coke and sat in the recliner.

About an hour later, Luke called, full of news about the people who'd escaped from camp. He seemed to be feeling both blame and excitement about it. Sort of like Travis and the coffin, she thought. "Did anybody get sick today?" she asked.

Luke's voice changed. "Yeah. We thought we were about done with it.

"Any of your buddies?"

"No." He paused. "We're anxious to see that list from the medical people. Fister swears it'll be posted in the morning."

"Not knowing is the worst," she said. Then she told him where she was, although she left out what Travis was doing. She just said he'd needed to go somewhere.

"I hope he doesn't bring the flu back with him," Luke said, sounding a little huffy about it. "Not after all you've done for his grandmother."

"I'm sure he won't," Maggie soothed. She hadn't thought of that, but she didn't think Travis would be seeing anybody, unless it was the sheriff when he got caught and then he'd be in jail anyway. What would she do then?

They talked until there was nothing more to say. Maggie kept her eyes on Annie who breathed hard one minute and barely breathed the next. When they hung up, Maggie looked at her watch. Travis had been gone an hour and a half. And it was another hour before she heard his truck. He knocked, saying, "It's me, Maggie," so she'd unbolt the door.

His eyes went to Annie first. "No change," Maggie said.

Then he went to the table and put two candy bars on it, lining them up just so. She could feel the thrum of nerves coming from him, hissing like a broken electrical line. "Did you get it?" she asked.

Nodding, he took off his jacket and pulled a kitchen chair next to the recliner. "Had to go to the funeral home on beyond Catesboro. Kingsford's was locked up tight as a drum."

Maggie didn't know these places. "Was anybody there?"

Patting Annie's arm, he shook his head. "Neither place, although I believe somebody'd been there earlier this evening, probably working on a body. Hell, there's nobody anywhere. If Wal-Mart is open at all, it isn't in the evenings. Not a car on the road. It's spooky."

"I ate a Nutty Bar," Maggie confessed.

He looked at her for the first time since he'd come in. "That's fine. I bought those candy bars for you too. Didn't know whether you'd like a Reese's Cup or a Hershey Bar better, so I got both."

"You bought them?"

He misunderstood. "I didn't go to a store. The funeral home has a little stand of snacks for people in the kitchen by the coffee machine. The money goes to the Lions Club or one of those organizations."

"You paid for them?" Maggie stared straight into his eyes.

He caught on and didn't like it. "Yes ma'am, I bought them. Left the money right there in the bowl." Bristling, he stood and glared at her. "And, yes ma'am, I paid for the coffin too. I may have broken in the funeral home, and I may have taken a coffin out of their basement, but I laid the money on the undertaker's desk, every damned dollar of it." His eyes narrowed. "What do you think I am?"

Ducking her head, Maggie said, "I don't know. How would I know?"

He exhaled. "I reckon I can walk you home now."

Feeling small and uncharitable, Maggie murmured, "I'd planned to stay. It may be a long night."

He'd been walking back to where he'd thrown his jacket but stopped. "You mean it? You're going to sit with her until. . . ?"

"Yes. And I love Reese's Cups."

Chapter Twelve

"Drew? Could you help me a minute?" The young man jumped to his feet and deposited the trash from his lunch.

"Where are we going?"

"To see Josh Monroe." Luke slid into his jacket. "I want your opinion." He told the EMT everything he knew about Josh.

Drew shook his head. "Not my area of expertise, but whatever."

"See if you can find some pills or a bottle." Drew nodded.

Luke tapped on Josh's door. No response. He opened it. The blinds were closed, making the room dim even at midday. Josh was an untidy lump lying in one bunk. All of his belongings seemed to be scattered on the other. Luke touched Josh's shoulder. "Hey, fella. It's Luke."

Josh mumbled. Drew stood behind Luke and whispered, "Is he sick?"

"Wake up. I brought you a sandwich." A fairly pitiful one. "C'mon. Wake up. Are you sick?"

The lump moved and Josh's head emerged from under the blanket. "I am not ill, and I do not wish to be disturbed," he announced. "Why is that man in here?" He pointed at Drew. "I do not want you in my room."

"Just wondering if you're okay." Luke felt like he was soothing a skittish animal. He looked back at Drew and blinked a couple of times. "Where are your pills, Josh? I'm the boss, right? You need to take your pills."

Josh swept the sandwich to the floor and pointed at the other bed. "Over there. But I'm not taking them. Need to be sharp now."

Drew edged toward the empty bunk and sat on it, moving his hands through the clothing, notebooks, and toiletries. Luke kept talking. "But how are you going to walk the perimeter if you don't get up and eat? We need you."

Josh shook his head and collapsed back onto the bed. "Not today. I can't do it today. Leave me alone."

Luke leaned down to pick up the sandwich and place it on a chair. He was buying time for Drew. "How about a shower? Bet you have sore muscles after all that walking." Actually the man reeked.

"No." He swung a listless arm at Luke. "Go away. I'm entitled to my privacy." Luke heard Drew clear his throat. Success.

"All right. But I'll be back later to give you your medicine." He paused. "I'm the boss, right?"

Only a garbled mumble came from the bed.

Luke and Drew shut the door. "What are they?"

Drew shook his head. "I don't know, but the scrip is for Depakote, 250 milligrams, three times a day." He opened the bottle and counted as they walked. "Ninety pills filled October 20, and all ninety are still here."

Luke shook his head. "What do you suppose the pills are for?"

"If I were to guess, I'd say they treat a mental health condition. From what you've told me, he's cycling between depression and mania."

"Bipolar?"

"Maybe. You want me to take these over to the medical building and see if they'll tell me anything? Connie is with Emma until three."

"Would you? That would be a great help," Luke said. "And get back to me. He's got to take his medication."

❖

Anxious to see a list, the next morning Luke was up by five again. Since the missing trio had been found, and then lost, Fister had no excuse for putting off his promise any longer. Just after the three took off, Fister had called him. Luke and French had been walking back toward the camp, and they'd grinned at each other like kids skipping school while Fister pitched what Oleatha would've called a hissy fit. Why hadn't Luke reported what he knew? Because he'd just learned it maybe two minutes before the plane took off, he'd said. Why hadn't Luke stopped them? With what, Luke had replied. His Halloween pistol? It hadn't taken Luke a minute to turn the accusations against Fister, reaming him out for breaking his promise about the list. Fister had more to answer for than he did.

For the second day in a row, Luke wandered alone out into the pre-dawn darkness. Several more had sickened last night before he went to bed, and more could have gone down through the night. Nothing was going well. He had a bite on his thumb from trying to get a pill down Josh Monroe's throat. Drew had been correct; the medicine was used to treat bipolar patients. Drew had laughed, saying they actually pulled a doctor from the back of the building to tell him they were unequipped to treat mental disorders. Drew had asked about Jack, but the doctor walked away.

Luke squinted at the door up ahead. Yes, there was a square of white against it. Luke loosened the tape holding the sheet so he could read it in the light from the window. Holding his breath, he read the list of dead patients, but Briley's name wasn't on it. He hadn't known the man a week ago, but he felt like family now. Eight dead; the four he'd already known plus four more. Jack was still okay and Pete. Then he read the list of patients.

Christ, last night must've brought a parade of ill people to the medical building. A bunch more sick, including little Emma. Damn, he thought, a child hardly had a chance against the ravages of influenza. He'd already known that Zachary was sick. Now the whole family had come down with it. And Alicia. His heart sank when he saw her name.

Hearing a noise, he glanced back to see Jill rushing toward the building, cradling her clipboard. "Well?" she asked.

"The little girl. And Alicia. Both sick." He swallowed. "Eight dead."

Jill shook her head, making notes on her roster. "It'll never stop," she said, her voice shaking. "Not until it's got every one of us."

"We don't know that."

"Oh, quit being Mister Brave and Wonderful," she spat. "In another few days all of us will be sick or dead, and then what good will lists or classes be?" She looked like she wanted to throw her clipboard at something. Or someone. "Dear God." She was crying and annoyed by it, dashing her fist against her cheek and shaking her head. Not a sound came from the medical building.

"Let's go get some coffee," he said.

"The mess hall won't open for over an hour."

"The recreation room then. I'll buy you a Coke." It was a feeble joke. Their soft drinks were free.

"You can't. The machine's been empty since yesterday afternoon."

He took her arm. "I'll tell Fister when I call this morning, but we can go there until the mess hall opens. It's too cold to stand around outside."

Although it was warm, the recreation room had the fusty smell of too many bodies. It was deserted, although someone had left the television on. Luke turned it off; Jill didn't need any more bad news. She sat on the sagging couch and sniffed, still angry at her tears. "I'm sorry," she said in a stiff voice.

Luke shrugged. "It's worth crying over."

She took a deep, shuddery breath. "Have you wondered what happens if the military and medical people get sick?"

"They're all doing their best to keep the hell away from us."

"Still, they go home or to a hotel or something, don't they? They eat, they see people. It's out there." She spread her arms.

"It's kind of hard to think about 'out there,'" Luke said.

"If they get sick, we'll have no medical staff or cooks or supplies." She tried to smile. "You won't even have Fister to hassle."

"I'd miss that." He smiled back at her. "I guess we'll do what we've been doing: coping with what comes along. But surely they'd get help for the sick."

The motor in the pop machine switched on, and Luke stood. Might as well try it, he thought. Sure enough, when he opened the door, rows of soft drinks filled the bins. "Hey, the Bunnies filled it sometime in the night. They're still doing their job. What do you want?" He brought her the Diet Coke she asked for and said, "Breakfast of champions."

This brought a genuine smile. "I haven't had soft drinks for breakfast since college," she said. "Great for hangovers."

Popping the top of his Dr. Pepper, Luke said, "I remember doing that. About a hundred years ago."

He wanted to distract her, just like he did when Maggie was upset. He thought of Costanza, Schultz, and Salyers and how they'd flicked off the world by escaping. "If they'd let you, would you have left in the plane with Salyers and the rest of them?" he asked.

"Sure." A little spirit came into her eyes. "I'm surprised you didn't. You and Jim French were right there, weren't you?"

"Yeah. "

"Would there have been room?"

Luke nodded.

"They weren't going the right direction though, were they?"

"No. French's family is in Cincinnati, and mine's down in southeastern Kentucky."

"Would you have gone if they were flying back to Cincinnati?"

"Probably not."

Jill sighed. "Don't you get tired of being good? Doing the right thing?"

Shrugging, Luke said, "It's what I do. I take care of people. I'd rather be taking care of Maggie and Jacob, but I know they're safe. Folks here aren't."

Her voice was bitter. "That simple, huh?" She stared at the blank television.

"You make trying to do the right thing sound like something bad."

"Maybe not bad," she snapped. "But not always smart."

He took a big gulp from his soft drink. It wasn't very cold.

Shaking herself, Jill apologized, "Sorry." She twiddled the cap of her pen. "Have you wondered about the blue pills and the red pills? And shots?"

"No." A lie.

"I've been keeping track. They don't matter. Nearly the same number of patients for both colors. Useless either way."

He didn't know what to say to her. All he could think of was breakfast and letting people know how many had become ill since supper the night before. Jill must've been thinking the same thing. "Pastor French's prayer group will be crowded this morning," she said.

"Have you seen the list of names on his prayer board? Everybody has someone up there."

She gripped her clipboard. "I know. French's daughters, my mother. Dozens of people to pray for." Luke touched her knotted hand. She said, "It's the only thing we can do."

❖

Maggie'd stayed awake way past midnight, eating her candy bar, talking a little to Travis, checking on Annie, but at some point she must've dozed off. Pushing away the fuzzy afghan Travis had thrown over her while she slept, she sat up and touched Annie's neck. The pulse was faint but still there. "Sorry," Travis said from the kitchen. "I didn't mean to wake you." He was making coffee.

She shook her head, trying to stir herself as much as dismissing his apology. Her watch said it was nearly four. "I didn't mean to drop off," she said, feeling stupid with sleep.

"It's okay."

Folding up the afghan, Maggie stood, suddenly unable to sit still another minute. She prowled around the room, glancing outside at the dark on the other side of the window shade, touching the backs of chairs. "I'm surprised," she said but didn't finish.

"That she's still alive?" he asked. "Me too." He turned on a burner under the coffee. "I reckon it's like childbirth. You can't predict when the baby's going to come."

"Did you and your wife have kids?" she asked.

He shook his head. "She didn't want them. That was one reason I got a divorce. That and her sleeping with a guy from the next county." He stared at the refrigerator and stuck his hands in his pockets.

Maggie was afraid he'd turn shy with her again. It seemed like he'd tell her something private and then clam up when he realized what he'd done. "Did Annie really call you Little Scooter?"

He smiled. "She did. And then Dad and Mom and everybody was calling me that. Don't know where she got it."

"I was Stinkpot."

This brought a laugh. "You're telling me way too much about your past, Miss Maggie." He sobered. "I've already been doing enough of that."

She lifted a hand and then dropped it. "Strange times bring strangers together. Luke's worried to death about a man he didn't know a week ago."

Travis nodded.

In the bathroom Maggie splashed her face and ran the edge of a towel around her teeth. She could all but feel last night's candy eating into the enamel. Running damp fingers through her hair, she tried to make it look like something other than a mess but didn't have much luck. She shrugged at her reflection and went back into the kitchen where the scent of coffee woke her more than the cold water had.

"Have you called your father and sister?"

He was rinsing the only two mugs in the house. "I'll call them when it's over."

"They wouldn't want to be here?"

"People aren't supposed to be traveling. I don't want them to bring the flu into the county, and, besides, I think they're content to let Mamaw be."

Taking a cup of steaming coffee from Travis, she went back to the recliner and held Annie's hand. It was cooling, as she'd known it would. It wouldn't be long now. Travis took his mug outside, to smoke probably, while Maggie kept watch. She knew he'd done the same for her all those hours she'd slept. It was her turn.

Just then Annie took a deep slow breath, and Maggie saw it coming. She nearly jumped up to get Travis, but there was no point. Annie spoke no final words, nor did she struggle. She simply quit breathing. Out of habit, Maggie noted the time and squeezed the woman's hand. Opening the door, she saw Travis's bulky shadow and whispered, "It's over."

He tossed his cigarette, a weak light arcing toward the road, and followed her in. For a long moment he stood by his grandmother and then bent over to kiss her forehead. Maggie didn't know whether to touch him. This was unknown territory. Normally she would've called the mortuary, prepared the body for transport, and finished the chart.

If he cried, she didn't see it, but Maggie figured he'd had days to do his crying if he was inclined toward it. He stepped away, went to the kitchen table, and drank down his coffee. "I'll have to wait for daylight," he said. "I reckon Roy might be able to help me." He seemed to be talking to himself. "I thought I could do it by myself, but as I was driving home last night I realized I couldn't." He rubbed at his face, starting with the bushy moustache and going down into his hairy jaw.

"Do what?" Maggie asked. "Can I help?"

Giving her a dismissive shake of his head, he replied, "No, too heavy."

"What? Carrying the coffin down to the grave?"

He nodded.

She hesitated, feeling she'd interfered enough. But she was already in it. "What if you and I carried the empty coffin down to the gravesite? And then you carried Annie down and we put her in? Is the coffin very heavy?" He'd loaded it in his truck; he'd know.

"No, it ain't heavy. I could carry it down there by myself easy if it was empty." He stared at the floor. "That would work except it would still take two strong people to lower it into the grave."

"You said you had rope."

His head jerked up. "Of course. I wasn't thinking." Frowning, he warned, "It'd still be awfully heavy for you."

"I'm strong," she said. "Unless you want Roy.'

"Rather not."

Silence hung between them then. What would they do until daylight? He poured himself more coffee, asked if she wanted any, and then leaned against the sink. There were no more candy bars or stories to distract them. From outside, she heard the distant crowing of one of the gaming roosters. It was nearly dawn but a long time until full light. Maggie smoothed the quilt over Annie's legs. "Do you have a dress or something you want to put her in?"

"I've been thinking on that," he said. "I don't have any of her clothes, but I want to wrap her in that quilt."

"Don't you want to keep it?"

"No. Dad'll give me another."

"Then is there a clean nightgown for her? I'll wash her."

Maggie knew that back before undertakers, in this part of the country anyway, the laying out of a body had been women's work. She'd heard Oleatha talk about it from childhood memories. She had described how the women would wash and dress the body, scenting it if they had anything to use, and arranging the corpse's hair. Travis seemed to accept that this was Maggie's job. He handed her a clean nightgown, the pink one. It smelled of fresh air and grass, probably the scents Annie had loved best. He ran warm water and gave Maggie a bar of soap and some towels. "Would you leave us now?" Maggie asked. He accepted this too and put on his jacket to go outside.

❖

When Travis came back to the house, he said that he'd already carried the casket to the gravesite. Maggie stepped aside and asked if Annie looked all right. Finding some plastic combs in a bathroom cupboard, Maggie had pulled Annie's sparse hair away from her face, exposing her strong bones. Before she worked the clean nightgown over Annie's body, Maggie rubbed sweet lotion into her skin. It was all she'd been able to do. Travis nodded and gently, carefully, he lifted his grandmother.

It was a fresh, bright morning, just cool enough for Maggie to see her breath. Clutching the bright quilt to her chest, Maggie thought they made an odd funeral procession. Sun glistened off the frosted grass. She feared that Travis might slip, but his steps were steady as he walked up a rise where what he said were redbuds and a holly tree clustered around the open grave. The hole in the earth reminded Maggie of a wound, but she knew it would heal, grass concealing the scar by spring. A light-colored wooden casket sat to the side, along with a sizeable pile of dirt.

She rushed ahead to open the lid so he could place Annie inside. Both of them fiddled with her, neatening her hair, arranging her hands, and then they both unfolded the quilt, a star pattern in pinks and blues and yellows. It smelled of dust and age. They spread it over Annie's body, tucking it in at the sides until there was nothing left to do.

Although she'd not given it much thought, lowering the filled casket into the grave was almost more than Maggie could handle. She feared she'd let the load slip, despite the heavy gloves Travis had given her to protect her hands. The casket wavered, wobbled, but they managed the job without mishap. And then Maggie wasn't sure what she should do.

Travis took off his hat. It was the first time Maggie'd seen him without one. His hair was black and wavy. Beautiful hair. He looked down at the casket and cleared his throat. "Mamaw," he said, "I know you didn't hold with preaching and religion and all, but I think you believed in God because you loved his world so much. You loved the mountains and the birds and the flowers as much as you loved anything." He smiled. "You even loved your silly chickens." He tapped his cap against his thigh. "Anyway, I know you loved me and I loved you back, and because of that I wanted you to lay in peace where there's the sound of birds and a creek flowing." One of the roosters down the road uttered its hoarse cry. Travis smiled again. "I reckon if you're not in heaven, I've given you the nearest thing to it."

Startling Maggie, he looked over at her as if he expected something. She had no idea what to say but licked her lips and stammered, "Rest in eternal peace, Annie Parker." By instinct she crossed herself and murmured, "In the name of the Father, the Son, and the Holy Spirit. Amen."

Travis seemed satisfied by this and put his hat back on. Turning from the grave, he said, "I'll cover it in a little bit, but I'd like to rest a spell first."

She nodded and moved toward the house, but he grabbed her hand and stopped her. "I thank you, Maggie Davies," he said, "for all you did for Mamaw and me." Then, his warm, callused hand squeezed hers, like he was trying to push gratitude into her.

❖

As Luke had expected, breakfast was grim. Jill read off the list of sick and deceased in an expressionless voice, and Luke half expected to hear a bell tolling. As he'd also expected, Jim French's prayer group expanded to where they needed to bring in more chairs. Just before it began, French asked Luke if he could hold a service the next morning.

"You know, like church," he said.

"I don't see why not," Luke replied. "Would you have it here in the classroom?"

"It could get crowded."

"True, and it might feel a little more like church up in the recreation room. We could move chairs this afternoon, push the couch and pool table out of the way."

"I like it." French smiled. "Especially having a pool table in the sanctuary."

Luke caught up with Ilse walking away from the building. "I need your help," he said and told her everything he knew about Josh Monroe, including the bite mark on his thumb. "You seem to have a way to make people do what they don't want to do. Would you give it a try?"

She gave him a regal shrug. "What would Bob say, 'might as well; can't dance'?"

Luke grinned. "He's a difficult guy. Drew asked the medical people if they would take care of him, and they refused." They entered the barracks.

Ilse frowned. "Unkind to Josh and us. Did you tell Fister?"

"He isn't answering my calls."

Luke eased Josh's door open and went into the increasingly foul-smelling room. Josh was in bed, lying on his back and staring at the ceiling. "I brought Professor Mayfield to see you, Josh."

Ilse towered over him, leaning until he couldn't avoid her gaze. "Get out of bed this instant, Mr. Monroe, and take a shower. You smell like a rubbish bin." Her voice was steel.

Josh blanched, moved his head, and stared back at her. "I do?"

"You most certainly do. Go with Luke while I find clothes for you."

Moving like a robot, Josh swung his legs off the bed and looked at Luke. "I have to?"

"Yes." Luke stopped short of touching the man, but Josh reached for Luke's arm. He seemed dizzy. Once they entered the bathroom, Luke started the water, found soap and shampoo, and put a clean towel on the edge of the sink. "Do I have to come over there and wash you?" he asked.

"No."

As Luke waited, Ilse hovered by the door and handed him clothes. "I'll strip the bedclothes and tidy a bit. Then we'll address the medication."

Washed and dressed, Josh looked dazed as he sat on the bare mattress. Luke had brought water. Ilse shook out a pill and handed the cup to Josh. "No games," she ordered. The man took the pill into his mouth and swallowed from the cup. "Do I need to check your mouth?"

Oh, God, she's going to get her finger bit off, Luke thought. But Josh opened his mouth and allowed her to peer in. "Now we will walk over to lunch," she said. "You must be hungry."

Docile as a pup, Josh strolled between them, and Luke thought, just like that. The woman had amazing powers. Problem solved.

❖

Wolfing down his four chicken nuggets and ten French fries, Luke left Drew in charge of watching Josh and dashed to his room to get Briley's picks. He'd been too busy to keep up the search for the weapon, although he felt certain Costanza had carried it to Vegas with him. He hoped the luggage in the next few rooms was unlocked; he didn't feel too confident about the picks.

He checked two more rooms in the men's barracks and the two rooms in the women's where the sweet little family had stayed. It broke his heart to see the toys and coloring books and tiny pink sneakers on the floor. Nothing was locked. He found nothing, not that he'd expected to, and returned to the clipboard. Several more to search, he thought. He couldn't do it during dinner because he was serving, but he'd get it done, he supposed. Even though it was less of a priority for him than it had been for Briley.

Restless, he prowled the camp. He paused outside the CO's house to see if there was noise inside that would disprove his suspicion that Fister was gone. Nothing. He wandered aimlessly, unable to settle even after he talked to Maggie and Jacob and heard all about Annie's death and the fish his son had caught. Expecting it to be empty, he went into the room where Ilse had her language classes, but she was sitting at a table, staring into space. "Are you all right?"

She gave him a long look. "I'm not ill, if that's what you're asking, but, no, I don't believe I'm all right."

Luke pulled up a chair. "Tell me."

She fluttered her big-knuckled hands and then pressed them to her eyes. "This is so dreadful. Just so dreadful."

"Josh Monroe?"

"Oh, that's bad. The man should be getting expert care, but he's simply a symptom, one part of it."

He waited. Ilse was far from young, but her crystalline eyes had always belied her age. Now they reminded Luke of lifeless old women huddled in nursing homes. "Alicia," he said.

"That's certainly part of it as well. I'd come to think of her as a troublesome grand-daughter." A hint of a smile crossed her lips and flew away. "She was bleeding when she went. Those are the ones who die."

"Sometimes I just want to give up. It's too much," he whispered.

"I know. And then I get very, very angry," Ilse said. "All this brings back terrible memories."

Luke didn't know what she meant, and she could tell. "I was born in 1934, Mr. Davies. In Germany."

"Ah," he breathed, realizing what she was saying.

She nodded. A wisp of silver hair worked its way loose from the twist behind her head. "We had a farm, dairy mostly. It was a lovely place, quiet and green. The land had been my grandfather's, and when my father came back from the Great War, he worked it." She stared ahead but was seeing something other than beige walls. "Although he was far from young, my father insisted on enlisting in 1939. First they refused him, saying his farm work was important and, besides, they had little use for a forty-year-old man. My brother Willi was another matter. He was nineteen, full of, how do you say it? Piss and vinegar?"

For the first time Luke heard an accent color her English. He smiled. "That's the expression."

"In 1940, they took my father for a desk job, supply clerk. And that same year my other brother, Karl, joined up as well. He wanted to be a pilot." Something about this made her smile again. "That left only women on the farm: my mother, my sister, and me. And I was only five. A woman from the village came to live with us, to help. Her husband was a doctor, an older man who'd also fought in the Great War and met her in France. He'd been pressed into military service, leaving his wife alone. She was called Laure, a Frenchwoman and thus suspect to most of the area's provincial minds, but to me she was glamorous and intriguing."

Ilse looked down at her hands. "We worked very hard. We milked, we hoed, we grew vegetables and raised chickens. Always, always, Hitler said we must grow more food. We tried.

"I didn't mind the work as long as Laure was there. She kept the house, did the cooking, tended the chickens. And she spoke French. My mother did not approve, but I begged Laure to teach me French. She liked me. She told my mother that because the Reich had conquered France they would need translators; I could have a wonderful profession." Shaking her head, Ilse said, "I wonder what it cost her to say that. She may have married a German and thus given up everything French, but no one likes to think of her homeland as conquered."

She paused, and Luke spoke, "It worked. You learned French."

"I did. Laure brought me books so I could learn to read as well as speak. Sometimes she would talk about France as we scrubbed the milk cans or did the dishes. I knew she missed her home, and she missed her family who had disowned her when she'd married a Boche." She smiled again. "She called us that but always with a little laugh."

"Was there fighting near your farm?"

Ilse said, "Only at the very end, and not much then. We were isolated, far from the cities where most of the bombing was. By then Karl was dead in Russia, and Willi was a prisoner in England. We ate better than most; my mother was a good provider, but we were always sad, except for Laure. She'd chosen to come to Germany, but I always wondered if she was secretly glad that we'd lost again.

"My father and Willi came home, and Laure went back to the village and her husband. The country was an open wound, throbbing with pain and guilt."

"For the Jews?"

She nodded. "For everything. I grew up thinking the Jews and Communists were to blame for every inequity we suffered. My parents said it; everyone did. It's human nature to blame others for our troubles, is it not? But my country turned blame into atrocity." Looking down at the table, she whispered, "I had no idea. Perhaps it was because I was a child, but I cannot believe my mother, Laure, and my father knew the extent of the horror. And now," she looked up, "I see it again."

"This can't compare," Luke said.

Her accent came through again. "How many will this virus kill? The method is cleaner; degradation and shame are not symptoms of influenza. The Jews suffered longer. Families were separated. Oh, of course the Holocaust was far more horrific. Still, what we are seeing now is yet another attempt to cleanse the world of a people perceived as evil, the ones who must be blamed for every misfortune. The flu, now the bombings in retribution." She stopped as if she couldn't speak any more.

"There's nothing right about suffering on either side, is there?" he said. "I felt that way in Afghanistan."

She shrugged, very European at that moment. "Oh, there is a right and wrong here. Those who made this virus, who plotted a way for it to be spread, are the evil ones. I wonder sometimes about Hassan."

"Who's Hassan?"

"The young man who died on the plane. Drew told me his name."

"Why would you think about him?"

"Because he was one of the believers, one of those who follow orders. I know his kind. I pity them nearly as much as I fear them." She stood. "It is the individual who saves us or kills us."

The drawn look returned to her face. "I did learn French. And when I turned seventeen, I went to university and met a G.I., who taught me English and healed my wounds. He brought me back here, where I often remember Laure, another person displaced by love."

"Did you ever write to her?"

Ilse shook her head. "No. I wanted nothing more to do with Germany." Again she shrugged, like this was a dishonorable confession. "I am American," she said. "And now it is our turn to experience hate."

Chapter Thirteen

After the long night, Maggie felt fuzzy all day Saturday. The cold rain that came in the afternoon hadn't helped, keeping them all indoors, and making her wonder if Travis was out in it, shoveling heavy, damp earth on Annie's grave. Jacob had thrown one of his tantrums, declaring he wanted to go home, now, and Maggie hadn't been able to calm him down. Wincing at the noise, Oleatha said he was spoiled, this was what came from being an only child, and Maggie nearly let her have it. Before she could start, though, Roy had bundled a tearful Jacob into Maggie's car, told her to drive, and led them on a quest for food.

They hadn't found any open stores but bought eggs from a scraggle-haired old crone who kept chickens on a hilltop farm nearly thirty miles away. Roy had been thrilled about the eggs, and being in the car improved Jacob's mood. It hadn't done as much for Maggie's, but she made it through the rest of the day without giving Oleatha a piece of her mind.

Her temper hadn't improved much by Sunday morning. Oleatha stood at the stove frying bacon and eggs. She wore a navy blue dress with a silver chain resting on her swollen bosom and gave Maggie a hard look when she came into the kitchen. "I don't reckon you brought anything decent to wear to church," she said.

Maggie looked down at her usual jeans and sneakers and pulled at her sweater. "No, I didn't."

Roy looked up from the table where he was waiting for his food. "Now Oleatha, I told you there'd be no church-going today." He wasn't dressed up either. "I doubt they're having services."

Oleatha declared, "Yes, they are. Brother Carter told Jane that we'd gather as usual, that we weren't to let the sins of the world keep us from salvation."

Roy rolled his eyes.

"Besides," Oleatha continued, "it wouldn't hurt that grandson of mine to hear the gospel." She turned back to the stove, muttering something about being brought up like a heathen.

Maggie's face turned red. Last night she'd vowed to keep her temper with her mother-in-law, but it wasn't easy. "I'll drive you to church," she offered.

"You will not," Roy thundered. "I'll not have you mixing with folks and bringing this sickness home, Oleatha. I don't care what Brother Carter says." He muttered too, and Maggie caught the words "self-righteous little banty rooster."

So, the eggs were eaten, and enjoyed, she supposed, although the atmosphere in the kitchen was chilly enough to freeze them. Jacob was the only cheerful one, gobbling his bacon and then going off with his grandfather to do some building, which amounted to hammering nails into scrap wood, and target shooting, which involved the new slingshot. The rain had stopped, and it'd turned warm enough for Maggie to sit on the porch, once she'd finished the cheerless chore of helping Oleatha clean up the kitchen.

Staring at the kudzu hanging now in wilted strands, Maggie supposed she was yearning for home as much as Jacob, and she couldn't help but wonder how long she'd have to stay. Nothing was right. Luke had called before breakfast, and although she was relieved to hear he was healthy, she couldn't seem to console him. Alicia, the girl he'd taken under his wing, had died.

She sighed and stared in the other direction, toward Annie's. She missed taking care of the woman and Travis too, for that matter. He'd been someone to talk to, but there was no reason for her to see him now and going to visit him might look odd to Oleatha who seemed determined to find fault no matter what. She and Jacob had stayed too long, but there was nothing Maggie could do about it.

After lunch Oleatha brought her crocheting out on the porch, but before Maggie could escape, the phone started ringing and Oleatha lumbered back inside. Maggie looked at the pile of yarn, a mass of tangled and knotted strings, disorganized, complicated. Just about the way life was right then. Oleatha's skill and shiny crochet hook had the capability to make sense and order out of the mess, but Maggie wasn't sure anybody could do the same for their country. Luke had told her yesterday that people on television insisted the president was sick or dead. No one had heard messages from him in days. It felt like no one was in charge. Food, cash, and gasoline shortages were hampering recovery from the illness and any kind of normalcy. Luke said he had no idea how much of it was true.

Maggie figured it was, and she knew they were lucky to have escaped both the sickness and the horrors of the outside world. But she was a little worried about food. Roy's two dozen eggs were great, but she had very little flour left. Oleatha had never forbidden her from looking in the cellar freezer, but she'd never encouraged it either.

Just then Oleatha crashed out onto the porch, breathing hard. She declared that flu had arrived in the county and there was a death. Someone had sneaked into a local funeral home and taken a casket. It had been all the talk at church that morning. Oleatha sniffed mightily, still sore about being forced to stay home. Maggie debated a second and then decided it was more important to squelch panic than defend Travis. Upon hearing the truth, Oleatha let out a deep breath and got up to phone her church biddies, as Roy called them. Her mother-in-law relished being the one to tell everybody what was going on.

While Oleatha was busy on the phone, Maggie sneaked down to the cellar. She glanced at shelves holding canning jars of tomatoes and the tomato juice she'd helped prepare. Lifting the top of the huge freezer she peered down at several ziplocs of homegrown green beans, some commercial bags of broccoli and peas, and four chicken pot pies. In the next section were bacon, a roll of sausage, and what looked like cubed pieces of ham, and in the last part were two whole chickens and three packages of ground beef. She supposed they'd eaten a lot of food in a week, but Roy had warned her that their stockpile was smaller than usual.

It was no more encouraging in Oleatha's pantry. Lots of homemade jam and dry pinto beans, some cornmeal and tuna fish, and several cans of soup. Maybe five pounds of potatoes. Jacob still had half a jar of peanut butter. Maggie heard Oleatha finish one call and make another. She peered in the cabinets and refrigerator. Rice and noodles. Margarine and mustard. They wouldn't starve any time soon, but she had no idea where they could get more. And if yesterday was any indication, Roy didn't either.

Oleatha had no more than come up for air when the phone rang again, sending her right back to the sofa. Maggie left her to it, going back out onto the porch, thinking how they could stretch the supplies they had. After a few minutes, Oleatha called her in, and with her hand over the mouthpiece, said, "Savannah's sick, and Marla wants to talk to you."

Maggie's stomach filled with dread. "Does she want to bring the child down here?"

"Yes, but I told her she couldn't. I said you'd give her advice over the phone. She's scared to take her to the hospital."

Maggie couldn't blame Marla for that. "Okay. I'll see what I can do."

On the edge of hysteria, Marla jabbered until Maggie had to yell to get her to calm down and answer questions about fever, symptoms, what she'd tried to do for the baby. "Has Savannah been exposed to the flu?"

"I had to get food. Went several places for formula, but couldn't get but a little bit. The groceries are closed." Marla paused for a second and lowered her voice. "I went to my restaurant, used my key, and took some yogurt and canned fruit. Don't tell Mama that I stole. I thought the baby could eat those."

Maggie tried to reassure her.

"With Carrie gone I don't know what I'm supposed to do. Should I try to take her to the hospital? They say the halls are full of people moaning and dying and I'm afraid the baby will die too if I take her there. I wish Carrie were here, but I think she's in Florida, maybe or…"

Maggie interrupted. "Has she been coughing?"

Marla said no. From what Luke had said, that was the one clear symptom. "Have you given her anything for the fever?" she asked.

Marla said, yes. Tylenol for children. And so it went until Maggie took in a huge gulp of air and said, "You know I'm not a doctor, Marla, and I can't examine Savannah, but my best guess is an ear infection. You might try calling her pediatrician to get an antibiotic."

"I'm afraid to take her to a doctor's office. We'll both get sick. Most of them aren't open anyway. Chicken-shit doctors are hiding out, not opening their offices. You don't know what it's like here. The end of the world, I mean it. Mama would say it's the apocalypse. People walking the street with guns and police nowhere in sight."

Marla stopped for a breath, and Maggie broke in. "I meant that he might prescribe something over the phone. Give her as much liquid as she'll take. Juice, water, anything. Do you have a food processor, blender?"

Marla said she did.

"Make baby food out of whatever you have. It may give her stomach problems, which isn't good with an infection, but she has to have calories if she doesn't have formula."

Maggie went on to tell Marla several tricks for respiratory or ear infections, things she'd learned from experience rather than nursing school. By then Marla had calmed down and asked if she could call again.

Of course, Maggie said, and hung up. She turned to Oleatha. "There's no way I can tell whether that baby has the flu." Rubbing her face, she said, "And there's no way I can help if it is the flu."

"I know," said Oleatha. "And I'll probably burn in hell for refusing to let my daughter and great-grand-daughter come home, but Lord help me, I don't want to be the one to bring the plague into this county." She twisted her hands. "And this house," she finished.

❖

Supper was so quiet that they could hear the military cooks running water and clattering pans. People were mostly pretending to eat the fish sticks and canned green beans set out for them. All afternoon the atmosphere had careened between a volcano about to erupt and a swamp ready to mire them all in despair. News from home was tragic. Television showed horror films of stacked bodies, ravished streets, and chaos. Luke had tried all day to get Fister on the phone, but the guy still wasn't answering. One improvement, though, was that Josh Monroe sat with Ilse and him and actually had a brief but lucid conversation. Thank God for the meds.

Outside, a cold, spitting rain pelted his head, but Luke walked anyway, making a beeline for the CO's house. He had a bad feeling about Fister and the management of this mission. There'd been no deliveries of any recent requests, the pop machines were empty, trash was piling up, and meals were adequate but meager. As he approached, Luke strained his eyes to see lights. He'd knock on the door whether Fister liked it or not. He'd keep his distance, stand out on the sidewalk so he wouldn't infect anyone, but he was going to have a come to Jesus with the man.

Behind its shroud of trees, the house was dark. Luke circled it, peering in windows to see if lights burned behind tight shades. Nothing. At the back door he could see through a partial curtain into the kitchen. Not even the light over the stove was lit. So he tried the knob. Locked. And he returned to the front porch to pound on the door and ring the doorbell. No response.

❖

Maggie'd no more than hung up Oleatha's phone when her cell jangled. A hysterical Tina told her that she'd just taken their mother to the hospital. "Flu?" Maggie asked.

No, she was having seizures and d.t.'s, and Tina couldn't cope. "I took her some cash and food two days ago, and she was okay," Tina wailed.

"She'll catch the flu in the hospital, even if she is in a detox ward."

"I don't care!" Tina shouted. "You're not here, and I don't know how to bring her out of those."

Taking a deep, shuddery breath, Maggie said, "Did you give her honey?"

Donna wouldn't take it, Tina said, and if Maggie didn't like what she'd done, she could just come back home and handle it. And then Tina burst into tears and apologized. "What if I've killed her?" she sobbed.

"She's been killing herself for years. It's not your fault."

Even though she kept telling herself those same words, Maggie cut the call short. She did feel guilty. No, Tina had never taken responsibility for their mother, but that was because Maggie had made sure she hadn't needed to. Leaning her head back until her neck popped, she stared up at the cloudless night sky, bracing herself before going back in the house. Maybe Oleatha had talked herself out on the phone and drained the snippiness out of her mood. But Maggie figured it wasn't a great time to bring up concerns about food.

Oleatha and Roy were sitting on the sofa with Jacob between them, engrossed in a rerun of *The Waltons*. Maggie lingered in the doorway. "You'll need to be going to bed pretty soon, big boy," she said to Jacob.

"We all do," Roy said.

"Soon as this show's over," said Jacob.

Maggie was turning away when there was a loud thump on the porch and both doors were thrown open, the screen door wrenched so hard the handle came loose. Two men crashed into the room. The taller one carried a short shotgun against the shoulder of his hunting jacket and wore a camo cap pulled over his eyes. He aimed his weapon at Maggie. The short one was younger with carroty hair and freckles and for one crazy instant reminded Maggie of Opie from Mayberry. The image vanished when he slitted his eyes and spoke. "Pills. Money." He spat the words like someone ordering burgers at a drive-though. Maggie's legs trembled. "We know you're a nurse," he said. "You're bound to have some vicodin or oxy laying around here somewhere."

Roy tried to get up, but the short guy shot him a glance as lethal as his buddy's gun. "Sit down, old man. We'll leave soon as we get what we need."

Oleatha squeezed Jacob into her bosom so hard his face turned red.

"I do not have pills." Maggie tried to sound as cool as a head nurse.

The tall one gave an ugly little chuckle. "Right."

It was her job to protect them, Maggie thought, her breath coming in strange little gusts. The old people and her son. Luke wasn't there. She had to manage this. She recalled the contents of her medicine cabinet back home, the pills and bottles she'd swept into the tote bag. There were a few vicodin pills from when Luke'd had his root canal.

Maybe if she dug those out they'd be satisfied. But she doubted it. They'd steal money and hurt people, especially Roy who would probably try to stop them. She couldn't let that happen. She still had two hundred dollars in her purse, her purse that was sitting right there on the side table where she'd left it after going for eggs yesterday. What had Roy said that day in Hazel's store? I take care of my own.

Raising her chin, Maggie repeated, "I don't have any pills." She reached for her purse. "But I do have money." From the television came the sounds of a jolly family dinner at the Waltons' long table.

The short one scowled. "You got pills. Nurses keep things like that."

"I'm a nurse, not a doctor," she said, her voice shaking. Inside the purse, her fingers fumbled but finally fixed upon the gun. She slid her index finger around the trigger like she knew what she was doing. Raising her right hand and dropping the purse, she said, "Get the hell out of here right now."

She heard three different gasps from the sofa, but she was concentrating on the tall man with the shotgun. "I'll shoot," she declared. "I really will."

The tall one tilted his head like he was considering it. Then, in one lazy movement he swiveled the business end of his gun away from Maggie and aimed at Jacob. A growl came from the depths of Roy's chest. "Maybe you'll shoot, maybe you won't," the tall one said. "But even if you do, I can still pull this here trigger before I hit the ground."

Maggie wasn't sure if she was breathing. Her right hand trembled, but she didn't lower it. They were waiting on her, but she didn't know what to do. Breaking what seemed like an hour's silence, the short one laughed. "Gotcha, Nursie. Now set down that pistol. You ain't gonna shoot nobody."

"She might not, but I sure as hell will." Travis's voice came from the front porch, right behind where the tall one stood by the door with his shotgun. Maggie saw the man's eyes flicker. "Put down the gun, Maggie, and step over by Roy." Travis sounded like he was telling her how to change a tire. She dropped the pistol to her side and walked on watery legs to the sofa, setting the gun on the coffee table.

Neither of the intruders moved. The shotgun was still aimed at Jacob, but the tall man was blinking. The short guy's eyes focused on Maggie's purse. "Now, lower that gun, Kyle Coughlin, and come on out of the house. You too, Red. I don't know your name, but you can be sure I'll find out."

The tall one lowered his shotgun to rest on his hipbone, his hand still gripped around its barrel. He thrust up his chin. "I know who you are too, Travis Parker, and I'll make you pay for this."

A deep chuckle came from the porch. "I don't reckon you will." The explosion made Maggie jump until she was leaning into Roy. He held her with a trembling hand. Coughlin's broken gun clattered to the floor and he yelped. Travis had shot the barrel, neatly taking off a chunk of Coughlin's finger at the same time. His voice still deadly calm, Travis said, "Sorry about the mess, Oleatha, but Kyle won't be shooting that gun anymore."

Coughlin held his right hand up in the air, blood dripping down his wrist and pattering on the floor in great, bright drops. The short guy was cussing, word after word, and edging toward the door. Travis motioned him out with his rifle. "Come on Short Stuff. Get your buddy home before he bleeds to death." He chuckled. "I reckon you could take him to the hospital and get some pills there, couldn't you? Of course you'd have some explaining to do."

As the two shuffled out, Maggie stepped away from the sofa and watched Travis motion the men off the porch. "I will be talking to the sheriff, Kyle," he said. They stumbled up the road. "Be careful walking home, you hear?"

Oleatha must've released her death grip on Jacob just a hair because the boy leaped up and ran to Maggie who knelt to squeeze him again and again, wiping away the tears that ran down his cheeks. "Dear God in heaven," Oleatha breathed, hoisting herself up from the sofa. She stared at the blood on her floor. Roy had tracked through it in his hurry to get outside to Travis.

Over Jacob's head, Maggie said, "I'll get that. I'll clean it up."

"You'll do no such thing," Oleatha retorted with a violent shake of her head. "You'll hug that child."

CHAPTER FOURTEEN

Luke buttoned his uniform shirt, laundered several days ago but ironed yesterday by Connie, who said she needed something to do. French's service was at ten o'clock, and Luke wanted to wear something other than sweats. After learning of Alicia's death, and little Zachary's, Luke felt like he was going to a funeral as much as church. He hadn't been able to tell Maggie about the little boy, so close to Jacob's age. He'd been glad that he was alone this morning when he'd seen the list. It was one thing to lose his composure to Maggie, but it would've shamed him to let anyone here see his tears.

Why, he asked himself as he combed his hair. Did he really take himself that seriously? The mirror reflected a mocking expression on his face. Maybe he'd let being the Mayor of Mickeyville go to his head. But maybe it had more to do with the way he'd been raised. He'd never seen Roy cry. Ever.

Plenty of people had been crying at breakfast when Jill reported the deaths. She was dry-eyed, right then anyway but had been so pale that Luke had asked if she felt all right. They'd gone twenty-four hours without any new cases, but that was little consolation. Luke didn't know how to help people cope with it. Hell, he didn't know how to manage it himself.

Ilse was managing one problem: Josh Monroe. He came to meals, he washed his clothes, and he spoke to people. Three times a day she found him and handed him a pill from her pocket. It seemed to be working. And on the other problem, he'd searched unsuccessfully for the missing weapon in another three rooms. He decided to quit worrying about it. It had to have been Costanza or maybe Briley had imagined seeing that orange tag. Luke put his jacket on. No, what was niggling his brain was that, like supper, breakfast had been sparse, sparse enough that he'd had to do some talking to dissuade people from breaking down the locked door into the kitchen. About to erupt, he thought again. Tonight, he told himself. Tonight he was going to take Bob Briley's lock picks up to the CO's house and see what he could discover.

In the recreation room they'd arranged chairs in a double circle with a single one where the television normally sat. The track lights that had illuminated Amanda the belly dancer now focused on French's chair. Ilse was already seated between the two Spanish passengers, although last night when he'd walked her back to her barracks, she'd confessed that her Spanish wasn't up to speed in theology.

More people came in, speaking quietly, touching each other's arms, just like they did at funeral homes. Within five minutes nearly every chair was filled. People whispered when they said anything at all. Mostly they looked around to see who might be missing. Luke was doing the same thing. He saw Josh, but he didn't see Jill.

French slipped between the chairs and sat in the middle, Bible in his hand. Starting with a prayer, he passed his Bible around, asking people to read the passages he named. Then he nodded at Connie who stood and sang "This Is My Father's World" in a clear, high soprano that brought to mind English choirboys in high-steepled cathedrals. A sadder song would've brought most of them to tears, but the simple words felt like healing. Then French handed the Bible to Luke. He saw that it was open to the Twenty-Third Psalm and said, "I bet most of you have this one memorized. Say it with me."

They did. After a quick word or two from Ilse, the Spanish couple recited it in their own language, and a haunting strength came from the words about faith and death and surviving troubles. Luke finished, and Jim French started speaking, saying he wasn't a preacher but wanted them to know that God was present even in an evil world and that faith was never misplaced. He hadn't spoken more than a minute or two when the door opened. Along with everybody else, Luke glanced over to see who'd come in late. And, along with everybody else, he couldn't help but utter a sound that was somewhere between wonder and joy. Accompanied by a grinning Jill, it was Jack, the EMT. Pale, thin, and looking like he needed to sit down real quick, it was Jack. Drew leaped to his feet and grabbed his buddy, easing him into French's chair. "Now this is a blessing," French said. "Please tell us how you are and about the others if you can. We're hungry for news."

Jack nodded and coughed, a long, hard series of barks that made Luke wonder how he'd be able to speak, but French gave him a bottle of water that calmed the spasm.

"I got well," Jack said, as if it still surprised him. "Or well enough for them to cut me loose. They needed my bed. People are on gurneys out in the hall over there. They only had beds for twenty."

"How's Bob?" Someone called and then all the names of the sick were shouted up at him from different sides of the room.

Jack shook his head. He was so young, Luke thought. It was nearly too much for him. "I don't know about most of these people," he said, looking miserable about it. "They had us separated off in different rooms and halls. I know some are on ventilators and some have pneumonia." He gulped more water. "The ones who hemorrhaged are already gone." His voice trailed off.

"The guy in the bed next to mine was a passenger. Dan."

Someone on the back row shouted, "Yes, Dan Royce. How is he?"

Jack nodded slowly. "He's doing good. He should be out soon."

"And my wife? Teresa Cimino?" It was one of the Broody Hens who still monopolized the television.

Adam's apple bobbing, Jack shook his head. "I don't know about any of the women, sir. They're on the other hall. I'm sorry."

Despite what Jack had said, people were still calling out names, squirming, leaning forward. Getting paler by the minute, Jack shook his head again and again.

French moved to Jack's side, putting his hand on his shoulder. "Did they take good care of you?" he asked in a voice so soft it barely carried to Luke.

"Oh yes," Jack said, but there was no assurance in his voice. He covered his face with both hands. "It's just that the doctors and nurses are starting to get sick now. They've lost at least one doctor and two nurses. I don't know who's going to take care of us."

❖

Oleatha was measuring coffee into the pot. "You sure were a brave girl last night," she said.

Maggie yawned. "But he turned it on me."

"No matter. It still showed courage."

Maggie'd never considered bravery as one of her virtues. She wasn't sure she had all that many virtues.

Oleatha started the coffeemaker. "Notice how Roy won't say nothing or even look at you?"

Maggie had, and it bothered her. She'd always figured that of the two of them he disliked her less. "Yes. I should've handled it better."

Oleatha sniffed and turned, resting hands on her meaty hips. "It about killed him that a little slip of a girl was defending the family."

"But," Maggie sputtered. She didn't want Roy irked with her.

Oleatha shook her head. "Don't you pay it no never mind. He'll get over it." The woman smiled, a kindly one that Maggie had never seen directed her way. "It's just that great big old male ego pinching his you-know-whats."

Maggie couldn't help but giggle, and then Oleatha chuckled too and touched her shoulder as she went to get the inevitable oatmeal from the stove, saving the last few eggs for the next day. So, Maggie sat and doused her gray porridge with sugar. Jacob raised his eyebrows. "Mom, you never let me put that much sugar on my oatmeal."

"Hush, boy," Oleatha said. "Your mama can do anything she wants." The woman raised her spoon and turned to Maggie. "I hate to bother you with another chore, but we're plumb out of bread with all that cinnamon toast."

To take Jacob's mind off the horrors of Kyle Coughlan and his buddy, Oleatha had made cinnamon toast at ten o'clock last night. Gooey, sweet, and delicious, it had brightened all of their spirits. Maggie swallowed and wished for more cinnamon toast. Oats were good for the heart and full of fiber. They were wholesome and nutritious. She hoped she'd never have to eat them again. "I noticed. I'll start some bread this morning."

Roy came to the table, spoke to Jacob, and patted Oleatha when she brought his coffee, but it was as if Maggie had disappeared. Despite Oleatha's words, it troubled her.

"Hello!" They heard a shout from the front porch. Roy jumped up and grabbed the shotgun he'd set in the corner. Maggie didn't know how he'd see to aim it. But this time it wasn't necessary. Travis came into the kitchen, and Oleatha fussed over him, making him sit and getting him a cup of coffee. He refused her offer of oatmeal. "I got up at the crack of dawn," he said. "Already had my breakfast." Smart man, Maggie thought. Probably something good like Little Debbies.

Once he sat down, Travis spoke to Roy. "Just wanted to let you know that I saw the sheriff this morning and told him about Kyle Coughlin and his sidekick. So it's on record."

"Will they arrest him?" Maggie asked.

Travis shrugged. "Doubt it. The law isn't real good about going after these characters even when things are normal. They must've been desperate, though," he said.

"How's that?" asked Roy.

"They don't usually come into occupied homes. They wait until people are gone and then break in. I heard they stole copper out of the air conditioner at the Methodist church in Catesboro. Of course, nobody was around."

Roy didn't seem to have a bit of trouble talking to Travis. "Yeah, but these days everybody's home. Makes it a little tough for them, don't it?"

Travis admitted it did. "Along with the fact that nothing's moving on the roads. Short supply. High prices."

"I wonder how they knew we had a nurse in the house," Oleatha said.

"Word gets around, I guess," Travis said. "You've told people, haven't you?" Maggie hid a smile, thinking of Oleatha and her church ladies.

"And maybe they'd seen the strange car parked up here or even noticed Maggie coming to help my grandmother." Travis shrugged again. "It was enough, I reckon."

"They must be stupid to think a nurse carries drugs," Maggie murmured.

Travis smiled at her, his eyes warm enough to make the flu, home invaders, and Roy's pique disappear for a minute. "They are stupid. Cunning maybe, but stupid and strung out enough to do most anything." His smile faded, and his deep eyes bore into hers. "Speaking of stupid, though, pulling a handgun on them was a damned foolish thing to do."

Maggie felt her face turn hot.

"Mom," said Jacob. She didn't know whether he was more shocked by her being scolded or the bad word. She patted his leg.

"I think she's brave," Oleatha declared. "A heroine."

"Maybe." Travis shook his head. "But Coughlin had a shotgun. And there were two of them. What if I hadn't heard them coming down the track and followed them?"

Maggie looked at her lap. "I don't know. I just thought I had to do something."

Roy made a funny noise. Oleatha cleared her throat.

Travis softened his voice. "Even a fool could tell you're too kind-hearted to shoot someone. I'm surprised you didn't offer to bandage up Coughlin's hand."

She raised her head, aiming her nose at Travis. "I don't help people who point a gun at my son," she said.

He started chuckling and then Oleatha, Jacob, and even Roy joined in. The old man gave her the warm smile she was used to and said, "We're gonna make a hillbilly out of this gal yet."

❖

Early Monday morning, Luke called, and Maggie told him about the home invasion, leaving out her part in it. He'd fuss. He'd really fuss. Even so, he still had what his mother called a conniption. "I sent you down there to be safe," he stormed.

"I don't think any place is safe," Maggie said. She sat on the back step, shivering as night cooled the hollow. "This afternoon your mother got a call from one of her church ladies who said that somebody in Catesboro has caught it. A man named Wilson."

"There's a bunch of Wilsons in the county."

"Well, I don't know which one." And she was too tired to try to remember. "Anyway, he'd been in Knoxville doing something and brought it home. Evidently Knoxville is overrun with cases." She looked toward Oleatha's dead garden and beyond where the wilted kudzu swayed. "It's just going to happen."

He told her about Jack and how everybody had pampered him all day until the young man looked as though he'd just about prefer being back in the medical building. She heard tempered hope in his voice, and that was about as good as it got these days. He begged her to keep everybody in the hollow, not to allow anyone to go to Catesboro. She promised.

❖

Arriving before daybreak at the medical building, Luke looked for the morning report, but there was none. He got the sense that everything was going to hell. Sure, Jack had come out, but, according to him, conditions in the medical building were chaotic at best.

When he checked in at the mess hall, Jill looked like she was ready to spit nails. "No list," she said.

"I know." Luke paused. He was almost afraid to ask. "Heard from your mother?"

"Finally," she said. "Sick but not dead." She looked away.

He scanned the room for Josh, who was sitting next to Ilse. Good. After the swings between anger, obsession, and wide-eyed childishness, Luke was glad to see that the man sat quietly, answering Ilse when she spoke to him.

Otherwise, there was no welcoming scent of coffee or bacon. A bin held individual boxes of cereal next to two plastic jugs, one of milk and one of orange juice. Somebody had flung a couple of loaves of bread next to a giant toaster, along with individual butters and jellies. That was it. People were grumbling, especially about the lack of coffee.

After opening a box of Cheerios and pouring milk over them, Luke went to sit with Ilse, Josh, and Jill, who was playing with a piece of toast. "Did you call Fister?" she asked.

"Still no answer."

Ilse said, "They've abandoned us." Her voice was calm, but the words were chilling. "Jack said the medical staff was getting sick even with their hazard suits; the others are too."

"We have to eat," Jill, said her voice rising. "We can do without the list, as much as we want it, but we have to eat and have medical care." She clutched her clipboard with fingers as white as her face.

"Anybody sick?" Luke asked between bites of cereal.

She shook her head.

"Maybe we've seen the last of it. Maybe it's going to be okay."

"We've thought that before," Josh whispered.

One of the passengers came up to their table. "Hey, Mayor," she said. "What's going on with breakfast? Why isn't there any coffee?"

"Don't know," Luke said. "I'll look into it."

"No sodas either. Haven't been for a couple of days."

"I know."

The woman gripped the edge of the table. "On the news this morning they said the vice-president has extended the ban on travel and declared a national emergency. National Guard units are being called up all over the place, but most of them are only at half strength. Everybody's sick. And they've finally admitted the president is incapable of doing his job."

"Dear God," Josh breathed.

"People are dying fast, too fast for them to keep up," the woman said. "Especially if they bleed, if it's hem, hemo, I don't know how to say it."

"Hemmorhagic," Luke said. Maggie had told him the word, Maggie who was holed up at the homeplace and safe, he hoped. Setting aside his half-full bowl, he touched the woman's clutched hand. "You're safe. We may have problems, but you're safe. Jack came out okay."

"He did, didn't he?"

Josh scooted his chair back. "Have to leave," he mumbled. Ilse frowned.

Another half dozen came to Luke's table, asking about the list or breakfast or Fister, some bewildered, some furious. He had nothing to tell them. But before people straggled out of the room, the wide double doors to the kitchen opened and two soldiers, one male and one female, stood well behind the cafeteria line. They both wore surgical masks and gowns over their uniforms. "Listen up," Luke shouted, pointing at the pair.

The man spoke first. "All the cooks are sick," he said. His voice was muffled by the mask. "They've been evacuated to hospitals. We're the only two left and I doubt they'll bring in more."

His partner took a step forward. "And me and Jimmy are running fevers so we'll be going in a few minutes."

A deep, collective sigh rippled through the room. Jimmy cleared his throat. "We don't want you people to starve so we're leaving everything unlocked. There's food back here. Some, anyway." He stopped to cough.

"What about food deliveries?" Ilse asked.

"We never know when they're coming. Usually they drop off stuff really early in the morning," the woman said. With the mask it was hard to read her expression, but her eyes were tired, glassy. "Haven't had one in several days." And she started coughing too.

"Thank you," Luke said. They turned to go back into the kitchen. "Good luck," he called after them.

The room sounded like a hive, and all the bees were looking at Luke. He considered Jill, but she had enough to do. Ilse was looking after Josh and teaching two classes and was, even though she didn't act like it most of the time, old. Someone would have to organize meals and get help preparing them. One of the TSAs, Angela, stood. As he recalled, she'd hooked up with the single Spanish guy who was so good at chess. Good for them. "I used to work in a school cafeteria," she said. "I know my way around a big kitchen."

"Thanks," Luke said. "She'll need helpers, folks. At least two or three for every meal."

One passenger said he'd worked his way through college as a grill cook, and Connie, dear Connie, raised her hand. "I'm no cook," she said in her crisp accent, "but I can wash up and do the bits and pieces."

Several more raised their hands.

"Come over here and let Jill make a list of your names," Luke said. "I reckon all of us will do KP on a rotating basis, so don't be surprised when your name comes up. We'll manage, folks. And maybe if you're lucky I'll fix you all soup beans and cornbread." They laughed, as he'd hoped they would. Christ, this was a mess.

Angela and several others went to explore the kitchen and inventory the supplies. Most everybody else drifted off. Jim French's Bible study would start before long. But Ilse, Jill, and Luke sat, all of them stunned. Finally Ilse said, "This will be all right, I suppose, as long as the food holds out."

"And the medical staff stays," Jill added.

"I don't know who to call," Luke said. "I can try talking to the soldiers at the front gate or to someone in the medical building, I suppose."

"Abandoned," Ilse repeated.

She and the others rose, leaving Luke to listen to chatter from the kitchen. They should send a replacement for Fister, even if the Homeland representative was sitting behind a desk in D.C. Sometimes Luke wondered if anyone actually knew they existed. What about medicine and coffee and toilet paper? They were in quarantine, not prison.

Angela stuck her head out the kitchen door. "There is coffee, Luke. Those two just didn't make it." She was smiling.

He heaved himself out of the chair, painting on a smile. "Good. Maybe Ilse won't be so cranky tomorrow."

"Want to come see what we have?" asked Angela.

He did. Guiding him through the walk-ins and store room and pantry, Angela chattered about what they could do. "I mean, there aren't that many of us now." She bit her lip. "It's not that much work, and there's food, if folks don't mind a few odd combinations."

No, there weren't that many of them anymore. He glanced into the kitchen office and gestured at the phone. "See what you can find, Angela. Numbers for suppliers, supervisors, anything military or otherwise. Remind them we're here. Tell them the uncollected trash out back is a health hazard. Most important, we need more food soon. Don't wait until it's desperate."

The cheerful expression drained from her face and she nodded.

"Also, hunt around for anything that might be useful elsewhere. Soap, bags, paper towels."

She blinked, anxious now. "Will do."

Luke spotted a can full of ballpoints and grabbed one. "Like this." Gazing around the small room, he saw something even more useful. "And this." He picked up the flashlight and left.

Chapter Fifteen

Maggie mixed up a batch of bread, using the starter she'd been feeding and babying for a week. She hoped she'd got it right. Ironic that the starter was ready just as she was nearly out of flour. Trapped in the house by a persistent drizzle, Roy and Jacob were playing checkers in the living room where Oleatha was actually finishing one of her abandoned afghans. Maggie stared out the kitchen window at the rain. She should call Tina to ask about their mother or Luke to calm him down, but she wasn't up to it.

The only good thing was that Roy was speaking to her again. Maybe that was worth the humiliation, but Travis's words still stung. She clenched and unclenched her fingers. She had other things to worry about than Travis's low opinion of her intelligence.

Oleatha lumbered into the kitchen and peered at the huge bowl of dough covered with what she called a tea towel. "It'll smell good in here after while," she said with a smile. "Don't you think you ought to catch a little nap? I bet you didn't hardly sleep at all last night."

Maggie had to admit she was exhausted. It was as if there was a string around her spine pulling her to the floor. "Maybe later," she said.

"And I need to think about what we can have for dinner," Oleatha said.

"How's the food holding out?" Maggie knew but didn't want to let on. Besides, she was curious about what Oleatha would say. Probably something about the Lord providing.

"All right, I reckon." But she frowned.

"Roy and I can go out again. Maybe some trucks have come in."

Oleatha shook her head. "You know they haven't. And meat that was anywhere a week ago's done spoiled by now."

❖

"Has Luke called tonight?" Roy asked later that evening.

"Right after supper," Maggie replied.

"Did they have food?"

"Yes," Maggie said. "They had tuna melts, macaroni and cheese, and peas. And cherry cobbler."

"He ain't suffering," Roy said with a grin.

"Could we have macaroni and cheese, Mom?" Jacob's eyes were big.

"No cheese, no milk," Oleatha said with tight lips.

"Oh."

"But I had pretty good luck making some of the bread dough into buns, young Jacob," Maggie said. "And Granny promised you hamburgers tomorrow night."

He brightened at this.

Maggie jumped when Oleatha's phone rang. Her nerves were as tangled as a bale of barbed wire. It was Marla. Listening to Oleatha's side of the conversation, it seemed that baby Savannah was no better, but Marla was still healthy. Oleatha was trying to persuade her daughter to stay in, to avoid people. But Maggie could hear Marla's protests across the room. Food, medicine, all of it. When Marla asked to speak to Maggie, she braced herself against the wave of emotion she knew was coming. Sure enough, Marla bombarded her with Savannah's symptoms and then complaints about the wretched state of their country.

"Can you get her to drink at all?" Maggie asked.

"She'll suck on popsicles I found. And she'll take a little juice. I still can't find formula."

"Oh, popsicles are good. I'm surprised you found them."

Marla huffed. "Had to go six places. And Mama can fuss all she wants but you gotta go out if you're going to get what you need. I know it's not safe, but I'm not gonna hide myself away from this crap. The government needs to do something to help us."

As soon as she could, she handed the phone back to Oleatha. Hiding herself away. That's exactly what Maggie was doing. But Luke would have a fit if she took Jacob back to River Hills even if she could make him macaroni and cheese there. It felt like Luke's plan for protection was making her into a coward.

❖

Luke set his phone to buzz at 2:30. He figured Rieselman would be totally dead at that time of night, except for the medical building where things might truly be dead. He grimaced at the dark humor. Grabbing the flashlight and lock picks, he left the barracks and sneaked between buildings toward the mess hall, veering around it while keeping an eye open for patrols. He needed to know the night-time patterns of the place: patrols, deliveries, movement. Other than the one time they were searching for the three who escaped, he'd never seen troops patrolling the area at all.

It was dripping a little rain, bringing a chill with it. The flat expanse of the camp made distances look huge. He wound around to the gate nearest the mess hall and used his flashlight to examine the padlock.

Nothing too difficult, he thought, but he made no attempt to unlock it. To the left and outside the gate was a stand of scruffy trees. The only trees on the post itself were those near the CO's house. A man needed trees, he thought. Something to rest his eyes on. And sometimes his back. Luke made up his mind to wait a while. Dousing the flashlight and pulling the hood over his head, he scrunched down to the left of the gate, figuring the pitiful trees would offer a bit of cover from anyone driving up to the gate.

Thoroughly wet, he heard a vehicle just after 4:00, and flattened himself against the grass, glad his jacket was dark. What looked like an old Jeep puttered along the perimeter road, turning right to shine its headlights on the gate, then backing up to continue down the road. Cursory check, he thought. He stood, shaking his jacket like a dog, and followed the fence on down to the CO's house. He had more than an inkling that their weapons were in there. He wouldn't mind getting his hands on some paperwork too. Since Sunday he'd been wondering why nobody had arranged transport home for Jack. The guy was well, immune, and another mouth to feed. He also wanted to know what they were doing with the dead. Families needed to know.

As before, not a hint of illumination came from the windows. The bare trees reached into the rainy haze like claws. Making no effort to be quiet, Luke climbed two concrete steps to the wooden porch and banged on the door before pushing the doorbell three times. He heard nothing but its echo. As he expected, the door was locked.

Around back, a ghostly swing set creaked its chains near a patio cluttered with cheap folding chairs and flowerpots full of wet dirt and cigarette butts. Luke shivered. It looked like the world had died. He rattled the back door, and pointed the flashlight through its window. Nothing.

Breaking and entering, he thought, as he fished Briley's lock picks out of his pocket. Setting the flashlight on a flower pot to shine at the doorknob, he pulled out the tools. He was clumsy with them but was sure he understood the theory. Patience. Finally he felt the mechanism give.

He swept the kitchen with his flashlight. He saw long counters and a good-sized table. The sink was full of cups soaking in gray dishwater. "Hello?" Luke called. "Fister?" The room smelled of stale coffee and dust with a hint of bad drains. Except for the brush of his shoes against vinyl and then carpet, the house was silent. Several desks were crammed into the living room, but they were all bare. A copier sat against beautiful built-in bookcases.

Luke made his way upstairs, calling out again, but the creaking steps were all he heard. Upstairs he smelled soap, maybe shampoo, and a whiff of disinfectant. There were four bedrooms, all currently unoccupied but furnished with unmade beds and wastepaper baskets full of used tissues, many of them bloody. No suitcases, no laptops, no signs of life. They'd left in a hurry, and they'd left sick, he thought. And there'd been at least four of them. He checked the two bathrooms but found only towels flung every which way and a forgotten tube of toothpaste. He touched the towels. They were dry.

He needed to check the basement, but on a whim he stopped again on the first floor. It would require a bit of space to store all those gun belts and weapons. A cabinet of some sort or a closet. There was nothing resembling either in the dining room. It was bare except for spiders in the corners, and the study was the same. Luke went into the kitchen and opened doors and drawers. He found paper plates, plastic forks, coffee, sugar, and an unopened package of Oreos he planned to pilfer.

Squinting at the desks in the living room, he saw that one had a deep file drawer. It was locked. Again, he took out the picks, and, despite the dimming light of his flashlight, he had it open in no time. Crappy lock.

The guns and belts had been jammed into the cabinet. Seen all together it looked like an arsenal. Okay, he should come back with a duffle bag and shove all of it in, returning guns to their owners. But many of the owners were dead or sick. He didn't want to arm nervous civilians. The flashlight was down to a dying glow, but he was able to find his belt almost by touch. It was different from the Customs equipment. He stuffed the gun in his pocket along with two clips. Latex gloves could be useful, as well as the pepper spray. He considered the handcuffs, but ended up putting them back in the cabinet. Couldn't really see any use for them.

His jacket was heavy, but his spirit was lighter. If he had to protect these people, at least he had the tools to do so. But they wouldn't be worth much if somebody didn't keep supplies coming. He relocked the cabinet, stuck the dead flashlight into the elastic of his sweats, and picked up the Oreos. He had a plan for them.

Chapter Sixteen

Before it was fully daylight, Roy fetched his tackle box and set out to fish. Jacob, of course, wanted to tag along. "This ain't for sport, son," Roy said. "I'll be going farther down the creek where there's deep water, a pretty fair walk for short legs."

Jacob insisted he could do it, saying Pop needed him, and Roy relented. Maggie started some laundry and called Tina. "You didn't call yesterday," Maggie said. "I was worried."

Tina's reply was a prolonged spasm of coughing. "I've caught it," she gasped. "Feel like the furthest reaches of hell."

"Oh, Lord. Does Andy have it too?"

"Not yet, but from what I can tell it's only a matter of time."

"Are you going to the doctor? You need the anti-viral medicine."

"Went yesterday and got it," Tina croaked, "although they're saying on the news that it's not very effective."

"Have to try though. How high's your fever?"

They dissected Tina's symptoms, and then Maggie asked about her mother.

"Still in detox, as far as I know." Tina paused to blow her nose. "I haven't tried to call. Didn't feel like it."

"Of course not."

"Dad called, though, night before last. He's caught it too."

Christ, thought Maggie. This virus could destroy her entire family. She listened to Tina cough, tightness in her own chest like steel bands.

"You should call him, Mag. You really should."

Afterwards, she cried. Gripping the sides of the washing machine, she spilled tears that splatted against the shiny top. She thought about calling her father, the man who'd abandoned his girls to a drunk. The whole time she was taking the wash outside and hanging it on the line, she thought about it. As she watched the stiff breeze billow the sheets and shirts, she tried to remember the last time she'd spoken with her father. But this could truly be the last time. In light of all the sickness, it seemed silly, cruel even, to be so stubborn, but she still didn't do anything more than take her phone out of her pocket. What time was it in Colorado? She thought for a second and realized it was eight-thirty, plenty late enough. Perching on the front porch step, she clicked on his number, stored in her phonebook but never used.

Her dad's wife Jody answered. Maggie guessed he'd been true to her; they'd been married now for twenty years. "It's Maggie," she said, her face turning hot. "Tina said Dad is sick."

Jody was a talker. It didn't seem to bother her that Maggie hadn't called her father since she'd announced that he had a grandson, nearly six years ago. The woman spewed out all the details, going on for quite a while before telling Maggie that her father was in the hospital. "He went straight to pneumonia," Jody said and finally took a breath.

This wasn't good. "But you're okay?" Maggie asked. She didn't really care; she had never met the woman.

It was another five minutes before Maggie was able to ask Jody to tell her father that she'd called and click off. She stared ahead at a bare tree, variety unknown, that clung to the bank of the creek, gnarled roots grabbing anything they could.

She told Oleatha about her dad and Tina over a shared can of chicken noodle soup. Oleatha gave her a fierce hug, said she'd pray, and took her crocheting out on the porch. It had turned warm again, feeling more like May than November. Maggie felt like her nerve endings were shredding. "I think I'll walk," she said. "Maybe I'll see if Travis has any more news about Coughlin."

Oleatha nodded benignly, but Maggie still felt like she was sneaking off. There was no real need to see Travis. She doubted he knew any more about Coughlin than he had yesterday morning. But climbing the hill felt good. Just in the few days since Annie had died, more trees had shed their leaves, and she was able to see the little white house sooner than before. She heard music too and a fervently uttered curse. Good, he was home. Scattered around his shining motorcycle were all kinds of tools and strange pieces of metal. Travis was hunkered down, his jeans low enough to show a stripe of white skin. "What are you doing?" Maggie asked.

He turned his head to grin at her. "Frustrating the everloving hell out of myself." He gestured at the porch. "Sit a spell."

She lowered herself to the rotten boards and sat in the sun. Within minutes she had peeled off her jacket to let the sun soak into her arms. "That looks complicated."

"It isn't. I'm just replacing the drive chain, but nothing's fitting together like it should." He stood, lighting a cigarette. "Want a Coke?"

"Sure, if you have enough. Things are starting to run out, aren't they?"

He stepped past her on the porch, his jeans close enough to touch and smelling of oil. "Well, I am out of Little Debbies, or I'd offer you one."

Maggie stretched her legs, willing herself to forget the horrors that nearly suffocated her. On the radio, a country singer was mourning the mistakes he'd made in his misspent youth. She never listened to country music, didn't know much more than Willie Nelson and Johnny Cash, but the song was pleasant enough, and the singer's rough voice sounded genuine and warm.

Travis handed her a Coke. "Everybody okay?"

No, she thought, but she nodded. "Roy went fishing, for real this time, and Jacob fussed until he took him along. Oleatha's crocheting."

"Big excitement." He grinned and then turned serious. "Fishing for real? Are you all running short of food?"

"Not exactly." She frowned at a quick pinprick of guilt. "I would've brought you some bread, but I made half of it up in buns."

He wouldn't let up. "I'm fine. What do you mean 'not exactly'?"

The song had changed to one about lost love. She supposed every type of music milked that theme. "We've gone through most of the meat Oleatha had, and we're out of canned milk and some other things. It doesn't matter."

He rubbed at his bushy beard. As always, he wore a cap. This one was dark green with what looked like a tan-colored bear embroidered on it. "I don't reckon there's a store anywhere around that's open. They said on the radio that the Red Cross was setting up a food station in Corbin in a few days." He flicked his cigarette at the road.

"That's a long drive."

"Not that long. If it happens."

"We'll be fine." She used her voice to underline the words. "Don't let me keep you from working. I'm just enjoying being out of the house."

He took her at her word and turned back to the Honda. Scrunching her neck until the bones cracked, she gazed at the sky above the rocks and listened to the radio. Even if the music was unfamiliar, it felt good to hear songs. She found herself trying to decipher the words, studying them like a foreign language. At one point, she chuckled.

"What?"

"Sorry," she said. "This song's pretty clever." The lyrics were essentially about the differences between men and women. "And true."

"Yeah. I like that one." He picked up a tool and started re-attaching the chain. "What do you normally listen to?"

"This and that. Rarely country."

His back was to her. "You're getting an education down here. What do you think?"

She considered. Although three or four songs didn't make her an expert, she said, "I like it. It's real and sentimental and sometimes funny."

"Yeah."

"I like the men singers better."

He chuckled. "Why's that?"

It wasn't hard to imagine that he'd been raised by a teacher. "I don't know. Some of the women sound like imitations of Dolly Parton, and she did it first. She's an original."

"Can't argue with that." His fingers, dark with oil and dirt, fiddled with the chain, pushed, adjusted.

"And some of the songs are sad and sensitive . .." She was searching for a word.

Travis stood. "Poignant?"

She looked up at him, his face hooded by the bill of his cap. "Yes."

"You surprised?"

"That country music can be poignant?"

"No, that I know that word."

She shrugged like she had in school when she figured any answer she gave would be wrong.

"My daddy made me read, made me do it until I liked it. You married Luke. You ought to know country boys aren't stupid."

She pulled her knees to her chest. "I never said you were."

After wiping his hands on a rag, he folded the cloth to a clean side and wiped the gleaming chrome. Damn, but he was prickly. And, torn by worries and short of sleep, she wasn't much different. "You're the one who called me stupid," she snapped.

"Sorry," he mumbled. "I really am." He turned to face her. "You know how you want to yell at your kid when he scares you? When he runs out in the road without looking or stays gone too long? That's why I fussed at you."

She gave him the tiniest nod, and he drank from his can, making a deal out of wiping his mouth on the rag and skittering his eyes away from her. This man didn't apologize easily.

There was an awkward silence until Travis finally asked, "So, isn't she a beauty?" He waved his dirty rag at the motorcycle.

"Beautiful. Shiny." She swallowed the last of her Coke. "I've never ridden a motorcycle."

"You're kidding. Never?"

She shook her head.

"Scared?"

"Maybe. Careful anyway. My cousin had a boyfriend with a Harley; I could've asked for a ride on his, I guess, but I never did."

Shaking his hairy head, Travis said, "Maggie, Maggie. You miss too much by being careful. Everybody needs to walk on the wild side a little bit."

"Not me. Life's dangerous enough."

In one quick motion he'd grabbed her hand, swallowing it with his rough, warm fingers. "How are you ever going to feel free if you're always trying to stave off trouble? Not one of us can control a damned thing."

He was hovering over her, blocking the sun. The warmth of his hand swam all the way to her belly. She shrugged. When did she ever feel free? She knew. The only time was when Luke was loving her, when he'd stirred her to the point where she cared about nothing else, just for an instant, just for a minute. Then she soared like a hawk gliding over the hollow.

She ducked her head. "I don't know."

Squeezing her hand, he released it, but stood close, not ready to give up the conversation. He was a remarkably persistent man. "Remember how tickled you were when Jacob smiled for the first time? How you told everybody? How you insisted it wasn't gas like everybody says it is? We were born to smile, girl."

She nodded and stood, unwilling to talk about it but reluctant to leave. He stepped back and grinned at her. "Think about it," he said. "I'll give you a ride one of these days. Nothing like riding a motorcycle to make you feel as free as the breeze."

Maggie looked down. "Okay. Well, see you later," she said, her voice very quiet against the radio. She could hear the eternal crowing of Coughlin's gamecocks. She was halfway home before she realized she'd forgotten to ask him about the robbers.

❖

Luke, Ilse, and Jack lingered after breakfast, listening to the kitchen volunteers washing dishes and singing along with somebody's phone. Finally, Angela came out, wiping her hands on her apron. Her hair hung in wild curls and her shoulders drooped, but she was smiling.

"Excellent breakfast," Luke said.

"Best we've had," Ilse agreed.

Angela ducked her head.

"How's the food supply?" Luke asked.

"We're okay for a while," Angela said, collapsing into a chair.

Ilse turned to Luke. "Nobody's called you?"

He shook his head. He slurped down the last of his lemonade. It wasn't orange juice, but it was okay.

"One problem," Angela announced. They all looked at her. "I don't want anybody to go hungry, but people are acting like this is their kitchen back home. We can't lock it up like the Mickeys did, so folks are sneaking in and getting into our supplies." She frowned. "I know the soft drink machines are empty, so I don't mind making up a few jugs of powdered lemonade and leaving it out on the line. And I found several bags of pretzels; I could leave those out too. But sometime between supper and this morning, somebody went through nearly all the peanut butter and saltines we had. There's just not enough extra for that to be happening."

All of them shook their heads, and Luke was about to say he'd make an announcement when the outside door opened. Bedraggled with rain, it was Jill, who'd checked in but not eaten breakfast. "They just posted a list," she said. The words seemed to be coming from her gut rather than her throat. "We have ten more deaths." She staggered.

"Sit," Luke said, taking her arm and pushing her down.

"Little Emma. Her mother. That whole family is gone."

Angela's hand went to her mouth

"Who else?" asked Jack.

"A couple of the TSA's. Two Customs people." She turned her stricken face to Luke. "McKenzie and Alvarez?"

He knew the names. God help them.

She checked her clipboard. "Mr. and Mrs. Whalen, passengers."

Ilse murmured, "The American bridge players. Oh my."

"And," Jill raised her head. Droplets of rain ran down her cheeks like tears. "Good old Pete, the guy who kept letting Bob Briley beat him at pool." She lowered her head. "And Bob Briley."

Luke covered his eyes with fists. No one spoke. Somebody sniffed, but no one looked up to see who it was. Luke squeezed Jill's cold hand. Finally, Angela scraped her chair back. "Forget what I said, Luke," she murmured. "I don't guess a little peanut butter matters."

Bob. Damn it to hell. Bob. Luke searched for his voice. "I know what you mean, Angela," he said. "But, unfortunately, it does. We can't be foolish." He turned to Jack. More than ever he needed to keep them busy, always keep them busy. "Go in the kitchen with Angela and see if you can rig up some kind of a lock for the pantry anyway. Maybe you could put most things in there."

"Except the ice cream," Angela said. "They haven't discovered it yet."

"There's ice cream?" Ilse asked, licking her lips and covering Luke's hand with hers. They laughed, weakly, but they laughed.

❖

Later that morning Luke grabbed the Oreos and his gun and sauntered up to the front gate. He ripped the end of the cookie package and stuffed two in his mouth. "Hey Troop," he yelled at the soldiers on duty. "Want a cookie? Don't have no milk, but they're still good."

He'd broadened his accent and plastered a stupid grin on his face. It wasn't the first time Luke had jumped behind a hillbilly to get what he needed. The soldier didn't move.

"It ain't like we're gonna storm the gates with AK47's," Luke called, reaching for another cookie. "We're just folks." He made sure his jacket covered the gun in his waistband. One soldier did blink, glancing at Luke and then looking away.

"See, we got a problem here. All the people cooking and doing for us have left. Well, that ain't a problem; we can hustle up some chow, if we had food, but we're almost out of grub. Y'all got plenty to eat? We don't. I found these cookies tucked away, and I'm willing to share 'em if you're hungry. Anyway, we got nobody to help us out except you all and the medical team. Those dudes from D.C. left." Luke paused to let the two absorb all this. They were young, male, and looked more intimidated than intimidating. "Guess you all already knew that. So," Luke pulled a slip of paper from his pocket and fed it through the fence, "that's got my phone number on it. I'd sure appreciate it if your commanding officer would give me a call and tell me what to do."

They didn't move.

"I'm Luke Davies. From Kentucky. And around here they call me the Mayor." He grinned. "Sure you all don't want a cookie? They're fresh, and I'm healthy as a horse."

He knew they wouldn't pick up the paper until he was gone. If then. Waving as he turned, he said, "Y'all have a good day." And he strolled away.

Stopping at the medical building, he rested the package of cookies against the outside wall and wiped his mouth. Here he'd be Officer Davies. Opening his jacket a little so the gun's bulge could be glimpsed if someone was looking hard enough, he went into the medical building. The small reception room was very warm and smelled of Lysol. It was also empty. A sign by the door said that no cell phones were allowed on the premises. On a table, Luke saw one of those little bells like hotels used to have, but he decided to wait another minute or two before ringing it. Maybe he'd see or hear something.

From a distance he could hear murmuring, he thought, but nothing else. Finally he depressed the bell's button, waiting another few minutes before a tall figure in a biohazard suit came into the room. "Are you ill?" Distorted as it was, he could tell it was a female voice.

"No." He straightened his shoulders, causing his jacket to flare open a little wider, and explained that Fister was gone, the cooks were gone, and the healthy residents of Ft. Rieselman needed food.

"I have nothing to do with that," she said.

"No, but you have superiors, don't you? And they might have phone numbers for people who can help us. Are you getting meals?"

The bubble-like helmet nodded. "We prepare our own food here."

"Are you getting food deliveries? Maybe you could talk to somebody about that."

Luke wasn't sure, but he thought she'd noticed his gun. He went on. "You probably don't want a bunch of hungry people coming up here and breaking in do you?" He held out another slip of paper. "I want someone with some authority to call me. Soon."

The detached voice was hesitant. "I'll see what I can do." Her heavily gloved hand took the paper. "We're really short-staffed." This wasn't hesitant at all.

"I appreciate that." Through the layers of plastic, he locked eyes with her. "Do it anyway."

As Luke walked back toward the mess hall, he saw Jack gently escorting Drew. He knew what it meant. "Damn, I'm sorry, Drew." Jack's pale face was whiter than ever.

"Thought the Angel of Death had passed over me," Drew whispered. "I just saw Josh. You need to help him; he's freaking out."

Luke nodded, touched Drew's shoulder, and kept walking. He didn't see how he could feel any lower. Briley and now Drew. But he'd better see if he could calm Josh down. Or get Ilse to help.

Chapter Seventeen

Somewhere along the line Luke had started thinking of himself and the others as prisoners, and nothing had changed his mind. No one called him. No one delivered food. But there was a list posted on the medical facility door, this time in the middle of the afternoon. Jill waved it under his nose. Good news. Scrawled in black marker were the words "One new case. No deaths." And Josh had calmed down and disappeared, probably to his room, Ilse thought.

But Jack was a mess. Angry and weak and grieving over Drew, at supper he suggested gathering everybody and attacking the front gate. With what, Ilse asked. Knives and forks? Luke knew where he could get all kinds of weapons, but he wasn't about to do it. Angela and her volunteers had turned out a decent supper, but Luke had little appetite for it. The cooks swore they had enough for a few days, but he was worried. He'd received no responses from his morning attempts, and morale was dropping by the hour.

It was nearly dark when he checked on Josh. He hadn't eaten supper, and, as Luke feared, was once again huddled up in his bed, covers over his head. "Let's walk over to the recreation building and have a game of checkers," Luke said.

Josh said no. At least he was talking. He blinked at the light Luke had turned on. "I want to go home," he said. "I don't understand why they won't let us go." He struggled to sit up. "They're going to starve us to death or poison us or maybe even shoot us. You know it's true."

The man met Luke's eyes and then dropped his head. "I haven't always been like this," he said. "It didn't get bad until ten years ago."

Luke was intrigued. "What set it off?"

"Oh, I always had problems, but not this bad. I managed to hold down a job for several years. Factory." He looked up. "I'm better at simple tasks." Then he showed a whisper of a smile. "But I do play Spanish guitar." He hugged an imaginary instrument. "That's why I wanted to go to Spain."

"But what made it worse, Josh?"

He looked at the ceiling. "Car crash. I was driving. Mother died." He folded up on the bed and turned his head away from Luke. "They should've let Jack and Dan go home," he said. "They're cured. Immune now, aren't they? Those two women too. Four people have recovered, and yet they haven't been sent home."

He was right.

"I'm scared."

"I know."

"It's a plot to kill us all."

More like screw-ups than plots, Luke thought. But that was almost worse. He left Josh, telling him to take his meds, relax. They'd make it. But he was losing hope too. He went to his room and called Maggie. He knew she was worried about her sister and father. Hell, she was even worried about her sorry mother. Maggie wore guilt like a medal of honor. "Hey, honey."

She sounded cheerful, although it probably was forced. That was Maggie's style. "Your dad and Jacob caught a big, old bunch of fish," she reported. "We've had a fish fry."

He asked what kind, and she told him, but she didn't seem to want to talk about food, which worried him. Oleatha had heard from Marla, she reported, and little Savannah was better. "So that's good news," she said.

"Absolutely," he said in a hearty voice.

She went quiet.

"How about your sister?" He'd dreaded asking her.

"She's awfully sick, but Andy was still okay this morning."

He made soft noises that were meant to comfort her, although he didn't see how they could. He asked, "Did you get a chance to speak to your father?"

At first she didn't answer. Then he heard her crying. "He called an hour ago," she said, her voice ragged. "Jody took a cell phone to the hospital so he could call Tina and me."

Luke waited.

"He's dying. I could barely hear him," Maggie said between sobs. "He said he misses me, that I'm still his little girl."

If Luke could've stormed the front gate, stolen a Humvee, and driven to Henley County, he would've done it right then. "Oh honey."

"He never should've left us. But." She couldn't talk.

"But he's still your daddy."

He heard a tiny yes.

Maybe Jack was right. Maybe he should arm people and break out, find a way home. He'd tried to comfort Maggie, but there was no substitute for holding her, for brushing back her thick hair, touching her cheek. Luke plugged the phone back into its charger and sat on his bunk, staring at his gun. He rubbed his face. He was tired, bone tired. He thought about taking a walk to clear his head but didn't and ended up falling asleep with his shoes on.

❖

Shivering, Maggie crept into the back bedroom and slid into bed next to Jacob. Worried about when they'd be able to get heating oil delivered, Roy had started guarding the thermostat like a Marine. But the bed was warm, heated up by Jacob's sturdy little body. He had his father's way of putting out BTUs like a furnace. She snuggled up to him, sniffing the skin on the back of his neck and rubbing her cheek against his silky hair. There wasn't much chance of waking him. Roy's fishing trip would've taken the starch out of a much older boy. The old man had gone to bed early himself.

Maggie stared at the window until she could see the gray slit around the shade. Her father would die tonight. Maybe he was already gone. A memory popped into her mind, a memory of when she'd been no more than four. She and her father had been out in his precious Nova, driving around downtown Cincinnati. He'd bought her a bag of peanuts, the ones in shells, and he'd shelled a few for her when she'd complained about how hard it was to do. After sucking on peanut shells and getting bored with using her teeth to open some, Maggie had thrown a peanut out the window at the car next to them. And then she'd thrown another. Her father saw her but didn't say a word. Soon she'd been pitching peanuts at cars all around Fountain Square, and he'd been laughing as hard as Maggie. For weeks after that he'd widened his bluey-green eyes, the same color as hers, and called her 'Peanut.' And she'd giggled.

Although she couldn't let go of years of anger at the man, perhaps she could summon pity for him. Living with Donna wasn't easy; she knew that. And the frowsy, vague hellcat her mother had become surely wasn't the fresh, young girl he'd married. He'd laid too heavy a burden on his older daughter. He'd been wrong to leave, but she couldn't blame him for wanting to be free of his drunken wife.

Free, she thought, rolling onto her side. She tried to remember what Travis Parker had said about being free. It was easy for him, she thought. He had no responsibilities, except those he chose, like taking care of his grandmother. But maybe he was right. Maybe God wanted people to smile. She just couldn't manage it now.

❖

Maggie dried the last of the breakfast dishes and stared out at the inevitable morning fog. Behind her Oleatha sat at the table, thumbing through a book of crochet patterns. She'd said her 'arthur' was bothering her this morning, and that's why Maggie had insisted on cleaning up.

"Nobody's called?" Oleatha asked.

Maggie shook her head. She'd thought she'd have heard about her father by now, but it was, of course, two hours earlier in Colorado, only a little after six. She fed sugar and the last of the flour to her yeast starter. Foolish optimism. She didn't know where they'd get more flour to use it. She wondered if she could do something with corn meal. Oleatha had plenty of that.

She called Tina who sounded dreadful but swore she was feeling a little better. Her sister didn't know anything. Donna had called saying she was sober and wanted to go home despite advice from the counselors. Tina had told her to stay; she was too sick to come get her. Should they call Jody about Dad?

They decided to wait, figuring Jody would call when there was news. So Maggie steeled herself to slog through the endless day. After lifting a little, the fog had turned to a slow, incessant rain, frustrating both Jacob and Roy, who roamed from room to room, carrying his shotgun with him. Oleatha's face was creased in a permanent frown. Maggie got out Roy's penny jar and played counting games with Jacob, who was cranky and bored. They worked through another ten pages of Luke's old reader.

"Look at that, Mommy. Daddy drew cars in the book!"

"I see that, and the girl in the picture has green hair. Daddy must like green-haired girls."

Jacob hooted. "Maybe you should make your hair green."

She was glad he was laughing. Noticing a band-aid on his finger, she asked, "Did you hurt yourself?"

He immediately hid his finger in his lap. "Uh, huh."

"How did you do that?"

He frowned. "I'm not supposed to say."

"Oh, you can tell me." She lifted his hand and pulled the covering off. It was a slit in the pad of his finger, white and clean.

"I hurt it when I was baiting Pop's hook. He can't see to do it." Jacob's face creased with concern. "But he said I shouldn't tell because you'd worry."

She smiled and shook her head. "Did it hurt?"

"Yes."

"Did you cry?"

"Nope. Not one bit."

"You're a brave guy, you know that?" She ruffled his scraggly hair. "And you need to be brave again now, Jacob. I'm going to cut your hair."

He chuckled. "Haircuts don't hurt, Mommy."

"Well, I hope not."

She'd finished the job right before Jody called. They'd tried a different drug on Bill, and it seemed to be working. He was still dangerously ill but alive and, perhaps, rallying. Maggie didn't get her hopes up. It was a plague, one of biblical proportions. Maggie thought that surely the signs along the road in Henley County were right. Jesus was coming. Trouble was, she wasn't ready.

❖

They stuffed themselves on the remaining fish: bass, blue gill, and one big, old catfish. Jacob chose two particular blue gill, insisting they were the two he'd caught, and Roy tousled his clean, short hair. There'd been cabbage too and corn, but, before supper, when she'd been sent down to the freezer to get the bag of corn, Maggie'd seen again how bare it was. Other than some packages of vegetables, the freezer blew its cold breath over one lonely roll of sausage and a package of hamburger.

At breakfast the next morning, Roy took a bite and declared, "Toast and jam. A body forgets just how good it is." His eyes met each of theirs. "You know what I mean? When you get used to fancy stuff like coconut cream pie and pepperoni pizzas, you forget how good simple things are. Like a hot shower on a chilly morning. Did you enjoy your shower this morning, Jacob?"

"I didn't take one, Pop."

"I did," said Maggie, "and it was wonderful."

Roy nodded like an old philosopher. "Hot showers, leaf buds in April, toast and jam." He took another big bite.

The glorified toast, along with fried Spam, made up their meal that morning and used up all the bread. Roy and Jacob set out once again to catch fish for their dinner. Oleatha sat in the front room answering phone calls from her church ladies and working on an afghan. She was nearing completion on a second, a complicated swirly pattern in three shades of blue.

Maggie supposed her father had lived through the night. Every hour on the new medicine would be to the good. She thought about Roy's little sermon on toast. They'd certainly returned to a simpler life, almost like those people on *The Waltons*. This reminded her of Kyle Coughlin and his buddy. Surely the sheriff would've come by to talk to them if he was going to arrest the guy. Of course nobody around here seemed to think the sheriff would do anything. That's why Roy carried his shotgun from room to room and Maggie had hidden her pistol and cash underneath a bunch of Marla's old sweatshirts.

Oleatha pattered into the kitchen. "You'll never guess what I've heard," she exclaimed but didn't give Maggie a chance to hazard one. "Somebody's been stealing catalytic converters off cars, just sawing them right off. And they took scrap metal from the construction site for the new bank. Ain't that a sight?" She gulped a breath. "Viola says you can get good money for scrap metal, so we're thinking it might be Kyle Coughlin or somebody else strung out on drugs and needing cash."

"Isn't the sheriff ever going to do anything about these people?"

"Viola's heard that the sheriff's sick, that at least half dozen people in Catesboro's caught the flu."

Damn, that was nearby, Maggie thought. There's no escaping it, a dire voice murmured in her head. "Well, doesn't he have a deputy or somebody?"

"He's not much count, but they have called the state police, although that won't amount to much either. They're all busy trying to get medical help for people and setting up food stations, those that aren't worrying with looting in the cities."

"It's just bad," Maggie said and wished she hadn't. Tears crept into her voice.

Oleatha ignored them or seemed to think they were perfectly warranted. "Yes, it's bad." Her voice softened. "You hear anything this morning?"

Maggie shook her head and went outside. A stiff breeze tossed the shriveled weeds on the other side of the road, making her hope Jacob was warm enough wherever he and Roy were fishing. She sat, blinking and swallowing to choke off her crying. Turning her head to the right, she stared at her car, ready to take her home any minute, provided she could find gasoline. And keep her catalytic converter. She could even drive to Illinois and get Luke, somehow. There was more food in her freezer than in Oleatha's just now. But she knew she wouldn't.

From up the road she heard a "hello," stretching into at least three syllables and loud enough to startle a jay over by the creek. She looked up in a hurry, ready to run inside and lock the doors, but it was Travis, carrying a bundle wrapped in newspaper and dripping, dear God, blood. She stood.

He was grinning and had a cocky swagger to his walk that made her think the bloody package was a trophy rather than an atrocity. "Brought you all dinner," he called as he neared the porch and set it on the rocks by Oleatha's flowerbed. "Better not carry it through the front room."

"What did you do?"

He wiped his hands down pants that were already smeared with gore. "Got me a turkey, that's what. You'll eat high off the hog tonight."

"Or the bird," she murmured.

He laughed. Oleatha came onto the porch. "What's this ruckus, Travis Parker?"

He pointed at the soaked newsprint and she clapped her hands. "Land sakes, wild turkey. That'll be a treat. Where'd you bag it?"

"North. Just this side of Pig's Eye."

Maggie couldn't take her eyes off his blood-rimmed fingernails. It was meat; she'd eat it, but it seemed brutish, uncivilized. Then she could almost hear Luke saying, "So if meat comes with styrofoam underneath and plastic wrap on top, it's not a dead cow or pig? C'mon, Maggie."

"You'll join us for supper, won't you?" Oleatha was saying.

"Don't mind if I do," Travis said.

Oleatha didn't have a bit of trouble picking up the ugly bundle and carrying it around the side of the house. "Come around five-thirty, you hear?"

Travis still stood in the yard, tilting his head to look up at Maggie. "You ever eat wild turkey?"

She shook her head.

"It's good. I left the skin on it, so it should stay moist. You'll like it."

"I appreciate it," she said.

"Where's Roy? Fishing again?"

She nodded. "They had good luck day before yesterday. Maybe they'll do as well today."

"Well, fish freezes, if they do." He seemed to be pinning her under some kind of microscope behind his bright blue eyes. "Luke okay?"

"Yeah. Worried about supplies for his people." She looked at the cupped floorboards of the porch. "But my sister's sick, and my father's dying."

"Ah, Maggie." His voice was a whisper.

Damn, the stupid tears were threatening again. "I'll be okay."

"Yeah, you will," he said. "I reckon we all will, some way or another."

❖

"Luke, I need to tell you something." It was Jack, serious and intent, with pink spots high on his thin cheeks.

"Go ahead." Luke motioned for him to sit next to Ilse and across from Jill. She was dreadfully pale too. Last night she'd had word that her mother was dead. And they were all hungry, had been for some time if Luke was honest about it.

"I'm going back to the medical building." Jack shook his head at Luke's frown. "No, I'm not sick, but I am immune, I suppose, and I do have some medical training. They're struggling over there."

"What a fine thing to do," Ilse murmured.

"Not so very noble. They won't let me go home, although I can't find a single, logical reason for it, and Drew's in there. I want him to have the very best treatment. He's like a brother to me."

Luke nodded. "Are you sure you're up to the work?"

Jack raised a shoulder. "I'll do what I can do." He pointed at Luke's plate. Breakfast had been a scoop of chocolate pudding and a slice of French bread. "And I'll get more to eat there than here," he said.

Jill shook her head. "That's not saying much."

"I'll work on that too."

"They won't let you go back and forth from here to there, will they?" Ilse asked.

"Probably not. Anyway, I wanted to say good-bye and thank you all for keeping us together." He shook hands with each of them.

Jill had just finished telling Jack, good luck, when the shouting started. Angela had emerged from the kitchen with a tray to carry bowls and spoons back to the kitchen when several people hollered her name. "You eat your fill back in the kitchen before you bring this out, Angela?" It came from a female TSA.

And then Derek, who'd seemed meek for weeks, yelled, "Yeah, how much you got hidden away back there? We're hungry."

Shouts came from every direction. Angela's eyes darted from one to another. She held the tray against her body. "I was afraid of this," Jill murmured. The shouters stood. But most people were saying nothing at all.

Luke stood too and strode to Angela's side. "Go back in the kitchen," he said. "Stay there."

Josh Monroe moved so close to Luke that he could see the sheen of sweat on the man's forehead. "I respectfully," he said, "respectfully request more food. Now."

The few people who could hear him started cheering. Two or three were hollering things like 'send us home,' 'feed us,' and 'we're hungry.' Luke waited. They would quiet down in a minute. He made eye contact with every one of them, including Josh who backed away.

He started quietly, forcing them to shut up. "The day the cooks left," he said, "Angela, Connie, and a couple of other people and I inventoried what was in the kitchen. It wasn't much. But Angela swore she would ration it out to last until we got food deliveries. Now, I've approached the military and the medical people about sending us supplies. So far nothing has happened, but I swear, Angela should be commended for doing the best she can for all of us."

He relaxed his posture a bit. "No one is hiding anything or sneaking larger portions. Most of you have helped out in the kitchen, and you know that's true." Many of them dropped their eyes. "I will keep trying to get food for us, but in the meantime, let's face this together." He smiled. "I'm hungry too. Hell, every step I take, I'm worried my sweat pants are gonna fall off my skinny ass." A few weak smiles and a welcome breeze of calm floated through the room. "But don't you dare." He strengthened his voice, chin, and posture. "Don't you dare attack Angela for making the best of an impossible situation."

Luke sat. "Defused," said Jack.

"For now," said Jill.

"I'll be going," said Jack.

And Ilse said, "I wonder if Josh is really swallowing his medicine."

❖

The turkey was tough even though Oleatha had worked butter under the skin, but Maggie enjoyed a small slice, drenched in gravy. She noticed that Oleatha and Travis ate small portions too. Roy and Jacob piled plenty on their plates.

"Mighty fine," Roy said, reaching for a toothpick from the little container on the table. "We surely do appreciate it, Travis."

He'd showered, his nails now rosy with health rather than gore, and he'd removed his hat so his curls, glossy and black as a crow's wing, glistened under the overhead light. "Happy to do it. Think I'll go out again in the morning and try to get me another one or maybe even a deer, as long as you've got freezer space, Oleatha." She nodded. Maggie couldn't help but raise her brows.

"You catch sight of a flock?" Roy asked.

"I saw three when I got this one. Shouldn't be hard to get another one, but there'll be more people hunting any day now. I was afraid I was late with it as it was." He took the last piece of the dreadful cornbread, made without milk or egg, and buttered it. "I heard shots yesterday and thought I'd better get my skates on."

Jacob laughed at this. "We got more fish today," he announced.

Travis turned his attention to the boy, man-to-man. "What did you catch?"

"Two blue gill. Those are my favorites. Pop got some bass."

"Nice ones too." Roy said.

They were such, well, men, Maggie thought, talking about their hunting and fishing. But they were keeping them fed. It felt as though her world, her century, had been turned upside down in some kind of movie-version time warp, but, regardless of Wal-Mart and cable television and drug-crazed burglars, she wasn't so sure the world down here had ever changed much. Oleatha mentioned the metal thefts.

"It was Kyle Coughlin who stole those converters and scrap," Travis said. "The sheriff's sick, but he wouldn't have done anything about Kyle anyway. Not unless he wanted his house set on fire or tires shot out. At least Kyle will be traveling for a day or two, staying out of mischief here. He'll have to take that scrap to Knoxville or Lexington or somewhere big to sell it."

"Maybe he'll get sick," Jacob piped up.

Travis chuckled. "Wouldn't be a bad thing, would it, boy?"

"I don't like hearing that sickness is in the county," Oleatha said, folding her arms across her belly. Everyone was quiet. It was like the boogeyman was camped out on the front porch.

Normally Oleatha would've been offering dessert about now, but, as Maggie cleared their plates, she knew there was nothing to serve. Without milk or eggs, it was hard to come up with anything resembling a treat. Travis must've been thinking along the same lines. "Oh, I brought you all something to thank you for the dinner."

"No need for that," Roy said. "You provided it."

Travis fumbled in his jacket. "You can't find a full Coke machine anywhere in the county, but folks haven't raided all the candy machines yet." Onto the table he splayed out four candy bars like they were a hand of cards. "Jacob gets first pick," he said.

Jacob's eyes grew round. "Candy!" He grabbed the bag of Skittles.

Maggie saw the Reese's Cups and knew he'd bought them for her, but she didn't reach for the orange package.

"Go on," Roy said to Oleatha. She grinned and took the Hershey's bar.

Travis reached out and slid the Reese's Cups to Maggie. He said, "Roy, did you know your daughter-in-law has never ridden a motorcycle?"

"Really?" The old man was much more interested in his Snickers.

Maggie slid her fingernail under the Reese's wrapper. "It's not like everybody's ridden a motorcycle."

"I have. Several times." Oleatha broke off a square of chocolate. "Remember that old bike you used to have?" She gave Roy a quirky smile that looked almost flirtatious. "Land, we'd go all over the county before the young'uns came along."

"I do," he said, smiling back at her as he chewed.

This led to a highly technical discussion of the old bike, its engine, and its fate. Maggie chose to concentrate on the sweet and salty flavors against the roof of her mouth.

Travis drawled, "Well, I was just thinking I might take our Maggie here for a ride some evening." That took Maggie's mind right off her chocolate bliss. She looked up in alarm.

"I think she should," Roy declared.

"Can I, Mr. Travis?" Jacob asked. Maggie shuddered at the thought; of course, she was shuddering pretty good at thought of taking a ride herself.

Travis said, "We'll see. Let your mama have her turn first."

"In the evening?" Maggie's voice was weak.

"That's the best time," Oleatha said. "Scarier, but that's part of the fun. I don't know how it would look, Travis, you giving a married woman a ride, but I reckon it couldn't do no harm."

Was this the Oleatha she knew? Well, Maggie thought, actually it was. She'd never known the woman to show fear. Spite maybe, but not fear.

Travis nodded as if this was settled and rose to put on his jacket. "I'll hunt again tomorrow, and then, if what I hear is right, I'll head to Corbin the day after to see what the Red Cross has to offer."

"I was going to go," Maggie murmured.

"I'd like it a fair sight better if you went with Travis," Roy said.

"I agree," said Travis.

He headed to the door, and after only a second of hesitation, Maggie followed him, catching up on the porch. "I have a favor to ask," she said.

He grinned. "Wanna go for that ride right now?"

She shook her head. "Take me with you tomorrow. I need to learn how to hunt."

He frowned. "You know I'll take care of you all as long as I'm able."

"I know. But I'd feel better if I knew how to provide."

He stared at her, his eyes probing for the truth.

"There's plenty of space," she said. "The freezer's empty."

"Be ready at five o'clock. Dress warm."

Chapter Eighteen

Waiting for Travis, Maggie knelt in front of the muted television to watch news channel scrolls across the bottom. Confirmed deaths were in the hundreds of thousands, soldiers were deployed to the largest cities to control looting, the vice president had okayed travel for emergency vehicles, the military, and food transport. Horrible facts raced across the bottom of the screen: bombings, foreign and domestic, troop fatalities, scams, robberies. Some people were recovering from the flu, but that didn't encourage her much. In another minute or two, Travis pulled his truck in front of the house, and she scurried out. She dreaded this. Guns and blood and killing. It went against everything she believed in.

"Good morning."

"Want coffee?" He gestured at a thermos.

She shook her head.

"I thought we'd drive south. Not so many people down there."

Not that any part of the county was over-populated.

"Heavily wooded. Might have some luck if nobody has cleared it out."

"Okay." The heater forced warm air into the truck cab. Almost cozy, if she could relax enough to think that way. Travis was talking about deer habits and habitats and then switched to the same topics for turkeys. His voice was low, soothing.

"Your father?" he asked, waking her into alertness.

"Doing better, actually." She'd talked to Tina after dinner last night. Although her sister could hardly talk for coughing, she'd said that Dad was going home today. He was better, and they needed his bed.

"That's great. And your sister?"

"I don't know. She claims she's getting well, but she's also complaining about shortness of breath and pain in her chest." Maggie took a deep breath like she was doing it for Tina.

"Still a worry, right?"

"Yes."

He drove past trailers and houses and churches and stores, all looking vacant in the gloom of dawn. They didn't see another car on the road. Travis slowed near one of the tiny churches and pulled into the parking lot. A sign read "Apostolic Church of Grace." It meant nothing to her.

"We're going to get out and do a little practice shooting here. I want to see how much you know and what kind of accuracy you have."

Maggie dragged herself from the warm cab. She'd asked for this.

"Do you prefer shotgun or rifle?"

She shrugged. "I don't know a thing about either one," she said. "I guess whichever one I do better with."

He pulled a rifle, a shotgun, and a bag of empty Coke cans from behind the seat. Handing her the rifle, he said, "It's loaded." Trotting behind him, she carried the gun awkwardly. "Stop there," he said and went on ahead to set Coke cans on a picnic table beside the church.

Joining her, he said, "Okay. Let's see what you can hit."

Maggie hardly knew how to hold it. He showed her, positioning the rifle into her shoulder, situating her arms and hands. He smelled like gun oil and coffee, cigarettes and male. "Okay, get a can in your sights and pull the trigger slow and steady."

Standing behind her, Travis held her shoulders, breathing into her hair. She gritted her teeth and fired. The cans stood still.

"You flinched. You can't do that, Maggie. The shot went way high. Roy taught me to shoot. He was always preaching site alignment and trigger control. You gotta practice both."

She nodded.

"Try again. Yeah, it's gonna be loud and it's gonna kick you a little, but not as much as the shotgun. You have to stay steady. Try again."

Steeling herself to stay still, she did better and hit the table this time. The damned cans mocked her. But by the next time, she hit one, and Travis patted her shoulder. "Okay, we need to move on before full daylight. We'll work with the shotgun next time."

"Is it easier?"

He packed up the cans and spent shells and shrugged. "You got buckshot with a shotgun, making it easier to hit something, but a rifle's cleaner." He grinned. "Oleatha won't have to pick pellets out of the meat."

He drove quite a ways, long enough for her heart to slow down, and then they walked through woods thick enough for briars to snag her jeans and branches to catch her hair. "Okay," he murmured. "For deer, you want the wind in your face, not at your back so they don't smell you. Let's hunker down here and see what comes along. We can't talk."

The sky lightened by inches. She heard rustlings and put her mouth close to his ear. "Snakes?" she whispered.

He shook his head. "Not this time of year," he mouthed.

She supposed hunting was a good lesson in patience and figured Jacob was learning it when he fished with Roy. Her stomach growled, bringing a smile from Travis. She wanted to check her phone, but kept it in her back pocket, turned off. Her feet were cold.

After what seemed like hours, Travis nudged her. In the clearing below a rabbit hopped into view and then was still. She positioned the rifle, took a deep breath, and aimed for its head. She missed and the rabbit scampered into the brush. "It's okay," Travis said.

"But if you'd shot, you would've gotten it."

He grinned at her. "You said you wanted to learn."

They walked again, up a rocky hill to a clearer area where there was a trickle of a stream, sparkling in the sun. She couldn't feel enough breeze to determine anything, but Travis seemed to sense things she couldn't. Again they waited, loaded and ready. She halfway hoped nothing would come their way.

And she got her wish. After another hour or so, Travis said they should give it up for the day. All the way home, he encouraged her, insisting she'd get better. Nothing like practice for improvement. In front of the house, he said, "Another early start tomorrow. Gotta get to Corbin before the food's gone."

She nodded. "Five again?"

"Sounds right."

Oleatha looked up when she came in shaking her head. Turning to Roy, Maggie said, "Will you help me learn to shoot?"

He grinned. "I can do that."

❖

The restless prisoners had been quiet for twenty-four hours, Luke thought. Of course it helped that Angela had come to the kitchen at five a.m. and managed to bake large muffins full of cinnamon and applesauce. Delicious. Ilse and Connie were cleaning up while he gathered the trash and took it behind the mess hall where other bags were stacked three deep, waiting for someone, anyone to haul them away.

He sniffed the morning air. Good thing it was cool or the garbage would be creating a massive stink. He checked his phone for about the fourteenth time. Nothing from anybody. Rieselman had fallen through the country's ever-deepening cracks, he figured, but he was going to keep trying. He'd pester the soldiers at the gate and the medical people again this morning.

Last night he'd actually sat in the recreation room watching the news with the last two Broody Hens. Coverage was focused on military action against suspected perpetrators of the virus. Bombings in the Middle East, round-ups of terrorists in Britain and France. Okay, retribution. But that wasn't feeding or healing people. They showed truckloads of rotting produce and meat lingering at warehouses, CDC scientists working night and day on a vaccine, the impossibility of keeping up with corpse disposal, and people robbing houses, stores, and businesses, looking for food.

He called Maggie. Last night she'd been bemoaning the fact that she'd missed getting a rabbit for dinner. Things down home were worse than she'd let on, he figured, although he couldn't imagine his mother running out of food in three weeks.

"Hello, honey," she chirped.

He heard music in the background and cheer in her voice. "You sound perky," he said.

"Travis and I are driving to Corbin for Red Cross giveaways," she said. "We're hoping for great things. Have you had any deliveries?"

"No." His little flash of jealousy shamed him. Luke was glad Travis Parker was helping out, doing what he would've done if he'd been there. But it had been 'Travis and I' an awful lot recently. "How's Jacob?"

She went on about everybody, sounding optimistic about her father and sister, laughing a little about shooting lessons with Roy. It made him feel hollow, but he continued chatting until her phone started breaking up.

He walked back into the kitchen. Of course, Maggie might misconstrue the hour he'd spent holding Jill while her tears soaked his sweatshirt, grieving for her mother, but it still bothered him about Travis.

❖

"This song makes me want to dance," Maggie declared, bobbing her head in rhythm to whatever country song it was.

"You like to dance?" Travis asked.

She nodded. "I never danced to music like this, but yeah, I love to dance." She gazed at occasional small houses, squatting down against the land, mountains dwarfing them. "It makes me feel free." She paused and smiled. "Like your motorcycle."

Travis smiled. "What kind of dancing do you do?"

"Oh, I don't anymore. But I took ballet for years until Dad left us and there wasn't money for it. Classical music. You know." Or maybe he didn't.

"I've never known a ballerina before. Pretty cool, Maggie."

She tossed her head. People around here wouldn't know much about ballet, she figured. No sense talking about it. "How much farther?" she asked.

"Maybe ten miles. On the way back I'm going to need gas."

She frowned. "Where can you get it?" Roy had said that gas stations in the area were all closed. Maybe not just in the area either.

"I got my little ways."

A long line of vehicles snaked around the high school, reaching all the way to the road and closing a lane. "And we thought we were getting here early," said Travis. He glanced at his watch. "They aren't supposed to start for another hour."

Maggie peered at the line. "Guess everybody's getting hungry." She told him about Luke's situation.

"It doesn't make sense that they're still keeping them locked in."

"No, but I guess they figure some of them might still get sick."

"People get sick out here too. Three deaths in Catesboro yesterday."

God, she didn't want to think about it. "They probably don't know how to get Luke and his people home even if they wanted to."

They inched forward enough that she could see the sign by the big red cross. 'Unlatch your trunk now. Then remain in your vehicle. Move slowly.' Okay, she thought. They could do that.

Her phone rang: Tina. Maggie threw an apologetic look at Travis and said hello.

"Well, she's done it again," Tina croaked. She paused to cough, a horrible-sounding spasm that hurt Maggie just to listen to it. "She talked the lady who lives upstairs from her into picking her up from the rehab facility. She's been home since last night and sounds like she's drinking again. What should I do?"

Maggie gripped the phone. "Not a damned thing, Tina. I mean it. If she kills herself, she kills herself. You're in no shape to be taking care of Mom."

"No, I'm not," Tina whispered. "Well, just wanted you to know."

Just wanted to transfer the guilt, Maggie thought, but for years the two of them had passed off guilt like a baton in a relay race. It was the way the Hausers conducted their lives. "Get some medical care," Maggie urged.

"I'm okay. Fever's gone. Anyway, they're saying nearly a fourth of the doctors are sick or dead. There wouldn't be anyone to help me if I did go somewhere."

"There would be help. Please Tina."

There was a garbled cough and a breathless good-bye.

"Is she bad?" Travis asked.

Maggie nodded. "And stubborn. I've tried to help most of her life, but she only hears what she wants to hear." She stared out the window. "And now my idiotic mother has skipped rehab and is back drinking."

"So your daddy left you all a long time ago?" Travis's voice was soft.

"Yeah. Way back." While they were waiting there was nothing else to do, so she told him about her family and all its problems. Keeping family secrets seemed silly, a civility that had no meaning in impolite times. He sympathized and reciprocated, talking about his failed marriage.

"I got everything wrong," he said, shrugging. "We met at a honkytonk. I was ready to settle down and thought she was. I wanted a kid and thought she did. Wrong on both counts. She cheated from the get go. I knew it but let it pass for a while, thinking she would straighten out. Wrong again."

It was her turn to make sympathetic noises and even pat his hand. The truck wound around the first turn of the school building. She was hoping for flour to make bread and maybe bacon or eggs or apples. It was apple season. Maybe even cider? She turned to glance at the truck bed. Empty and spotless, ready for a big haul. Travis had fastened a sign to the back window that said, "Two families." It was sort of true.

"I hope everything's okay back home," she said.

"Northern Kentucky home or Roy's?"

"Here. I hated to leave those three on their own."

"I sneaked down to Coughlin's last night and nobody's there yet."

After two hours of idling in a crawl, Maggie grew impatient. She needed a bathroom. Constant country music was getting on her nerves. But Travis seemed serene, like a man used to waiting. When they finally reached the distribution point, a woman in surgical scrubs and mask lowered the gate, and a similarly dressed man heaved a box and a couple of bags into the bed. The man hit the gate with his gloved hand, and Travis pulled forward, moving faster than they had in hours.

Maggie let out a long breath, and Travis said, "Bet you're dying to see what's back there."

She grinned. Pulling into an empty Wendy's parking lot, he stopped the truck, and they got out.

The two sacks were five pound bags of pinto beans and rice. Useful, she thought, but not exciting. Travis pulled items from the box.

"Dry milk, a huge chunk of cheese, butter, noodles, five cans each of green beans and peaches."

Disappointed, Maggie nodded. "Better than nothing, I guess."

"It'll help."

"At least Jacob can have the macaroni and cheese he's been wanting."

Chapter Nineteen

Travis didn't follow the same route back, so there was no way she could tell how far they'd come. She was squirming to the point where she'd have to ask him to stop the truck soon, when he pulled into a gas station that looked as old as a black and white TV. It was deserted.

Travis had about a thousand keys on his ring but knew the right one for opening the door. "Bathroom's that way. I'm gonna pump some gas."

The cubicle was clean enough, except for a thick ring of gray mold in the bowl. Hadn't been flushed in forever, she thought, and closed her eyes in relief. After washing her hands, she looked around the old place. It still had a two bay garage for repairs. No attached convenience store. No lottery tickets. Behind the counter a rack of maps and a stack of motor oil cans stood on a shelf filled with auto belts and bulbs. Functional, but not helpful for a woman hunting and gathering for her people.

"Hang on a minute," Travis said. He went to the counter and jotted something on a legal pad. "Before you start thinking that I'm stealing again, I've left a note for my buddy, telling him how much gas I pumped." He threw her an evil grin.

She smiled back. "I'll never accuse you of stealing again."

He opened the door into the garage and motioned for her to follow, pointing to a dilapidated vinyl sofa with its stuffing poking out. Then he went to a closet and brought out two canned Cokes. "Warm but better than nothing." Turning, he switched on a radio sandwiched between an air compressor and an ancient, red battery tester. She remembered seeing one like it in her grandmother's garage. He handed her the Coke. "Don't know about you, but I need a little rest."

She popped the top and drank long and deep. He lit a cigarette.

"Who's that singing?" she asked.

"Reba. You've heard of her, haven't you? Even up in the big city?"

He loved to tease her. "Yes, even way up there."

He narrowed his eyes against the smoke. "I work some weekends down here doing repairs for the owner. We take care of each other."

"Where is he?"

"At home in Catesboro, I suppose. I haven't called him."

"Are you going to move back there?" She dreaded his answer.

He knuckled his beard. "Not anytime soon. I can't see people coming in for timing belts and new tires. My boss said to give it another week, and I sort of like living down in Mamaw's house. Besides, I don't like leaving you all down there with Coughlin and his crew."

"I worry anytime we're gone from there. Do you think he'll come back and bother us again?"

"If he needs money for his drugs, yeah, he'll be back."

Maggie shuddered, gesturing toward the radio to cover it up. "And who's that singing?" She didn't want to think about that gun aimed at Jacob.

"Alan Jackson."

She listened, feeling the beat, and looked around the shabby workplace, oil spots on the concrete floor, light dimmed by grubby windows. It felt warm in a weird way, though, a place where men would sing along while they worked and eat their lunchtime sandwiches with stained fingers.

"Want another Coke?" Travis asked.

"No, thanks."

He walked over and turned up the volume on the radio. "So you said you can dance ballet. Did you wear those funky shoes, the ones with the squared off toes?"

"Toe shoes. No. I wasn't old enough, but the teacher said I'd be going into them the next year. If I'd stayed." She had to smile at the thought of Madame Roberta, a fat old monster who'd once danced with the Cincinnati Ballet. She'd worn swathes of shawls that probably should have gone in a Good Will bag. Actually, Madame Roberta resembled a Good Will bag. "I did wear a tutu a few times."

He knew what one was. "Bet you thought you were hot shit."

Grinning, Maggie nodded. "A princess. I danced between the Schuler twins at the Lions Club Christmas Party. Those old coots gave each of us a bracelet that turned me green the first time I wore it."

"Do you still do it?"

"Dance?" She hooted. "No. But I do remember the five positions."

"Let me see."

She gave him a skeptical look.

"No, I'm serious. Show me."

After an exaggerated sigh, Maggie stood. "First position," she said, arranging her hands and feet just so. It felt strange to do it in gym shoes, so she slid out of them and then shed her socks. The concrete was cold under her feet. "Now second." Travis smiled like her dad used to do when she'd show off. She moved again. "Third and then fourth." She assumed the fifth position and raised her chin, pretending she was the Sugar Plum Fairy. "And fifth."

"That last one twists you up like a pretzel, doesn't it?" he asked, laughing. Then he clapped. "Bravo, Maggie Ballerina. Now do a little dance."

She'd already slid back onto the sofa. "I couldn't do that. I don't remember anything."

"Betcha do. Come on. There's nobody here but us chickens."

The music right then was lively, a conglomeration of fiddle and guitar with a man whooping it up about women in Texas. Ballet could certainly be lively, but she sure as hell wasn't up to that. "I need slower music," she said.

"I know just the right song." Travis went out to his truck, coming back with a cd and inserting it into the radio. A few bars of sweet, melancholy piano came through the speakers. "Now. No more excuses."

The tune was in three. She straightened, remembering to let the center of her body have all her power. Then she began a series of steps, a *plie*, a few more steps, a *releve*, an *arabesqu*e, a change in the combination, and then a modest pirouette. While it was a far cry from Tchaikovsky, the music moved her. At one time music, and dancing, had meant everything to her, but she'd forbidden herself from thinking about it after her father left. The male singer sounded sad, but she paid little attention to the lyrics other than noticing that he was talking about a dance. She tilted her head, shaping her neck like the stalk of a flower as Madame Roberta had said they must do, and moved a bit more to the right and then to the left. Then, as she heard the singer finish and the song resolve once more into bittersweet piano chords, she posed, hands gracefully twisted in front of her, and bowed her head. Not half bad for an out-of-practice, old woman, she told herself. Her turnouts were still pretty good.

When Maggie raised her head, Travis was watching her, eyes intent and mouth open like he'd had a shock. Then he smiled and clapped, pausing only to bring his fingers to his mouth and emit a shrieking whistle. She'd always wanted to be able to do that. "Jesus, Maggie. You should've kept up with it." His voice was soft, like he was in church rather than a shabby gas station. "You ought to start back. They have classes for adults, don't they?"

A little breathless, she sat, shrugging off his compliments. "I guess. Maybe I should. It's terrific exercise and would be a lot more fun than going to a gym." She was sweating under her hair.

He touched her cheek with one finger. "You're amazing. I've never seen anything like it."

She didn't suppose he had. Her feet were black but she stuffed them back into her socks and shoes. "Don't you think we'd better be getting back?"

It was like she'd shaken him awake. "Yeah."

❖

During the rest of the trip, she pumped Travis for more information.

"I figured with Roy and the boy being gone so much, you and Oleatha might've been watching the television."

"Oleatha never offers to turn it on. I think she's scared and that has more to do with her saying we can't watch than Jacob. Tell me."

"Are you sure? You've got enough troubles."

She nodded, and he started talking in clipped sentences. Hospitals were overflowing. In the big cities they were using schools or hotels to house patients. And the flu had invaded Europe, mostly France and Spain. No one terrorist group had claimed responsibility for the virus, but there was speculation that it might be a united effort between two or three of them. They'd identified all of the twelve carriers who'd left from three different European cities. They were dead. Some places were banning funerals. The governor of Kentucky had cancelled school until the first of December. She bowed her head during his recitation and was staring at her clasped hands as he wound down. And no one knew what to make about the president's absence. The vice-president refused to take the oath of office.

Travis folded his hand over hers. "I knew you wouldn't want to hear it."

"Maybe Oleatha's right not to listen. Ignorance, bliss, all that."

"Maybe so. But they are saying that most people who die from it do so in the first forty-eight hours. That's good news for Tina, isn't it?"

She looked up. "Yes, if there are no complications. My dad ended up with pneumonia."

"And he made it, didn't he? Try not to worry."

❖

"This is like Christmas," Oleatha declared, peeking into the back of the truck.

"Is it Christmas?" Jacob asked.

"It's not even Thanksgiving yet, Jake." Travis mock-punched the boy's shoulder. He gave him the chunk of cheese, nearly as big as his head.

Roy took the beans and rice. Maggie lifted the box of canned goods. "Don't guess dry milk is much punkin, but it beats a blank." Travis handed this to Oleatha.

"I'm glad to have it," she said. "And you must join us for supper every evening."

Travis was protesting when Maggie's phone rang. She didn't recognize the number or the voice at first. She hurried to the front porch.

"Maggie?" Andy's voice was ragged as a ripped shirt. "It's Tina." He didn't, or couldn't, say anything more for a second.

"What? What?"

She heard a raw, rattling breath. "I took her to the hospital right after she talked to you this morning. She couldn't breathe; she was almost unconscious." He paused again. "We had to wait and wait, her just lying there on the stretcher gasping for air."

"Oh Andy." Maggie knew what was coming.

"Pulmonary embolism, they said. They put her on a respirator, but they told me it wasn't doing any good. They needed the machine for someone else." He paused. "Did I do wrong? I said they could take her off."

Maggie couldn't possibly know, but she remembered Roy and Oleatha's discussion about prolonging life. "No, you didn't do wrong."

"She died an hour ago, Maggie." He said her name on a sob, and she clutched the post.

"Are you all right? Are you home?"

"I'm not sick," he said. "Yeah. I'm home." His voice had gone so quiet that Maggie squeezed the phone against her ear. "No funerals, they said. Just dump her in the ground." He cried now, really cried, the athlete who'd been a high school football coach for two years now. Tina's cocky, tough, over-protective high school sweetheart, just the kind of husband she'd choose.

"I'm so sorry, Andy. Call someone to come over, you hear?" Tears flooded Maggie's cheeks. She didn't have any words for him, any comfort to give him. "I, I'll call you back," she faltered. "I can't talk any more right now."

She stuffed the phone in her pocket, barely aware of Oleatha and Travis hovering at the front door. "Not Luke," Oleatha murmured.

Maggie didn't turn around. She shook her head and strode off the porch and down the road, toward the creek. "My sister," she said and kept walking, fast. Behind her she heard Oleatha say, "Maybe she wants to be alone," and Travis growl, "The hell she does."

Maggie paid them no mind. For some reason she was thinking of the night after Dad left, when Tina, a great big ten-year-old, had climbed into Maggie's bed and asked if the monsters would get out of their cages now that Daddy was gone. She'd hugged her little sister and said that of course they wouldn't, that Daddy had given Maggie the keys to keep them locked up.

It'd been childish for a girl that old, but Tina'd always been childish. Maggie'd made sure she'd been allowed to be.

She stumbled over a rock in the road and nearly fell. "Hold on," Travis said from behind her. "Slow down, Maggie. You're gonna bust your knees."

Head bowed, she stopped beside the rock where she and Jacob had sat on that warm day a few weeks ago. Travis had caught up to her. "I promised Daddy. I told him I'd take care of my little sister. I promised."

The words gushed from her mouth like the tears from her eyes. "When Mom set the apartment on fire, I got Tina out. When Mom's horrible boyfriend tried to touch Tina, I threatened him with the police. I tried. I moved her in with me as soon as I could afford an apartment and made sure she did her homework and got through college." She looked up, not at Travis who was standing by the rock but at the stubbled field across the creek, winter barren and desolate. "And for what? So she could die of this horrible flu?" A muscle twitched near her eye. She shivered.

Travis wrapped his jacket around her, guiding her arms into the sleeves. It was his hunting jacket and smelled of leaves, woods, and tobacco. It held his warmth. "Maggie," he murmured.

She kept talking. "Just a month ago she told me that they were trying to have a baby. They'd been saving and were going to buy a house close to her school. With a yard for a baby."

He coaxed her into sitting on the rock and then sat beside her, pulling her close, using his body as shelter. She rested her head on his shoulder. "She was always Dad's girl, not me. She mourned and mourned when he left. I was glad to have the fighting over, but Tina wasn't. She wanted to move to Colorado to be with Dad, and it broke her heart when he wouldn't let her. Mom didn't care one way or the other." Maggie sniffed. "Or maybe she did. Mom said so many crazy things when she was drinking that I never knew."

Travis held her, not telling her to hush but making little sounds like the ones she used to calm Jacob. She lifted her shirt tail and wiped at her nose and wet cheeks, trying to calm down. "Poor Andy," she whispered into Travis's collarbone. She felt him nod.

"You did take care of her," he said. "You gave her the best life she could have, even if it was short. You spared her the worst of it, you know you did. You stood up and took the punches for her, didn't you?"

She nodded. She'd have to call Andy back and Dad, if he was in any kind of shape to hear such dreadful news. And Mom. She'd bet Andy hadn't called her. He considered Donna the worst sort of mother. And he was right. She must call Luke. He'd always liked Tina. She amused him with her little jokes and flirty ways, running from anything serious like the monsters she'd once feared. "She was the pretty one," Maggie murmured. "I was the smart one."

"Smart keeps; pretty spoils," Travis said.

Despite her sorrow, a choked little chuckle caught in her throat. "You make it sound like food."

"Not much different."

Maggie concentrated on the creek, burbling as it flowed over rocks and spread wider into the deep water where Roy and Jacob caught their fish. "The world's going to be a different place after this sickness," she said. "We're all going to lose people. We'll all be wounded."

He squeezed her, just for a second. "That's why we gotta take care of the ones we have."

Suddenly she was too anxious to sit. "I have calls to make."

"Sure."

They eased up the hill. Travis kept his hand on her back as if he could transfer something to her. She didn't know what.

"There were a few more things in the truck," he said, pausing to peer in.

"Roy must've gotten them." Maggie gave him his jacket. "Thank you."

"I'm sorry," he whispered and pressed his lips against her temple, right at the hairline.

Chapter Twenty

He and Angela had heated up canned beef stew for breakfast. She turned up her nose at it, but they served it anyway. He'd hardly slept for worrying about Maggie. Tina, that bright little butterfly of a girl, dead. He couldn't speak for his anger, raging at the world, the military, the government, God. When Luke slopped stew on French's plate, the man murmured, "Okay?"

Luke had said no, his sister-in-law was dead. And now, as he was washing congealed stew off the giant pot they'd used, it took all his discipline not to throw pans and lids. He was scrubbing hard when Jill raced up behind him. Lord, she looked bad. Thin, gray, unkempt. Ilse had been commenting on this last night, but Luke didn't know what he could do about it. Hell, he couldn't do a thing about any of the problems, big or small.

She was screeching. "Hurry! Josh at front gate." She had no breath. "Connie. Hostage. Gunpoint."

He flew through the mess hall, dripping water behind him. He didn't wait for Jill. He wished he had his gun, but it was in his room. Up ahead, he saw Josh, right at the gate, his left arm holding Connie in front of him, his right holding a pistol to her neck. Maybe a dozen people stood well away from him. He registered Ilse and French. The soldiers were poised to shoot. "No," Luke shouted. "Let me talk to him." He slowed his pace, holding his hands away from his body. "Josh. Hey, Josh. It's Luke."

Josh stood steady, facing the gate. Connie whimpered. The gun was dull silver, double action. Less likely to fire from a nervous twitch. Hell, why hadn't they found it in Josh's room? Was it loaded?

"Stop, sir." A command from the other side of the fence, a sergeant. "Now, sir."

He stopped. No way Josh could see him unless he turned his face, and he wouldn't do that, Luke was sure. "Stand down, buddy. We can work something out." He made his speech slow and soft. "Drop the gun. You wouldn't want to hurt Connie. We all love Connie." The sun glistened off her tear-soaked face.

"I am hungry and I want to go home." Josh got louder. "Arrange transport for me and I will release her."

Luke glanced at the soldiers. The sergeant was listening to his phone. The others were taut as trip wire. "Where's home, Josh? Is it much of a drive from here? Will we need a plane?"

He watched the man shake his head a touch. "St. Louis. Not so far."

The sergeant looked at Luke. "Keep him talking. We've got this."

A wave of nausea swept through Luke. No, he thought. No. "We can talk this out, Josh. I'm the boss, right? We can get you to St. Louis."

"No, you can't." Josh nodded at the gate. "They can."

"Well, okay. We'll work together." Luke stared at the sergeant, mouthed 'no' and shook his head. The man didn't respond.

"Please drop the gun, Josh. Please."

Silence.

"What are you waiting for?" screamed Josh. "I'll kill her."

Luke heard moans behind him. He stepped forward.

"You must move back, sir," barked the sergeant.

He took a step back. He knew. God, he knew. "Please, Josh. Now, for God's sake. Drop it now."

"Please." Luke said to the sergeant, not Josh.

Where would it come from? Not the gate. He was afraid to take his eyes off Josh to look for the sniper. Could he rush him without Connie being shot? Maybe, maybe. And then a crack split the silence and Josh was down, pulling Connie with him.

In seconds, French was helping Connie up and enveloping her. Ilse knelt by Josh, checking for a pulse. There wouldn't be one. The sniper had fired a neat surgical bullet in the side of Josh's skull. Ilse rose and strode to the gate. Tears running down her cheeks, she grabbed the metal. "You didn't have to do that," she shouted. "We could've handled it. He's sick, not evil."

Jill grabbed Luke's hand. "Not your fault. You tried."

He couldn't move, let alone speak. Like drowning a puppy, like stepping on a bug. "Will they give him dignity now?" Jill asked.

Luke shook his head. French had Connie up and walking. The pilot spoke to Angela, "Is there tea or anything?"

She nodded.

"Come on, folks. Let's go to the mess hall," French said and led his dispirited flock away from the scene.

Luke couldn't move. Ilse was still giving the sergeant hell, questioning his ethics and demanding food. When she ran out of steam, she grabbed Luke's arm. "Come. There's nothing more to do."

Luke shook his head. Raising his hands above his head, he moved to Josh's side. The soldiers were watching him. He picked up the pistol, pointing it down. They'd shoot him in a second. He locked the slide back and checked the chamber. Empty. Luke tossed the gun toward the gate. "It wasn't even loaded," he screamed. He screamed it again and walked away.

In the mess hall, people had gathered around Connie and French was praying. Luke went into the kitchen where Angela was boiling water for tea and making coffee. He headed back to the sink where he'd left the dirty stew pot and stared out the window at the stacked garbage, waiting and rotting.

He stomped out the back door, picking up two of the garbage bags and marching down the long path. Right at the gate he heaved first one, then the other bag over the fence, listening to them land with satisfying plops, hoping they would burst and spew their noxious contents. He strode back and got two more and then two more. His shoulder muscles protested the throwing; sweat drenched his face. He wore no coat but he was on fire. Josh, Bob, Tina, thousands, maybe millions more out there suffering and dying. Two more and then two more. One broke, spreading coffee grounds and chicken bones and a ferocious stink that fueled his anger. Maggie's broken voice. Josh's broken body.

He went back for more, ignoring those who were watching him at the doorway. French said something, but Luke ignored it. He grabbed bags. He threw bags. His hands shook. Sweat clouded his eyes. Over the fence again and again until all the garbage lay outside the fence like dozens of body bags in a pile. And then he stopped.

❖

They were good to her. Oleatha made her a cup of tea, adding a huge dollop of honey to it. Roy and Travis put the food away. But Maggie made macaroni and cheese for their dinner, telling Oleatha she needed something to do. Jacob was thrilled, but Travis didn't show up. Maggie hadn't the energy to wonder why.

She called her father. Dad had been too weak to talk, so Maggie'd told Jody who, for once, was shocked into near silence. Nobody answered the phone at Donna's, and Maggie felt a jolt of worry. She'd tried two more times without getting an answer but didn't know who to ask to check on her. Certainly not Andy. Maggie had felt better about him when she called back. She heard relatives and friends in the background, but he was still agonizing over his decision to take Tina off the respirator, and nothing Maggie said seemed to ease him. Finally she'd repeated Roy's observation about health care a hundred years ago, and Andy said, "I hadn't thought of that. It's true."

So far the hardest thing had been telling Jacob. He adored his pretty Aunt Tina who'd finger-painted with him and let him do whatever he wanted when he came to visit. One time she'd let him have a spoon and a whole container of Rocky Road and refused to let Maggie take it away from him. His only experience with death had been a goldfish or two who'd floated ominously at the top of the bowl, but he did understand that it was the sickness that was causing all this. He fretted that his daddy might get sick, and Maggie didn't know how to reassure him.

The next day Maggie was drinking another cup of tea while Oleatha rooted around in her cabinets. "I wonder why Travis didn't eat with us last night. I made it plain that we expected him."

Maggie shook her head. She wanted to hide, to crawl down into the warm mug and stay there.

"Here," Oleatha said, setting down a plastic bowl and a lump of something covered in foil. "I want you to take some macaroni and cheese and cornbread up to Travis. I bet he don't have anything much at his place."

Maggie knew what Oleatha was doing. She'd fabricated a reason to distract Maggie and send her out in the fresh air. Maggie didn't want to move, but she went to find her jacket.

Fog had filled the holler all day. It was like clouds had drifted off from their partners and gotten lost there, trapped. She stepped into it, unable to see more than a few feet ahead. Other than Coughlin's roosters, she heard no birds, but as she came closer to Travis's house, she did hear the screech of nails being pulled from wood and the thunk of boards thrown in a pile. Maggie stopped to watch him tear up the front porch. His back was to her, and he wore a grimy sweatshirt and his UK Wildcat hat. To the side of the porch was a stack of blistered, broken boards along with at least half a dozen empty beer cans. "Hello," she called out.

He didn't turn around. "Go home, Maggie," he said. "I ain't in a mood for visiting." His soft accent had turned into a rough mountain growl.

"Oleatha sent you food. She expected you for supper last night."

He took his pry bar to the porch like he intended to kill it. "Thank her for me." A board shrieked.

She walked past him, setting the food on the hood of his truck. "Maybe you'll want it later," she said and started back the way she'd come.

He faced her, his eyes glittering. He muttered, "I ain't fit company."

She waited.

"Drunk," he mumbled. The fog was close, shutting them off from everything familiar about the place. "Know you got a problem with drunks." He turned away from her. "Sorry."

She kept waiting, half expecting him to start railing about the state of the world, about how death was seeping into their lives like fog in the holler, but he kept silent.

Giving it a vicious tug, he ripped the board up with his hands. "Seems like I never deal with nothing that ain't broken," he muttered. "Can't ever build nothing new. All I'm good for is fixing things for other people."

"Travis."

"Get out of here," he snarled. "Can't be responsible." The last words were a whisper.

❖

It was after dark when Maggie's phone sounded, gave up, and sounded again. She was alone in the kitchen, putting beans to soak for the next day. Heart racing, she rushed out the back door, hoping for better reception. It rang again.

"Maggie?" His voice was weak, but it was her father.

"I'm here."

"Are you okay, honey?"

"I'm okay, I guess."

He cleared his throat. "I can't believe we lost Tina. This damned flu." He sounded angry. Maggie supposed that was all right, but she was too numb to feel anything at all. He went on. "I called Andy. He's holding up."

"Yes. But I can't reach Mom. She left rehab, but she's not answering her phone. I don't know where she is." Maggie imagined her mother lying dead in her apartment.

"Can't worry about that." Maybe he thought that sounded harsh. He repeated himself. "You can't. She makes her own decisions. Always has."

"I know. But."

"No buts. You're healthy? You and Jacob?"

"Yes."

"And Luke?"

"Yes. But he's a million miles away."

"Jody told me. So sorry."

She chewed at her lip.

"I'm getting better. Eating now and starting to get a little strength. When all this is over, I'm coming to see you and Luke and Jacob. Maybe we can have a memorial service for Tina. Would that be a good idea?"

"Andy would probably like that."

"Then that's what we'll do."

There wasn't much more to say. She clicked her phone and wandered into the living room where Jacob turned wide eyes away from the television. "It's okay, Jacob. Your other Grandpa is getting better and wants to see you soon." She turned to Roy. "You think we might have another shooting lesson tomorrow?"

The old man nodded. "If the fog'll hold off."

❖

The rest of the morning, Luke hid himself in his room. Still boiling but resolute, he skipped lunch to hike back to the CO's house, to unlock the back door and leave it that way. He hadn't told anyone where the guns were, but he was going to. They might need them. Nearing the front gate, he saw a kind of cross, made from what looked like unscrewed table legs. Attached was a sign written in red crayon: HONOR JOSH MONROE, GIVE US FOOD AND SEND US HOME. He glanced at the disinterested sentry. "Make sure your sergeant sees this, soldier. That's an order."

He shook his head as he walked to the women's barracks, to a room at the end of the hall where the deceased's belongings were stored. Jill had made a personal ritual of sorting through the items, labeling and packing them in the bags and backpacks of the dead. Clearly written nametags and dates of death were attached to each. Like a sort of dog tag, Luke thought. No one knew how the medical facility disposed of bodies.

He found the kid, Todd's, backpack and unpacked it, making a neat pile of his things with the label on top. It was a good bag, sturdy and large with comfortable straps. He looted other bags, finding some clean socks in one, a Swiss army knife in another. Grabbing a heavy sweater that looked about his size and a small travel pillow with airplanes on it, he stuffed it all in the bag. The pillow had belonged to one of the kids, he thought. He silently apologized. Back in his room, he packed Briley's money and his own toiletries and underwear. He was ready.

❖

All apologetic, Travis showed up the next night for supper, with an air pistol and bb's for Jacob and a box of Jello for Oleatha. He wouldn't meet Maggie's eyes.

"Did you listen to the speech this afternoon?" Roy asked, dishing up pinto beans and rice. The vice president had spoken; actually he was president now. The previous one was alive, he said, but had resigned the position.

"Yeah. For what it was worth," Travis said. "They're going to get supplies running again, but then he said folks should stay home for at least another week. You know people will get out the minute they think there's gasoline or food. It doesn't make sense. And the past guy is a coward. Great leadership." His mouth turned down.

"They said his daughter died, that he couldn't face up to his duties after that." Oleatha had heard it all from her cronies.

Roy sniffed. "Not man enough for the job. I didn't vote for him."

"Can I hunt something with this?" Jacob asked. The pistol sat next to his plate of untouched beans. He'd eaten the rice.

"Well, no," Roy said. "But you can work on your aim for when you're big enough to shoot a gun."

Maggie scrunched her shoulder, feeling the soreness from her lengthy shooting lesson with Roy. He said she'd improved a lot, was actually turning into a 'darned good shot.' She stared at Travis until he looked at her. For a second. "How's the porch coming?"

"I've taken off all the boards and begged some wood off a buddy of mine." What she could see of his cheeks reddened. "I wondered if I might borrow your power saw, Roy."

Roy said he could, but there were three kinds of saws up in the shed. They spent some time discussing what Travis would need.

"Three bites," Maggie whispered to Jacob. "Or no dessert."

The boy gave her a long look and then tried out his grandmother who raised an eyebrow. Sighing, he took a bite of beans.

"Are you fixing up the place so you can live there?" Roy asked.

"Maybe. Nothing else to do right now." Travis wiped his mouth and smiled at Oleatha. "Mighty good food," he said. "I called my boss today, and he said that he went to the dealership last week and didn't see a soul."

"There's peach crisp," Oleatha announced. It was actually canned peaches with crumbled cornmeal, butter, sugar, and cinnamon on top. Jacob had tried the beans, so she nodded at him.

"I'm full as a tick," Travis said. "Not big on sweets anyhow."

This was a lie but Maggie figured he was trying not to eat much of their food. He was thinner than when she'd first met him, but then her jeans were held up by a belt she'd found in Marla's things. In her head she could almost hear Tina joking, a weight loss opportunity! Lord, she missed her.

Travis put on his jacket. She remembered its warmth. "Heard from Luke?" he asked as he passed her, meeting her eyes this time.

And this time she was the one who looked away. She had no idea why Travis Parker had been drunk or ugly to her the day before, but she wasn't going to give him much. "Not today."

"Well, thanks for supper," Travis said. "I spotted a couple of wild turkeys up at the head of the holler. You want to come with me tomorrow morning, Maggie?"

"Yes."

"Bet she gets one," said Roy.

Travis patted Jacob's head. "You get your grandpa to set you up some targets and practice with that pistol. Before long you'll be hunting turkeys."

Jacob beamed, but Maggie turned to the sink.

❖

Luke made himself lie down, doubting that he'd sleep, but he did and even dreamt. This time he was on patrol in Afghanistan, and a tiny, old man had jumped out in front of them and started waving his arms, babbling away about something. Their translator yelled, "Stop!" and the driver did. "He says there are IEDs down this road."

"But our orders say they've been neutralized here," Luke said.

"Fuck the orders," said the translator. "Turn back."

Barren rocks enclosed the road. "I can't turn around," the driver said.

In the dream, Luke shook his head. "We have to go on. There's no place to turn."

"Turn back!" screeched the translator. The old man was still gesticulating, his withered face full of terror.

Luke's phone buzzed. He was at Rieselman, not Afghanistan. With a shaky hand, he picked it up. It was someone in the military saying there'd be a shipment of food in two days. Luke sat on the edge of his bunk, pulling himself out of the dream, the fear. Good news about the food, he supposed. Made him feel a little less guilty.

It was late afternoon. He'd decided the perfect time would be an hour or so after midnight. People were asleep by then. He'd found some batteries in the kitchen for the flashlight so he didn't need daylight to pick the lock. He considered stealing a bit of food but didn't want to leave the camp with less to eat even if they were delivering supplies soon. He wished he had internet so he could see a map. His phone server had cut off access weeks ago. He glanced at his water bottle, a disposable one that he kept refilling from the faucet. Yeah, he'd fill it and stuff it in the bag.

❖

They walked up the hill, Maggie carrying Roy's Enfield. She liked the feel of it better than Travis's rifle, although he'd laughed and asked if she was going to an antique show. Neither of them said much as they climbed. She could hear roosters and asked Travis if Coughlin was back. "Yeah," he said. "Yesterday."

That news tightened her chest, but she couldn't worry about it now. They needed meat, and she meant to get some. Travis gestured for her to follow him off the gravel into a thicket. Maggie had borrowed a ball cap from Roy; it had a Cincinnati Reds logo on it, a gift from Luke to his father. It kept the branches from grabbing her hair. Ahead of them a shallow dip in the land turned into a field of tangled weeds and dead wildflowers. Dawn painted it pink, so it looked prettier than it was. Travis crouched down at the edge of the clearing and motioned for Maggie to join him. "They were here yesterday," he whispered.

She wondered if that meant the turkeys would revisit the spot today. She ran her fingers over the rifle's stock, trying to remember everything Roy had taught her. But her mind slipped into its usual round of repeating worries: Andy, Coughlin, Luke. Roy was out of his blood pressure medicine; she'd finished her contraceptive pills a week ago, not that it mattered. Jacob flatly refused to eat more than a few beans, and that was nearly all the protein they had. Her mother was God knows where. She wondered how Donna was getting her hands on liquor these days. The sky lightened a bit more, allowing her to see the entire field.

Travis looked at her. "Okay?" he murmured.

She nodded. It seemed like they were breathing together. Synchronized. Maggie took a deeper breath to break it. She wondered about his demons, why he'd been so crazy drunk the other day. He was better today. Shifting a little, she disturbed the leaves and stilled herself. She closed her eyes for a minute.

Then Travis touched her hand with a finger and put it to his lips. A deer moved from the trees on their left onto the field. A doe, Maggie saw. Too far away for accuracy. She expected Travis to raise his shotgun, but he waited.

The deer grazed, her tawny hide blending with the colorless field. Bowing her dainty head into the grass, she foraged and moved a little closer. What was Travis waiting for? Then he turned to Maggie, nodded, and pointed at her. He wanted her to shoot, but surely the deer was too far away. She raised her eyebrows. He held up his hand. Wait. She shouldered the rifle.

Inching closer, the doe turned so she was in profile. A beautiful animal. Every part of Maggie's soul fought against killing her. But when Travis touched her hand again, pointed to his head, and nodded, Maggie took a deep breath, held it. Her fingers were cold. The trigger was cold. She let out the breath and pulled, the noise an insult to the morning. The deer was down.

Arms shaking, Maggie lowered the rifle. Travis walked out to the doe and examined her. "One shot, Maggie. Right below the ear." He grinned. "Roy will be proud of you."

This made her smile, and she joined him. The wound was neat. She was pleased. "Let's walk down to the house, and I'll get my truck and come back to dress it. I need more than my knife."

Maggie shook her head. "I'll stay with her."

He gave her a puzzled look but shrugged and took off into the woods.

Chapter Twenty One

Luke stuck the lit flashlight in his mouth and started working the padlock with the picks. Patience. It took longer than it did on TV. Keeping his ears alert for approaching vehicles, he fiddled with the tiny tools. It was like doing a job by Braille. He thought he had his timing right. It was just before one o'clock in the morning. Coal mine black. He wanted to be well down the road before the four o'clock patrol.

Feeling the tumblers slip, he opened the padlock and pulled the gate towards him. Good deal. He slipped through the opening, trying not to step on the fetid garbage bags. He closed the gate and reset the padlock. Straight ahead was pretty much due south, the best he could figure. He just needed to find a road heading that way or to his left: east. First he crossed the perimeter road and then headed across a field, mowed but not often, and then he all but ran into a fence, wood, not chain link like Rieselman, but he'd just as soon not climb onto someone's property.

So, he turned left, hoping he was too far from the main gate to be noticed. There'd be a road leading to it, which he hoped to avoid. As he walked through the rough field, he saw lights at the front gate, far enough away to leave him in the shadows. Yeah, there was a road straight to the main entrance. He kept to the field, and sure enough, another road running north and south intersected it. He turned right, trying to keep a map in his head. He'd have no directions until the sun rose, and that was hours away. Adjusting his backpack, he picked up his pace and followed the two-lane road to the south.

❖

With one finger, Maggie touched the doe's coat, giving over to sentimental thoughts about Bambi and fawns. But she stifled those images immediately. This was meat, that's all, and it was meat her son would eat, she hoped. She was proud of what she'd done. The sun moved higher but brought little warmth. She thought about Luke and hoped Rieselman would get supplies soon. He wouldn't admit it, but it sounded as though they were going hungry. Damned government.

Marla had called last night with more good news about little Savannah, although she still hadn't heard from Carrie. Maggie figured that only their food shortage had prevented Oleatha from urging Marla and the baby home for Thanksgiving. But it wasn't safe. The virus was still cutting people down like an evil machine. And there were desperate, dangerous people out there. Travis had told her that all over the country looters were breaking into homes and stores to get food, not valuables. Now that transportation was permitted, she hoped trucks were on the road delivering food everywhere, not just Rieselman and Henley County. But mobility was going to make contagion worse.

After longer than she'd expected, she heard Travis's truck, pulling as close as he could to her and the deer. He emerged from the trees with a rope, coolers, and a saw. He'd expected a turkey, not a deer. "You okay?" he hollered.

"Fine."

"You're amazing Maggie." He unsheathed his knife. "Absolutely amazing, but this part is sorta gruesome unless you're used to it."

"I need to learn."

Travis shrugged. "Okay. We gut it first. Then we skin and quarter it."

She moved beside him, watching him unzip the deer's belly with his knife, then separate the intestines from the membranes around them. He used his hands to dig deep into the deer's belly. When he had gathered up the bundle of organs, she held out her hands. "Throw this in the brush for the coyotes and buzzards?"

He nodded. The guts were still warm, and she did feel her stomach rise for a second. But she'd never in a million years let Travis Parker see her puke. She crossed the clearing and deposited them in the weeds.

Sounding like a teacher, he explained how they would hang the carcass from a tree to skin, quarter, and butcher it. Fashioning his rope into a noose for the doe's legs, he hung it, head down, from a poplar standing across the field. Occasionally he would ask her to hold a leg to keep the deer from swaying. He kept talking about the process, about shooting, and about Roy's rifle. "Where did he get that thing? I mean, it's World War I."

"It belonged to Luke's grandfather. I don't know any more. Roy said that he customized it for hunting."

"Yeah. I can see the modifications." He was easing the skin from the deer's leg. "My father would love seeing that."

The skinning was nearly done, and Travis explained how he was going to quarter it. Maggie nodded, wondering if she could ever dress and butcher a deer. Maybe she'd never have to with Travis around, but she paid attention.

Finally he got to the point where he was trimming and cutting what he called roasts and tenderloins, making the dead animal into meat. He dropped the segments on ice in the coolers. "Had to raid Oleatha's fridge to get more ice," he said. "This part here isn't good for much more than hamburger. Tough and sinewy. But this," he picked up a strip of meat, "this here is the tenderloin. You can fry it or roast it. Use a little Worchestershire sauce or marinate it. Really good." He dropped it into the cooler. His hands dripped gore. "I reckon Oleatha can tell you all about the cooking. You don't need me for that." And he turned silent, lines crossing his forehead.

The curious and changeable moods of Travis Parker, she thought. She grinned at him. "Guess we'll have deer rather than turkey for Thanksgiving." He'd been so cheerful. She wanted him to stay that way.

Travis corrected her, "Venison." He looked away from her, closed up the cooler, and cut the carcass down.

Again, she tried. "Okay, venison." Said with another big smile.

Travis didn't respond. Maggie waited while he squatted next to the deer and touched it. She'd thought he was finished, but he seemed intent upon the eviscerated doe. He rose, his hands dripping blood. When he gazed into her eyes, serious now, there was no chatter left in him. "You won't need me now," he said. "You can do it all yourself."

She started to protest, but his expression and gruesome hands stopped her. He came up to her, so close she could smell him. Raising his fingers, he painted blood on her cheeks and forehead. "You've killed. You've been blooded." It was a ritual. He was the hunter. She was the initiate.

She tried not to shrink from his touch, from the blood. His eyes were steady at first and then hot and fierce as lightning. He grabbed her shoulders and pulled her to his mouth, all teeth and tongue and fire. She fought against him, but her attempts were weak, useless. His lips stifled her cries as he pushed against her. Down the length of her body she felt his heat, but she didn't know how to stop it. She moved her head from side to side to break off the kiss but thought the motion might resemble reciprocated passion. Finally she managed to utter a choked no. And again, no.

He released her, making her stumble. Mumbling apologies and something about how he'd tried, God knows he'd tried, Travis turned away, returning to the deer and heaving it over his shoulder to dump in the woods. Maggie wiped her mouth with the sleeve of her jacket. She didn't understand, and yet she did. Staggering to the coolers, she carried one to the truck while he took the other. Their eyes never met, even when they grabbed the rope and tools and picked up their guns. He drove to the house where he placed the coolers on the grass in front of the porch.

Full of questions and excitement, Oleatha, Roy, and Jacob rushed out, wanting to know all about the hunting. Jacob asked why there was blood on her face and jacket. Travis never said a word. He threw his hand up in a silent goodbye and drove away.

❖

Luke trudged down the empty, endless road. He hadn't seen a vehicle yet, and he figured he'd walked about eighteen miles. Of course, it was five-thirty in the morning, not a fit hour for much of anything except sleeping. It would get better. Occasionally there was a lit porch or a pole light shining down on a farmyard, but it was vacant country and dark. His mind had little to dwell on except a litany of guilt about his Rieselman people, with as many transgressions as Maggie had beads on her rosary. He'd joked with her once, asking if Catholics counted up their sins that way. She'd rolled her eyes and spat, "Stupid Baptist." With a grin. Ah, Maggie, he thought, I'm breaking all kinds of rules and oaths for you and Jacob. I've lied, stolen, looted, and abandoned people who counted on me. Who knows what I may have to do before I get home? But it's for you; to protect you and Jacob.

And as soon as he thought this, he knew it was a lie too. He wanted to go home. He was worn out with the government's inefficiency and the damned inequity and cruelty of attacks against innocent people. He'd take care of his own. That was the only duty he respected. But he felt guilty as hell when he thought about distraught little Jill and stoic Ilse and honorable Jim French. He'd left French a note, confessing that he was running off and hoping that French would guide the Rieselman people to a good ending. In case things weren't so good, he'd told him where the guns were. He'd promised to do what he could for them from the outside. If his feet would carry him to any sort of solace at all.

He could see a vague lightening of the eastern horizon, not even close to dawn yet, but encouraging. He'd spotted few houses and those were dark. Sleeping. Or dead. It felt as though he was the only man alive. Don't be so freaking dramatic, he told himself. Keep walking.

About an hour later, his feet protesting and cold seeping through his coat, he heard a vehicle behind him. Turning, he saw headlights and moved to the side of the road and raised his thumb in the classic pose. It was a pickup and it slowed, shining headlights on him.

When Luke approached the door handle, the driver sounded his horn and turned on the interior light. He was middle-aged, bald, and was shaking his head. The passenger window inched down. "You sick?" the driver said.

"No, not sick at all. Just trying to get home."

"Where's home?"

"Southern Kentucky."

The driver shook his head. "I can take you a ways, but then I have to turn west."

Again, Luke reached toward the door, but the driver hollered no. "You can get in the back. I ain't risking the sickness even if you say you are healthy. There's a tarp. You'll be warm enough under it."

With a grunt, Luke climbed in and crawled under the tarp. Boxes filled most of the truck bed, but he was able to squeeze between them. It didn't take a minute to realize the boxes were full of apples. Two deep breaths and Luke was nearly drunk on their sharp, sweet scent. Easing off the backpack, he was able to lie on his side, listening to the road beneath him. The tarp bubbled with wind above his ear. God, it felt good to get off his feet even for a little while. His stomach growled, and he explored the boxes nearest him. All apples? No, he felt one box of turnips, and in the front corner he touched a few loose pumpkins. His mouth watered. He'd pay the guy for an apple, damnit. He had to eat something.

❖

Maggie escaped to the bathroom where she started the hot water in the shower. She caught a glimpse of herself in the mirror and almost cried out. A thin-cheeked woman with an eerily painted face stared back at her. Her eyes were huge. Her lips were reddened nearly to the color of the doe's blood. She wondered why Jacob hadn't run away from her.

Inside the shower she scrubbed her face raw and washed her scraggly hair until it squeaked. She should be angry with Travis or even afraid of him, but she was neither. The moment had been primal, visceral. It wouldn't happen again. She let the water pelt her shoulders and took a deep breath. They had meat for several days now. She'd provided it.

Her face as clean as a baby's, she wandered into the kitchen to find Roy and Jacob discussing whether they should fish and Oleatha dealing with the venison. "Aren't you hungry, girl?" Oleatha asked.

She was. Ravenous, actually, but she said, "I'll help you."

"You've done plenty," Oleatha said. "Get you some grub."

There wasn't much. She cut off a small wedge of cheese and finished a dab of the sweetened peaches. Even with the deer, there wasn't much food. Roy turned to Jacob, "All right. We'll go see if the fish are biting. But let me carry in the other cooler for your granny."

"And I need the food grinder from the cellar," Oleatha said.

"I'll go," Maggie offered.

Roy stood and put his hand on her wet hair. "Sit."

After they grabbed their fishing poles and left, Maggie watched Oleatha rinse the meat and cut what she called 'silverskin' from it. Tendons, thought Maggie, or ligaments. Finally Oleatha did allow Maggie to package the venison in heavy plastic bags for the freezer. "This piece needs to go in the fridge for our Thanksgiving dinner," Oleatha said. "It's the tenderloin, the best part."

"Travis said something about marinating it."

"Well, you can do that, honey, if you've a mind to."

Honey? How things had changed over the past few weeks.

"Just wish we had more to make a special dinner. No potatoes to mash. No sweet potatoes. I've been holding on to a can of pumpkin, hoping we could have a pie for Thanksgiving, but I don't reckon we can. I love pumpkin pie."

Maggie put the bag in the empty refrigerator. "They say that food trucks are out again. I could go to the store and see."

Oleatha shook her head. "I don't want you going out there. Sickness. Mean people. Ruth Ann said that two men walked into Preacher's house, bold as brass, and took nearly everything they had in the pantry. Preacher's not a young man; he didn't have the strength to stand up to them. She sent over a chicken from her freezer."

Maggie took the empty cooler and emptied the bloody ice and water across the road. And while she was rinsing it out, she had an idea. "Oleatha, do any of your friends keep chickens or have a fair amount of food left?"

Oleatha looked up from her gory work. "Jane's got hens. She locks them up in the garage at night so nobody can steal them. Made nests for them up on the shelves. That woman loves her chickens like they're children."

"Any reason we didn't try to get eggs from her?"

"I offered to buy some a couple of weeks ago, but she said they weren't laying much right now, and pretty much ignored me." Oleatha lifted a shoulder.

"Hmm. What if we traded some nice venison for a few eggs and a bag of flour from her? I could make a pie."

Oleatha looked up like she'd been pinched. "Lordy, Maggie, that's a good idea." She kept rinsing. "Let me finish this piece and I'll get right on the telephone."

Maggie stretched and yawned and thought she might just get on the telephone too. She wanted to tell Luke that she'd shot a deer.

❖

The loud knock woke Luke. The scent of apples had lulled him to sleep. Emerging from the blue haze under the tarp, Luke saw the driver, standing several feet away. "No closer, buddy, all right?"

Luke nodded.

"Sorry I can't take you any farther, but I need to head west here on the interstate." The man pointed ahead. "You follow this road another six miles or so and there's a little town, Seton. You'll do better finding food and rides than you would on the interstate."

Luke gazed at the ramp onto the highway. Not a vehicle in sight. "I ate an apple. Let me pay you for it."

The man shook his head. "Naw. I'm taking this stuff into town and hoping to get a pretty penny for it, but I can spare an apple." He took a wide path to the front of his truck. "Good luck to you."

He drove off, and Luke looked at his watch. It was only seven-thirty. The sky looked like dishwater. Hitching his backpack over his shoulders, he started walking. He passed a large farm with silos and several barns. A neat white house sat to the side of it with trucks parked in front. He wondered if there were people inside, huddled up against the sickness or if it was abandoned, the occupants dead or sick or if someone was making a huge pot of tasty soup. His feet kept working.

Seton wasn't much: a couple of churches, maybe two dozen widely spread houses, a gas station. On the other side of the town he spotted a grocery and quickened his pace. Apple or no, his stomach was eating itself. When he reached the store, it was dark, no cars, no people. He tried the door, but it was locked. No use getting out the picks. He pressed his face to the glass and saw empty shelves. Not a crumb anywhere. Other than knocking on someone's door, there was nothing for him there. And he'd probably be met with a shotgun if he tried. He kept walking, drinking all his water just to fill his stomach. He kept listening hard for the sound of an engine. Hard to believe that no one was driving anywhere.

So bare. A raw wind blew over empty fields on both sides of the road. What few houses there were crouched down under the low sky. Luke made up his mind to knock on the door of the next house. He'd stolen and lied; he might as well beg too.

It was on his right, grey siding and a white door. Empty flowerpots and plastic toys littered the muddy yard. Not a pretty place. He knocked on the door stepping back so people inside could see him through the window. Someone twitched the curtain on the right. He held his empty hands out to his side. "Go away," came from the other side of the door.

"Just wanting a little food," Luke said. "I can pay."

He heard the unmistakable sound of someone racking a load into a shotgun. "Get off my porch." The voice was male, rough.

"Okay, okay," Luke mumbled. He walked slowly back to the road, hoping he'd hear the door behind him open and something edible set on the doorstep. No.

He was shaking from cold, hunger, exhaustion. The road stretched out forever. He never imagined it would be this difficult. Another half mile down the road he saw a church sitting off to his left with an empty parking lot. On the other side were several trees with a few picnic tables under them. All set for church dinners in fair weather, he thought. It looked welcoming to Luke. Near the front door was a sign that said Pleasant Grove Baptist Church. He liked the name. Walking around the side, he found a back door and unloaded his picks. Might as well add another crime to his list.

The lock was surprisingly easy. Inside, the church smelled of old coffee and dry hymnals. The room he entered was the kitchen, and he started opening cabinets like a crazed man, finding more dishes for those church dinners than he did food. A container of the funny little crackers they used for communion, powdered creamer, and sugar. Inside the fridge there was grape juice, also for communion, and strangely enough, a pack of Kraft singles. He tore into this and guzzled the grape juice. While he ate, he walked into the small sanctuary, dead silent, and sat in a pew to unwrap piece after piece of cheese. After a bit, a furnace came on, warming the place a little. Good stewardship, he thought, remembering the words from the years when Oleatha had dragged him to church. Keep the heat low when no one's at church. He stopped shivering and drank more grape juice along with all the communion wafers. It was just past two in the afternoon, too early to stop for the day, but it was a temptation. He smiled at himself. Tempted by a church.

But once he'd finished the food, he gave into it. Considerate of the Baptists to furnish their pews with cushions. He'd rest a bit and get back on the road. Just long enough to let his food settle.

He awoke to his ringing phone. Maggie. He struggled to push air and strength into his voice before he answered. God, it was four o'clock. He'd slept for two hours. "Hello, sweetheart," he said in what he hoped was a hearty tone.

"Hello, yourself." She sounded cheerful.

"Everybody okay?"

"Yes. How about you? Did the food delivery come?"

He lied. "It sure did. We'll eat fine at Rieselman tonight." She mustn't know he was on the road. She'd worry more than ever.

"That's good," she said. "We'll be eating fine here too. Guess what?"

"Wal-Mart's open?"

"No." She actually giggled. "I shot a deer this morning."

Unbelievable. She'd always treated firearms like poison. "Well, that's great, Maggie," he exclaimed. "Buck?"

"No, a doe, but a pretty good-sized one, according to your dad."

"Did he go hunting with you?"

"No." Her voice turned a little funny. "Travis did. Oleatha and I have been busy with the venison all afternoon."

Travis again. She kept chattering, talking about pumpkin pies, and grinding meat and stuff that made his mouth water despite the wodge of cheese in his belly. He made up some stories about Ilse and Jill, and then clicked off. They were hungry, he thought. He needed to get back on the road.

Chapter Twenty Two

"Wish Travis was going with you," Roy said over yet another breakfast of rice and butter. "I'd be happy to, though."

Maggie shook her head. She'd tried calling Travis, both last night and this morning, but he wouldn't answer. "I want you here with Oleatha and Jacob."

Oleatha was vibrating with excitement. "I drove a hard bargain, didn't I? Jane didn't know what to do but say yes." Maggie had heard the story five times now. "But she's got plenty. It's not like we're depriving them."

"We're gonna have pie?" Jacob asked.

Maggie nodded. She wasn't sure Jacob really knew what pumpkin pie was, but Oleatha had spoken of it with such reverence that the boy was in awe.

Maggie picked up the plastic bag containing two pounds of ground venison. Oleatha had added two quarts of her canned tomatoes to sweeten the deal. "I may drive around a little, see if anything's open."

Roy nodded and then looked pointedly at the rifle. She nodded and picked it up. "Just in case," she murmured and saw him smile. She had the pistol in her purse and the rifle wedged next to her as she started her car. Luke would be amazed.

Roy had started her car occasionally to keep the battery going and siphoned gas from his truck to her tank, but she hadn't driven it but once since the night she got here. It felt odd. Out of curiosity, she turned down the lane to Annie's house, just to see. No truck, nothing, as she'd figured. She supposed he was ashamed of attacking her, well, kissing her. In the voice mail she'd left him, she'd said that they must get past the 'incident.'

Fiddling with the radio, she found a news channel and listened as she pulled onto the road. Evidently there was controversy about lifting the travel ban. One man said it was reckless and downright dangerous to allow travel before a vaccine was ready. Another said that people were going hungry. She shook her head. Everything was dangerous. She wondered what she would have done back in River Hills these last few weeks. A different kind of coping, for certain. Would she have stormed a grocery and stolen for her son, possibly exposing them to the sickness?

Following Roy's directions to Jane's house, she drove onto a gravel driveway that led to a small house far from the road. She parked behind a Chevy sitting in front of the garage turned henhouse, and an old dog rose from his patch of sunlight to bark at her. Hens picked at the ground inside a fenced pen. A tiny woman came out on the back porch. "Hush, Rambler," she said to the dog. "Maggie?"

"Yes, I'm Maggie. And you're Jane."

Sunlight glistened from her glasses. "Oleatha's told me about you and that son of yours. Thinks mighty highly of you."

A recent change, Maggie thought. She held out the bag, and Jane motioned her inside. The kitchen was a jumble of egg baskets, bags of chicken feed, and old junk mail, strewn over the counters and table. A man, older than Roy, sat there with a pistol resting on a seed catalog. He gave her a solemn nod. "Here you go," said Jane, pushing bags at Maggie. "The eggs are in this one, so be careful with it."

"I will."

"Good for you, getting a deer. Some's been hunting over this way. I've heard the shots. Don't know if they've had any luck, though." Jane smiled, wrinkles pleating her face. "It'll be good to taste some deer meat."

Back in her car, Maggie looked through the bags. As promised, half a dozen eggs and a ten pound bag of flour. She smiled. Oleatha had done well.

She drove on, heading to Wal-Mart, just to see. Nobody in Oleatha's phone network had said it was open, but nobody was moving around enough to find out. Catesboro had sickness, more cases every day. She did see a few cars, several actually, in front of the local clinic. But that wasn't good news. The Wal-Mart parking lot was empty. At least the store was intact. She knew that stores in cities hadn't done as well. Circling around to the back, she hoped to see a big, old truck full of food. Nothing.

So she drove by memory, trying to find Pig's Eye and the little store she and Roy had visited. Changing the radio station to music, she rolled down the passenger window just a little, savoring the morning breeze. One of those little pleasures that Roy talked about. Being by herself was good too. After a couple of wrong turns, she saw Hazel's place up ahead. No cars, so she pulled closer and swallowed hard. The door hung open at an odd angle, and the front window was smashed into shards. Glass twinkled in the dead leaves. As far as she could tell, the store was bare to the walls. No point in exploring. She hoped Hazel was all right.

Maggie pulled away and turned off the radio. The danger was far from over, and she still had to take care of them. As she drove, she decided she'd ask Oleatha to take over Jacob's lessons today, which would delight the woman. At breakfast, Roy had said there'd be no more fishing expeditions for a while; everything was fished out. Jacob had moped, but Maggie bet Roy would come up with some fun alternative after the lesson. And while they were working with Jacob, she'd concoct some kind of marinade for the venison and make a batch of bread. She wondered if her starter was still good. She smiled at the thought. Such little worries.

❖

Luke slipped a twenty under the Bible on the pulpit and locked the church door behind him. His legs felt like noodles, but at least he had a full belly for the moment. Walking down the center of the road, he scanned the scenery for an abandoned car, a helpful stranger, anything. But all he saw were flat fields. By now, they would've missed him at Rieselman. He wondered if they were pissed off or just as happy there was one less mouth to feed. He considered calling them; he had Jill's number and her phone was the most dependable, but he didn't.

A day that had never been bright crept to sunset. Two cars, an hour apart, passed him but never hesitated. He spotted lights at a few houses, way off the road, but he figured shotguns were at the ready everywhere. Rubbing his face, he felt stubble that was only going to get worse. He'd look like a real reprobate by tomorrow. But tonight he had to find someplace to shelter, especially since a few drops of cold rain were hitting his jacket like pellets. Hell, maybe it was sleet.

By eight o'clock, he was thoroughly soaked and shivering. But he was also seeing a few more houses. Maybe there was a little town on down the road. It would be a hell of a thing to be immune to the flu but die of pneumonia. And then up ahead he saw a small house, porchlight on, but dark inside. Brick, nice shutters, and a detached garage. Luke staggered to a stop. This was as good as anything. He'd see if he could get into the garage.

Stumbling down the driveway, he tried to raise the garage door, but it was locked. He glanced to the side and saw a window and a regular door. The knob turned. Hallelujah. Even in the dim light he could make out the shape of the one car inside—a Volkswagen Beetle. Too cramped to sleep in but small enough to leave a little laying down room in the garage. Shrugging off his backpack, he found the flashlight, keeping the beam low. The VW was Pepto- Bismol pink, of all things, and he had to smile. He piled up bags of grass seed and fertilizer to make a bolster between him and the wall and changed into the heavy sweater so he could cover up with his coat. Pulling out the kid's pillow, he laid it on the backpack and snuggled down onto the concrete floor.

❖

He'd thought he was tired enough to drop into a near coma, but the cold floor was a killer and he kept being afraid someone would find him. And then his appetite raised its greedy head and demanded food. So way before daybreak, Luke, stiff as an old man, sneaked out of the garage. He walked softly down the driveway to see if the porch light was still on. It was. He didn't think anyone had come home. Maybe the owners had holed up somewhere else. Maybe they were in the hospital, or worse. But maybe there was food inside. He crept onto the back porch, ready to get the picks out, but at his touch the doorknob turned and opened to a kitchen. He clicked on the flashlight. The house smelled dirty. Greasy water half covered a pile of unrinsed dishes in the sink. Moving quietly, he checked out the dining room and living room. Silent. Dark. He crept down the hall to the bedrooms. The doors were open. Beaming the flashlight at the floor, he peeked into the first bedroom: unmade bed, clothes thrown on top. Next to it was a bathroom, towels littering the floor. He shone his light at the sink and saw blood congealed in its bowl. Oh, God. And the towels were rusted with it.

Crossing to the other bedroom, Luke saw a female body in bed, huddled up like she thought that would make the pain go away. He turned on the bedside light. She was young with long, dark hair glued to her gruesome pillow. He checked for a pulse, although he knew there wouldn't be one. The blood wasn't completely dry; she hadn't been dead too long. Her thin hand clutched a wad of tissues. She'd been alone, he guessed. Or maybe not. Maybe her death chased away the person who slept in the other room. At Rieselman, at least people had died with someone taking care of them, even if the caregivers were strangers. Luke's legs gave way, and he slipped to the floor, his back against the girl's bed. Great sobs shook his body. He couldn't do a thing for her. Nobody could. All the deaths, all the grief piled onto him like giant stones, grinding him into despair.

He finally cried himself out and scrubbed his face with his hands. He found her purse and then her wallet. She was Melanie Anderson, aged twenty-four. She had credit cards and an expired student ID from a college in Indiana. Fifteen dollars and change. Her phone was out of juice, and Luke was glad for that. He didn't want to know any more about her. But he glanced around her room, seeing goofy photos with friends tacked to the walls and cheap trophies for softball tournaments. On her desk were colorful, thin books and several folders. An elementary school teacher, he guessed. Just starting out.

He thought about searching the other bedroom to determine if there'd been one or two people there, if they were her parents or what. But he didn't. Jaw set, he went back to the kitchen and prowled through the refrigerator and cabinets, loading what he could find into his backpack. There wasn't much. Digging in his wallet he pulled another twenty from Briley's stash and placed it on the kitchen table. And then he noticed the keys beside the salt shaker. VW keys with a fuzzy pompon attached to the ring. Twitching his nose like the odor had suddenly worsened, he put the keys in his pocket and returned to the garage. He pressed the door opener and squeezed into the Beetle, adjusting the seat as far back as it would go. He started the engine and was relieved to see a half tank of gas. He used her opener to shut the garage and said aloud, "I hope you don't mind, Melanie. I'm sorry."

❖

Maggie turned into the holler and listened to the gravel's crunch. She heard a crow complaining, and then she heard the crack of a gunshot. Close. And then another. She accelerated down the hill, stopping just shy of the house and throwing the car into park. The scene flashed into her head like a photograph. Oleatha screaming on the porch. Roy crumpled at the porch steps. Kyle Coughlin halfway between Roy's truck and the house. Coughlin lowering a pistol and staring at her. Legs sticking out from under Roy's truck. Blood.

She grabbed the rifle and opened the car door in one motion. Settling the gun into her shoulder, she fired just as Coughlin was raising his pistol toward her. He dropped. Under the truck, the legs scrambled backwards, and a young man, not the redhead, stood, hands raised. "You better run far and never come back here," she shouted. Her voice sounded as rough as the gravel under her feet.

He might've nodded, but all she could see was the back of his black jacket. Oleatha was still screaming and praying. Where was Jacob?

Maggie reached in and turned off the ignition with a palsied hand. Then, still clutching the rifle, she bent over Coughlin's still body and checked his pulse. Blood blossoms stained his shirt. Chest shot. Dead. Oleatha was cradling Roy. "Good God, Roy. Lord help us." She gulped for air.

`Jacob rushed out of the house sobbing, "Mommy, Mommy, Mommy." He ran to Maggie and cried into her hip. She bent and squeezed him to her.

"Get towels, Jacob," she said. "Lots of towels."

He raced off, and Maggie went to Roy, ripping open his plaid shirt. Oleatha sat on the step, holding his hand. "Chest shot," Maggie said. "But to the side. Not his heart." Oleatha nodded.

Roy's eyelids fluttered open. "Good shot, gal," he whispered.

Not an arterial bleed, she thought, although there was plenty of blood coming from near his armpit. "Coughlin?" asked Oleatha.

"Dead."

A wisp of a smile lifted Roy's lips. Jacob came running back with bath towels, dish towels, and a filthy dustcloth. She smiled her thanks and tossed the dirty one aside. "Pack them in around the wound," she told Oleatha. "And put pressure on them. I'll call for an ambulance."

Roy's voice was surprisingly strong. "No hospital. I'm not gonna die from that goddamned flu."

Oleatha jerked.

"Roy, you need fluids and antibiotics and surgery. I can't do that."

He shook his head. "No hospital."

Maggie winced. Oleatha said, "Then we better get him in the house. Jacob, honey, hold the door open for us, will you?"

Somehow they managed to get Roy upright and steer him to the bedroom. "Your bedspread," Maggie mumbled, easing Roy onto his good side.

"No matter."

"Scissors, tweezers, alcohol, cotton. Do you have antibacterial soap? Hot water in a bowl." Maggie squinted at her father-in-law. "More light, if possible. He's shaking; he's going into shock. Blankets and hot tea with tons of sugar."

Oleatha blinked at every item and pulled a comforter and a quilt from the closet. Maggie spread them over Roy and watched Oleatha go to the kitchen in a near run. At her elbow, Jacob whispered, "Can you fix Pop?"

"I'm going to try." She gave him all the smile she could muster. "Would you clear all the stuff off this bedside table, Jacob? And then I have another job for you to do." She lifted a towel. The bleeding had slowed. She saw bits of Roy's shirt in the wound. Would she be able to get them all out? The exit wound looked worse than the entrance, but at least no bullet was lodged in him. His face was pale and the shivering was increasing. Jacob cleared the small table while she ran to the back bedroom, got her bag, and took Roy's blood pressure. Low. Too low.

"Good, sweetie. Now get in bed with Pop and spoon up next to him. Remember how we spoon sometimes? Real close. Keep him warm."

While Jacob scooted next to his grandfather, Oleatha bustled in with everything but the tea and hot water. "It's heating." She was out of breath. "What else do you need?"

Maggie started cutting off his shirt. "Some paper towels and a couple of lengths of some kind of thick thread." She shook her head.

"Carpet thread. And a needle to fit it, right?"

Maggie nodded. "And then you need to call the sheriff."

Oleatha frowned.

"Stay where you are, Jacob. I've got to scrub my hands."

When Maggie had finished, Oleatha came back; she had the needle and thread, tea and hot water. Although Roy wasn't much more than semi-conscious, Oleatha used a straw and managed to get some of the tea down him. Jacob snuggled back in, and Maggie began the tedious process of cleaning and picking the wounds. She'd never done anything like this before. Of course, she'd never shot a man dead before either. Taking a deep breath, she put that out of her mind.

"Make that call, Oleatha," she ordered.

"But," the woman hesitated. "What if they arrest you for killing Coughlin? Should we make it look like Roy did it?"

Maggie looked up to see Oleatha pleating the fabric of her shirt. "It wouldn't work. Roy was using a shotgun; I had the rifle. That kid under the truck would know better. The angle's wrong." She smiled at Oleatha. "You learn things when your husband's a policeman."

Still, Oleatha waited. "If they arrest you, who will take care of him?"

"They won't arrest me. Self-defense. He was raising his pistol to me when I shot. You saw him. Go on. It gives me the creeps to know there's a dead body in the yard."

Roy whispered, "She's right."

That settled it. "Go with Granny, Jacob. Pop's warming up."

Maggie packed covers around the front side of Roy to keep Jacob's heat close. And kept working.

Chapter Twenty Three

Luke felt a naïve wonder at how the car ate miles he would've so painfully walked. He dug in his bag for a Sunny Delight and a granola bar. Almost a sensible breakfast. Now if he only had a map. But judging by the weak sun rising on his left, he was still going pretty much due south. Eventually he'd hit the Ohio River.

In another hour, he saw signs for I64 and decided to risk it. The pink VDub stood out like a princess in a coal mine, but he figured law enforcement would be too busy to hunt for stolen cars. If he drove I64, he'd travel a ways in Indiana, and then he could cross the bridge into Louisville. He'd be hugging and kissing Maggie and Jacob by nightfall. He smiled and turned on the radio. Most stations were playing programmed music, but the NPR station, weak as it was, seemed to be broadcasting news and views. Evidently truck drivers were refusing to work, saying that sure, people needed food and supplies, but they were risking their lives exposing themselves to the sickness. There was some talk about the National Guard doing it. Regular military had been called to various cities and were, in many cases, on stand-by for the escalating actions against several terrorist groups claiming a grand alliance. Luke sighed. People were sick, angry, despondent. He hoped governmental leadership was up to the task, but after what he'd witnessed at Rieselman, he wasn't betting on it. Hell, the president had thrown up his hands and quit because the task was too big for him.

He'd expected to see traffic on the highway, but Luke was the lone cowboy. He watched mile markers, feeling a little giddy as they added up. He glanced at the rearview mirror and saw nothing but the Mardi Gras beads and dreamcatcher Melanie had hung on it. Luke checked his watch. He'd left her house two hours ago. Enough time, he hoped, and dialed 911 to report a death at Melanie's address. He refused to give either his name or location. "Best I can do, Melanie," he said to the sparkling beads.

Up ahead, he spotted a speck on the shoulder. He slowed a bit, letting the speck gain definition. Probably male, rather tall. In a dark gray or black jacket and jeans. Dark hair, light skin. He slowed to a stop and lowered the passenger window. Cold air poured in. The guy had to be freezing.

"Need a ride? I'm healthy."

The guy bent down and peered in. Skeptical, he took in the car's color, the beads, dreamcatcher, and bobbing daisies on the dash. Then he nodded, and folded up his long legs to fit in the seat.

"I'm Luke."

"Joe."

It probably wasn't his name, but he didn't care. As long as the fellow didn't shoot him for his car. Melanie's car. "Where you heading?"

"Atlanta."

"Good Lord. On foot?"

Joe shrugged.

"I can take you a fair part of it. I'm going to southern Kentucky."

Joe nodded. Not a chatty fellow.

"Where'd you start out?"

"Chicago."

"Illinois for me too." Luke figured that telling him the tale of Rieselman would just make him more leery. "Guess you're healthy."

Another nod.

"There's a little food in my bag, but go easy, okay? All I've got." The bag was in the floorboard. Luke reckoned he should stow it in the VW's non-existent backseat to give Joe more room, but he liked having it near.

"No, thanks."

"How many vehicles have you seen today?" Luke hadn't realized how starved he was for conversation.

Joe squinched his eyes. "Maybe eight, ten since sunup."

Luke nodded. NPR was interviewing someone who'd made a makeshift hospital for flu victims in Oklahoma. She said it was hitting the Native Americans particularly hard. Joe stared straight ahead at the concrete. A pickup actually passed them.

It was tempting to push the Beetle as fast as it would go. Probably not that fast, and speed sucked gas. He guessed he would have to start exiting every ramp to see if he could find fuel. "You see any open gas stations?"

"One early this morning. Can't always tell from the highway, though."

"True."

Joe shifted, opened his mouth, and then shut it again.

"Whatever it is, say it," said Luke.

"Is this your car?" He was frowning.

Luke started laughing for the first time in what seemed like years. "This priss pink roller skate?"

Joe tried to smile.

"With beads and doodads and flower bobble-heads?" Luke was still chuckling. "No, Joe. It isn't mine. I, uh, requisitioned it."

Now Joe grinned with bright, white teeth and sunlight in his eyes. "Would've done that myself if I'd had the chance. When did you get it?"

"This morning. I walked all day yesterday."

"Me too. My feet are so sore."

"Mine too. Haven't you had any rides since Chicago?"

"A couple. Semi carrying automotive shit took me about fifty miles. People need brake pads real bad, you know?"

Luke grinned.

"And then I hitched a ride with a guy in a van. Maybe he was carrying dope or something. Sketchy. He kept his heat right on his leg. Freaked me out but it was another fifty miles."

Luke felt the weight of his firearm in his right pocket. "Whole lot of bad going on. I'm just trying to get to my family, but I didn't dream it would be this difficult to hitch rides."

They tried two exits with no luck. Luke thought about driving into the small towns beyond the interstate but didn't figure he'd have any better chances at finding gas there. At one point he stopped the car and dug in his backpack, taking out two pop top cans of peaches and two bottles of water. "Here," he said, handing one of each to Joe.

"Thanks."

They slurped peaches for a while, and Luke drove to the next exit, a good eighteen miles. The gas gauge was sending him to panic mode. "We're nearly to Louisville. Surely there'll be something open there."

Joe didn't answer.

The closer they drove to the river, the hillier the country was. Bare trees towered over the highway, and the VW sped down and plodded up the road. Luke took his foot off the gas and coasted when he could. According to the signs, the next exit offered bunches of restaurants, motels, and gas stations. "This one has to work," he muttered when he pulled off. The gas tank warning light had been on for five minutes.

At the end of the ramp a homemade sign read 'Gas Here'. Luke let out a breath. He dreaded relying on his feet again. "Probably charging a fortune," he said. "But I don't care." He felt in his left pocket for his wallet.

Luke slowed the car and pulled into a huge truck stop with what looked like a hundred pumps. A semi was at one of them, but there were no other vehicles. A hand-made sign partially blocked their way into the station. Luke read the words aloud:

CREDIT CARDS ONLY
RESTAURANT AND STORE CLOSED
NO BATHROOMS
PRAY FOR REDEMPTION

"This is redemption as far as I'm concerned," Luke muttered as he turned off the motor. Once outside, he heard a loudspeaker blaring over the cold concrete. A preacher was exhorting people to accept Jesus and be saved. This was the Apocalypse, the hysterical voice said. Luke slipped his credit card into the pump.

The semi driver started his truck and pulled away. He wore a gauze mask over his face and latex gloves on his hands. Luke didn't see another soul. He couldn't tell whether the emotional speaker was inside the store or whether it came from a recording. The preacher was quoting scripture; *Revelation*, he said. "I looked up and saw a horse whose color was pale green. Its rider was named Death, and his companion was the Grave. These two were given authority over one-fourth of the earth, to kill with the sword and famine and disease and wild animals.'"

A raw wind blew across the field on the other side of the road and blasted through his jacket. Luke shivered, his hand like ice on the metal handle. "Repent," the voice shrieked.

On and on the shrill voice cried, beseeching, scolding. It made Luke's head hurt. Finally he filled the tank and replaced the nozzle. "Spooky," he said to himself.

He twisted the gas cap back on. Wind blew into his face. He turned to wait for the receipt and heard the Beetle's ignition strike and watched the car move away. In the driver's seat now, Joe raced to the edge of the truck stop, threw Luke's backpack to the ground, and sped off.

❖

Roy grimaced as he swallowed. "Yum."

Maggie had crushed two Vicodin tablets and mixed them with sugar and a little water. "This next part is going to hurt. Maybe the pills will help a little."

He raised a heavy hand. She had to stitch him now as best she could. Flesh was missing. She didn't know how tight she could pull his skin; she might only be able to close part of the rear wound. "I'll give this a little time to kick in." She dipped the carpet thread into a small bowl of alcohol to let it soak.

He mumbled something and Maggie went to the kitchen where Oleatha and Jacob looked up at her with white faces. "All done but the stitching," she said. "So far, so good."

"Are you hungry?" asked Oleatha.

Maggie shook her head. The deputy had come, questioned her and Oleatha, and attempted to interview Roy who kept his eyes and mouth shut. Playing possum, Oleatha said, but it was just as well. The deputy hadn't taken her away in cuffs, but he'd scolded her for not detaining the other guy. Maggie shrugged, working kinks out of her neck, and put water on for tea. The deputy hadn't taken Coughlin's body away either, although he had spread a tarp over it. She couldn't rest easy until he was gone.

Jacob fidgeted. He wanted to see Pop. He wanted to go outside. He wanted to crawl into his mother's lap. She allowed the last one and petted him until the water boiled. Oleatha jumped up to fix the tea.

"I was going to make bread today," Maggie said, stirring a little honey into the cup. "And marinate the meat for tomorrow."

"Doesn't matter," said Oleatha.

"No. Oh, I forgot about Jane's food. It's still out in the car."

Oleatha patted her hand. "I got it. We'll still do Thanksgiving tomorrow. Roy will be better."

Maggie doubted it. She could practically see bacteria multiplying in his wound. She'd found a chip of rib bone and wasn't sure whether the bullet had knocked off a bit of lung tissue. It wasn't a life-threatening wound yet, but it could be in twenty-four hours. They were still adamant about the hospital.

She closed the bedroom door before stitching him, but Roy made only soft grunts when she punctured his skin. Stopping occasionally to check his blood pressure, she worked with steady hands, trying to make it as quick as she could. She didn't like his low numbers at all. Once she yelled for Oleatha to make more sweet tea and spoon it into his mouth, and he tried to swallow it. And then vomited it back out. Finally she taped thick gauze over her work and positioned clean towels under it. He wanted to lie on his back, he said. Maggie threw all her instruments and trash into the water bowl and told Oleatha to watch him and give him sips of sweet tea when he'd tolerate it.

Then her hands shook. Jacob had fallen asleep on the sofa. The sun was deserting the holler. She washed up and boiled the scissors, needle and tweezers. She might have to go back in. It was crazy to home treat a bullet wound. She went out the back door and stared up the hill, letting the chilly breeze blow the strain off her. She hadn't heard from Luke all day but didn't feel like she could call him without breaking down. He didn't need this kind of worry. She couldn't tell him about the shootings. For a minute she shut her eyes and saw Coughlin and felt the thud of the rifle against her shoulder. God help her, she'd killed a man.

❖

Receipt fluttering in his hand, Luke stood stock still for a minute, watching the pink Beetle fly away. Son of a bitch. Over the monotonous tirade on the loudspeaker he heard another voice yelling, "Get off the property! No loiterers." He moved. He picked up the backpack and walked to the ramp and then onto the highway toward Louisville. It couldn't be many miles to the bridge. A big city like that, he'd find some sort of transport. Hell, maybe even jump a train if they were running. His knee was starting to complain, along with his sore feet, but he shuffled on, mentally kicking his own ass for leaving the keys in the ignition. And then he stopped, opened the backpack, and searched. Joe hadn't taken the time to stuff Luke's phone into it. He had no way to call Maggie. Or anyone. He wanted to hit something.

As he trudged along, his mind jumped back to when he was a kid, sitting on his grandparents' porch in the summertime. His dad and grandfather both had guitars and were playing while his granny, a hard-cheeked woman with white hair stretched into a bun, was singing one of the old songs. "I'm just a poor, wayfarin' stranger, a-travelin' through this world of woe…" Granny's voice cracked and strained, but her pitch was true and honest. He remembered the tune but no more of the words and sang it until a hill took his breath.

A car passed him and then two semis. The most traffic he'd seen. Up at the entrance to the bridge was a roadblock, but the personnel were neither military nor law enforcement. The guys wore hunting camo with semi-automatic rifles and shotguns. Luke felt the outline of the pistol in his pocket. He saw no other pedestrians, but there were five vehicles waiting to pass through. He waited beside the first one. Joe had probably gone through quite a while ago.

A bridge guard questioned the first truck from the passenger side, keeping his distance and glaring at Luke. "Where you headed?"

The driver said Knoxville. Oh, that would be perfect, Luke thought. He stepped a little closer.

"What you carrying?"

"Paper products. Wanta see my manifest?"

"Naw. Go on. Do not get off the highway in Louisville. We'll be watching for you." The guy pointed his weapon at the traffic camera attached to girders above the bridge.

"Hey," Luke shouted. "Hey, can I hitch a ride? I'm heading toward Knoxville. I'm healthy."

The truck started creeping away, and the guard turned his rifle toward Luke. "No pedestrians. Move."

"What do you mean, no pedestrians? I need to cross the river. Where am I supposed to go?" Luke yelled. He fingered the pistol. Damn it.

"Don't care if you climb under a rock, but you're not coming into Louisville. Get the fuck out of the way."

All of the camo guys were focusing on him now. If he took so much as a step, he'd be dead. Long before he could pull out the pistol. He raised his hands and turned his back. The next vehicle, a Toyota SUV, pulled forward, the driver deliberately not making eye contact with Luke. He walked slowly, thinking about boats and how far it was to the next bridge. He wasn't sure. The sun was sinking into the treetops. Another night coming.

❖

It was dusk before an ambulance came to take the body. Soon after, the deputy called and said no charges were being filed. "Don't know whether that speaks to the reputation of Kyle Coughlin or Roy Davies," Maggie remarked. She stood at the open refrigerator door trying to figure out some kind of marinade.

"Both, I reckon," said Oleatha. "But it also has a lot to do with how bad things are around here. Break-ins. Sick people. Desperate druggies. Law enforcement's got their hands full."

Maggie nodded. She heard the theme song from the *Waltons* from the living room where Jacob was watching. It made her shiver. She chose Worchestershire Sauce, bottled lemon juice, and hot sauce to go with the oil and honey sitting on the counter. "We still have garlic powder?"

Oleatha nodded and got up to get it. "You want anything else?"

"Maybe some cinnamon."

Oleatha frowned.

"It'll be good, I promise."

"Honey, I guess I trust you with anything now." Oleatha handed her the spices. "What I want to know is why Travis didn't come down and help out. He had to have heard the shots."

Maggie mixed the ingredients. "Travis isn't at the house."

"Really? How do you know?"

"Went by there this morning when I was going to Jane's. God, that feels like a year ago. Anyway, deserted. Locked up. I bet he went back to his apartment in Catesboro." And she knew why.

"After all the work he's done there? That's a surprise."

"Would you check Roy's dressings, see if he's bleeding through? And try to get more liquid down him."

Oleatha picked up the sweet tea cup.

"I'm going to start some bread for tomorrow, so would you mind dividing your time between Jacob and Roy?"

"Of course not, but it'll be the middle of the night before you finish."

"That's okay. Don't think I'll be sleeping much tonight anyway. I'll want to check Roy every little bit."

Oleatha smiled at her. "Whatever would we have done without you?"

Hours later, Jacob absolutely did not want to go to bed even though Oleatha had shut her bedroom door, and the house was quiet. "Call Daddy and make him come home," said Jacob. "We need him."

Oh, how she yearned to do just that. "Daddy's a long way away. We'll be okay. I promise."

Jacob shook his head. "Last time, Mr.Travis came."

"Yes. But this time I came. Sweetie, it's okay." She smoothed the covers over him. "I'm going to be up for a while tonight, checking on Pop. So don't get scared if I'm not in bed beside you."

"Check on me too?"

"Of course. I always do."

She went back to the kitchen and peeked under the dishtowel. The bread wasn't in a big hurry to rise. She put a kettle on and chose a teabag from their dwindling supply. She was tired down to her bones. From the front bedroom, she heard Oleatha murmuring to Roy. Her mother-in-law seemed to think Maggie had everything under control. Fifteen minutes ago, she'd checked his dressings, blood pressure, temperature, and heart rate, and they'd been okay. He was a tough old guy, but Maggie couldn't build much optimism. Maybe she could persuade Oleatha to get him to the hospital tomorrow.

She called Luke while she let her tea steep. She was past concern about him worrying; she'd tell him everything even if it did drive him crazy. But she'd tried three times now, getting nothing but his voice mail. Maybe he was busy. Or maybe he was sick. She bobbed the teabag. She didn't recall Luke telling her about any new cases of the sickness for a while now, but she supposed it was possible. Carefully laying the teabag on a saucer for another use, she added a scant teaspoon of sugar and raised the cup to her nose to inhale the steam. Then she called Travis again, hoping he'd be over his embarrassment, or whatever it was, and at least talk to her. He had his little ways, as he said. Maybe he could get his hands on some antibiotics. Again, voice mail. In a terse voice, she told Travis to call her. Jacob cried out in his sleep, and she hurried to hold him. The kid had seen too much, even if Oleatha had made him crawl under his bed when Coughlin showed up. "Bad guys, Mommy," he sobbed into her chest.

"They're gone, baby boy. Mommy isn't going to let anything hurt you."

He clutched her hand. "You'll shoot them?"

"Yes."

"Shoot them dead?"

It took her breath. "Yes, I'll shoot them dead."

"I want Daddy. " His head drooped back onto the pillow.

"I do too, Jacob."

"When's he coming home?"

"Soon, baby. Soon." A lie. A wish.

Then everything was quiet again. She heard the hum of the refrigerator and the soft roar when the furnace came on. She'd tiptoed to the front window and glanced out the back every few minutes all evening. It was like working night shift at the hospital. Guarding the patients under her care from the deadly stillness of the night when bodies were vulnerable. Yet, there'd been something warm about it too, like when she'd fed Jacob in the middle of the night. Dim lights and soft blankets. She sipped her tea and waited to make her rounds again, to finish the bread, to comfort.

Chapter Twenty Four

Luke staggered up the empty interstate, retracing his earlier steps until he was at the entrance ramp from the bizarre truck stop. This was the lowest he'd felt. Cold, hungry, and with no idea of what to do next, he squatted on the harsh pavement and waited for the sun to set. Not for any particular reason. He just waited. He couldn't even call Maggie and confess his stupid plan. He pulled his hat farther down over his forehead. He supposed he could walk back down the ramp, avoiding the truck stop, and wander down the road. He'd glimpsed fast food joints and other commercial places, all closed, he imagined. For a minute, he considered it, but his knee was throbbing hard now.

He squeezed his eyes together. He'd been so sure it would be easy to hitch rides. He hadn't seen a vehicle in any direction for thirty minutes, let alone one that would dare to pick him up. He wasn't sure *he'd* pick himself up. Long hair, scruffy beard, kinda big. Scooting over to sit on the shoulder's grass, he pulled the last of his supplies from the backpack: a can of tuna fish and a tiny bag of pretzels, and ate them. He amused himself by using the pretzels as a fork and settled in to wait. Maybe he'd try something else later.

The sky turned ink black, and Luke watched the moon. Louisville's lights were too bright for a star show. He saw headlights from a semi and stood, arms outspread. The driver gunned the engine. He silently thanked the apple truck man for his courage yesterday. He dozed, curled up on the ground with the kid's pillow under his head, ready to jump up at the sound of a vehicle on the highway or ramp. About midnight, he woke up alert and angry. He had to make this happen, next chance he got.

The next chance appeared about an hour later. A white delivery truck struggled up the ramp from the truck stop. Luke eyed the door and its handle. No toe hold. Nothing extra to help him. As the truck wheezed into gear, he started running, keeping his eyes on the passenger door just the smallest bit ahead of him. Ignoring his knee, he kicked into overdrive and grabbed for the handle with his left hand, using his right to pound on the window. Both feet were planted against the moving door.

He heard a terrible shriek from inside. And then he heard the squeal of brakes. The driver stopped and giving him a hard stare, unlocked the passenger door. He got in.

She was a well-upholstered African-American woman, probably his mother's age. Lights from the dash glinted against her gold-rimmed glasses. Her mouth was wide open and gearing up for another scream. He held his hands up. "I'm healthy and I mean you no harm, ma'am."

She was terrified. He dug in his coat pocket for his badge and airport ID that he'd pulled from his backpack while sitting on the ramp. "I'm an airport policeman and I'm healthy."

"Can't say that makes me feel any safer," she whispered.

He nodded. "I'm trying to get to my wife and son in southern Kentucky. I've been on the road for better than two days now. Nobody will pick me up."

"That's just them showing good sense."

"I agree, and I wouldn't have jumped your truck except I've already been down to the bridge." He gestured. "They won't let pedestrians cross. I'm desperate."

She didn't say anything for at least two minutes, just stared ahead at the empty road. "You got a gun?"

Luke nodded.

"Let me see."

He took it from his waistband, pointing it at the floorboard. He couldn't figure out what she wanted. She reached for the ID tag. "Luke Davies," she said. "Why aren't you at the airport in Cincinnati?"

He grinned. "Because no one's at any airport anywhere."

She laughed. "I'm Vanessa. I'll take you across the river, and then we'll see." She put the truck into drive. "Are the people at the bridge gonna recognize you?"

"Hope not."

She tilted her head and started driving while Luke took off his jacket, putting the pistol under the seat. She asked, "Is it military or police or what at the bridge?"

"Redneck militia, armed to the teeth. They'll want to know your destination and see your manifest if you have food or valuables."

"Don't have no manifest. This is a charity run. Did you see the side of the truck while you were getting ready to scare the bejesus out of me?"

He shook his head.

"It says 'God's Pantry,' and I volunteer there. People are starving. Some of the Amish people who help us now and then said we could have a truckload of non-perishables if someone came and got it. I said I'd take the truck up to Indiana and get the stuff for Thanksgiving. Didn't dream things would be so rough out in the country."

"Where do you live?"

"Nashville. Believe you me, it's rough there. People lying dead in the streets from the sickness and other causes. Gangs ruling neighborhoods. Police just gone. Crazy."

"My sister lives in Nashville."

"Lordamighty, I hope she's okay. Where does she live?"

"Don't know." Luke shook his head. "You're a brave woman, Vanessa."

"No, I'm a scared to death woman, but for now you're gonna be my protection from those white thugs on the bridge. Get out that pistol and display that badge. I'm telling them you're my bodyguard." She drove at a good clip, straddling the lanes of the highway.

"They're going to think I hijacked the truck."

"From what you say about them, they'll trust you more than me."

In minutes they were approaching the bridge. It was well-lit with huge pick-ups parked to narrow the road to one lane. As they neared the roadblock, two guys got up from their cheap lawn chairs and held their guns ready. A double-barreled shotgun and a semi-automatic. Luke tensed. The guys stepped in front of Vanessa's truck, motioning her to stop.

"Here goes," she whispered and rolled down her window.

"Where you headed?" the bald one asked.

"Nashville with food for a church pantry," she said. "So folks can have something to eat on Thanksgiving."

The other man wore a camo cap and stood behind baldie. "Got a manifest?"

Vanessa shook her head.

"Then we'll need to search the truck."

Luke bent down so they could see him and put a little bit of a smile on his face. "I don't think so."

"Who are you?"

Vanessa spoke up. "He's my bodyguard, an off-duty policeman." She picked up Luke's badge and showed it to them. Luke moved the pistol a bit.

"How about sharing some of that food with us?" Baldie's smile was evil. "We're hungry too."

Luke gripped the pistol, making sure the guys could see him do it. Camo hat raised his shotgun, but he was too close to the truck to lift it enough to aim. "Floor it, Vanessa," Luke said in a sharp whisper. And she did. There were two shots. Luke thought one went wide, but the other pinged off the back end, probably the bumper. Thank God they hadn't hit a tire.

Vanessa was driving fast and babbling faster. "Good Jesus, what if you hadn't been with me? Did they want to kill us? For what? Food? Is it that bad for everyone? Jesus, Jesus, Jesus preserve me."

"You're safe, Vanessa. Calm down. We're okay. They had no legal right to search the truck. Black market profiteering, I'd say." He patted her hand gripping the steering wheel. "We need to watch road signs and make sure we don't get lost."

She gulped air. "Do you think there'll be more roadblocks? Lord God, I didn't know I was heading into a war."

"Don't know," Luke said. "You didn't run into any on your trip up?"

She shook her head. "If I was a drinking woman, I'd take me a big swig just now." Slowing a little, she peered up at the signs. "This way, right?"

"Yes." Luke glanced toward the city and saw flames in the distance.

"Lord, the world's a mess."

"Won't argue with you about that." He could hear distant sirens.

She took a huge breath and exhaled. "I know you want to go home, but you gotta stay with me until I get to Nashville, you hear? We'll find you a car, or maybe one of my nephews can drive you in a couple of days. You can help distribute the food. Might have some trouble then too."

Luke's spirits fell. Nashville was way too far west, and Vanessa's plans were too vague. He was grateful to the woman for coping with his sudden appearance, he thought her mission was good-hearted, and he wasn't sure how soon he could get home on foot. But no. "I can't. Much as I want to, Vanessa, I can't." He tried to see a map of Kentucky in his head. From nearby Elizabethtown, he could go east to Lexington. Still pretty far north, and she was traveling south. Wait, he thought. She would be going through Bowling Green, and there was a highway from there to Somerset. Not a well-traveled road in the best of times, but it was a more direct route.

"Tell you what," he said. "I'll stay with you until Bowling Green; you're nearly to Nashville there. And then I'll go east on the road that heads to Somerset. We've got quite a bit of time together."

"All right, all right. I understand, but I'd feel a lot better with you and that pistol riding shotgun." She grinned at her joke. "Now I want you to tell me how you got separated from your family, and what you've been doing since the sickness started." She pointed at a bag between their seats. "Get both of us a sandwich and talk to me. I gotta get my blood pressure down."

❖

Maggie woke with a start when Oleatha walked through the living room toward the bathroom. She'd fallen asleep on the sofa while watching out the front window. Creeping into the bedroom, she touched Roy's hand. Warm, not hot. And she quietly took his blood pressure. "G'morning," he said.

"Good morning yourself. How are you feeling?"

"It hurts like sixteen kinds of torture, gal."

Maggie smiled. "I'll get you another pain pill in a minute." His pressure was high now. Probably the pain, but it was really high. Before he could say anything else, she stuck the thermometer in his mouth. "How about a nice egg and toast for breakfast?"

He grunted around the thermometer. Low grade. Nothing alarming yet.

"Why do you all do that? Ask people questions when they have a thermometer in their mouths? Dentists do it too."

Nice and cranky, Maggie thought. She rolled him onto his good side to check the bandage. Some seepage, not too bad. "I don't know," she said. "Maybe we just want to torment you."

A small chuckle came from his chest. "Don't feel much like eating, but that does tempt me a little."

Thanksgiving morning, she thought as she opened the front door. Heavy frost coated everything in sight. She wanted to wash down the wall where Roy's blood had dripped and rinse off the grass where Coughlin had fallen, but she guessed she'd wait until it warmed up. Oleatha was relentlessly cheerful while she cooked an egg for Roy. Jacob smeared jam on his toast but didn't get any on his shirt. Maggie reckoned there were a lot of things to be thankful for; she just couldn't seem to do it.

She'd finished rolling out the crust for Oleatha's pie when her phone rang. Luke, she hoped, or Travis. Somebody to relieve her worries. It was her father. "Happy Thanksgiving, Maggie," he said. His voice was strong.

"Same to you, Dad. How are you feeling?"

"Good. You?"

She told him about shooting a deer. She told him about the pumpkin pie. She could never tell her father that she'd killed a man. They chatted a while, and then his cheer disappeared. "Maggie, I have some bad news. I don't know why they called me, but my number was still in your mother's phone as an emergency contact."

Maggie grimaced. "What? Who called?"

"The Cincinnati police." He paused. "Your mother is dead. They found her in a car alongside the road out near the Indiana line."

Maggie shut her eyes. "Car wreck?"

"No. I guess she passed out or it was alcohol poisoning or something. They can't tell without an autopsy, and I told them no. You agree?"

"I agree. When did she die?"

"That's just it, baby. She's been dead a while. They didn't check the car until yesterday when someone complained about it sticking out in the road."

Oh God, Maggie thought. What a gruesome death.

Her dad went on speaking. "The officer apologized but said they'd been so busy trying to keep the city under control that things have slipped through the cracks."

Her mother, a crumb to be swept into a crack. "I guess I can see that," she said, trying to keep her voice steady. "Things are bad everywhere."

He said, "They are. We've had fires here in Denver. Other cities too. Of course looting. People scared, hungry. An angry crowd took over a hospital south of here. Demanded treatment when there was nobody to give it. Medical personnel are dying. The news said that sixty percent of the sick people needing ventilators don't have them. Just not enough." His last words trailed off.

Maggie's hands were shaking so hard that the phone skittered against her ear. "So what do we do about Mom? I'm down here, you're in Denver," her voice caught, "Tina's gone, and we can't lay this on Andy." Tears ran down her face like rain on a window.

"I paid for them to cremate her. A lot of people being cremated these days. Hope that was okay with you."

Mostly it was easy. For him. He didn't care. "It's okay," she mumbled.

"I'm sorry. Maybe we can have a service for Tina and your mother at the same time."

After Tina's death, this had sounded sweet. Not anymore. Maggie's stomach tightened with anger. "It's okay," she repeated. "Talk later."

Throwing on her jacket and finding a brush and a sponge, she marched to the shed and grabbed the hose, connected it, and turned on a full blast of water. She scrubbed the siding. She found the bullet that had pierced Roy's body and pocketed it. She watered down the dead grass where Coughlin had fallen. Crying and silently screaming, she washed and washed until big puddles spotted the yard. It was hers to do. The killing, the protecting, the healing, the feeding. She wouldn't shirk. She would work and fight until there was nothing left of her. She wasn't her father.

❖

Luke was warm, full, and sleepy. He was pretty sure he'd dropped off in the middle of a sentence, just like Jacob sometimes did. But when Vanessa jabbed him with her meaty elbow, he was instantly awake. "This road goes to Glasgow and then Somerset," she said. "Is this the one you want?"

"Yes" He focused on the signs and then saw something he liked better. "Highway 90," he said. "That's even more direct. Let me out here."

She took the turn onto 90, and kept driving, peering at the few closed businesses at the junction. "This is an old state highway," she said. "You're not going to get any traffic on this road."

"Probably not, but there'll be shelter every now and then. Not like an interstate." He patted her arm. "I'll be okay. I'm not but seventy-five or eighty miles from home here."

She shook her head. "That's a long walk, Luke. I'm gonna get you ten miles down it and then turn around and leave you to your nonsense."

"That's taking you out of your way and using gas."

She sniffed.

When she stopped, she handed him a peanut butter and banana sandwich and a bottle of water. "You be safe," she said.

"Thanks for everything, Vanessa." He kissed her cheek and made her giggle. It sounded good.

And then he was alone again. It was three in the morning, solid black, and cold. He wasn't sure his knee could sustain five miles an hour, or even three, but he'd give it his best. It was deep country here with scarce habitation. He heard the melancholy sound of a train whistle, and that cheered him. Something was moving, but it certainly wasn't cars on this road. Luke had never approached Henley County from this direction and had no landmarks. He thought about Maggie. He'd been tempted to call her on Vanessa's phone, but it was the middle of the night. And he wasn't sure which would worry her more--him walking home or silence. He imagined Maggie's smile when she saw him. He felt Jacob's arms around his neck. A waking dream, he thought and chuckled: a walking dream.

The sky was no lighter at six. His legs ached like they were pulling a truck. He arrived at a little cluster of modest houses. Two had lights shining behind shades. A deserted gas station with a mini-mart was the only business he saw. Detouring into its lot, he went to the door and read the hand-scribbled sign. NO FOOD, NO MONEY, NO GAS. He wondered if it was true. Circling around to the back, he got out his picks. He didn't want money, had no use for gas, but he could stand some food or even a spot to eat his little sandwich out of the frigid breeze.

Glancing around, he saw nobody. His weakening flashlight revealed the back door and its knob. Luke's hands were too cold for such precise work, but he made up for it with determination. After a good ten minutes of fiddling, he unlocked the door and walked in, halfway expecting to hear a security alarm, but the mini-mart was silent. The sign had told the truth. He walked from shelf to empty shelf, even going so far as to get on his knees and shine his flashlight under them. This netted him a single packaged cinnamon roll living in swirls of dust. The coolers were empty and warm. Oh well, he thought. He'd eat the sweet roll, wash his face, and move on.

There was no power, no heat, but it was warmer inside than out. Sitting on the floor beneath the open and empty cash drawer, he took a bottle of lemon tea, the last item from Melanie's house, and chewed up the stale cinnamon roll. Everything hurt. Muscles, joints, head. Be some kind of fucking justice for him to get sick now, he thought. He was just tired, he told himself.

A single passing car woke him two hours later. Furious with himself for maybe missing a ride, he hitched on the backpack and went to the bathroom, a pure luxury, he thought, but not enough of one to delay his trip. He scrubbed at his hairy face and risked just enough battery to flash the mirror. He looked like some beast that lived in a cave. He'd probably scare the wits out of Jacob. Nothing he could do about it.

❖

Maggie shed her wet shoes and opened the front door. Red-faced, Jacob was rolling on the sofa trying to mute his giggles. In the bedroom, Oleatha was shouting. "I know your legs ain't hurt, but you're going to use this walker to get to the bathroom. And I'll hear no more cursing from you, Roy Davies."

Jacob whispered, "Pop said a bad word."

Maggie couldn't help but smile. "Which one?"

His eyes widened at the thought of saying it himself. "D-A-M."

"Oh, well. He's hurt." She hugged her son, thinking that as bad as things were, she had this boy. And yes, she would kill for him.

"All right then, old woman. I'll use your precious walker," Roy bellowed, and the sound of thumping steps, faltering now and then, came from the bedroom. Oleatha had been wise to think of it.

Later, when they had the Thanksgiving feast on the table, Roy used the walker again, saying he was perfectly capable of sitting at the table. His face turned gray after the exertion, and, although he praised the food, he didn't eat much. Maggie was still worried. She'd brought up the hospital again, but neither would consider it. She was happy that Jacob liked the venison and pleased that Oleatha had her pumpkin pie. For a minute all was well. She'd hidden her emotions as best she could, but they overwhelmed her when she was doing the dishes. Staring out at the cold, gray afternoon, tears burned her eyes. She'd thought she was alone in the kitchen, but Oleatha murmured, "What's wrong, honey?"

Maggie shook her head, sending a teardrop into the dishwater.

"Oh, come on. We got maybe five teabags left. You want to share one?"

"Okay." She could hear the murmur of Jacob reading to Roy. They'd both be napping in a few minutes, she reckoned. She finished the roasting pan about the time Oleatha had the water boiling.

"It's about Coughlin, isn't it?" Oleatha asked.

"I've never even thought about killing someone. I'm a nurse. I heal."

"And you're doing a fine job of it with Roy. But Coughlin would've killed you, and Lord knows what he would've done to Jacob and me." She passed the teabag to Maggie. "He'd already shot Roy. You had to protect your kin. Nobody'd argue with that."

Maggie rubbed her face red. "I know. But it's wrong to take a life. Wrong." She dropped her head. "And I'm worried about Luke."

"Still not answering his phone?"

"No. I haven't heard from him in days. I don't know whether he's sick or been moved or anything."

"Maybe his phone's broken. Them things break sometimes, don't they?"

"Yes, but he could borrow one." Maggie shook her head. "I don't know what to think." Oleatha waited. Sipped her tea. "And I'm afraid somebody will hurt us again. Really afraid."

"Reckon we all are. I heard little Jacob in the night. And Roy's fretting about it too. But all we can do is keep our eyes and ears open. I wish Travis would come back."

Maggie shrugged. "I've been calling him, but he doesn't answer."

"Don't know about that boy." Oleatha shook her head. "Not like him to let us down." She patted Maggie's hand. "We'll get along without him, although you're wearing yourself out taking care of Roy and guarding the house. Bet you didn't sleep much at all last night."

"I'm okay," Maggie said and realized she wasn't. Tears welled up again. "I heard this morning that my mother's dead. She'd been dead for days before they found her."

"Oh, Maggie." Oleatha pulled her halfway into her lap and held her. She smelled of cinnamon and nutmeg, the perfume her grandmother used to wear. Maggie cried. And Oleatha patted her and said soft, murmuring words.

"It's too much," Maggie whispered.

"It is, for a fact. She got the sickness?"

"No." And Maggie told her, about her father and her mother and her childhood and Tina. Oleatha poured more hot water over the sad, single teabag, and they drank tanned water.

She let Maggie tell it all without interrupting until she ran out of words. "Well, I got one thing to say," Oleatha announced. "If God gave you all of that to endure, you're strong enough to handle anything we got going on now."

"I'm not strong."

"Then you're doing a mighty good job of acting like it." Oleatha settled her sweater, used a napkin to clean her glasses, and cleared her throat. "You got us now, gal. Don't you forget."

❖

He'd forgotten about hills, how they'd slow him down and chew up his muscles and force him to rest. There was something seriously wrong with his right knee. Since mid-morning, pain had gripped and circled around the joint with every step until it had turned into a constant burn.

When he stopped to eat half his sandwich at noon, the sky looked the same as it had all day. No hint of sun. Cold. Since morning, there'd been two pickups on the road, and both had ignored him. The little settlements he'd passed had been locked up tight, and he didn't have the strength to bluff his way into a house. Luke considered resting at a church, like he'd done before, but he couldn't see much difference between sitting by the side of the road and sitting in a cold church. At least outside he could try to flag down any passing vehicles, and it took fewer steps.

He passed a house with a yard full of cars. And probably a house full of guns. He wondered if they had some kind of Thanksgiving dinner on the table or if someone would give him a ride, maybe just ten miles up the road. That wouldn't be a lot to ask, would it? But he didn't stop. They were probably staring at the hairy man limping up the hill and shaking their heads. Or maybe they were gathering to say good-bye to someone with the sickness.

He had to sit. But he wasn't going to eat the other half of that sandwich. Just catching his breath, he told himself. Lowering his aching body to the cold road, he massaged his leg, trying to stop its shaking. If he still had his phone, he'd call Maggie and have her come get him. He probably wasn't but sixty miles from home. Might as well be two hundred at the speed he was traveling. He made himself stand and started limping down the hill. He could see a house or a small business up on the next hill. That was his goal. Maybe there'd be some kind of shelter there. It would be dark soon.

As he neared the place, Luke saw that it was a small used car lot, decorated with limp flags. He counted ten cars. What had been a small house, now an office, filled the rest of the lot. There was nothing to either side of it. Low tech, deserted. Maybe he could steal a car. He shook his head at his crimes. Upstanding law enforcement officer, my ass, he thought.

The last stretch of uphill climb about killed him, but he kept saying, "Suck it up, Davies. Suck it up." Aloud for God's sake. The cars and trucks in the lot were modest, older, nothing to brag about, but if he could find keys and get one started, he didn't care. He staggered across the blacktop and opened the storm door of the office. Thank God for the lock picks. But as soon as he touched the door, he heard ferocious growling from the other side. Hell. He worked at the lock, thinking about how he'd manage an attack dog and how its presence meant that someone must visit the place regularly.

The growling turned to howls. He felt the tumblers turn and eased the door open, jerking his elbows forward to absorb an attack. But the dog whined and rushed out the door, nearly knocking Luke down. It was mostly black with some brown and white markings. Skinny. The dog ran to the grass, squatted, and came back, tail down and whining.

"Hey buddy," he crooned, giving the dog his fist to sniff. He could see the dog's ribs, and its movements, after the first rush, were sluggish. "Bet you're hungry too."

As he entered the office, the stink of dog waste hit Luke like a bomb. There was just enough light to let him see the piles and puddles. Lots of them. "You've been locked up in here for days, haven't you?" he said. Walking carefully, Luke moved around the chairs and desks, in what had probably been a living room. He turned on the light in the hallway and saw a closed door that the dog had ravaged, shredding the fake wood. "Let's see what's in here," Luke said. The dog sidled up to him, panting and snuffling.

A half full bag of dry dog food sat on the floor of a closet. "Enough for you and me, buddy," he murmured. Better not to give the dog too much at once, he thought. He dribbled a handful of kibble on a clean spot on the floor. "There you go. Let's take it easy." The food disappeared.

He moved into the kitchen. A small table sat in the center. A coffeemaker and some mugs rested on the counter. Luke opened the refrigerator, hoping he wouldn't have to share dog chow with this poor mutt. He saw some bottled waters, a jar of pickles, and half a loaf of green bread. Damn. But the pickings were better in the freezer: a small pizza and a microwave spaghetti dinner. "We hit the jackpot," he said to the dog.

Even better, there was a bathroom that still had a rusty shower and another office with a couch and a TV. A pegboard with car keys hanging like little treasures was on the wall. "It's the Ritz, boy." The dog whined.

Water, Luke thought. He dragged his leg back to the kitchen and found the dog's bowls. He put a little water in one. "Slow and easy," he told the dog, who lapped every bit. Luke opened his backpack and reached in for his half sandwich. Pulling out a kitchen chair, he fell into it. The dog sped to his side. "This is mine, buddy," he said, unwrapping the food. "But I can share a little, I guess." He pinched off a corner, and the dog plucked it, dainty as you please, from his fingers. He ate, rubbing the dog's head the whole time.

He kept busy, slowly moving around the place and cleaning up the dog shit and puddles. Every little while he doled out more dog food and water and let the dog out. He showed no signs of running away. The tap in the shower gurgled and spurted, but by dripping a little liquid hand soap and drying with paper towels, Luke was able to get blessedly clean. He couldn't face the task of shaving with the useless razor left from Rieselman. Like shaving with a hedge trimmer. He put on his cleanest clothes, which happened to be his uniform. Then he heated the little pizza. He was so hungry, it tasted as good as Maggie's roast beef. He gave the dog a bite of crust. "You know, if I keep feeding and talking to you, I'd better give you a name. You probably already have one, but there's nothing on your collar, and, besides, I don't want to call you what your owner did. Is he sick or useless? How about Buddy? I say that all the time anyway. Do you like Buddy?"

He took the tail wag as a yes.

It was full dark, and Luke was leery about turning on lights. He turned the television on and set the sound to mute. That gave him enough light to limp into the front office where there was an old analog phone. He was optimistic enough to call Maggie. In the morning, he would confiscate a car and be home before noon. Maybe he'd bring Buddy. Jacob would like that, and he'd sweet talk Maggie into accepting him. He picked up the phone and got nothing. No lights, no sounds even after checking the connections.

Disappointed, he struggled back to the sofa. Buddy immediately jumped up beside him. "It's just a few more hours, Buddy. And then we'll hop in a car." He turned up the volume a little and watched a news station. They showed massive military action in the Middle East and Africa, led by the Navy carriers and destroyers. Luke reckoned the Navy would have supplies on board to feed their crew and could avoid the virus better than land forces. They showed riot squads in Chicago and Philadelphia battling mobs of people. They showed firemen in New York fighting block-sized fires. There were devastating scenes of sick babies. It was spreading, spreading like the violence and chaos the terrorists had intended. Every country in the world was prohibiting entry by Americans, with Mexicans and Canadians reinforcing borders with their militaries. Wall Street and banks had been closed for weeks. ATMs had been empty forever. And then the newscaster smiled just a tiny bit. Behind her was a video of a convoy of Kroger rigs and another one of Wal-Mart trucks taking off from warehouses. She said, "Happy Thanksgiving."

Chapter Twenty Five

Oleatha had bathed Roy, and Maggie had heated bottled lemon juice, water, and honey to make him a soothing bedtime drink. He sat on the edge of the bed. "This is pretty good," he said. "Beats the water you've been pouring down my gullet all day." He tried to twinkle.

"You need fluids," she said in a very nursey voice.

Roy nodded. "This isn't as bad as I thought it would be."

Maggie shrugged. She didn't want to tell him that he wasn't out of danger yet. Attitude meant a lot.

Roy murmured, "I know you want me to go to the hospital, but I'm getting fine care here. And no flu."

"Antibiotics, fluids, pain medicine. I don't have any of those. That's the last pain pill." She gestured at the tablet on the bedside table.

"I'll be okay. Got my own private nurse, don't I?"

Maggie smiled.

He touched her cheek with a shaky finger. "You heard me tell the Lord how thankful I am for you."

She nodded. When he'd said grace before dinner, he'd said it loud and clear. "You're a blessing, Maggie."

Smiling again, she handed him the cup. "Finish this and let's get you comfortable." Before she left she leaned down and kissed his bristly cheek. "Thank you. It means everything, Roy." And she left, ready to take up her post in the living room, straining to hear anyone near the house.

Maggie made her rounds first at eleven and then at one and three. Each time, she tiptoed into the back bedroom and cuddled Jacob until he smiled in his sleep. She patrolled the kitchen, scrutinizing what she could see from the windows and backdoor. Then she slipped into Roy and Oleatha's room to check his vitals and see if he needed anything. Bless her, Oleatha slept through it all, but Roy was never deeply asleep.

So, Maggie nearly jumped off the sofa when, at five, Oleatha touched her. The woman's face was wet with tears, and Maggie knew it was bad. She rushed into the bedroom, turning on lights and breathing hard. "He sorta shook," Oleatha gulped, forcing the words out between silent sobs. "And grabbed at me."

Roy's good arm was still clawed into a clumsy embrace. Maggie checked for a pulse, a heartbeat, anything, but he was gone. His mouth was twisted into a grimace on the right side, and she knew what had killed him.

"Was it infection?" Oleatha whispered. "He didn't have much of a fever last night, did he?"

"He had a stroke, Oleatha. See how his right side is contorted?" She folded her arms around the little woman, trying to give back the love they'd shared in the kitchen yesterday. "It was sudden, real sudden."

"I'd prayed that the Lord would ease his pain." She massaged her swollen knuckles and hung her head.

"No pain." Maggie took Oleatha's hands between her own and warmed them. "How are we going to tell Jacob?"

Oleatha whispered, "Roy knew, I think. Last night he told me that if something happened to him, he wanted the boy to have his guitar and you to have his rifle."

Maggie shut her eyes.

"What do we do now?" Oleatha's voice was plaintive.

"Call a funeral home?" She looked at her watch. Five thirty. She didn't know whether mortuaries kept business hours or not but figured they were staying plenty busy these days.

Oleatha nodded. "I can do that. But how will I go on without him? Married forty-seven years. We'd said we'd do something special when we got to fifty." She blotted her face with the bedsheet.

"You'll get through this morning and then this evening and then the day after that," Maggie said. "We're all getting a lot of practice with that one day at a time idea. And you've got me."

Oleatha hugged Maggie hard.

"Let's shut the door and try to keep Jacob out once he wakes up."

"I'm going to call Bobby Kingsford. The sooner they take him away, the better we'll be. Especially Jacob." She took a deep breath. "But I want to take a minute and pray with Roy."

"Take as long as you need."

Maggie shut the door behind her and went to the kitchen. After peering out into the pre-dawn darkness for signs of danger, she moved around, filling the tea kettle, cutting bread for toast, setting out butter and jam. Little tasks, not worth mentioning in light of the horrors. The terrorists had lived up to their name. Everywhere fear floated like dust with no clean wind to blow it away.

❖

Warm and relaxed on the old sofa, Luke slept hard. Buddy snuggled right next to the sofa and occasionally whuffed in his sleep. Luke touched him and the dog settled. He wasn't aware of sunrise, and it took Buddy's warm tongue against his hand to wake him. "You hungry again, Buddy?" He yawned, but when he tried to stretch, his knee made him yelp. He moved gingerly, aiming toward standing up but not getting too far with it. Damn, he hurt.

He couldn't put weight on his right leg without it screaming and him doing nearly the same. Touching walls and doorframes, he made it to the kitchen and poured out some food for Buddy. Catching sight of the coffeemaker, he looked in the cabinet behind it and found coffee. That would be a treat, he thought. But even better, he found a sleeve of soda crackers.

Buddy gobbled his kibble, and Luke made his tortuous way to the door to let the dog out. He'd better be able to get one of those vehicles moving because he sure as hell couldn't walk. Buddy circled and sniffed until he performed his functions. It was way past daybreak. Luke looked at his watch and was shocked that it was ten.

Buddy followed every slow step. After the delight of hot, strong coffee and stale crackers, Luke visited the pegboard. Pick one, he said. The car of your dreams. He grabbed two key rings, put on his jacket, and limped out into sunshine. The number on the first key ring matched a small, red Kia. He unlocked it and took a deep breath. Buddy sat by the car looking anxious. Luke turned the key. Click. Click. Nothing. The other key matched an old brown Corolla with a rip in the seat. He wondered if it would even make it to Henley County. Same story. No juice.

After two hours of trying every car on the lot, he and Buddy collapsed on the sofa. Now what? He couldn't remember being more frustrated, even at Rieselman. He didn't bother searching for jumper cables because what good were they without a car that would start? He wished he'd been like Travis Parker and other guys who grew up under the hoods of cars. Maybe there were tricks. A lot full of cars and not a damned one that would run. After a bunch of cussing, Luke heaved himself up, determined to search every inch of the building for a new battery he might be able to install.

There was a small shed behind the building. He'd start there. Buddy galloped around the back and sniffed every blade of dead grass. Luke wished he could move like the dog. Shivering in the cold sunlight, he had no trouble picking the padlock on the shed. He didn't expect to see much inside, and he was right. A lawnmower. A few cans of motor oil. There were jumper cables but no sign of a fresh battery. And there were five large cans full of gasoline, which seemed like four more than you'd need to maintain a lawnmower. Luke grinned. Whoever owned Hilltop Motors was a sly cuss. He'd probably put just enough gas in a tank for a quick test drive and a short piece down the road for the new owner. Otherwise, the cars sat on E. Maybe that was the problem.

With Buddy prancing beside him, Luke hauled a can and his right leg back to the lot and his favorite of the cars, a slightly newer Ford Fusion. He fetched its key, wishing Buddy could do it for him. After pouring all the gas in the tank, he tried starting the car again. No. Of course not. Stupid idea. He slammed the door shut. The dog whimpered. "I'm not going to hurt you," Luke said. "You're the only good thing about this fucking place."

❖

Oleatha's voice rose with every word. "What do you mean? Bobby, I taught you Sunday School. You know Roy and I are good for the money." A pause. "Reckon it'll have to do, if you say so." Another. "Thank you, Bobby." She set down the receiver with a loud click and stomped into the kitchen.

"They don't know when they'll be able to get Roy. And when they do, they're putting him on an ice truck and sending him to a cold storage warehouse in Corbin. He said they don't have a single casket left." Oleatha slumped into a chair. "Twenty-five deaths in the last week, he said. Lord help us, Maggie."

She poured hot water for Oleatha and went out onto the frigid front porch to call Travis. Didn't wait for voice mail and called him again and again. Finally he picked up. "Maggie?"

"Roy's dead. We need help. The funeral home doesn't know when they can get him, and it's hard on Oleatha and Jacob for his body to be laying here."

"Roy's dead?" His voice was clogged with sleep. "Jesus, Maggie."

"I don't care what you think about me or what your inclinations are, but these are your neighbors. Go over to Kingsford's, get a body bag, do what you can. I'm afraid to leave them here alone."

"How did Roy catch the sickness?" Travis sounded more alert.

"He didn't. Coughlin shot him. I shot Coughlin and killed him. Would've thought you'd have heard about it." Her words were shards. "Roy died from a stroke, not the wound."

Again he said, "Jesus, Maggie. Yeah, I'll get there as soon as I can."

She was shivering when she screeched back a kitchen chair and sat by Oleatha. "Travis is coming. He's going to check with Kingsford and do something." She passed her hands over her face. "I don't know what."

Oleatha made a strangled noise. "Too late for real help."

Maggie nodded. "I'm going to wake Jacob and tell him. Better now than when we're moving Roy out." She stood, already weary. "Get some toast. You need a little something in your stomach."

She crawled into bed beside Jacob, savoring his warmth. With little touches and kisses, she woke him gently, but waited until he yawned and opened his eyes before she spoke to him. There was no easy way to do it. She held him when he cried, wrenching sobs that probably killed Oleatha's heart. She whispered love words and talked about heaven and Aunt Tina and how she'd bet Pop was singing songs to her. Nonsensical, theologically absurd things. Later she made him dress and let him eat toast with gobs of jam, but he wouldn't say anything more than yes or no and quickly hid back in the bedroom with the door closed.

It was over an hour before Travis came with a body bag and paperwork for Maggie to sign. Bobby had told him that, as a registered nurse, she was qualified to sign a death certificate. He wore his usual ball cap, pulled low over his eyes. He was thinner. Who wasn't? And he spoke no more than he had to. He did hug Oleatha and went back to speak to Jacob. Maggie hoped he said good things. She made Oleatha stay in the kitchen while she and Travis wrestled Roy into the bag. Somehow they got him out of the house and into the back of Travis's truck. He folded one of Oleatha's afghans over the bag.

"I'm taking him straight to cold storage in Corbin," he said. "It may be a couple of weeks before they can get him buried."

Maggie nodded.

"There's a couple of guys in Catesboro who've set up shop making simple coffins. That'll speed things along a little. Bobby says Oleatha's already got plots up at the Baptist cemetery."

"Yes."

"Bobby will let her know when they catch up." He finally met her eyes. "You killed Coughlin?"

"I told you I did."

He shook his head. "You've become quite the woman, haven't you?" He offered a smile. She didn't return it.

"I'm sorrier than I could ever tell you," he whispered.

She lowered her head. A hard breeze blew her hair. "Before you leave, I want you to check Roy's truck and see how much damage Coughlin's buddy did before I stopped him."

Travis nodded. "I mean it, I'm sorry. It was the moment. I was a fool."

"Could you check it now?" She stared at Roy's truck.

"Okay." He scuttled under the truck, touching its belly and then scooting out. "It's fine. The guy barely got started."

"Good." Maggie turned away. "Thanks."

"I couldn't stay up here close to you, Maggie." He lit a cigarette. She wondered how people could still find those. Behind her back he whispered, "I'm in love with you."

"No excuse for abandoning us." She raised her right hand and walked into the house.

Oleatha was in the back bedroom, cuddling Jacob but stood when Maggie came in. "It's done," she said.

Oleatha let out a long breath. "I'll start making my calls then."

Maggie nodded. "I'm going to work on your bedroom. Come on, Jacob. It's sad work, but we need to do it."

Chin down, he watched while she bundled up linens and threw away used supplies. She stripped the bed and found fresh sheets. Abruptly, Jacob pointed at Roy's guitar, propped in the corner, and said, "Mr.Travis shoulda taken the guitar. Pop'll be wanting it."

Maggie stopped stuffing a pillow into a fresh case. "Oh, they have all kinds of musical instruments in heaven. Harps, trumpets. I'm sure they have guitars too. Really fine ones." She fluffed the pillow. "Besides, that's your guitar now. Pop said you should have it."

His eyes widened. "Really, truly, mine?"

"Yep."

He picked up the guitar and headed back to his room. She could hear the pluck of a string every now and then, accompanied by Oleatha's tearful talk with Marla. There was no way to tell Luke. Her stomach tightened.

❖

Luke searched every drawer, cranny, and cabinet of Hilltop Motors for anything useful. Buddy stayed at his heels, looking up at him with warm eyes. His first find was an old broom which he turned into a kind of walking stick by decapitating it with the Swiss Army knife. He found business cards for Hilltop Motors, with a photo of the owner, Larry Hampton. And then, in the desk drawer he found a bottle of ibuprophen. He washed down four tablets, hoping for some relief. He would have to start walking again, but he was going to give himself a day of rest before setting out. He counted three vehicles that passed, but there was no way he could run outside to hail them.

He'd hoped to find a working flashlight and did, under the sink of all places. And that was where he unearthed an old box of rawhide bones. Buddy seemed tickled about that. As daylight waned, he heated up the spaghetti and fed the dog, picking out a piece of kibble and trying it. Bland, but edible. Tomorrow he'd have coffee and the rest of the crackers for breakfast and carry dog food in his backpack for him and Buddy. Taking ice that he'd frozen earlier, he went to the sofa, iced his swollen knee, and snuggled the dog while he watched newspeople scroll a long list of famous people who were now dead. Not helpful, folks, he thought. Although he imagined the Broody Hens back at Rieselman enjoying such gruesome coverage. Luke wondered if they were still locked up, if they had food. He thought about poor Josh Monroe and where he'd come by a gun. Maybe he'd bought it in Spain where no one knew about his condition.

By morning, the knee wasn't quite as swollen, although every step stabbed him. He limped to the door to let Buddy out, and, using his stick, moved around the kitchen to feed them. The sky was white. Looked a little like snow. Luke hated the thought of leaving the heated office for a miserable day on the road. Suddenly Buddy started barking like crazy, running back and forth between the front door and Luke. A car had pulled onto the lot.

It was black, some kind of big-assed SUV. The driver parked it nearer the path to the back than the front door. Hurrying as best he could, Luke put on his jacket, leaving it open so the guy could see his badge and gun, grabbed the half empty bag of dog chow and shoved it into his backpack, shouldered the pack, and hobbled to the back office to get the keys to the Ford. He hid his stick behind the desk where it couldn't be used against him. Buddy had outsized his barking to howls. The driver got out of his car and paid no attention to Buddy's noise. Luke recognized him: Larry, the owner of Hilltop Motors and probably Buddy as well. Son of a bitch, treating an animal like that. Luke limped from window to window to see what the man was doing. He was bald-headed, short, chubby. He looked like he might be late forties to early fifties. At the shed, the guy stopped, fiddled with his keys, opened the door, and picked up two gas cans. His own private gas station, Luke thought, except the man wasn't going anywhere until he jumpstarted a car.

As soon as the man's back was turned, Luke opened the office door. Buddy leapt out, jumping on the guy until he nearly dropped the can. He whirled around to face Luke. "What the hell?"

"Yeah, what the hell," answered Luke. "How ya doin', Larry?" He unholstered his weapon and pointed it at the ground.

He could tell the man was putting together the uniform, the gun, and the attitude, and wasn't quite sure what to make of it. "What are you doing here?"

Luke lifted a lazy shoulder. "Keeping warm, taking care of the dog. Figuring out which of your fine cars I'm going to requisition." He stood still, reluctant to reveal his limp. Buddy was by his side now and on alert. But it wouldn't be smart to count on the dog's loyalty however badly his owner had treated him.

"Shit. That ain't happening." Larry lifted his double chin.

Luke raised the gun, just a little. "Maybe the one you're driving. It won't have to be jumped." He grinned. "And you're gassing it up all nice for me."

"You can't come in here and steal one of my cars."

"Reckon I can." Luke raised the gun until it was aimed at Larry's knees. "Of course if I take your car, it would look like stealing. I said I was going to requisition one, rent it. Return it to you if I have the time."

"You're going to shoot me if I don't?"

"Might. I ought to shoot you for the way you neglected this dog. Don't you have a conscience, Larry?"

"Don't you?"

Luke shook his head. "Lost it about the time the virus cut loose." He pointed the gun at the lot. "I kinda like that black Ford Focus over there. I'm going to pull your big gasburner over in front of it, so we can give it a charge."

"What if I don't let you?" Buddy growled at this.

"Then I'll shoot you and you'll end up in the hospital with all those people dying of the sickness. And I'll do the jumping myself. Easy."

Larry blinked, thought about it a minute, and reached for the door handle. Luke figured there was probably some kind of weapon inside. He really didn't want to shoot the guy, but he would. God help him, he would. "Guess you know how bad the law would twist your balls if you shot a cop, Larry. Especially in these troubled times. Give me your car key."

"You're not a cop." He kept his hand on the door handle.

"Oh, I am. Come look at my badge."

Instead, Larry threw Luke the keys. He caught them left-handed. "Now stand over there in the grass," Luke ordered.

Trying his damnedest not to limp, Luke kept the gun on Larry and started his car, maneuvering it close to the Ford and leaving it running. He opened the SUV's door and stood, aiming the gun toward the shed.

"Now you need to get the jumper cables. I'll be watching."

Larry took slow steps toward the shed. Luke shifted so he could see him. He didn't think he'd missed anything in the shed, but there might've been a tire iron or wrench he hadn't noticed. Not much defense against a handgun, especially when the stakes were nothing but a used car, but people could be stubborn. Buddy stood with Luke and kept his eyes on Larry.

He didn't seem to be carrying anything but the cables. The guy was sincerely pissed off but fearful too. His mouth was working hard at keeping words inside. "Get 'er done, Larry," he said, unlatching the Ford's hood. "And then I'll leave you alone."

When the Ford's motor caught, Luke took a deep breath. He'd put nearly two gallons of gas in its tank yesterday but wondered if he could force Larry into another task. But that wasn't happening. As soon as Larry disconnected the jumpers, he hopped in his SUV and screeched off. "You know what, Buddy? I'd rather be lucky than good any day of the week." Luke rubbed the dog's head and limped to where Larry had left the gas cans. Holstering his weapon, Luke struggled to carry the full can and emptied it into the Ford's tank. He opened the passenger door and said, "Jump in, Buddy. We're going home."

❖

"Daddy's dead too, isn't he?"

Oleatha's hand went to her throat. "Oh, child, don't say that."

Maggie swallowed hard. "No, Jacob. Daddy's not dead. We just don't know why we can't call him." She'd divided the remaining pumpkin pie into three slices and served it for breakfast. The sweet spices made her feel nauseous.

"He needs to come home now," Jacob said, tears spilling from his eyes.

"He'll get here when he can," Oleatha said. "Eat your pie, Jacob."

Maggie touched the soft flesh on Jacob's wrist. "Granny's right. He'll come."

The kitchen was so quiet that Maggie could hear dead leaves blowing against the siding. She ate one more bite and put the rest in the refrigerator for later. "I've been thinking," she said. "I'm going to move the truck and car right in front of the porch where we can keep an eye on them."

Oleatha nodded. "I hate that you've been sleeping on the sofa to keep watch. Maybe I should move my things to the back bedroom, and you and Jacob could move to the front. You'd be able to hear more from there."

Maggie had thought the same thing but didn't want to say it. "Good idea," she said. And it would give them something to do. After making dozens of calls yesterday, Oleatha had holed up in Roy's big chair and read the Bible for hours. Activity would be good for all of them.

Logically, she didn't think anyone would be bothering them. The fact that she'd killed Coughlin would be a big deterrent for anyone who knew about it, but she wondered if the county drug addicts had as active a communication line as Oleatha's church ladies. She couldn't imagine feeling safe leaving Oleatha and Jacob when she hunted or eventually went to town for groceries. Maggie shook her head and took a pile of Oleatha's clothes to the back bedroom.

Oleatha sat on the bed, sorting through Marla's clothes. "Look, Mom." Jacob pointed to a box of plastic soldiers.

"I see," she said. "Bet those were your daddy's."

Oleatha nodded. "They were." She held up a plaid flannel shirt. "Think you would wear this? You didn't bring much with you, and it's colder now."

Maggie hugged the flannel to her. "Would Marla care?"

"No. Besides she'd never fit into it now. Take it. There's more stuff here. Give it a glance."

"What we need is more clothes for a growing boy," Maggie said, picking up a pair of brown jeans that looked like they'd fit her.

"And we might just find us some, although they'd be in the big room."

Maggie doubted that Oleatha could find anything in that jumble.

Oleatha went on. "I'll work in there tomorrow. It's a sight how bad I've let it go, but Jacob's going to need his own room once Luke comes home."

The boy didn't say anything, but Maggie could tell he liked those words. She wasn't sure that she did. Home was River Hills, their house. Oleatha was assuming they'd live down here forever. And yet, they might have to. She unfolded another flannel shirt, this one green and aqua, and slipped it on over her turtleneck. It felt good.

Then she heard something. A vehicle coming down the road. "Stay back here," she hissed and headed for the front door, grabbing a hat and the rifle on her way. Before the vehicle was in view, she was posted at the porch railing, rifle at her shoulder. Then she relaxed. It was Travis.

He wore latex gloves and carried a large envelope and a paper bag. "I'm not coming close," he said. "Been around a lot of bodies, dead and alive, and I don't want to infect you all."

He stepped between Maggie's car and Roy's truck to lay his items on the ground. "Good idea." He gestured at the vehicles.

Maggie nodded.

"The envelope's got paperwork for Oleatha. She'll need it when Bobby can get around to burying Roy."

"Okay."

He pointed to the lumpy bag. "An old man outside Corbin was selling potatoes. Thought you all might like some." Only then did he look up at her, his deep eyes wanting anything she could give him.

Maggie met them. "Thank you."

He gave her a quick nod and turned back toward his truck. "Reckon you can call me if there's a problem," he said. "I'll get here next time."

She didn't say anything. He got back in the truck and started the engine. Her eyes followed him as he turned around and headed up the holler.

❖

Perched in the passenger seat, head up like he was doing the driving, Buddy let his tongue loll and did a good impression of a canine smile. Luke reached over and scratched his neck. "We're doing okay, aren't we fella?"

He was on familiar roads now and making good time. No Thanksgiving weekend traffic, he thought and grinned. The Ford was okay. The brakes seemed soft, but it would get him home. He was starving, and his knee was throbbing from being bent toward the accelerator, but he was riding, not walking. He planned to throw Jacob up in the air until he giggled, hug his parents until they begged for mercy, and kiss Maggie until she melted. Oh, Maggie, he thought, barely seeing the road for thinking about her eyes and mouth.

And Jacob, he thought, smiling a different way. Jacob and Buddy were going to be the best friends ever. Every kid needs a dog and every dog needs a kid, he thought. Near Monticello, he saw a pickup traveling in the opposite direction and wondered if old Larry had told anybody about him. He didn't figure it would be too much of a problem even if he had. Luke slowed through the town, watching for any kind of activity. A few cars were parked near the courthouse, but nothing was happening anywhere else. He wondered when groceries and banks would start opening up. When they did, more people were going to get sick, but you couldn't starve folks.

Buddy finally eased down and settled his head against Luke's thigh. A few flakes of snow hit the windshield. He saw a house with a cow chained to the porch railing. By the lake, he noticed two fishermen with lines in the frigid water and shivered at the idea. He'd have work to do once he got home. But for quite some time, he'd been all but sure he was immune to the sickness. He could go out and get things, forage, steal if he had to.

Luke turned down country road after country road, each of them narrowing until they were little more than single lanes. He was in Henley County now. He looked at his watch. Two o'clock. More snow flitted down. He didn't want to think past the next few hours. His job, River Hills. It was too much to grasp with too many contingencies liable to foul things up. He wanted food, company, his family. More than enough for now, maybe forever.

Turning down the gravel road to the holler, he slowed way down. He wasn't too sure about the Ford's tires, and there was a touch of snow glazing the rocks. The dog's head snapped up. "Almost home, Buddy," Luke said.

When he neared the house, he could see someone he didn't recognize standing at the railing, his dad's old rifle at the ready. He blinked and realized it was Maggie, a ball cap pulled close to her eyes, flannel shirt flapping in the breeze. She didn't recognize him or the car. He beeped the horn, but she didn't move. A warrior, a sentry defending the homeplace. He turned off the ignition and opened his door. She shifted the rifle up, ready to shoot, and he yelled, "Maggie, I'm home."

ACKNOWLEDGEMENTS

For medical knowledge, I thank three fine doctors: Nancy Swikert, Lisa Miller, and Michael Bowlin. For the ins and outs of airports, U.S. Customs, and flights, I am grateful to Elizabeth Belli, Ann Purdy, and Beth Burks. Andrew Morison and Kevin Sterner contributed military details. And I learned all about deer processing from Jim and Tricia Boh. Any errors here are mine, not theirs.

For believing in this story from the get-go, I thank talented writers Pamela Duncan and Sharyn McCrumb. T. M. Williams, another gifted writer of fiction and songs, gave me insights and invaluable advice. I'm always grateful to my Wise Women readers: Cheryl Eschenbach, Annabel Ihrig, and Joyce Hurst for their suggestions and encouragement. And although we're purveyors of words, I cannot come up with enough of them to thank my friend and staunch supporter, Gwyn Hyman Rubio.

With thanks for his amazing design and formatting skills, I salute Evan Sharfe.

And last of all, I thank Jim and Matthew Cooper who smoothed every rough spot along this journey. All my love.

About the author:

J.T. Cooper is the author of another suspense novel, RUNNING, and has received the James Still Award for Short Story. She lives in Kentucky with her husband and a smiling corgi.

To learn more about Cooper's work or to contact her, visit

jtcooperauthor.com

CPSIA information can be obtained
at www.ICGtesting.com
Printed in the USA
BVHW08s1931270618
520186BV00009B/682/P

9 780692 111079